THE MOMMY CLUB

a
novel
by

SARAH
BIRD

DOUBLEDAY
New York London Toronto Sydney Auckland

T H E

MOMMY

CLUB

PUBLISHED BY DOUBLEDAY
a division of Bantam Doubleday Dell Publishing Group, Inc.
666 Fifth Avenue, New York, New York 10103

DOUBLEDAY and the portrayal of an anchor
with a dolphin are trademarks of Doubleday,
a division of Bantam Doubleday Dell
Publishing Group, Inc.

"SH-BOOM"
(James Keyes, Carl Feaster, Floyd McRae,
Claude Feaster, James Edwards)
©1954 UNICHAPPELL MUSIC, INC. (Copyright Renewed)
All Rights Reserved. Used By Permission.

Library of Congress Cataloging-in-Publication Data
Bird, Sarah.
The mommy club / by Sarah Bird. —1st ed.
p.   cm.
I. Title.
PS3552.I74M66   1991
813'.54—dc20   90-26159
CIP

ISBN 0-385-41123-5
Copyright © 1991 by Sarah Bird
All Rights Reserved
Printed in the United States of America
May 1991

Book Design by Claire and Nick Vaccaro

1   3   5   7   9   10   8   6   4   2

FIRST EDITION

To Diane Campbell and George Jones,
for getting me through.

To Gabriel,
for telling me how the story ends.

To Colista McCabe Bird,
for what I know on this earth about being a mother.

ACKNOWLEDGMENTS

For time to write, I thank Laura Davis.

For inspiration, Meredith Edwards and Dave Hickey.

For insight and improvements,
Leticia Baldonado, Judyth Rigler, Paula Allen,
Marion Winik, Ernest Sharpe, Sally Furgeson,
Tom Bird, Richard Zelade,
Casey Fuetsch, and, of course, Lucy Herring.

THE MOMMY CLUB

1. Nearly all of the seven dwarfs of pregnancy have shown up by now: Sleepy, Queasy, Spacey, Weepy, Gassy, and Moody. The only one who hasn't checked in is Happy. But then, this isn't exactly a normal pregnancy.

Being pregnant and living here with Hillary and Victor Goettler in the famed Schier mansion in the King William Historical District reminds me of the bus trip Sinclair and I took to the Yucatan Peninsula. I'm nauseated all the time, everything I want to eat I can't, and I'm never sure of what's going on or how I should act. At least it smells better than a Mexican bus.

No, I'm happy to be sniffing the scents of lavender sachet tucked into cedar-lined drawers, of sheets washed in Ivory flakes and dried in the sun, of tung oil massaged by well-paid brown hands into furniture that has been on one side or the other of Victor's prominent San Antonio family for over a century. I'm particularly grateful to be surrounded by the smells of sunlight and subdued wealth, as pregnancy has turned me into a giant nostril attached to a hair trigger gag reflex.

Still, that Mexican bus smell, that blend of diesel fuel and the cheapest room deodorizer mixing with an on-board toilet that has been overflowing for fifty miles, can even now make my heart ache with longing. I've always longed for the wrong things. Junky things. Things of no value to anyone else.

I wonder what human breast milk tastes like. Probably a lot like powdered baby formula from a canister. I drank quite a bit of formula that first time. I knew I was pregnant then because I suddenly couldn't stand the taste of black coffee and added formula to cut the bitterness. I wouldn't admit that I was pregnant that first time, although I did go out and buy the baby formula.

I would heap that sugary formula into my morning coffee and drink it in the kitchen, since that is the only room in my apartment that gets any light. Toward the end of the off-and-on year we lived together, I spent a lot of time sitting in the kitchen in the morning waiting for Sinclair to come home. Sinclair David Coker, a freelance mystic with a lot of enthusiasm for the carnal. He thought we made a gaudy combination of the sort that would enhance his reputation as a man dancing in stardust. Pregnancy was far too flatfooted for Sinclair, and he was in the process of dancing off without me.

That special kitchen light comes in through the window above the sink in the morning and lands in warm, friendly puddles on the top of the Formica dinette table. I try to keep that table cleared off since I am so fond of the swirly aquacolored patterns in the Formica and the way the sun hitting them reminds me of the ocean around Isla Mujeres. Sinclair and I once snorkeled out so far that the grass shack where we were renting hammocks for a few pesos looked like a matchbox. In the warm pastel water we took off our suits and made love. This was something Sinclair had always wanted to do but he had never found someone with enough "lubrication." He was impressed by my "lubrication." I've heard that the hammock shacks are all gone now, replaced by condominiums.

So I would sit there with my elbows in the Formica ocean and spoon baby formula into my coffee. I could tell by the color the coffee turned how long it had been in the percolator. Of course, a creamy café au lait was the best color; that meant fresh coffee. It got muddier the longer it sat until it started going from any tone you could call brown right into gray. The oldest coffee actually had hints of purple in it. When I saw that murky purple, that's when I knew it was time to start on a new pot.

It's important to make things last when a person has no

money. This trait, however, can cause problems in other areas. I tried to make Sinclair last even after it was over between us. He'd told me it was over. Repeatedly. He was getting back with his old girlfriend. She'd started seriously dating someone else and, of course, her being chased by another man fanned his flame like nothing else could. There were more and more nights when he never came home. Still, I clung like a limpet. This panicked Sinclair, since our entire relationship was based on the myth that I was a free spirit with many another ticket to ride.

Having the father patching things up with his old girl-friend put a serious crimp on my pregnancy. As the days went by, I spooned more and more formula into less and less coffee. Pretty soon it was mostly hot water with just a few drops of coffee in it for color. I'd carefully float a tower of formula on the coffee water and watch it turn milky as the powder dissolved, an island crumbling into the sea in speeded-up motion. Toward the end I didn't even bother stirring the formula up in hot water, I ate it straight out of the can. It turned to taffy in my mouth and stuck to my teeth.

Since babies live on formula, I was certain that this must be good for the one growing inside of me. I thought that and kept eating formula even though I knew from the first time I threw up in the morning that I was never going to keep the baby. I couldn't. I didn't have any money. As most everyone who knew me agreed, I wasn't levelheaded. And, of course, the father *was* patching things up with his old girlfriend. The situation was far from optimal. So, I made a deal with the baby. I asked for a rain check. If he would go away, I'd try to engineer a suitable life for him to come back to in a few years.

And that's how I ended up where I am now. Sitting on a four-poster canopied with an ethereal floral print. Listening to the Brandenburg concerti. Sipping a special raspberry leaf, uterus-toning tea. Nibbling occasionally on a Carr's Water Cracker. Sniffing lavender sachet and tung oil. Looking out on the San Antonio River from the second story window of the famed Schier mansion in the heart of the King William Historical District.

The baby, Sweet Pea, came back last year to collect on his end of the deal and this was the best situation I could find for him. I think I did pretty well. For a surrogate mother.

2. My real home, my apartment on Laurel Street just off of San Pedro, on the other hand, always reeks of the burned plastic stink of Sculpie clay baking into my latest project.

Still, I miss it. I miss the view from my second story

bedroom window. It looks down on an empty lot where the eponymous Laurel Theater once stood. Sinclair and I used to sneak in the side door and spend entire days in the air-conditioned darkness. I even miss my view of Gil's Used Tires. Gil also offers Delicious Barbacoa and Free Water and Air. Across San Pedro is the Quik-Pik Ice House and its perennial specials: Little Debbie Cakes 49¢, Armour Corn Dog 39¢, twin pop Popsicles, asstd. flavs. 19¢. Summers in San Antonio require many twin pops, primarily in the coolest of the asstd. flavs., lime and grape.

So much for the old neighborhood. The views from the windows of my bedroom here at the Schier mansion are radically different. From the amplified spiels of the tour buses that troll the streets, I've learned more than I ever wanted to about the King William Historical District. For starters, it was built by a bunch of rich German merchants in the 1870s. Ernst Altgelt, founder of the Pioneer Flour Mill that still stands at the end of the block, named this street and the whole neighborhood for his beloved king of Prussia, Wilhelm I. Perhaps that's why Ernst's seven-story-tall mill looks like a castle with its crenelated tower and American flag snapping at the top.

King William had over half a century of glory days before it began a long, gradual slide. By the sixties the rich Germans' mansions had deteriorated into flophouses and dope dens. But money eventually calls to money, I suppose, because the neighborhood staged a comeback and was returned to the rich people. Now the Germans' mansions are the restored homes of lawyers and bankers who need permission from a neighborhood board before they can change the color of their porches.

From my back window I can see the San Antonio River

making a slow olive-colored bend. I feel like a Peeping Tom every time I look at it. As a young girl growing up in San Antonio, the river, little more than a gutter running through town back then, was something shameful. The nuns warned us about "going to the river," and we all understood the code, if not the technical details, for the moist and impure activities that can occur in such moist and impure places.

That's all changed. Now the river is contained within pristine cement banks and plied by tour boats filled with visiting families. The operators always idle their engines behind the Goettlers' rolling expanse of lawn with its fountains, and rose arbor, piles of jasmine, pots of red geraniums, magnolia tree with blooms the size of carving platters, and rows of palm trees three stories high. The tour boat operators point out the "magnificent" cypresses, the "stately" pecans.

"Stately" and "magnificent" are not conditions I've previously had much acquaintance with. They put me on edge. That's pretty much where I've been since I moved in two weeks ago. It's not as if a certain degree of alienness is new to me. Pariahhood has been a constant of my life except for two periods: one, when I went to high school at Our Lady of Sorrows and Aurelia and the rest of the Mexican girls were my friends. And two, when I had my first and, to date last, art show in the early eighties.

The owner of Tesoros Gallery, Beatriz Luna, came to one of the craft fairs I used to enter and fell in love with my work. In the catalog Beatriz wrote that she thought my work "made profound and witty and profoundly witty statements about the often blurry borders between treasure and trash." I met Sinclair at the opening. The show didn't exactly sell out, but it was reviewed in both papers. "Idiosyncratic" was used in both reviews. For that brief flicker in time I was a local legend and the recipient of many date offers. The many date offers were what piqued Sinclair's interest in me. Sinclair has never wanted a woman unless at least one other man also wanted her. And, for a while, I was in demand. Then the attention faded. Then the old girlfriend started getting rushed. Then there was Sweet Pea. By the time I got back to my projects, Sinclair was gone and Beatriz's gallery was bankrupt. I can't say I cared much, as I'd lost the desire to exhibit my work and worked on projects only for my own consolation.

I have always had my projects. Give me a hot glue gun and a tub of Sculpie and I don't care who's around or who's *not* around, for that matter. Sinclair, of course, was the exception. But except for the few months, not quite a year, we were together, much of *that* off and on, I've always relied on my art to keep the sand running through the hourglass. That's what I miss most about living here at the Goettlers, my projects.

My projects require a lot of materials: found objects, crafts supplies, assorted junk. They keep my place fairly crowded. My landlord, Mr. Braithwaite, asks every time he sets foot in my apartment if I've ever heard of the Collier brothers. After he asked for the third time, I did some research and found out that they were a couple of fabled pack rats back in the thirties who crammed their New York apartment with towers of junk that eventually avalanched and buried them. I don't think my apartment has ever gotten to avalanche danger stage, but I do see his point. There has never been much open floor space at my place.

From the tour operators I've learned that Hillary's house, the famed Schier mansion, has ten fireplaces, five bedrooms (stairstepped so each one catches the prevailing evening breeze), a ballroom, a card room, a billiards room, and at the center a staircase winding up to a giant skylight that is opened in summer so that warm air can escape. I've learned that speaking tubes connect the master bedroom and upstairs hall to the servants' quarters. It's just not a projects kind of place.

Back at the apartment on Laurel, I can take in every square foot of my abode and inventory all my possessions without ever leaving my bed. Since the Quik-Pik supplies most of my needs in the way of edibles, the kitchen area is given over to my projects. The counter is stacked with jars of Phlexglu, polymer-latex gesso, and neoprene. I have a couple of lazy Susans that I use for brushes next to the box of doll's eyes I just bought. You can get forty percent off on all doll parts if you order a hundred dollars or more.

I have a long work table next to my bed. I left my latest project spread out on it, the Tortilla Goddesses. I love my Tortilla Goddesses. I bake the tortillas out of Sculpie then scorch on El Virgen de Guadalupe with a propane torch. I'm also currently involved in Dino-Sardines, little baby pterodactyls made out of Sculpie and packed into sardine cans. Tackle boxes are great for various tiny components: the ball bearings for warts and moles, the glitter to make silicone caulking look like soap foam, the clothespin I rigged up with a piece of brain coral so perfect for pressing skin texture into Sculpie. I even have some of the first projects I ever did. A family of sharecroppers with pecans for faces. A mosaic of a butterfly on a lantana flower made out of crushed eggshells. Rock paperweights painted with signs of the zodiac.

Of course, last year's Rey Antonio costume contest entry dominates the place. A seven-foot hand with complete digital mobility does sort of tend to take over an efficiency apartment. I won over $1,300 with the giant hand. The upthrust middle digit was a definite crowd-pleaser. As I'll be nine months pregnant when the Rey Antonio costume contest comes around next June, I might have to skip this year's competition.

3. "Trudy! Oh, Trudy!" Hillary calls up to me. "Dinner's here!"

This is the first time in my life that I haven't been happy about mealtimes. Even my mother's weak-blooded concoctions of cyclamates and iceberg lettuce could always bring a bounce to my heart. Going into my arrangement with Hillary I thought that three catered meals a day would be a slice of heaven. Guess again.

Hillary, after a lot of research, found a stringently healthful restaurant called Eat for Your Life. The owners put nutrition way way above taste. This is an order that I have always reversed in my previous dining.

Hillary went to Eat for Your Life with eight prenatal nutrition books and a lot of ideas of her own and they worked out this diet for me that's health cubed. Health to the nth power. All the whole grains and dark, leafy greens reassure me that I have found the absolute best situation imaginable for my baby. I'm certain that this food is the best thing on this or any other planet for a baby. I know these things for facts since I hate this food so much.

"Trudy! Little Mama! It's not getting any warmer!"

I pray it's not a Bonus Meal. As soon as I leave my room and start walking down the stairs, I can smell that it *is* a Bonus Meal. I've spent nearly every moment since conception with my peristaltic waves lapping in the wrong direction. I walk through the day like the unhappiest passenger on the *QE II*. The smell of the food meets me on the stairway and brings me right to the brink. I pause to gauge whether a bolt for the bathroom will be necessary. Several deep breaths and concentrating on how good this meal will be for Sweet Pea keeps me going.

As usual, Hillary has my place all set up in the kitchen. Like the rest of the first floor, the kitchen was done over several years back in southwest decor. Talavera tiles brightly painted with blue birds in flight, red radishes, brown cows, yellow sombreros, and bunches of green onions are embedded in walls crusty with built-up plaster meant to look like adobe and washed with a fish bait orange paint. The floor covered in terra-cotta Saltillo tile is as bumpy underfoot as a creek bed. The copper light fixture overhead has a punched-out design depicting Quetzalcoatl, the Aztec's plumed serpent. It hangs over a massive kitchen table of pickled pine. The table legs, big as phone poles, are carved with Hopi Indian designs. The effect is a kind of Oaxaca/Santa Fe/Taco Cabana look.

A few months ago Hillary spotted sand paintings and a howling coyote cutout at J. C. Penney's home furnishings department and decided it was time to redo again. "French country" is the motif she's come up with this time. There will be lots of copper pans on the walls, a red brick floor, special tiles with fleurs-de-lis glazed into them. She and Victor have even ordered a woodburning stove from France for baking French bread the authentic way. Mercedes, their housekeeper, swears she will never use it.

"Next time you see me cook with wood, you better look around for them guys with the pitchforks, 'cause you gonna be in hell!" Mercedes assures me regularly. "Day I left Los Indios was the *last* day of my life on this earth that I *ever* cook with wood."

I believe her. Mercedes is not the kind to go back on her word. She is round and brown with teeth whiter than George Hamilton's and not a sliver of gray in her crackling black hair even with eighteen grandchildren, a sizable number of whom now live with her. She tells me stories about Los Indios, the miserable little scrap of America that she and her family and neighbors clung to when they reached this side of the border.

"Back in them days you show me a toilet, I put carrots in

and make soup!" Mercedes is emphatic about most everything she says. "I didn't even *see* no indoor plumbing till I'm
fifteen!"

That's how old she was when her second baby dug his
heels into her womb and wouldn't come out for four days.
The *comadrona* tried everything. She covered every mirror in
the house so that the new spirit wouldn't see itself and be
afraid to come out. She made Mercedes drink yerba buena
tea. She beat the girl's rock-hard belly with willow branches.
Finally, the *partera* told Mercedes's family that the baby was
dead and that they would have to take their daughter to *la
clínica* run by the Baptists to get the gringo machine to pull
the dead baby out or Mercedes would die too. The Baptists
saved both the baby's and Mercedes's lives.

After the Baptists saved her life, they asked for
Mercedes's soul. She let them dunk baby Luis, but, even at
fifteen in a strange place that gleamed whiter than heaven
itself, Mercedes declined. She was already spoken for. She'd
let the bishop slap her cheek and, as I've said, she wasn't
one to go back on her word.

"Mercedes!" Hillary calls to the housekeeper as soon as
she sees me. "Microwave off!"

Hillary likes split-second timing, but Mercedes is cultur-
ally indisposed to speed. Mercedes takes her time getting to
the microwave and shutting it off. Hillary read in one of her
dozens of baby books that microwaves could, potentially, be
dangerous for fetal tissue, so they've been outlawed whenever I'm around. It's a reasonable request. I just hate to be
the cause of rapid motion for Mercedes. Actually, Hillary
asked Mercedes to stop using the microwave altogether, but
Mercedes keeps forgetting. Mercedes has a memory that
makes life easier, not harder. She can, for instance, remem-

ber the names and birthdays of all eighteen of her grandchildren, but not which button to press to make Hillary's cordless phone work.

Hillary takes my plate out of the microwave and brings it to the table. She likes to do that herself. Just like she insists on setting the giant kitchen table with fresh flowers and their best silver and china. It is weird having my former boss set the table for me, but she says she enjoys doing it for "us." She beams at my stomach when she says "us."

"All right, now, Trudy," Hillary says, straightening my silverware on the linen napkin, then pulling back my chair. "You just have a seat right here." She pats the chair. I can't take my eyes off of my dinner. Not only is it a Bonus Meal, it is *the worst* Bonus Meal of them all, liver Stroganoff made with yogurt.

I make the mistake of smelling it, and what feels like a golf ball comes up the back of my throat.

"What a treat for the baby this is going to be!" Hillary's enthusiasm is one of the qualities that made her such a success at her job as director of the volunteer docent program at the San Antonio Museum of Folk Art that she was promoted to assistant director. When I was working there as her assistant I had many opportunities to see how good she is at motivating people. Especially women from Alamo Heights whose children have recently left home.

But all the enthusiasm in the world doesn't keep my stomach from heaving as I stare at that grayish plop of liver and yogurt sitting on a bed of whole wheat noodles. The strips of glazed carrots sitting in a pool of orange oil don't help the color scheme much. The salad with the little basket of whole wheat buns beside it looks pretty good. I think I can eat that. If I don't have to put the sesame yogurt dressing on the salad. But Hillary is already pouring it on.

"Loaded with calcium." Calcium is Hillary's mantra these days.

"Just think." Hillary slides my napkin out and pulls it across my lap. "The baby is going to get *double* nutritional benefits from this meal."

Double nutritional benefits is the concept behind Bonus Meals. Given a choice, I would rather eat two hamburgers or twice as much pizza to accomplish this doubling effect. Luckily for Sweet Pea I *don't* have that choice.

"Well, dig in." Hillary stands behind me and waits. I fiddle with my fork and take deep breaths through my mouth so that none of the liver smell will reach my stomach.

"I know what's missing." Hillary zips over to the refrigerator, a big black Sub-Zero, and comes back with a fresh, crisp sprig of parsley to nestle on my plate.

"Thanks, Hillary," I say.

Hillary puts her hand on my shoulder. "When *you're* happy, the *baby* is happy. Now, eat, eat, my child." She laughs. When I worked for Hillary, I used to look forward to her laughter. She seemed to take a tiny vacation when she laughed, to forget for a second about keeping her job and her body and her appointment calendar under control and just let loose. She's stopped doing that since I moved in. Neither of us knows how to act now that she's not officially my boss and I'm not officially her employee. It's tense.

Feeling Hillary's eyes on me, I take a bite and turn around to smile at her. "Good," I say, keeping the bite packed away in the side of my cheek as far from any taste buds as I can get it.

Hillary smiles back at me. I grin out of the side of my

mouth that's not packed with liver glop and nod enthusiastically as if actually tasting something edible. Hillary smiles and returns my nod. I am about to start up the whole cycle again when the front door opens. Victor is home.

Hillary pats my shoulder. She never used to touch me so much. Touching people is something she makes herself do when she is nervous. I appreciate the effort, but it makes me miss the old days when being around me didn't require an effort. She brushes off the front of her blouse and goes to meet her husband.

The instant she is out of the room, Mercedes pops the top off the garbage can and brings it over to the table.

"*Ay-chee, madre,* I wouldn't make a dog eat that mess." She holds the can open for me. I hesitate. I've seen the bills from Eat for Your Life. The liver Stroganoff is $9.95.

Mercedes urges me on. "Here or in the bathroom. No way you keep that down."

She has a point. I scrape my dinner into the garbage can.

Mercedes whisks the can away, then comes back and quickly breaks up some rolls to scatter around my plate. "Make it look like you been eating."

Hillary and Victor come into the kitchen. Victor is carrying the cellular phone from his car. He often has to bring it into the house to receive calls from clients who think he is still in transit. I start to stand but stop myself at the last minute. Victor brings out my subordinate side. I haven't been around men like him very much. Men who wear suspenders and carry real leather briefcases. My father carried a black vinyl pouch, but it was just for show since he kept it filled with Pringle's and Chicken Bones candy. Even though I'm older than Victor, he makes me feel like a child. Not a particularly quick child either.

He starts to speak to me, but the phone rings and he holds up a finger. "Got to grab this," he apologizes. "Chick? That you? . . . No, I'm home now, but go ahead. What'd Allied General do?"

Hillary and I study Victor as he listens to his caller. He presses the phone between his ear and shoulder and takes his suit jacket off. I love the way his shirts, fresh out of a dry cleaner's bag every morning, wrinkle after he's had them on all day. I especially like the wrinkles under his suspenders. Victor is not nearly as enthusiastic about surrogate parenthood as Hillary is.

"No way, Chick! If *you're* underwater on the multifamily, *Allied General* is underwater." Victor punches his index finger into the air for emphasis. "They're not going to let you sink, because they'll go down with you."

Victor is in real estate law, which means in Texas, lately, bankruptcy law. Reorganization. Chapters Seven and Eleven. Even though he works for the law firm that his great-grandfather started, Victor puts in long hours. Obviously, it's not for the money, since he could easily live off his trust fund and spend his whole day polishing his tennis serve like his alcoholic brother Ted. For that matter, he could live off of Hillary's money. Her father is Jack Murkoff. *The* Jack Murkoff. San Antonio is the only city in Texas where family counts more than money, and between them Hillary and Victor have always had plenty of both.

You'd know Hillary came from wealth the moment you saw her. She just looks like someone who would be at home in jodhpurs. It's in her bone structure, delicate and finely made, except in the places where it counts—cheekbones, jaw, shoulders, clavicles—then she comes through with just the right amount of character-defining mass. She's not as tall as she looks, about my height, five six, but she's slender. Not skinny in the bony, knobby way that I am, but slender with a naturally shoulder-padded physique.

"Uh-huh. Listen, Chick, we'll go spread the shark repellent tomorrow. Bash a few snouts, see what we can do. Don't worry. . . . Yeah. . . . Okay, Chick, talk at you later."

As he hangs up, Hillary asks, "Was that Chick Farley?"

"Um." Victor makes some notes on a pad he pulls from the inside pocket of his suit jacket.

"So, he's going to be all right?"

Victor clicks shut the ball-point pen and tucks it and the notepad back into his suit jacket. "Friend Chick? 'Fraid not. Stick a fork in Chick Boy, he's dead meat. Trudy," he turns to me—"how are we doing today?" He speaks to me in a booming voice.

"Oh, you know. Okay." I shrug and my mouth twitches.

Victor put up this wall of heartiness between us right after the first insemination. I guess the thought of his sperm, still warm from his body, being put into mine, even if by way of a kitchen utensil, sort of threw our relationship off kilter. It's hard for a man to know how to act in front of his wife with the woman who's carrying his child. Still, he doesn't need to put up that kind of sound barrier. I mean, if he's worried that I think that he was dreaming of *me* while he was beating off into a test tube, he can forget that. One look at Hillary would put *that* idea right out of anyone's head.

Besides the great bone structure, Hillary has dark hair that shines like mink cut blunt along her good jawline and a body with tone to spare. They both keep in perfect shape. Victor has a perfectly flat belly which he occasionally slugs when he imagines fat is accumulating there. Which it isn't. His hair is nearly as dark as Hillary's, except that it has glossy brown highlights like a wet seal pup's fur. His eyes are a nice mossy color somewhere between brown and green but tending more to green. His jawline always looks polished from shaving, and there are high spots of color on his cheeks. I suppose his only flaw is that his nose might be a tiny bit too large, but there's nothing wrong with a big nose on a man.

Luckily, the reverse holds true for women, since mine is so small that I have to wad up twists of toilet paper to clean it since I can't fit a finger into my nostril. Not far enough to do any good. I wonder if my nose will win or if Victor's will. The button or the beak. Or if the baby will split the difference and come up with an absolutely average nose. I certainly hope he gets Victor's thick dark hair.

My own pumpkin-colored baby-fine mop is really more tufts than actual hair. It responds more to air currents than to gravity. If I stand under a ceiling fan, my hair squashes down on top and billows out around my neck. If I walk across a vent in the sidewalk, all my tufts waft skyward. Mostly, though, I'm prey to the usual assortment of changing wind directions and my hair swirls around my head in licks and eddies going every which way. I enjoy the variety.

"The nausea any better today?" Victor booms at me.

"Oh, well. I guess so. The color schemes seem to be improving. The lentil loaf I blew yesterday just really wasn't one of my best pieces, if you know what I mean." Being nervous and talking is always a losing combination for me.

"It certainly looks as if you're feeling better," Hillary says, staring at my plate. At first she beams at me for eating all of the Bonus Meal. But then her eyebrows crinkle together and she steps forward, still staring at my empty plate.

I wish Mercedes had left a little of the liver behind for more realism.

"I mean," Hillary says. "I was only out of the kitchen for a minute or two and you managed to finish off your entire dinner?"

She knows. There's no point in lying. "Well, you see . . ."

"Oh, man," Mercedes breaks in just before I confess. "Don't let looks fool you. This little *flaca*'s a chowhound and a half. I coon belief my eyes, the way she was packing it in. I said, 'Hey, slow down. Take you a breath or two. That cow ain't going nowhere!' " Mercedes laughs.

"Well, good," Hillary says. "I'm sure Trudy has the baby's best interest foremost in her thoughts and would never even *consider* cheating it nutritionally."

"Naw," Mercedes answers. "She'd never even consider doing that."

"Okay, then, good, if you ladies will excuse me, I've got to . . ." Victor points over his shoulder and edges toward the door. Hillary beams a final smile at me, puts a slender hand on Victor's upper arm, and follows him out.

Mercedes is unpacking the white Styrofoam boxes that the Goettlers' dinner was delivered in. They've had their favorite restaurants fix take-out dinners for them every night for the past two weeks, ever since I've been living with them. Tonight is grilled amberjack with pineapple-tomatillo salsa from Cappy's Heart Healthy menu. The take-out dinners are part of Hillary's new regime. She and Victor are practicing staying at home in preparation for having a baby. Hillary knows that they won't be able to eat out *every* night like they usually do, but she also feels that their lives don't really have to change.

"Parenthood," she likes to tell me, "is mostly a matter of organization. It's a time-management problem."

Mercedes spoons portions of amberjack and tomatillo sauce onto the Goettler family china with the Goettler family herald glazed onto them. The herald involves a stag with enormous antlers and other Teutonic elements. Mercedes puts a plate in the microwave. I move back out of the way of the waves.

"Thanks for covering for me," I whisper to Mercedes.

She shrugs. *"Por nada.* I like to lie. It's my hobby. Now, you"—she points her metal slotted spoon coated in mushroom sauce at me—"you. I bet you couldn't tell a lie if your Sancho was hiding naked under the bed and your husband was standing there with a thirty gauge."

I smile but don't answer. There have been lies, plenty of lies. A person either has to be fearless or rich not to have to lie. Oh, yes, there have been lies. I tiptoe over to Mercedes for a whiff of the fish. For the first time in weeks my stomach doesn't knot up at the smell of food. Without a word Mercedes pulls out another plate, scrapes what is left in the Styrofoam boxes onto it, and hands it to me.

"Here, get you your nutrition off this. Plenty calcium and it don't look like the dog already got through with it." She shoves the plate into my hands.

"Mercedes," I hiss, glancing around to make sure the door is still closed. "This is *their* dinner."

"Orale, huisa, you don't want it. Give to me. Arnufio likes it when I bring these hotty-totty things home for him."

I hesitate.

"Hey, you seen 'em out there." She points to the dining room. "He eats about half what he got on his plate, then he does like this." Mercedes presses her lips together and punches herself in the stomach, imitating Victor abusing his imaginary flab as if he's telling his body that if it dares to make any fat, he'll beat it up.

"And *her.*" Mercedes rolls her dark eyes upward until the brown spots in the white show. "She does like this." Mercedes purses her lips prissily and touches the corner of a napkin to them. "'Oh, I coon eat another bite,'" she trills in a falsetto that doesn't sound a bit like Hillary's cultured voice. "And you know she's so danged hungry she wants to put her face down in that plate and just in-*hale!*"

The microwave pings. Mercedes pulls out one antlered plate and sticks in another. "Hey, I used to give them the whole thing. Just have to come in next morning and scrape it off the plates straight into the garbage. So, *come, come.* Eat, eat!" The microwave pings again. She grabs the other plate and plows into the dining room with it. The swinging door hasn't even slowed on its hinges before Mercedes is back. I am still staring at the fancy dinner in front of me.

"You want to hear?" Mercedes climbs up on the second rung of my stool and pulls the grating open on the duct above my head. Most evenings we tune in on their conversation.

Like the sound track to a wonderful movie from the forties, Hillary's voice filters down from above my head. "I told the Klagles that the eighteenth is impossible."

I imagine them out in the dining room. Like the kitchen, the walls are plaster-caked. Out there, though, they've been painted a brooding oxidized green. They have a Mission-style table covered with a vivid turquoise wash that is even more massive than the one in the kitchen. Their chairs, rudely cured Mexican leather affairs that a local artist has painted in gum-drop fiesta colors, squeak every time they move. A crudely carved *retablo* taken from a chapel altar in northern New Mexico sits on the sideboard, another Hall of the Giants piece of furniture, this one carved with Zuni Indian designs.

Hillary plans on having the walls scraped and bringing back the brocade wallpaper and spindly Goettler family antiques that were in the dining room before.

"Good. Good," Victor mutters. "What's our story?"

"You're conducting a seminar on reorganization for multi-family investors."

" 'Conducting?' You sure you don't want to have me heading an institute or something."

"Victor." Hillary's tone sharpens a bit. "If I'm going to have to do your lying for you, I don't want my fiction critiqued. Oh, I just remembered. I haven't done my assignment yet for my Power of Myth class at the Jung Center tonight."

"Assignment?"

"Victor." Hillary is exasperated. "I told you. We're supposed to write up a description of our parents in terms of gods and goddesses."

"Bamsie and Jack? Gods and goddesses? Of what? The 'highball at nightfall'? Patchwork golf pants?"

"Victor, don't sneer. If we're going to have a child, we first have to liberate ourselves from the child within. There's a lot of profound work we have to do, and we aren't going to get it done by sitting back and sneering. When you become a parent, you surrender the luxury of sneering."

"You're right, Hillary. You're deeply, mythically, right."

"So, you're going to come with me?"

"Love to, babe, but, jeez, I'm buried. You know I've got that deposition tomorrow. Monfort just went over the falls without a barrel. We'll be picking up body parts for the next month."

"Okay." Hillary relents. "But when we start dealing with what Campbell has to say about the mother as hero, about the heroic deed of giving your life over for another, I want you to be there."

"With bells on," Victor agrees in a way that precludes any possibility of his ever appearing at a Power of Myth class.

In a low voice Hillary asks, "Do you think Trudy really ate her dinner? All of it? In two minutes?"

"She said she did, didn't she?"

"Well, no, *she* didn't actually say that she had. Mercedes more or less answered for her, which leads me to believe that—"

Hillary's words are lost in the sound of a car honking outside the kitchen.

Mercedes bustles to the back window. "Ay, Arnufio's here."

I join her as she flags a wave to her husband in his old Pontiac LeMans. The car looks like a pinto horse from all the spots where the paint is worn or rusted away to the primer. Arnufio acknowledges the wave by slinking down a little in the driver's seat, a *cholo* cruising in his lowrider. He has the look of a wild young man wearing a grandfather's mask of wrinkles and gray hair. Three of Mercedes's grandchildren, the little girls, Eulalia, Samantha, and Nikta, are in the backseat of the Pontiac grabbing a comic book away from each other. Arnufio ignores them. Even though it's thirty degrees outside, he's got the window rolled down and is resting his forearm on it. He picks through the hairs on his arm, pulling the flesh up for a closer look, stops, and honks again.

"*Chee-wah-wee-tah!* Keep your shoes on!" Mercedes mutters in her husband's direction.

A second later Hillary picks up the little ceramic bell by her setting and we hear a far-off tinkling that is Mercedes's signal to clear the table.

"About time." Mercedes throws her blocky bottom against the door, bursts into the dining room butt-first, and has her apron off before she gets back into the kitchen with a teetering stack of plates and glasses which she dumps into the sink to wash tomorrow.

"*Hasta mañana, flaca.*" Mercedes grabs her black vinyl purse and barges out the back door. Mercedes gets in back with her granddaughters and all three cuddle around her. Arnufio blams out, his pinto car blasting unmufflered farts into the King William air.

I go back to my dinner and replay my last glimpse of Victor's face. Needless to say, his physical characteristics are much on my mind lately. I think about the way his jaw bunched up when he was on the phone. I hope Sweet Pea inherits one hundred percent in the jaw department from Victor. My lips and jaw are on the small side. I guess I wouldn't mind if the baby got my eyes. Maybe not quite as big as mine. But then again, why not? They're the one thing I've always been complimented on.

There's no chance that Sweet Pea will inherit my most distinguishing characteristic. My voice. It's high. Stratospherically high. One of Sinclair's friends, a Latin America studies major who always called the U.S. "this country" as if he had came from somewhere much farther south than his hometown of Darien, Connecticut, asked me the first time he heard me speak, "Did you just breathe helium?" Sinclair actually liked my voice. It reminded him of the high-pitched, strangled way real old-timey cartoon characters like Krazy Kat used to talk.

No possibility of a Krazy Kitten. Sweet Pea won't even ever hear my voice.

My voice is probably responsible for my spotty education. School itself I never minded, and there was quite a bit I actually liked: extra credit reports on marsupials. Salt maps of the world. Baking soda and vinegar volcanoes. Recess was what I hated. And lunchtime. And the walk to and from. My voice became a social liability very early on. When the other children outgrew their baby simpers and mine lingered on, its keening, almost pleading register doomed me to certain roles within the playgroup. I could be, for example, the one all the other little girls ran away from. Or I could be the object of various chants, such as:

> Nanny, nanny boo-boo
> Trudy smells like poo-poo.

I'm sure there were other factors besides my voice. Perhaps people like myself excrete a hormone that signals to the group that you are the one to be run away from. Who knows? In any case, school slipped very far down on my list of preferred activities. I didn't plan, in the beginning, to stop going. It just seemed that other forces took control and preempted school. I would set out in the mornings and, before I knew it, I would find myself strolling through a Solomon's mine of treasures. The pickings were especially lush on trash days: pots of only slightly wilted chrysanthemums, a game of

Chutes and Ladders minus a few markers, a pair of ruby-red heels cracking just the tiniest bit across the instep, a metal-flake lampshade. Once, gleaming in the morning sun, I even found a pair of cut-glass salt and pepper shakers with silver lids. The treasures people put out with their trash had their own geography that lured me farther and farther away from formal education.

When my truancy was reported to my mom, Randi, she would sigh and say, "Trudy lives in her own world. She always has. Her father and I have just never been able to reach her."

Then, for a while, my father would drive me to school. We left early, after I finished a small pink plastic bowl of Special K moistened with bluish skim milk and barely sweetened with the one level teaspoon of sugar that my mother measured out. Once we were out of the house, away from Randi, my *father's* treasure hunts would begin: Dunkin' Donuts for creme-filleds. Seven Eleven for honey buns. IHOP for Belgian waffles. Denny's for link sausage and over-easies.

My father weighed 380 pounds at his peak. My mother never asked how he could have bulked up to such an astounding degree on the diet of Special K and broiled fish that she served. My father never let me eat so much as a crumb of buttered toast when I was with him. We both understood that we each had our own treasure maps to follow and couldn't expect anyone else to understand the paths they took us down.

After a week or two of being driven to school, the crisis would seem to be over and, soon, I'd be walking to school on my own. Then dawdling, then meandering, then failing to show up altogether. Fortunately, my father, a salesman who was particularly hard on the suspension systems of company cars, could never hold a job for long and we'd move before any official action could be taken.

4. I first met Hillary two years ago. My counselor at unemployment, Mrs. Navarro, was getting fed up with me. Like many others, she didn't think I took my professional life seriously enough. I, on the other hand, didn't see how *any-*

one could take seriously the kind of job she found for them. At my last place of employment, my boss would put some numbers on a form, staple the pages together, carry the form to my desk, and deposit it in my In box. I would then unstaple the form, photocopy it, restaple the form that had just been stapled and unstapled, and file it. If for one second I had taken *that* job seriously, I would be lining up for lunch at someplace where the inmates are not allowed to have forks.

"Trudy, I see no evidence that you are applying yourself to the job search," Mrs. Navarro told me. She reviewed my employment record. "You have a pattern of staying on a job just long enough to collect benefits, then getting fired. How does that happen, Trudy?"

"Beats me," I answered. I tell almost nothing *but* lies to authority figures. What's my choice? Should I have explained to Mrs. Navarro that there is no way on this earth that I am ever going to save enough to take a vacation, so I let unemployment provide them for me between the time I go from one interchangeable job to another? Besides, it isn't as if I go off on a Caribbean cruise. I take the time to work on my art.

Mrs. Navarro, who had a new perm, shook her tight gray poodle curls and sighed. It made me feel bad that she took my case so to heart. She slid a three-by-five card across the desk toward me. "Did you notice this listing?" she asked.

All the jobs were posted in thick notebooks. On the weeks when I was giving myself a vacation I would come in and pick the three most unsuitable out of the "Clerical" book to apply for. Then, if by some unwanted miracle I was called back for an interview, I would go in and drop hints about how the sexual harassment suit against my last boss was going. Or, if the interview was with a woman, I'd mention apropos of nothing, that I had no bitter thoughts, angry feelings, or deep, festering resentments about taking orders from one of my own kind, from *just another* woman.

Sometimes even that wasn't enough, though, to deter potential employers. One office manager, for example, was so out of it that she had actually asked me back for a second interview. I had to show up in a dirty sweat suit and not brush my teeth for three days to head *that* threat of gainful employment off. But, this time, my benefits were running out, so I took the card Mrs. Navarro held out to me and looked at it.

"I thought it might interest you," Mrs. Navarro said. "Given your academic background."

"Wow," I whispered to myself as I read the particulars. "The San Antonio Museum of Folk Art." The Folk Art Museum is where I hope I'll go when I die.

I set up an interview as soon as I could even though it meant foregoing my last couple of days of benefits. I found out that my interviewer and potential boss would be Hillary Goettler. Several days before the appointment, I went on a reconnaissance mission. I wanted to check the office out, see what people wore, especially this Hillary Goettler, so that I would have a better chance of fitting in. I have sporadic bursts of focus like that when I get really determined about something, but they're so exhausting that I don't do them very often and my life quickly slips back into chaos.

I arrived at the Folk Art Museum just as a thin young woman in fashionable black cotton was unlocking the front door. For an hour I was the only person there. I wandered through the exhibits, enjoying the cultured hush and the morning light streaming in from windows three stories above my head. My life would be perfect if I could come here every day.

Usually when I visit the Folk Art Museum I am intent upon the exhibits. Typically, I carry a sketchbook to jot down designs I want to copy in my own projects. But that day I could barely pretend to look at the handcarved dolls from Armenia, the Zingu feathered headdresses, the Indonesian batiks, the Yoruban burial masks, the Inuit food-stirrers, the New Guinean peanut-grinding boards, the Maori fish eye pluckers, the Kwakiutl winnowing trays. My reconnaissance mission was uppermost in my mind.

Gradually, I made my way over to the administrative offices, and when no one was looking, slipped in. There was a large reception area where the secretaries and other underlings sat. Private offices for the bigwigs opened off it.

I don't know if it's how I dress or just my whole being, but the way a leopard disappears in a jungle, that's how I am in an office. Clerical coloration, I guess. I picked a pile of folders off the first unoccupied desk I passed and ambled in using my going-to-the-Xerox-machine gait. It's a walk that's slow but not reluctant because, believe it or not, for a lot of us clerical types, going to the Xerox machine is the most entertaining thing that happens all day. Almost a social outing with the prospect of running into someone from another section whom you don't actively hate the way you hate all your immediate work neighbors.

I peeked into all the offices I passed, studying how everyone was dressed. When I saw the name Hillary Goettler and the title Docent Coordinator written on a door, I stopped. I didn't want my potential boss to so much as glimpse my face. I pressed as far back against the door frame as I could without attracting attention, then slowly peeked around the edge. I was just drawing a bead on Hillary's empty desk when she came up behind me and asked, "Are you looking for me?"

I jerked away from her to hide my face, and the entire contents of the file folders I clutched slid down my front. Grabbing them as they reached my crotch, I ducked my head and mumbled into my collar, "No, no, no. Standard documentation rerouting. Prioritization of print facilitation. You know, S.O.P."

The folders slid past the barrier of my hand and continued inching down my thighs. I squatted so that there wouldn't be as much of an incline and halted the avalanche of files just as they reached my knees. Papers escaped and fluttered about me. I looked like Chuck Berry as I duck-walked to the door, still mumbling, my face buried in my collar. My eyes at about waistband level, I noticed that Hillary was holding the door open for me.

"Implementing executive directives," I muttered wildly, swiveling my head from side to side to deflect her gaze.

"Here." Hillary stooped down and gathered up a pile of the fallen papers. "You lost these. . . ." We both glanced at them at the same moment. They were crayon drawings from a file labeled "Creating the Creative Child." ". . . 'directives,' " Hillary finished dryly.

"Um, um, yes, well. Thank you." I grabbed the drawings and scuttled away.

Though not without a price, I *had* achieved my main objective: appraisal of the boss's outfit. In our few seconds of contact I burned every detail of Hillary's ensemble into my memory. I stepped into the crisp November sunshine muttering to myself, "Speedskater-looking black unitard. Chunky ziggurat earrings. Lizard elf boots." The effect was quite arty.

Naturally, when I returned to the museum for my interview later in the week, I was wearing my version of that very outfit. A budget version. A black aerobics unitard from Solo Serve. Nubbly "lizard-look" elf boots from Kinney Shoes. A great pair of chunky earrings I made myself from discarded computer chips. It was a reasonable facsimile.

I went into the interview praying that Hillary wouldn't remember me. My prayers were not answered. She took one look at me and asked, "Weren't you in here the other day?"

I've had more than my share of bosses, probably half of them women and none of them exactly what you'd hope for. In the way of most bosses, particularly in state work, they were second-raters who created more problems than they ever solved. But Hillary was entirely different. From my first glimpse of her it was obvious that she was a first-rater. I couldn't dismiss her the way I had my other bosses. And I couldn't lie to her. At least not then. I admitted that I had been the person clutching papers to my crotch.

"Why?"

"I . . ." I shrugged and winced. "I really want the job."

Hillary stared at me for a long moment while she wiggled a pencil between her long fingers. No fingernail polish. Antique wedding ring. Finally she smiled. She had perfect small teeth in a wide dental arch. "You were checking us out!" She cocked her head, seemingly delighted by this realization. "Now, *that's* resourceful. You really do want this job, don't you?"

"Oh, yeah. Lots." It was a heartfelt answer.

She tapped the eraser of the pencil decisively on her

desk. "I like that, I like that a lot. Any drone can come in here and type and file. But you, you"—she checked my résumé—"Trudy! You've got that extra spark that can't be taught and can't be learned. It's that spark that I want in my assistant."

I thrilled to her use of the word "assistant" rather than secretary.

She breezed through my résumé. "Received your bachelor of arts six years ago in, well, perfect. Perfect! Art education!" She looked up at me, her eyes glittering somewhere between gray and blue and asked, "Could there be a more perfect background for the assistant to the coordinator of volunteer docents?"

I smiled with relief and delight. "Probably not."

"The spark *and* the background. I don't think I need to look any further, do you, Trudy?" She shut my personnel file, giving the impression that a shoot-from-the-hip devil-may-care executive decisiveness was one of her hallmarks. That she left things like thorough readings of résumés to the "drones" and acted on finely honed intuition. I learned later that Hillary did indeed like to give that impression, but only because thorough research had revealed to her that seventy-three percent of executive respondents considered such decisiveness a prerequisite for any top management candidate.

She narrowed her large, intelligent, now solidly gray eyes at me and smiled. "We're going to make a great team, you and I. We're going to put this docent program on the map."

I had the job!

Hillary's cavalier dismissal of my résumé was one of those tiny slips that end up changing lives more than all the degree planning and career counseling in the world can. But neither one of us knew it that day. Or for a long time afterward. At first all *I* knew was that for the first time in my life I didn't get up on a workday morning with my stomach hurting.

I loved working with Hillary. I learned from her. Just being in her presence was like taking graduate courses in style. She had her own way of dressing that made all the rich women who came in to volunteer look like jumped-up sharecroppers. Everything she did or wore was exactly right. She could pile her hair up on top of her head and run a pencil through it and look like she was ready for a *Vogue* magazine layout. She could pin a toy out of a gum machine onto her blouse and have the director of the Dallas Fine Arts Council begging to know where she could get a "witty piece" just like it.

Best of all, she always made me feel as if we really were a team. I know that it was just a management technique, but that's like saying that the Civil War was fought for economic reasons more than to free slaves. The effect in both cases was that the slaves were freed. I wasn't just removing staples. I was helping Hillary create a top-notch docent program so that visitors to the museum could get as much as possible out of it.

Together we started a recruitment drive, and even more women from rich neighborhoods poured in wearing long denim prairie skirts with boots and loads of jewelry from their last trip to Santa Fe. The docents all adored Hillary. I think she was exactly who they wish they could have been if they'd been able to start their lives about twenty years later in the century.

Just a few well-placed remarks from Hillary about the dire straits the museum was in and how tenuous her job and the future of the entire docent program was, and the checks flooded in. It seemed too easy. But, as Hillary explained to me, "Women like that are more than willing to pay to have a purpose in life. I mean, it beats sitting around at home looking up the Spanish word for toilet so you can criticize the way the maid's cleaning the commode."

She had a point and the women could certainly spare the cash. This sudden spurt of contributions yielded two results. First, the museum got an excellent new exhibit of paper burial goods from Singapore. Great stuff. Paper radios, paper shirts, paper cars. And always the best brands: Sony, Arrow, Mercedes-Benz. No cheap shit in the afterlife. The grieving family commissioned all these incredible tissue creations, then burned them up so that the deceased would be better furnished in the next life than he had been in this one.

That was one result. But the real result, the one Hillary had been angling for, was that she was appointed assistant director. "Now," she said. "Now! Things will start happening."

And they did. I loved coming in every day to find out what energetic new plan Hillary had dreamed up and how I could help her carry it out: A mailing to the Opera Guild. An exhibit of "Tactile Surprises" especially for the seeing-impaired. A proposition for the city council to have September twelfth through the nineteenth declared San Antonio Folk Art Week. All my life I'd wanted to be part of a team doing something important, and I finally was. Plus, I was getting lots of ideas for my own art. For the first time in my employed life I wasn't plotting out how to get fired so that I could collect unemployment for a few weeks. I happily settled into a job.

I suppose it was this feeling of permanence that triggered the dreams. Maybe job hopping had even been a way to keep them at bay. Who knows? All I know is that I began again to dream about the baby I hadn't had. About Sinclair's baby.

In my dreams the baby looked like Sweet Pea from the Popeye cartoons. He wore a long, flowing baby nightgown that hid his feet. Sweet Pea reminded me that I had promised him that he could come again and that time was ticking away. I let the baby know that I was quite aware that time was passing and apologized that I hadn't done a better job of getting myself into circumstances in life that a baby would like. But I hadn't. I ate Vienna sausages cold from the can for dinner one night, then the next I'd have the jelly spread on toast for a second dinner. I couldn't remember to feed a cat. My apartment didn't have room for a crib, and there would be even less room when I started working on my Rey Antonio costume. My crafts projects involved the use of many solvents that would surely crinkle a baby's delicate lungs. The water in my toilet was permanently ringed in fuzzy green. I simply didn't think my life was one a baby would care to share. I loved it, but it was clearly unsuitable for a baby.

Sweet Pea let me know that he wasn't interested in excuses. That he wanted to get into the game and pronto.

That was when I was forced to mention the one inescapable fact about my setup that made his demands impossible. I'd have to point out that my arrangement was entirely lacking in a male, father-type individual to provide the vital spurt needed to propel a baby soul into the material world.

Sweet Pea answered that this lack was just awfully poor

planning on my part and that I'd better start rectifying matters. P.D.Q.

I'd wake up burdened yet relieved after these dreams. Sweet Pea's demands were certainly justified; there simply wasn't a thing I could do about them. I was thirty-eight. I hadn't had sex since I was thirty-five. There was no way for me to have a baby. My life, my perfect life, could go on.

These dreams make it sound as if, deep down, I secretly and desperately yearned to have a baby. I didn't. I never have. Even when I was a little girl, I didn't like playing with dolls. I liked *making* dolls or taking mine apart and gluing their eyes and hair onto my autograph dog. But I never liked doing anything that would resemble mothering them. It seems to be a hormonal thing that you either have or you don't have, and it strikes the most unlikely people.

I've been told all my life how good I'd be with children. I even believed it long enough to take a job as a helper at a day care center. What I quickly discovered, though, was that I didn't want to show a bunch of preschoolers how to make Christmas bells out of cut-up egg cartons. I wanted to make bells myself and to paint them with Etruscan designs I'd found in a Dover catalogue. I was utterly bewildered when they cried or shrieked or looked to me for guidance.

I thought that when I got older, some sort of instinct would take hold of me and I'd go from wanting to make Christmas bells to wanting to make babies. It never did. There were only the dreams of Sweet Pea, ordering me to march a path my hormones hadn't laid out for me.

It was near the end of my first year that Hillary started to have weekly doctor's appointments at her lunch hour. Usually she came back from lunch all charged up, ready for the second half of the day. Except on the days when she had

"Dr. Appt" marked on her calendar. On those days she'd come back an hour, two hours late, shut her door, and not take any calls for the rest of the afternoon. If I did have to go in for some emergency, she'd always be staring out the window, dreamy and distracted.

I put two and two together and figured out that Hillary was having an affair. I mean, anyone who gets up at six in the morning for a high impact aerobics class can't be feeling all *that* puny. A tragic, doomed affair was the only force I could think of that would take the wind out of Hillary's sails so badly. I imagined a secret Hillary, one who could be "released" only by a secret lover. A muscular day laborer, perhaps, who kept his wallet on a chain? A boy, a tender young sapling with three hairs under his arm? A woman? I tried then to imagine what fatal flaw her apparently perfect husband was hiding that drove Hillary into the arms of another. Premature ejaculation came to mind.

I understood love affairs that drenched a person in regret and depleted their energy. I didn't harbor the tiniest shred of disapproval, only curiosity about what sort of man or woman could put Hillary so far off her Minute-Minder. I might even have been a little jealous of him. Or her. Every time she came back from one of her long lunches, I got a little more curious. That's why one day when she bolted out of the office saying "I may be a bit late getting back," I followed her.

This was more daring than it sounds, as I don't own a car and I had to do my sleuthing by bicycle. But the snarl of San Antonio's creeping downtown traffic played in my favor, and I actually ended up having to hang back on Navarro Street so that I wouldn't pass her silver Volvo.

I'd hoped for a glimpse of the mystery lover as he or she

waited in the shadows; instead, Hillary pulled the Volvo into the parking garage of a building with a plaque outside that read NIX MEDICAL BUILDING.

My heart froze. Hillary actually *was* sick. My perfect job was in danger. I raced back to the office and began calling every doctor with a Nix Medical Building listing saying I had an urgent message for patient Hillary Goettler. I didn't have to fake a wobbly note of panic when I called the one office listed under oncology. I knew that it was entirely possible that Hillary would keep up with her high impact aerobics program in the face of a cut that did not heal, a mole that changed color or size.

I breathed again when the receptionist said in a snippy tone, "No. No Hillary Goettler has been in today."

The last listing that had any entries in the Nix was women's reproductive systems. I dialed the number of a Dr. Meador V. Wiegand, and the receptionist told me that Hillary had just left.

"I can probably still catch her," she offered, caught up in the spirit of my frantic request.

"No, it's better that I tell her in person," I said, spurred on by the receptionist's sympathetic tone.

In the general listings I found a small display ad that read WIEGAND, MEADOR V., FERTILITY SPECIALIST, and it all fell into place: Hillary had stroller lust. This confirmed my theory about hormonal urges striking the most unlikely of women, since it was hard to imagine Hillary doing anything as unfastidious as even chewing her cuticle. Forget about giving birth and changing diapers.

Of course I'd peeked at Hillary's personnel folder, but even if I hadn't, I would have known that she was the kind of person with a sort of four-wheel-drive attitude toward life, churning over obstacles in a higher gear than most of us manage to work up to. I imagine that's how someone ends up in the Who's Who of High School Women. Captain of the debate team. Undergraduate degree in art history from NYU. Master's from Harvard in museology. With a lawyer husband from one of the most socially prominent families in San Antonio.

So, with this Bigfoot approach to life mudbogging over problems, I can imagine how frustrated Hillary must have felt when she decided to do something simple, something that almost anyone with ovaries could do, something even *I* could do and she could not accomplish it.

I'd read women's magazines where they talk about the "anguish" of infertility, so I had to assume that part of Hillary's frustration was anguish. Actual real pain. But I could only assume, since I've never had any of the feelings the magazines talk about. The yearning to hold a little body next to yours. The emptiness of a life without someone to care for. The joy of watching a little one grow up. It just always seemed to me that these voids could be filled nicely with a kitty. Not that I'm even that great with cats. I tend to forget to feed them and they tend to run off and find, I hope, better homes.

Once I pieced all this together, that Hillary wanted a baby, that Victor was apparently ready to father one, my dreams changed. Sweet Pea stopped demanding and began to gloat. That's all he did, simply watched me with one nearly invisible baby eyebrow cocked and waited. It infuriated me that he wouldn't tell me what he was waiting for, but, two weeks later, I woke up and knew. I can't say I was happy about the knowledge. I even prayed for a few days for an early menopause. But my feelings in the matter were beside the point. Sweet Pea pointed out that I now had a way to make good on my promise. That all the key players necessary for bringing a baby into the world were now present in my life. How I got them together was entirely my problem. He'd been waiting almost ten years and, after all, a deal *is* a deal.

5. Once I decided that Hillary and I were going to collaborate, one of my rare fits of focus came over me. I saw clearly that Sweet Pea's plan would not work unless Hillary thought it was all her idea. And that it would work a whole lot better if she felt she had to talk me into it. So I started dropping hints.

When Maureen, head of museum security, who was eight months pregnant with her third baby, would waddle past our open door, I'd sigh and say to Hillary, "Oh, to be heavy with child." (I've noticed that babies give a person license to more lyricism than is usually allowed in everyday life.) Then I'd laugh and add quickly, "Of course, what would *I* do with a child?"

I carried on like this for a couple of weeks, but all that happened was that Hillary asked if we needed to have the ventilation system looked at.

The problem with really smart people like Hillary is that they ignore the obvious. I was afraid Maureen's baby would be potty-trained long before Hillary took the bait. But finally, after another two weeks of Maureen waddling past, then me sighing, Hillary clicked. It was a memorable moment. For the first time in months, she brightened up. Her face glowed, her eyes twinkled and she said, "You know, Trudy, you're right. Every woman should have the *experience* of giving birth to a child. Not that every woman is necessarily fit to *raise* a child."

This is another characteristic of smart people, they tend to work from the general to the specific. They seem to feel better if they make a law then force themselves to obey it.

"To say the least," I agreed heartily, snorting a little laugh. "Look at me, for instance."

And that is just what Hillary did. Looked at me. For a very long time. I knew what she was thinking too: Not the best, but with Victor's genes and an enriched atmosphere, I think we might be able to overcome the genetic handicaps.

Which is pretty much how I had the whole deal figured as well.

A week later, at about 1:30 in the afternoon, Maureen's water broke and soaked her secretarial chair with pinkish fluid.

"Wow, I guess it wasn't the bean burrito," she announced, having earlier ascribed certain heaving and churning sensations to lunch at Taco Bell.

Everyone scurried around mopping up with soggy handfuls of brown towels from the restroom dispenser. I was the one who thought to call her husband, Chuck, at the auto parts store he managed. Then we all settled down to watch Maureen. About every ten minutes she would roll her eyes up, open her mouth like a hooked bass, suck in air, clench spasmodically at her desk blotter, then gasp, "Hoo boy! That was a good one!" as she let the air hiss back out.

Hillary watched her too. By the end of half a dozen contractions, Hillary looked worse than Maureen, pale, trembling and sweating. You didn't have to be a mind reader to see that she considered this an experience to be avoided. I agreed. But then, for me there wasn't much choice involved.

"Where is that husband of hers?" Becky from Security asked every time Maureen clenched up. Then Becky would stride off officiously, holding the walkie-talkie she wore on her belt against her beefy hip so that it wouldn't bang against her.

"He's here!" Becky announced just about the time we were all starting to get seriously worried and the number 911 had begun cropping up in our conversation.

Chuck was late because he'd had to borrow a car after he put his truck into reverse when he was leaving the auto parts store and had impaled it upon a concrete stanchion. By this time things were moving along pretty swiftly and Maureen had switched from "Hoo boy!" after each contraction to "Goddamn cocksucker!" which Chuck assured us meant that the time was drawing nigh. We followed them down the hall, then watched from the window. As every tiny movement caused Maureen considerable pain, we knew she probably didn't enjoy it when Chuck stuffed her into the tiny sports car he'd borrowed. Or when he rammed the car into the building before pulling out. He probably thought he was in reverse.

We were all still clustered by the window, watching Chuck skitter and jerk out of the parking lot when Hillary called me into her office.

"Could you . . ." She nodded at the door behind me. I knew she wanted me to shut it, but I pointed to it anyway so she would have to nod before I shut it.

"Trudy, what I'm about to suggest is going to sound very strange to you at first, so I don't want you to say anything. Just take some time, Trudy, to think about my proposal. To really consider it. Now, Trudy, I'm going to tell you something that I would like kept in the strictest confidence."

She had never used my name so many times in a row. It gave me a tiny power thrill to hear her playing up to me. Hillary looked away from me and the fine skin over her fine bone structure tightened. I knew she was about to reveal her big "secret."

I wanted to stop and tell her that she didn't have to spell it out for me. Or, really, for anyone else at the museum, since Maureen had a friend who went to the same fertility doctor as Hillary and the friend had told Maureen months ago about seeing Hillary there with Victor. About Victor filling his specimen jar. Naturally this all became the hot topic of conversation in the lunchroom among those of us who brought sandwiches.

Maureen, who is obviously ga-ga about kids, offered the opinion that Hillary's "barrenness," as she called it, was a great tragedy that no amount of money or success or even an incredibly sexy husband that *she* wouldn't kick out of *her* bed for eating crackers could ever make up for. I didn't see the big void, but the coffee room women, the ones with children, told me I just didn't understand.

"Bearing children, that's what it means to be a woman," Becky said. She has four. They're all either in special ed or on parole. Still, all the bearers nodded and said their silent prayers for Hillary. Anyway, we were pretty well versed in Hillary's dilemma. I didn't think, though, that knowing that most of the museum's hourly wage staff has been pulling for her all this time would make Hillary feel any better, so I kept my face a blank while she revealed her dark secret.

"I have a fertility problem."

I guess I succeeded with the blank look too well. "Fertility," Hillary prodded. "I can't get pregnant."

"Oh," I said, crimping my mouth into an "O" of belated understanding. "And you want to. Have children."

"Yes. Victor and I have thought about it and discussed it a great deal. The timing is perfect right now. The bulk of Victor's clientele is coming out of reorganization, and for me, a brief professional hiatus would be beneficial."

She meant that Mr. Vogel, the director, was retiring and the executive board might ask her to take over as *acting* director while they conducted a nationwide head hunt for a seasoned director. A well-timed absence would give the board an opportunity to appreciate all Hillary did before they had a chance to decide that she was too young and had risen too rapidly.

"Anyway," Hillary continued. "This is an ideal time for Victor and me to start our family, but because of certain . . . problems, it's impossible."

Hostile cervical mucus was Maureen's guess. She described her friend's treatment to overcome just such a difficulty. Betty had wondered about Victor's motility.

I tried to think how I would react to Hillary's news if I didn't have secret plans of my own. What I would say if I weren't trying to herd Sweet Pea into her life? Helpful, I decided. I would probably try to be helpful.

"Aren't there all sorts of new techniques for problems such as this?"

Hillary's face knotted up and her eyes opened wide. "No!" she said with a startling firmness that made me remember how pale and trembly she'd gone watching Maureen in labor. She had the same expression on her face except that this time I realized what it was: fear. Hillary was terrified of labor.

She blinked twice, the muscles relaxed, and she said again, softly this time, "No. I looked into those procedures. Sperm washing. Testing the viability of sperm on hamster eggs. In vitro. Gamete intrafallopian transfer. Zygote intrafallopian transfer. God, think of how many times a person would have to take her clothes off in front of strangers. And even then there's no guarantee of success. Can you believe that? None of these programs will give me any guarantee. I mean, I have friends who have been at this business for years. Years! Their lives just grind to a dead halt. No, the lab-rat routine is out. Besides, the women in my family tend to develop varicose veins when they're pregnant. Awful, horrible, spidery things. All blue and bumpy and—" Hillary shuddered.

So it wasn't just labor. Hillary was terrified of *anything* that meddled with her body. I understood the feeling.

"Well, adoption," I said brightly.

"Mmm, yes, that's a possibility, Trude. But really, Trudy, don't all couples yearn to see a bit of their genetic impress upon their offspring? In my case, I'm afraid, it will never be mine, but it would mean everything to Victor to be an actual, biological father."

"Whew, that's going to be kind of tough," I said sympathetically.

"Well, yes, it would be. Unless . . ."

"Unless what?"

"Unless a woman of extraordinary generosity. A woman not bounded by convention. A woman with . . ."

I almost expected her to say "a high squeaky voice" to speed up this narrowing-down process. Instead, Hillary patted herself on the black jersey of her Norma Kamali top slightly beneath her Ugandan bridal necklace and finished. *"Mucho corazón.* Unless I find that woman, it will be more than 'tough' for Victor to ever be a father. As long as we're together it will be im—" She faltered, her chin quivering. "Impossible."

One perfect tear slid down Hillary's cheek. She cried the way I've always wanted to cry, with luminescent dignity. When I cry, I snort and gulp in such overblown quadripedal suffering that any potential comforters are put off by the burlesque quality of my blubbering. But there was Hillary's misery, glistening flawlessly as a diamond on her cheek. She brushed it aside and got down to cases.

"Trudy, I've seen your desperate yearning to bear a child

and I've heard your acknowledgment that you could never provide that child with a proper upbringing. Victor and I, on the other hand, could offer a child the best life imaginable. Yet I can never bear that child."

I nodded as if I were trying to keep up with her but falling just a bit behind. "Boy, just doesn't seem fair." I nodded with sad resignation. I wasn't going to make this easy for her.

Hillary's aristocratic nostrils quivered at my obtuseness, and she tried again. "You know, Trudy, sometimes two women working together can accomplish vastly more than either can on her own."

"Are you going to hire an assistant for me?"

That might have been too thick, because Hillary finally burst out with "Trudy, you have the baby and I take it off your hands and raise it."

I didn't have to fake a look of puzzled annoyance. *Take it off your hands* was pushing it. This was my Sweet Pea she was talking about, after all. My feathers unruffled, though, when I saw that Hillary was struggling to hold herself together. She often talked tough when she wanted to put some snap back in her garters.

"I know it's a difficult concept to get a handle on," she allowed. "Take your time to get used to it."

I did. I held out for Sweet Pea's sake. I wanted him to be the object of much desire. A week later Hillary called me into her office right as I was headed out for the lunchroom and again asked me to close the door. On her calendar she had marked through "Dr. Appt."

"Well?" Hillary asked.

I'll admit it, I enjoyed having the upper hand. Having

Hillary approach me so delicately. Having something she wanted. I held up my lunch sack.

"Mind if I eat while we talk?"

She said she didn't and I pulled out my can of jalapeño-marinated mushrooms and an opener. It's a good, quick lunch which I accompanied with a Big Red soda. Hillary watched with a worried fascination as I opened the can, then speared the spicy mushrooms with the toothpick I had packed for that purpose. Another reason I like this lunch—no dishes.

"Well?" Hillary asked again.

"Well?" I answered. I had a duty to Sweet Pea to make this difficult for her. To put out a few hurdles for her to jump over. Hillary folded her hands and gazed at me warmly.

"We'll pay all your medical expenses and see to it that you get a good, long maternity leave before helping you find another job."

My staying on at the museum was never a possibility. I knew that. Still, Hillary's offer sounded more than fair to me, but while I pretended to mull the proposal over, she upped it to three months before delivery off.

I agreed. What we were doing seemed so abstract, all I could focus on was the time off. With three whole months off I could launch my latest project. I was so excited that I told Hillary about it.

"God, it would be great to have some time to work on the Missile Toads."

"Mistletoes?"

"Hey, that's exactly what you're supposed to think," I said, pleased that my pun had worked. Of course, Hillary still had no idea what I was talking about. I'd made it a rule to keep my projects to myself, but she seemed genuinely interested. Besides, I was pretty proud of this one. "Actually, it's two words. Missile and toads. Missile Toads. They're these Christmas decorations I make out of Sculpie, sculpturing dough. I have about five different little toads in elf costumes I make. Then I put them on the back of Minutemen missiles decorated with holly. Missile toads. Get it?"

"Ee-yeah. Sounds like fun."

"I think I already have a buyer. The woman at Noel Noel is quite interested."

"That's great."

I popped a couple more mushrooms, then held the can out to Hillary. She waved them away. I continued.

"Of course what I'd really like to do is hook up with a novelty outlet that would market the Toads for me nationwide. Royalties are really the only way to make any money at crafts. I mean individual creation is basically a fun way to starve to death, isn't it?" I'd wanted to discuss my projects with Hillary for a long time. Get her professional input. Who knows? Maybe some leads. Of course I didn't want to abuse my personal relationship with her, but a small exhibit, just something off in a corner between the Sumatran enameled nail guards and the Peruvian quill pipes, could really put me on the map.

"You know," I went on. "I did have a show once. Tesoros Gallery. They're closed now. Did I ever show you the reviews?"

"Is that all you're having?" Hillary asked, staring at the empty mushroom can.

"This?" I pointed my toothpick, now tinged with green jalapeño grease, at the can. "Well, I'll probably go to the machine later on and get something for dessert." I was thinking along the lines of a Peanut Plank or one of Tom's other treats. Then I noted the look on Hillary's face. "Or maybe," I quickly amended my disgraceful menu, "I'll just go to the coffee shop and buy an apple."

"And your Missile Toads, what do you paint them with?"

"Hobby enamel?" I answered tentatively. I knew from the way her eyebrows pinched together that this was not a pleasing answer either.

"It's safe for kids," I offered. "They use it to paint models. Especially little boys. They don't sell the stuff you can get high on anymore. Even though it really gave a lot better finish. More impermeability. Humidity now can be—"

"I think you should move in with us. As soon as you get pregnant."

I hadn't considered leaving my apartment. I'd been there since I started on my degree at San Antonio College twenty years ago. Way before the neighborhood got trendy and rents skyrocketed. My landlord, Mr. Braithwaite, held the line for me at $175, asking me not to tell the other tenants what I pay.

"Is that absolutely necessary?" I asked. "I mean, I'm pretty settled where I am. All my stuff's there. I might not, you know, transplant too well." My voice had gone all squeaky and pleading.

Hillary glanced again at the empty mushroom can in my hand. I knew she was thinking about monitoring my diet. "Wouldn't it be kind of fun to live with us? Have all your meals prepared for you?"

"Oh, no question. It's just that . . . my stuff . . . my projects . . ." Panic fluttered through me. I forced myself to stop thinking about what I was doing.

In the end, Hillary agreed to come over and check my place out. We left immediately, zipping up San Pedro toward my neighborhood, Laurel Heights. Most of the important parts of San Antonio are laid out in the shape of a butterfly with two loops of highway supplying the wings on either side of downtown. So, if downtown, where Hillary and I were coming from, is the butterfly body, Laurel Heights is somewhere in the vicinity of the left antenna. (The river, incidentally, would be a stream of butterfly pee pouring out of King William district, the butterfly urethra.) I like living in the antenna area, the spectrum is broader. The rest of San Antonio follows a much stricter color scheme. After work, most blacks go home to the east side, most brown citizens go to the west and south sides, and the pink people head north.

"Did you read where San Pedro was voted ugliest street in the city?" Hillary asked, glancing out the window at the fast food places, the copy shops, the thrift stores, the many old houses redone into lawyers offices.

"It was? What's so bad about it? I can think of lots worse streets." I didn't like having my neighborhood slammed. "Sometimes I think San Antonians don't deserve their city. Maybe it was the same poll you're talking about, but every year they ask people their favorite restaurants and places like Pizza Hut win. They asked for favorite street names, and, here we are, living in a place with street names like Gomer Pyle and Thoreau's Way, and Bikini Street, and guess what won?"

Hillary shrugged.

"Guess," I prodded her.

"Blue Star?" She named a street near her house.

"See, another great name. No, Broadway won. Broadway." I really was disgusted with San Antonio voters. We came to Gil's Used Tires. "Take the next right." We turned onto my street, Laurel. "Was that so ugly?"

Hillary laughed as if I were only pretending to be upset. She stopped laughing when she beheld my apartment building. I was hoping she'd notice the lovely green and tan mosaic work outlining the front doors. Or the incredible poinsettia Mr. Braithwaite had planted last Christmas, how it reached almost to the second floor. Or the cunning miniature doors cut into the big doors that the milkman used to push glass quarts of milk through. But instead, she noticed the dead cottonwood tree and the rust stains dribbling from the air conditioners bulging out of the windows and the graffiti on the sidewalk beneath our feet that told the world that "La China Is a Fucking Bitch and a Dog Whore!!!!"

We went upstairs to my apartment, the place I wanted to live while I was gestating the child I would carry for Mr. and Mrs. Victor Goettler of the King William Historical District. Hillary didn't say anything for a long time. When she finally spoke she asked, "Have you ever heard of the Collier brothers?"

I pointed out to Hillary that, to my knowledge, clutter had little or no effect on fetal development, but her attention was riveted by the giant hand. "What is that?"

"Oh, this?" I hefted the hand up and slid it over my head. "This is my last year's Rey Antonio costume contest winner. I waved to her.

"God! It moves. How on earth do you make it move?"

"Oh, that." I had to yell to make myself heard through the costume. "I used flexible dryer vent tubing for the knuckles and covered everything with stretchy knit fabric and liquid latex so that all the fingers could move. Then I've got a bunch of ropes and springs in here that make all the

joints move. See." I tried to raise the middle finger to dem-
onstrate the bird-shooting ability, but my ceiling was too low
for a full extension.

Hillary made no comment at all. I began sweating and
took the giant hand off.

"Is this supposed to be . . . ."

"Yeah, a human hide." I touched my genuine, deluxe
Huma-Hyde, a rug I had cut out of flesh-colored latex so that
it looked exactly like it had been skinned off a human. Complete with toes and fingers and ears. Another visual pun sort
of piece.

"Here, let me move this out of the way so you can have a
seat." I picked up the skeleton sitting in my Goodwill armchair. I'd dressed him in a hillbilly outfit of overalls and
straw hat. "I call him Abner Cadaver," I said, but Hillary
had already continued her tour of my place.

She stopped and examined the manger scene I had set
up on the kitchen bar. "Oh, I thought those were real." She
touched the little plastic ants I'd glued onto baby Jesus.

"Do you get it?" I asked.

"Get what?"

"The Anty Christ."

"Oh. The Anty Christ. Okay."

Hillary moved on barely glancing at my Dino-Sardines,
the little pterodactyls made out of Sculpie packed in a sardine can, or the Cornyation scene, a mosaic of the crowning
of the King of Riverfest done in candy corn. It wasn't as if I
expected Hillary to offer me my own one-woman exhibit on
the spot or anything, but I was hoping for some sort of
acknowledgment.

All she said, though, was "You've got some really fun
things in here."

I was starting to see that "fun" had replaced "interest-ing" as the all-purpose brush-off. "Kind of folk artish, don't you think?" I suggested hesitantly.

"Folk art?" Hillary touched a scorch mark on one of my Tortilla Goddesses. "Don't you think, really, that folk art has to be the expression of the upwelling of a cultural im-pulse? That it has to come out of a community?"

"You mean unsigned?" Signed versus unsigned was a big issue at the museum.

"Well, by definition, isn't folk art *of* der volk? That would imply anonymity."

"But what about when we did the Luther Crompton show?" Luther Crompton was a gas station attendant in ru-ral Georgia who had built an exact ten-foot-high copy of the Mormon Tabernacle and covered every inch of it with the foil liners from the packs of Salem cigarettes he smoked. Only one spire was left unfoiled when his lungs finally gave out. "His name was on it."

"Yes, but Luther was very explicit about merely being a conduit for a higher power. That he wasn't acting on his own inspiration."

"I guess I'm just not religious enough to be a folk art-ist."

I would have liked Hillary to disagree with me, but she was peeking into the kitchen. The sink was filled with purple dye and the giant eggplant curtains I was batiking. I had all my Missile Toad stuff—enamels, Sculpie, half-finished toads and missiles—spread out across most of the counters. There wasn't an edible anywhere in sight.

"Trudy, we'll pay you ten thousand dollars when the baby is born if you'll move in with us. We'll pay all your living expenses and give you a generous allowance and pay your rent here while you're gone."

"Move in with you? You know, Hillary, I think it might be disrupting, upsetting, for me to move. I'm sure that a disrupted, upset mother would be bad for a baby, wouldn't she? Wouldn't it be better if I stay here in familiar surroundings?"

"Trudy, you have a really good point. I'm really pleased that you're putting the baby's well-being above all else. Why don't you move in right now so you'll have plenty of time to adjust before the actual pregnancy starts?"

This was not going at all well. "I . . ."

"Trudy, look around. Really look."

I did. I looked at my place through Hillary's eyes. I looked at it as an incubator for her baby. It *was* unsuitable.

"You're right," I had to agree.

Still, leaving would be hard. I'd grown attached. The Formica dinette set with the top like the ocean around Isla Mujeres and all. It would be hard to leave.

6. I woke up sobbing this morning at four-thirty. My mini-sized bladder has shrunk recently to micro size. All my life I've been able to confine dark thoughts to my sleeping mind. Something in prego hormones has liberated the gloomy ruminations I usually manage to sleep through.

I wake up knowing clearly that I was never meant to be a mother. Even biologically. That my arrangement is a mistake. That it has ruined my relationship with Hillary. That I hate being trapped in the Schier mansion. That I will retch if I have to face another Bonus Meal. I ache to be back in my little apartment crammed with all my stuff. The gravity in this room is too low for me. The canopy above my head makes me feel as if I'm floating away. I need the pressure of my things crowding in on me, holding me down.

Maybe I *am* a Collier brother. I think that the problem with us pack rats is we don't generate enough gravity on our own. That we need to borrow some heft from the treasures tossed away by ordinary people who are tacked down more firmly. I want to leave. To go out in the thin light before dawn and ride my bike around, beating the garbage trucks to the good stuff that normal people have left out on their curbs. I want to glue and stitch and make parts of one thing work on another. I want my old life back.

I lay in bed for hours planning how I will sneak out before anyone else is up. It is clear that I cannot go through with my end of the deal. I would have gotten up right then and there to commence packing except that every time I lift my head off the pillow, waves of nausea roll me right back down again.

Around seven that morning the phone rings. That is not unusual. Desperate one-time tycoons are always making early-morning and late-night calls to Victor. Victor talks to these men who are about to lose their fortunes in his butt-slapping jock way, reassuring them that every means is being employed to keep as much of their money as possible away from the people to whom it is owed. But instead of the usual locker-room camaraderie, there is silence, then a soft tapping at my door.

"Trudy, are you awake?" It is Victor. "Ah. You have a phone call. You want to take it?"

I'm on my feet, pulling on my robe, before the first taps end. I open the door because I can't imagine yelling at Victor from my bed. "No," I tell him, pulling the sash on my robe. He is already fully dressed in his weekend outfit of khaki pants, flannel shirt, and tie-up boat shoes.

"No, I'll take it." *I'll take it,* as if I have been dodging a flood of calls and only this one lucky call has made it through my elaborate screening process. In fact, this is the first call I've gotten in the three weeks I've been here. Hillary offered to pay for call forwarding, but I didn't want it. I hadn't decided if I wanted to tell anyone what I was doing. I still haven't. Besides, I didn't want Hillary to see how few calls there would be to forward. Since I have an unlisted number, there wouldn't even be the usual calls from salesmen who are "talking to homeowners in the neighborhood." Not being listed costs a little extra, but it's cheaper than the sales calls. I'm an easy mark. I guess because fake friendliness reminds me of my father.

Victor moves away from the door when I come out. He treats me as if I might be carrying a thermonuclear device instead of his child. I start downstairs and he says, "I could bring the phone up here. Plug it in in your room so you can have some privacy. Or I could get the cordless out of our bedroom."

Even though I'd rather do either of those things than trudge to the bottom of the stairs where the phone is, the choice and subsequent command seem too difficult to make. "No, that's okay. Thanks."

Victor disappears. I notice that now that I'm out of bed and on my feet, my outlook is considerably improved. I pick up the receiver, wondering who could have found me. The few friends I do have are like me, a noticeably nonpersevering group with no idea how to do tricky, everyday things such as keep a checkbook balanced, cook meals at home, or trace a lost friend. The caller turns out to be Randi, my mother.

"What are you doing at your boss's house at seven o'clock on a Saturday morning? Make sure and ask for overtime."

"How did you know I was here?" I ask, dodging her question. Most conversations between me and my parents consist of me dodging their questions. I learned early that my answers only made them unhappy.

"I've been calling your apartment for a week." In the last few years my mother seems to have picked up the dodge mode of communication so that our conversations are a series of blips on separate radar screens.

"Two days," my father corrects her on the extension. "Three tops." Most of my parents' long distance phone dollar goes to pay for the arguments they have with each other on the extension phone.

"Whatever, we've been worried sick. We called your boss to find out if you got fired again."

Again.

Randi goes on. "I never expected you'd be there in person. What are you doing there? If it's work, make sure you get overtime. You're entitled. You let everyone take advantage of you. You always have."

Randi was old when I was born. Forty-three. Maybe that's too old to pick up the habit of making friends, even with your own child. Twenty years ago my parents moved away from San Antonio back to Indiana, where they'd both grown up. My mother always hated the city. Hated the heat, hated the chaos, hated the inefficiency, hated, to be blunt about it, the Mexicans. She never got over her homesickness for Lafayette, Indiana, and went back the instant she was free. Which is to say, the instant I left the house. Out of politeness they asked me to go with them. But they didn't really want me to come and I certainly didn't want to go. I loved San Antonio. Chaos and inefficiency are my natural milieu. I would have stood out in tidy, Anglo Lafayette even more than I did here in S.A.

"Has she told us what she's doing there?" my father asks.

"Well, I don't know, Gordon, I think it has something to do with work. A rush project of some sort. Is that what you said, Trude?"

I don't know if the words exist in English that could have explained to my parents that I was living in the home of my former supervisor because I was pregnant with their artificially inseminated child. If the words do exist, I don't know them, so I was grateful that my mother had, as usual, found an explanation she could understand: a rush project at work.

"That's right, Mom. We're cataloguing a new show we just got in. Fijian burial tapestries."

"What did she say?" my father asks. "Figgy berry pastries?"

"No, Gordon. Fijian burial tapestries."

"Burial tapestries? That doesn't sound too promising."

"Listen, Mom, Dad. I've got to run, the delivery boy just came in with another dolly of shrouds."

"Well . . ." my mother says. "You put in for your over-time."

"Okay. I will. Thanks for calling."

"Trudy"—in a rare moment that leaves me stunned, my father addresses me directly—"get a husband. You're too old to still be playing the field. You're going to wish you'd settled down when you're our age eating cat food in a welfare hotel."

Hillary comes in the front door, freshly showered and glowing pink from her early-morning aerobics class at the health club. I smile broadly, as if my father has just said something warm and witty.

"Oh, Dad, you silly old Pooh bear, you."

"What did she say? Sell me blue hair?" my father asks my mother.

Before she can answer, I trill a cheery good-bye and hang up.

"Your father?" Hillary asks.

"Oh, yes," I answer fondly. "And Mom too. Just check-ing up on me."

Hillary and I smile at each other. "You know, of course, that you're free to use the phone as much as you like. We can even put in another line."

"Oh, no. What I like best about being here is not having the phone ringing all the time. I mean, it rings, but it's wonderful knowing it's not for me."

Hillary huffs out a little breath of acknowledgment. "What a luxury *that* would be." She shakes her head at the burden of being both socially popular and professionally in-dispensable, then she shifts back into the early morning peppiness that is worse than a whiff of cat food for my nausea. "Hey, how about a walk. It's really gorgeous outside. Crisp. Not too cold. Get that oxygen exchange going."

At the very mention of exercise, I want to crumple onto the stairs behind me. Practically from the moment sperm met ovum I have been paralyzed with exhaustion. Every step has become an effort. I feel as if I am on Jupiter or some other planet with strong, soggy gravity.

"Gosh, Hillary, I don't know. I'm kind of prone to earaches at this time of year. I'd hate to get anything that would require antibiotics."

The truth is that I am so tired that clomping up and down the stairs for my meals and naps and bedtimes has been almost more than I can handle. But being tired is just not something Hillary understands. She believes that if you're tired, it's because you need more exercise. That energy is like egg whites, the more you whip it up, the more you will have.

"That's a very valid point," Hillary says. "How about a few miles on the Life Cycle, then?" They have a virtual gym in their paneled basement. Back in the days when I was Hillary's assistant, I would have ridden to New Delhi on her Life Cycle if that's what she'd wanted. But there must be some sodium pentothal in with all those prego hormones because I tend these days to actually say what *I* want instead of just what it is I think Hillary wants to hear.

"What I'd really like to do is work on my projects. Ones without solvents."

Hillary nods slowly. She is careful with me these days. Even when I'm cranky, she is nice. Apparently being her incubator is a promotion from being her assistant. "That shouldn't be any problem at all. I'll drive you over whenever you'd like. We want you to be happy."

She touches me on the shoulder. It's odd that now, with so much effort being put into making everything right for me, it all seems so wrong. Everything started off so chummy in the beginning.

Right after I agreed to have a baby for Hillary, while we were still working together at the museum and I was still officially her employee, we were like sisters. Or like what we imagine sisters to be, since both of us are only children.

For that brief period before I'd even met Victor, when this whole scheme was just an agreement between Hillary and me, we each had what we thought we wanted. It seemed that as soon as I said yes, Hillary plumped out, not physically, but with an air of expectancy. She glowed like a pregnant woman and I basked in the reflection. It was a daily wonder to me that I had it within my power to give Hillary Goettler something that could make her so happy.

This giddy state didn't last long. The very instant I became pregnant, biology stepped in, fired us both, and we found out who was really running the show. Does any woman who's never been pregnant really know what she's getting into? I don't believe it's possible. How could she? First of all, it's one person who says, "Oh, why not?" Then, after the hormones and nausea do their nasty work, it's an entirely different and far less carefree person who has to, literally, carry the load.

The sparkle dimmed as soon as Victor with his big, booming voice became involved. That was at the beginning of last September, the cruelest month. Everyone is exhausted by four, possibly even five months of summer, but all we get for relief are catalogues and ads meant for kinder parts of the country, showing frost-nipped children jumping in heaps of fallen leaves in their full-fashioned one hundred percent Shetland wool sweaters.

The first mistake was arranging the official meeting with Victor at Goettler, Paxton, and Jones, his father's law firm, where he is waiting a decent interval before becoming a partner.

"Okay, just ignore Victor if he gets too lawyerish," Hillary warned me as the elevator hummed us up to the twenty-third floor. "He can really be an old wingtip sometimes."

I giggled, feeling as if we were two girls out on a double date and Victor was no more to us than someone to buy the popcorn. The elevator doors slid open and we faced a wall covered by expensively framed prints of Edward Curtis Indian photos.

"Real adventurous, huh?" Hillary said. Her sarcasm made us collaborators.

"Yeah," I sniffed. "Maybe they'll update and get some R. C. Gormans."

The floor was empty except for a preoccupied junior shareholder who scurried past us on the way to the Xerox machine. Victor had a corner office with a view of the River Walk. He looked up, startled, when we walked in. In his dark gray suit he seemed like the father of the boys we were going out on the double date with. Then Hillary kissed him. That kiss signaled the end of my sisterly time with Hillary.

"Hi, babe," Hillary said, struggling to be breezy in the sober surroundings. She turned and gathered me toward her. "Trudy, this is Victor."

Victor took my hand, shook it, looked gravely into my face, and said, "Trudy."

All the double-date frivolity went out of me in that instant. Because of a life spent in mostly temporary clerical positions, I don't shake hands much. I mean, unless you belong to one of those gregarious kinds of churches, secretaries just don't shake hands much. Anyway, it threw me off. I could feel my vocal cords clenching even tighter than usual. This was a bad sign. Whenever the social pressure is on, I'm guaranteed to squirt out tiddledywinks of inanity. In the silent office I squeaked out, "So you're the sperm donor."

Victor inclined his head toward me, checking that he'd heard correctly. "Pardon me?" He let my hand drop.

Hillary's gray eyes found mine and asked what I was doing.

"The firm loner," I corrected myself. "You're the *firm loner*, up here all alone." I tittered out a strangled laugh. "Firm loner."

Victor chuckled, but he cut his eyes to Hillary with a look that asked her why she had chosen an addled ninny with a Minnie Mouse voice to be the mother of their child. Hillary ignored his glance and took a seat on the couch.

"Trudy"—Hillary patted the off-white couch beside her —"come have a seat."

I sank down into the puffy couch and noticed that I'd been walking around all day with black grease from my bicycle chain smudged along the inside of my leg. I tried to fold one leg over the other to hide the grease marks and succeeded only in smearing them even farther. I looked up and caught Victor glancing away from where his pale couch stood in peril of my greasy leg. I slid forward until I was perched on the edge and the couch was out of danger. Victor pulled a chair around.

We sat there in silence, trying to figure out how to breach

the topic of how to get a lawyer's sperm into the body of his wife's secretary.

"Well," I heard myself say, a horrified ventriloquist listening to her marionette come to life. "No point in *beating around the bush,* is there?"

Hillary and Victor smiled smiles of a matching polite thinness. Hillary was determined to make this work. "Trudy has a point. We need to establish some sort of framework for what we're planning to do."

My cords unclenched and I relaxed as I listened to the sweetly reasoned tones of Hillary's voice; there would be no further outbursts for the moment.

Victor leaned forward in his seat; he was a man born to establish frameworks. He held out his hands to us as he cited cases and statutes from different states. I studied Victor's hands instead of listening to what he was saying about birth-mother rights. The nails, pared to exquisite half moons, wrapped around nearly the entire top side of each long, expressive finger. I thought they were the loveliest hands I had ever seen and that it would be a shame not to keep such hands circulating through some gene pool. It is a sad testament to the willowy insubstantiality of my mind that Victor's hands occupied my thoughts much more thoroughly than anything he said about legal technicalities.

"Frankly, we're charting unknown waters," he concluded after citing several cases with contradictory rulings. "While the Texas legislature has adopted statutes modeled after the Uniform Parentage Act of 1973, which define the activities of A.I. . . . ."

Victor started citing cases and I zoned out. When I focused again, he was saying, "At best what they have is an inconsistent patchwork of rules based on the existing structure of tort, contract, and family law."

I nodded. I'd given no thought to the details of this arrangement. Like cutting your hair on an impulse, I felt it was something that should be accomplished swiftly and with no further thought. Impulse is, however, legal antimatter.

"Recent rulings in favor of the contracting parents notwithstanding, A.I. may in fact be an unworkable paradigm," Victor warned us. "Because it potentially places the private contractual agreement among the participants regarding parental rights and responsibilities above what many courts might interpret as the best interests of the child. This could cause big problems in courts theoretically bound by stare decisis."

I nodded as if stare decisis had been much on my mind lately.

"We've never had a major A.I. case here in Texas. And, frankly, with an issue this emotional, I wouldn't bet the farm on getting a surrogate contract upheld."

I had not even considered that a contract would be involved. I didn't understand why one was needed.

"Basically," he concluded, "the whole thing is still a crapshoot."

Now, crapshoot I understood. This metaphor helped me to grasp that Victor was worried about me welshing on the deal. A good lawyer, he wanted to tie up an airtight contract, but the courts were leaking like the Hindenberg. I thought I saw a way around the whole question.

"Maybe just a handshake?" I asked. "No contract? No courts? I have the baby. You raise the baby."

"Hillary?" Victor flipped his palms up, deferring to Hillary.

"Why not?" Hillary asked. "I mean, this isn't a real estate deal. What we have is a very unusual, very human agreement based on trust and love and generosity." Hillary scooted over and put her arm around my shoulder. "This woman's incredible generosity."

I glowed. The whole idea seemed wonderful again.

"What do we need a contract for? If any one of us isn't happy at any time, there's no reason to go ahead, is there?" Hillary looked at me. "Is there?"

"Not a one," I agreed, pleased that I wouldn't have to learn what stare decisis meant in order to get Sweet Pea set up.

Hillary turned to her husband. "Victor? Is there?"

Victor sighed, then smiled for the first time. "Jeez, if I ever had a client who did this . . ." He shook his head at his own mad folly.

In the end Victor agreed that if the legal system wasn't firmed up on this issue, there was no point in skating out on thin contractual ice.

"None whatsoever," Hillary said triumphantly, heading for a large rosewood cabinet in the corner of her husband's office. She pulled out a decanter of brandy and poured us all snifters to seal the deal. Then she brought up the next hurdle we had to clear. This one definitely would require more than an after-dinner drink.

"I guess all that's left now is to figure out the best time of the month for the insemination."

There is nothing like the prospect of a new acquaintance's semen being injected into your body to take the frivolity out of a meeting.

"You mean, fertilitywise." I took a studiedly casual sip of my drink. It went down the wrong pipe and hit me like a slug of paint thinner. I held in the cough but succeeded in forcing brandy up into my nose.

Hillary jumped up and fetched a paper towel. "Do you chart your cycles?" she asked, daubing at my sweater.

I shook my head, which had turned the color of a cooked tomato, and continued hacking into a napkin.

"Listen, we'll get you all set up with a basal body temperature chart. I'm a pro at it. I brought all the stuff with me." She pulled an Ovulindex thermometer and several large sheets of graph paper out of her purse.

I kept coughing.

"You okay there?" Victor asked.

I bobbed my head vigorously to differentiate the gesture from the coughing.

"Heimlich?" he offered, cradling his fist in his hand. I waved away his offer and left, still hacking. That was the end of my first official meeting with Victor, and I can't say we ever became much cozier. But, from that day on, Hillary and I became mercury sisters linked by the rise and fall of the slender red column in the Ovulindex.

Once the deal was on, the first thing Hillary asked me when I came into work every morning was what my temperature was. Was I sure I had taken it before I got out of bed? Had I been drinking the night before? Was I getting a cold? She soon took to keeping her own chart, a better, more detailed chart than the one I kept. Naturally, I stopped bothering with my chart after a while. It was so much more satisfying to go into Hillary's office first thing in the morning to report the day's number and watch her carefully place a bead on the graph that she then linked to the last bead.

On the first day of October, after ten days or so of beads in the 97.8 degree range, I came in and announced a reading of 97.5. Hillary grabbed the phone and called Victor.

"Clear your schedule and meet us at Dr. Wiegand's ASAP," she told him, and hung up. "Trudy, this is it!"

I was swept away by Hillary's enthusiasm to such an extent that I didn't dwell on specifics. I grabbed my purse and followed her out to the car at a brisk trot.

I had a lot of time to study the fertility doctor's office while Hillary filled out the new patient forms for me, crossing through large sections as she muttered, "Doesn't apply." The wallpaper was printed with tiny violets. Tiny, framed portraits of all the tiny babies the doctor had coaxed into the world hung in neat rows.

I was so absorbed in the little lumpkins that it wasn't until Victor burst in that the full implications of what was about to happen hit me. He seemed frazzled and distracted as he stood at the door, glancing around the room. Before he could come over to us, a nurse intercepted him, handed him a test tube, and directed him to a room down the hall. He stared at the test tube for a moment, then disappeared down the hall.

"A test tube?" I whispered to Hillary. "I figured he'd at least get a Dixie cup or something."

"It's only a tiny amount. Most of it would end up clinging to the sides of anything larger than a test tube."

"Oh." It was impossible not to imagine the logistics involved. I was trying not to when the nurse called Hillary's name. I assume she was a nurse, though she looked like an aerobics instructor in her black stretch pants and a skintight fuchsia top.

"That's us," Hillary said brightly.

"Okay, you're going to need to take off all your clothes," the nurse instructed me in the examining room. "You can put this on. Opening to the front. Lie down on the examining table and the doctor will be right with you." I took the gown she handed me. It was soft and prematurely worn from a lifetime of being washed every day after only a few minutes of wear.

After lying down on the table for several minutes while Hillary leafed nervously through an old copy of *Sports Illustrated,* I sat up. "They always say they'll be right with you, but your feet have turned purple from the cold by the time they show up."

"Actually, it's probably Victor who's holding up the show."

I thought of Victor with his test tube. Did he have all his clothes on, I wondered. His wingtips? His tie? His suspenders? Did he just have his fly down for a quick, efficient jerkoff? How was he going to catch it in that tube? What if he dribbled on his pants? Was the room specially equipped with porn videos and devices available only to fertility doctors?

There was a tap at the door, then the doctor came in, flipping through my file. He was a lot younger and cuter than I had expected him to be. His hair was in one of those rock star poodle dog kind of cuts that are short on the sides with a big pouf of curls on top. He looked like he should be wearing black leather instead of a white lab coat.

"Hillary, good to see you." Hillary stuck out her hand so that he had to juggle pen and chart to shake it. "I just checked in with Victor. Our specimen should be right out. And this must be Trudy." Neither one of us tried to shake hands.

He put down my chart and sat on a stool that he wheeled up to the end of the table. "Now, Trudy, if you'll just scoot your bottom all the way down here"—the paper crinkled as he patted my destination—"and put your feet in the stirrups. Just a little farther down." I wriggled into place. "There. Okay, that's good. Now, if you'll just lie back and let your legs flop open."

Hillary was hovering behind the poodle-cut doctor. Even though all we'd talked about for the past two weeks were my bodily functions, I just could not bring myself to "flop open" in front of her. Hillary noticed my hesitancy and moved away from the pertinent areas. I assumed the Thanksgiving turkey position and the doctor inserted the speculum.

"All right," he said, twisting the wings into place, then peering in. "Your mucus looks very good. Very promising. We'll just wipe away"—he dipped a long-handled cotton swab in saline solution and slid it in—"some of this excess discharge on the cervix. Then insert this"—he threaded in a thin, flexible piece of plastic tubing—"and we'll be all set."

He sat up and looked at the door. "The specimen will be here in one minute. The nurse was on her way with it when I came in." One minute, two, three minutes passed. They could have been hours. The doctor picked up the tubing that was hanging out of me and examined it as if it were something on a hardware store shelf.

"We'll be injecting the specimen through this tube just as soon as it arrives." He looked again at the door. After a few more minutes he jumped up and stuck his head out the door.

"Angie!" The aerobics instructor nurse appeared. "Could you check on Mr. Goettler?"

The nurse looked from the doctor to Hillary, then whispered something in his ear.

"But we're all ready to go here," the doctor responded, then turned to Hillary. "If I might have a word with you." All three of them stepped outside, leaving me with speculum and tubing hanging. After airing out for about ten minutes, I sat up, unscrewed the speculum, took it and the tubing out, and peeked into the hall. It was empty. I was about to go back inside, when I heard Hillary's voice coming from around a corner.

"Are you sure?" she asked plaintively. "Even if I helped?"

"Even if you pumped me full of Spanish fly and did the Dance of the Seven Veils." Victor's whisper was a strained hiss. "It is just not going to happen. Not in here. Not in that goddamned test tube. I mean, a *test tube*, for chrissake. I'm supposed to be a sharpshooter on top of champion stud? Not with Wiegand and that gum-snapping twat of a nurse breathing down my neck. Jesus, I played the guy last fall in the club racketball tournament. Hopeless serve."

I hadn't noticed the gum.

"Did he beat you?"

"What has that got to do with anything?"

"Just trying to isolate the inhibiting factors here."

"Goddammit, Hillary, don't go psychotherapeutic on me. Here. *You* try coming in a Pixie Stick with the fluorescent lights buzzing overhead, someone snapping their Juicy Fruit on the other side of the door, and a couple dozen drooling babies flashing their gums at you. See how hard it is then to 'isolate the inhibiting factors.' Here. Take it." The tinkle of glass breaking could only mean that Hillary had not taken the test tube.

"Are you certain you're not trying to sabotage us?" she asked calmly.

Victor made a strangled sound. "I'm leaving before I say something I might regret."

I scurried back into the examining room just in time to hear the heavy tread of angry wingtips pass by. The door opened and I grabbed the *Sports Illustrated,* pretending to be absorbed in an article on Richard Petty's contribution to the sport of stock car racing. It was Hillary.

"Oh, I'm glad you went ahead and . . ." She waved at the speculum and tubing. "Sorry I kept you waiting. There's been a little snag."

I hoped she wasn't going to tell me about Victor's failure to perform. I hoped it so fervently, in fact, that I made it into a little test. If she told me, I was going to seriously reconsider going ahead.

"Oh?" I said, all innocent, impartial interest. I like to keep my tests as unbiased as possible.

"Yes," she answered, too readily I thought, too eager to roll over on Victor. No, this wasn't the solid parental team I wanted for Sweet Pea. Victor's inhibition was a sign. "The test tube broke," Hillary finished.

A perfect answer, neither a lie nor a betrayal of her husband. She passed.

"Listen," Hillary went on. "This setting, a doctor's office, it's got to be uncomfortable for you. Maybe we could just do this whole thing at my house. So much less . . . you know, the speculum, the stirrups . . ." She gestured at all the gynecological torture apparati.

"I've read up on this. We don't need a doctor. There are other ways. At home. Would you want to give it a shot? This evening? After work?"

Hillary was always at her most appealing during those rare times when she was uncertain, when her sails luffed a bit and she gave ordinary mortals like myself time to catch up with her.

"Sure." Sweet Pea would be able to learn a lot from a mother like her.

I went home with Hillary that evening and my body became her own personal laboratory. That was the first time I set foot in her house. A burnished, golden light of a haunting, antique quality streamed in the warbly windows. Hillary was explaining to me about the lead content of old glass, when Victor returned home. He had obviously not been clued in about the evening's experiment, and Hillary pulled him into the back parlor for a private chat. She was beaming when she came out fifteen minutes later holding a shallow, wide-mouthed plastic cup about the size and shape of a party favor cup. "Do you use the diaphragm?"

"Well, not as much as I should. Apparently that's a big part of my voice problem. I've been to a couple of speech therapists and they both said that I don't project enough from the diaphragm."

Hillary looked puzzled, and I realized she meant the other kind of diaphragm.

"Come on." She beckoned me to follow, and we went upstairs to the bathroom. "Could you keep this warm in your hand?" she asked, handing me the cup. I cradled it carefully in my palms, and a familiar mushroom smell filled my nostrils. "Babies," Hillary said, turning from the cabinet she was rummaging through to point to the cup in my hands. "Millions and millions of babies. All right! Here it is." She pulled out a dome-shaped blue plastic case and popped it open. Inside was what looked like a giant, blunt-nosed baby bottle nipple.

"Cervical cap," she explained. "I got it as a fallback position. I can see now that the do-it-yourself approach is going to work a lot better for us." She carefully poured the semen from the party favor cup into the cap. "Why do we need a middleman? The statistics are just as good without them. So you do use the diaphragm."

I didn't want to tell Hillary that holding that warm little puddle in my hand was the closest thing to sex I'd experienced in years. My apartment seems to discourage suitors. So I said, "Diaphragm? Sure." I paused as if giving myself a moment to ponder the lucky legions who'd battered at my rubber beanie. "Yeah. Pills always made me break out."

I had in fact used a diaphragm. One had been responsible for Sweet Pea's premature visit to our planet. I shouldn't blame the diaphragm. Actually, my incompetence with the little rubber disc was responsible. I could even recall the decisive moment in the losing match. There I was in the bathroom back in my place on Laurel. Sinclair was waiting for me in the bedroom. Knees spread, the diaphragm slick with contraceptive goo, I was just about to wedge it in when it slipped from my grasp and went sproinging through the air.

If I'd ever been the sort of person who stuck with things and saw them through to the end instead of being distracted by momentary pleasures, I would have peeled that sproinged diaphragm off the powder blue mosaic tiles and wrestled it in. Of course, if I'd ever been that kind of person, I would have done better in school, gotten my degree on time, and had a career instead of drifting from one dead-end job to another. I certainly wouldn't be here fulfilling a ten-year-old pact with a baby. But Sinclair began plinking on the African hand harp he was learning to play and I knew that if I didn't get out there soon, his attention would have drifted fatally to the rhythms of Botswanaland.

"Good." Hillary was pleased with my alleged diaphragm familiarity. She handed me the cap. "This works on a similar principle. Just fit it up next to your cervix, then we leave it in place for six hours, *et voilà*. Do you need some help?"

I firmly deflected the offer. Hillary seemed to like meddling with bodies quite fine as long as it wasn't hers being meddled with.

"We'd better get a move on then. It's not good to let these little baby minnow cool down."

I was even worse with the cap than I'd been with the diaphragm. Several hundred battalions of babies sloshed out before I admitted defeat. I watched out the upstairs window until I saw Victor leave the house. He sat in his parked BMW for quite a long time, speaking on his car phone before driving away. When he was gone I went downstairs. Hillary's face fell when she saw the slippery cap. Without saying a word she led me into the kitchen, opened a drawer, and pulled out a common household utensil, a turkey baster.

"This isn't quite what I had in mind," she told me. She turned the implement over to me. "Maybe, if you could just sort of ad lib. You know, suction up whatever you can and, well, you know. . . ."

If I didn't know, I was to get a lot of practice. Hillary decided on a saturation bombing campaign to cover the next five days. So I spent my lunch hours for the rest of the week waiting for Victor to fill the party favor cup, then suctioning up what I could and dispatching the baby minnows to wriggle their way upstream. Afterward, Hillary always had a bushy salad or a roast beef sandwich sent in. She emphasized the importance of folic acid and iron in the early stages of fetal growth and felt I was delinquent on both counts.

That Friday night, after five days with the turkey baster, I had a dream in which Sweet Pea lifted up his gown and showed me two chubby infant feet that had never been walked upon, then he vanished and the phone was ringing.

"What's your temperature?" Hillary asked. It was Saturday morning. I told her I would call her back, but she preferred to hold for the full five minutes she insisted I keep the thermometer under my tongue.

"You still have it under your tongue?" she asked every thirty seconds.

"Uuummmaaahhh," I answered, and that was pretty much the extent of our conversation until I read the mercury and reported, "Ninety-eight point seven."

"Still elevated!" Hillary cheered, and hung up.

And it stayed up, right until the bleeding started. Hillary took the news harder than I had expected she would. Knowing my own inability to accomplish any of the normal milestones in life, I was not surprised. In fact, I'd never held out much hope for our experiment. Hillary's disappointment lasted only a day, however, before her mercury habit kicked back in and she was asking for my temperature first thing every morning.

I quickly lost interest in this biology experiment I was the object of and started making up temperatures when Hillary called rather than lie there for five minutes with the thermometer in my mouth. I had planned to start again really taking my temperature, but my cat of the moment batted the tiny baton out of my hand when I was shaking the column of silver down. With eerie accuracy the thermometer found the one path cleared on my cluttered floor and skittered along it straight to the heating grate, where it disappeared forever.

I fully intended to buy a replacement. In the meantime, I simply reported whatever number was on the chart from the previous month. On Halloween Day, my favorite holiday of the year, I reported a nose dive in temperature, the signal that an egg was about to drop. Hillary whisked me home at lunch with her. Victor appeared and I was sent upstairs with the warm party favor cup, the baster, and instructions to lie down for twenty minutes in what she called the Laura Ashley room when I was through.

I spritzed myself, then lay down beneath the floral-printed canopy on the four-poster and thought about the only time when there had ever been enough sex in my life, my time with Sinclair. My favorite times with him were in the old International Harvester truck he drove. The odometer had stopped at 293,000 miles. I loved rambling around in that old truck, looking down into ordinary cars, having room to stretch out completely in the front seat. Sinclair and I took full advantage of that last feature because, with Sinclair, there was no telling what along the highway might trigger a fit of concupiscence.

Once, on a drive north, for example, the sign for the turnoff to a town called Noodle Dome stiffened Sinclair up more than a year of *Penthouse* letters so that we had to search for the first available deserted roadside stop. The instant Sinclair switched off the rackety engine, the night turned quiet and still. He pressed me back against the long seat and I was sandwiched between the heat of the truck beneath me and his on top. The smell of diesel fuel mixed with Sinclair's own urgent scent and the sweet fragrance of

the honeysuckle clumped along the tumbledown fence outside the window.

Sinclair had read once that Warren Beatty made love
four, five times a day and, as far as Sinclair was concerned,
Warren had thrown down the gauntlet. Sinclair secretly believed that by all rights he should be a movie star. Many of
the steps required to achieve screen stardom are either not
apparent to the general public or else they involve a lot of
work. But sex four or five times a day was one requirement
that Sinclair could meet. And so he did. I was pleased to
help. Sinclair might have indulged himself that often even if
he weren't trying to keep up with Warren Beatty, as he made
it a rule never to deny himself anything. He said it was
because he was an only child. But I was an only child and I
ended up scavenging from curbs.

No, Sinclair's mother, Arlene, was the reason Sinclair
turned out how he did. I'm sure that Arlene divorced Mr.
Coker when Sinclair was barely a year old because she
wanted to be completely alone with her beautiful son. Before
childbirth ruined her figure, Arlene had been a model. Sinclair showed me some of her old magazine ads, mostly for
Clairol: "Only Her Hairdresser Knows for Sure." She was
incandescent, a female Sinclair with creamy skin and velvety
black hair.

Arlene had raised her son to believe that he was destined
to become the star that only his birth had prevented her
from being. Arlene was the first one to notice Sinclair's resemblance to Warren Beatty. Sinclair, however, was the one
who decided that the place to sharpen that resemblance was
the bedroom (or truck cab, or elevator, or dressing room, or
waves off Isla Mujeres). They were all fine with me.

"Trudy." Hillary called upstairs to me. "Whenever you're ready, we need to be getting back to the office."

"Be right there."

That night only one group of trick-or-treaters made it up to my apartment, and they were a gang of tough preteen boys in Rambo fatigues and camouflage makeup who yelled for cash instead of candy. I gave them all quarters and ate the bag of miniature Mounds bars myself.

For most of the month of November daily body temperature readings were enough, then Hillary wanted more. She wanted mucus tests. On the day before Thanksgiving she brought a Bunsen burner, some slides, and counterslips into work. Then, dressed in a Norma Kamali cowl-necked black mini accessorized by amber dowry beads from Ghana, she set up shop. I was wearing my giant hand costume with a big red crepe paper wattle taped onto the thumb in honor of the hand turkeys we all made in elementary school. The Folk Art Museum is the kind of place that encourages such holiday festiveness in its employees.

"We'll just start with a simple Spinnbarkeit test." From the way she hocked out the syllables, I assumed this test came from Germany. You think of things German as being white-jacketed and fastidious, but this test just involved fishing a finger around inside myself and applying what I retrieved to the slide. I lost several tail feathers in the process.

Hillary eagerly slid the gooey smear between two slides and pulled them apart like a researcher testing a denture adhesive. "Not very stretchy. Not much resilience," she confided, pulling apart the first slide sandwich. I was ashamed of my flabby cervical mucus. "Let's try a burn test."

Hillary held the smeared slide over the Bunsen burner's blue flame for a minute, then twisted the neck of her desk lamp so that the naked bulb pointed upward. She inspected the slide carefully, her finely wrought brow furrowing. "The book says that if it turns a light- or dark-brown color, that's indicative of nonfertile mucus. Transparent means we've got fertile mucus. What do you think?" She handed me the slide. It looked semitransparent and caramel colored. We decided it was too close to call.

Even after a week of mucus tests, the results never got any clearer, so Hillary had to fall back on the alleged temperature readings I gave her every morning.

"You are remarkably consistent," she said halfway into the second week of December as she placed the chart she was working on on top of last month's chart and found that they matched perfectly. "These graphs are identical." I still hadn't gotten around to buying a new thermometer.

Even though my mucus refused to stretch or char to an unambiguous transparency, Hillary exalted when my reported temperature nose-dived, signaling that it was time once again for a squirt of egg drop soup. It was the day before Hillary was scheduled to leave for a resort at Banff, Canada, famous for its recreations of authentic Victorian Christmases, so she just phoned Victor, then left half a day early and whisked me home with her.

Victor, called out of an important hearing, appeared shortly afterward, unbuckling his belt. Hillary followed briskly with the party favor cup. She left me with a spinach salad sprinkled with dessicated liver instead of Bacon Bits. Even dried, the smell of the iron-rich nuggets made my stomach wobble.

I looked around. The house was decorated with boughs

of pine tied with plaid ribbons, and candles in clear glass holders sat everywhere. A huge tree decorated with red chile pepper lights and Mexican milagros reached almost to the ceiling. Several pottery nativity scenes from Ocumicho were displayed prominently. Ocumicho is a Mexican village that likes to put the devil into most lineups so that, in their Christmas creations, horned and tailed creatures poke in between the Three Wise Men, tempting Mary with a bottle of tequila. Hillary thought Ocumicho pottery was "fun" and had lots of it around her house all year round.

As I picked the liver bits off and hid them in my pocket, it suddenly occurred to me that I had stopped having dreams about Sweet Pea. The last one had been almost three months ago, at the beginning of October, when he'd shown me his chubby feet. I was wondering if this meant that Sweet Pea had changed his mind and that I didn't have to go through with this after all, when I heard Victor speaking on his cellular phone as he made his way to the car.

Hillary popped in a moment later holding the cap brimming with warm semen and the bulbed baster. I trudged up to the bathroom, preoccupied with this latest revelation: Sweet Pea wasn't going to demand that I make good on our deal. I all but danced up the stairs when I realized the implications: I didn't have to have a baby.

I very cheerfully dumped Victor's yield that day into the toilet, then tossed the turkey baster into the trash. I was a free woman. Hillary wouldn't be annexing my ovaries after all. I was planning my celebration—a can of marinated mushrooms for dinner washed down with a daiquiri from Quik-Pik's freezer section—when a sheet of damp perspiration chilled me. I barely made it back to the toilet before the mulched-up plop of salad I'd just eaten reappeared.

I didn't want to think about these new implications, but the knowledge crept right up from my uterus and flowed through me, letting me know precisely why I had stopped dreaming about Sweet Pea and why he had shown me those dimpled baby feet at his farewell appearance: He was getting ready to march back into my life again. I should have known he wouldn't tolerate welshers.

7. "Trudy got a little mixed up on her dates," Hillary explains to the obstetrician, sitting on a stool at the foot of the examining table where I'm perched. "That's why we didn't get in to see you during the first month."

This examining room is much more workaday than the fertility specialist's. It's all almond metal drawers and cabinets. The only decoration is a laser photo of the kind of flaming red and yellow autumn leaves we rarely see in San Antonio.

The obstetrician nods and makes a note. Dr. Worley. Dr. Antoine Worley. He's supposed to be the best in the city. At any rate, the best in the city come to him to help them spawn the future best in the city.

Perhaps, I think upon meeting him, Dr. Worley's success is due to his remarkable resemblance to that totem of breezy birth, a giant chubby rabbit. His puffy-pink mid-sixtyish face rests on his chest with only the barest interruption of neck. His large front teeth push out slightly onto his lower lip. His white hair is wiry and coarse in front and ends at a series of small black scabs on his forehead which, if connected, would form a matinee idol hairline. The last thing I notice about him is that his tie tack is a tiny fish of the sort that advertises the wearer's Christianity. His hairline recaptures my attention.

I stare at this odd stippling a bit too intently. For the first time, Dr. Worley looks at me, then bends his head down as if searching in the pocket of his white lab coat for a pencil and brushes the curiously wiry hair forward over his hairline. His embarrassment unfolds the mystery: hair transplant.

"Okey-doke"—he glances down at the patient-information form I filled out during the first five of the fifty minutes Hillary and I sat in his waiting room—"Trudy. Let's take a peek."

Hillary tactfully moves out of the line of sight and he scoots his flabby bottom over on the rolling stool. I assume the position. There is the usual probe and Dr. Worley, lips pursing in bunny puzzlement around his protruding teeth, glances at his notes.

"The date of your last period was?"

I figure that I am about to be found out. "Well," I lie, "there were a few speckles last month around the fifteenth." That would be the fifteenth of January. It is now February. I stole a month from Hillary after heaving in her bathroom. I wanted to finish up my Missile Toads before Christmas and see Mr. Braithwaite's poinsettias reach the second story. In fact, I needed the extra time to pretend that none of this was happening. As I suspected she would, Hillary had me installed beneath the canopy and booked with San Antonio's finest ob the instant that I reported I'd felt, oh, a twinge of nausea.

"My periods are so erratic that it's hard for me to know what to count." Vague and dumb is one of the lying variations I do best. My naturally distracted temperament make it a credible favorite.

"Well, darlin', I'd say, judging by the height of the fundus and general condition of things down here, you're well into your fourth month."

That was pretty much what I'd figured. I turn a look of bafflement on Hillary.

"Fourth month?" she echoes, looking at me, horrified by my deficiencies in folic acid, iron, and calcium, to say nothing of simple record-keeping. "That's not possible. She just started getting morning sickness." Hillary is not going to accept this without a fight.

"Hormones are mighty individualistic critters," Dr. Worley says. "They don't always read the book to find out precisely when they're supposed to show up."

"That must mean—" Hillary stops herself, but I know

her thought. That means that I bingoed on my first date with the bulb.

Hillary does not voice this revelation since Dr. Worley does not know that I am a stand-in. Given the thin legal ice that Victor has told us we are skating on, they thought it best to cast me as a downtrodden single mother with Hillary playing the part of my only friend in the world. I, personally, like my waifish role quite a bit. Hillary's, unfortunately, tends to make her appear like a colossal buttinsky.

We adjourn to the doctor's office, where he sits behind a massive dark walnut desk, twin nautical prints framed on the wall behind him, and asks some general questions about the condition of my health.

I reply negatively to his questions about kidney disease and rheumatic fever. Then he moves on to my parents' general state. I know that Hillary is already worried about the unsupervised months I spent in my apartment eating popcorn for dinner, so I feel this is not the time to reveal my father's diabetes, the hiatal hernia, tendency to obesity, and fallen arches. Or about my mother's sciatica, colitis, and gum disease.

"Excellent," I tell him. He is only too glad to cut that portion of the interview short and draws a line straight down the "none" column for both maternal parents.

He asks about other relatives, and I recount a series of peaceful deaths from hearts worn out by an overabundance of brimming good health. The stories seem to please Hillary, so I overreach and add a great-uncle who was Cape Cod sea kayaking champion in his eighty-seventh year.

"And the father?" Dr. Worley asks. "What do we know about his health?"

"Excellent," Hillary answers. "I mean—" She looks at

me. "Isn't that what you said, Trudy? The father is in very good shape?"

"Oh, the best. He's a surfer from California." It wasn't one of my better lies, but it was the healthiest sort of individual I could think of on the spur of the moment.

"And the rest of the family? Could you get in touch with him to ask if there is anything we need to watch for?"

I look at Hillary, she tries. "He . . ." A lifetime of getting what she wanted by being herself has left her lying skills desperately undeveloped.

I intercede with the obvious. "He's married."

"Oh." As I was certain it would, that information closes the case for Dr. Worley, who moves quickly on to other matters. "So, have you thought about amnio?" He closes my chart and screws the cap back on his fountain pen.

"Amnio?" Hillary repeats carefully.

"Amniocentesis. It's a relatively simple procedure whereby we withdraw—"

"I'm familiar with the procedure," Hillary interrupts, the creamy, cultured sound of her voice curdling the slightest bit. "What do we need with am-ni-o-cen-te-sis?" The way she pronounces each syllable with chilling distinctiveness puts me on my guard.

The doctor, trying not to look befuddled, opens my chart again and skims through. He finds what he's looking for. "It's fairly standard these days for mothers over thirty-five. Unless, of course, there are moral concerns. Which I certainly support wholeheartedly." He fingers the fish tie tack and beams approval.

"How does any of that apply here?" Not much takes Hillary by surprise, and from the snappish tone she has adopted with the doctor it is clear that she is not enjoying the sensation.

As for myself, a nauseated feeling that, for a change, has more to do with foreboding than hormones, leaves me clammy as I see the misbegotten pieces fitting together.

With exaggerated patience the doctor turns the chart around so that we on the far side of the desk might examine it. "Is this an error?" He taps "age" where I have written in the number that causes Hillary's flawless skin to pale from ivory to ash.

"Thirty-eight?" she reads the awful number out loud, then turns to me. "No. You can't be thirty-eight. Trudy? You just got your B.A. six years ago. That makes you what? Twenty-eight. *Twenty*-eight? Twenty-nine if you were real slow and took five years to get your degree."

She makes a very good case, and I am willing to cede the point. I *should be* twenty-eight. My life *is* at least a decade behind schedule. "Well," I explain. "I wasn't exactly one of your shortest-distance-between-two-points sort of scholar. It took me"—I wince as I squeeze the number out—"twelve years to graduate."

"Twelve years?" For possibly the only time in her life, Hillary's mouth hangs open in amazement.

I suppose I should have seen it coming. People generally take me for about a decade younger than I am. It's my voice and not wearing makeup combined with a few other things like not having a driver's license. Mostly, though, I just don't generate as much gravity as people who've been on the planet for almost four decades.

"I thought you knew," I whisper. "My birthday is on my résumé." Age is one of the things I've never lied about. Besides the fact that my thirty-eight years are too amply documented to edit successfully, I've just never cared that much about how old I was.

"I never *read* your résumé," Hillary wails, and I see her again in memory, closing my personnel file in that one ill-fated show of executive decisiveness before she declared us a "team." "No one takes *twelve years* to get a B.A. In art education of all things. Thirty-eight? Jesus!"

Dr. Worley tucks his chin a bit more deeply into his neck and touches the fish tie tack.

Hillary continues to edge toward the thin side of a full-blown rant. She holds up her long, elegant fingers and begins ticking off the disasters I'm forcing her to court. "There's Down syndrome. Increased risk of all other kinds of chromosomal abnormality. I don't believe this. Ten goddamn years."

"Mrs. Goettler?" Something in the doctor's tone, kindly as it is, causes the words "church deacon" to form in my mind.

Hillary stares at him as if trying to figure out who he is. "Thirty-eight? I can't deal with this." With that Hillary walks out.

In the vacuum of silence that falls upon us in Hillary's wake, Dr. Worley draws heavily on forty years of dealing professionally with erratic female behavior to keep his composure. Since I'm the hormone-riddled one, his job is a bit tougher. "Couvade," he says as much to himself as me. "Sympathetic pregnancy. An adoption of all the symptoms. Nausea, bloating, violent mood swings. It doesn't always have to be the father. Just someone close to the mother."

"Mmm. Couvade." I nod and stand, sensing that the appointment is over.

The air in the parking garage underneath Dr. Worley's

office building is dense and cool as a basement. Hillary is waiting in the car. Neither one of us says anything as she screeches the Volvo down the switchbacks. As we pull into the sunlight a man in a quilted hunting jacket who's missing most of his front teeth pushes a bouquet of discouraged Tyler roses toward Hillary's window.

She guns the Volvo past him into the downtown traffic. We creep along, the street narrowed to half its width by construction. The asphalt skin has been peeled back to the rock and dirt beneath. Loops of ductwork poke out of the exposed earth like so much tubing stuck into a hospital patient. A skinny man in a safety orange jacket waves for us to turn off Commerce Street. The street is closed ahead.

Hillary bows her head with exaggerated patience. "Perfect. A detour. I haven't missed enough work already, I *need* a detour. Perfect."

We fall in behind a line of stalled cars, then move, slowly as a funeral cortege, past Dillard's, which used to be Joske's, where Randi brought me to shop for school clothes until fourth grade, when I started taking the bus and shopping on my own. We crawl past the Menger Hotel, where Andy, the guy in the apartment below mine, works as a bartender at the Theodore Roosevelt bar. Then we are smack-dab in front of the humpy dun-colored arcades of the Alamo. Inside the museum is my favorite exhibit in the city, the resting place of Unknown Bones, dedicated to the unheralded heroes who perished at Santa Anna's hands.

Though I struggle to concentrate on Unknown Bones, on what a great name for a blues singer that would make, I can't turn back the peristaltic waves that have already begun reversing direction. I cork my mouth with my hand and search frantically for the handle to roll down the window, but there is none. Hillary fumbles for the button and opens both back windows before lowering mine. I lean out and succeed mostly in flinging my used breakfast over the side of the Volvo. When I sink back into my seat, Hillary has a wad of tissues ready for me and a stick of gum.

I towel off, apologize for what I've done to her car's finish, then say, "Look, you can just drop me off right here. It's just a couple blocks to Navarro. I can get the San Pedro bus. Practically stops at my front door. Even the North St. Mary's would work."

"Why? Do you want out of the deal?"

"Well . . . don't you? It's not . . . I mean, *I'm* not what you expected."

"Okay, so we've run into an unexpected contingency. Conditions may not be optimum." We finally break free of the tangle at Alamo Plaza and break for Houston Street. We make it as far as Navarro before hitting a light. Hillary stops and four young women in navy blue air force uniforms cross the street. Each one has a shoulder bag slapping her hip and a cap tucked under an epaulet. They look like modern nuns in their navy blue A-line skirts and black flats. "It's still Victor's child you're carrying. What were you planning to do?"

"I didn't really have a plan. I guess I should have realized you'd want a younger mother. I'm sorry."

"It's not your fault. It's not anyone's fault. We had a communication foul-up is all. We'll have the amnio and decide where to go from there."

Hillary perks up and roars off the line slightly before the light turns green. She nearly clips a young noncom who whirls around and shoots a bird at the silver Volvo. Hillary doesn't notice, she is busy formulating alternate strategies. I wonder briefly about the life I would have had if I'd ever stopped to formulate even a primary strategy. I'm certain it wouldn't have included stand-in motherhood.

8. " 'Feed the baby in the mother's stomach or feed the prisoner in the jail cell,' something like that," Mercedes says, flipping away the translation with a wave of the black-streaked rag she is using for her chore of the day: polishing all the silver frames in the house. There are dozens. Nearly every frame holds a picture of a Goettler. Every day Hillary leaves Mercedes with an assignment, something to keep her occupied full-time in a house where food is never cooked and clothes never washed. Mercedes rubs away at the silver border around a sepia-toned shot of a prosperous burgher with glasses pinched onto his nose and a celluloid collar digging into his double chin.

"It's better in Spanish. Basically means you don't satisfy your cravings, you gonna have one mean baby. Prolly end up doing time."

I'd confessed to Mercedes that I was dying for *pan dulce* from Mi Tierra. Specifically a *ricardo* with cream filling and pecans embedded in the white icing spackled on top. I hadn't had any cravings until I moved into the Goettlers' house. This makes sense, since craving involves denial and I don't practice that skill in my normal life. But since I have been here where every bite I put into my mouth is monitored, all I have been able to think about is that *ricardo* with the custard filling oozing out. They were always Sinclair's favorite.

I even mentioned the craving to Hillary to see if, just this once, she'd okay one load of empty calories. Instead, she had Eat for Your Life whip up something that she claimed was "even better." Cheesy-Oat Bars they were called, and a bigger gyp I've never sunk my teeth into. I don't know if this is fact or just a figment of my slatternly mindset, but the instant a food shows even the merest hint of nutritive grit, its treat value is erased. The whole-grain apple-juice-sweetened low-fat ricotta-cheese-filled facsimile made me yearn all the more for the feel of hardened powdered sugar icing breaking like crusted snow under my teeth.

The moony, sugar-starved look on my face finally cracks Mercedes. "Come on." She throws down her rag, leaving a couple of generations of Goettlers unpolished. "You got my sweet tooth awake now. We'll take the trolley." It was handy having a tourist conveyance running less than a block from the house.

"I don't know. . . ." I waffle. For the past week, ever since the appointment with Dr. Worley, when the rings on my trunk were counted and Hillary found out what a bundle of damaged goods she had had foisted off on her, I've been tentative, hesitant about everything. It's a natural state for someone in limbo. We're waiting until the amnio next week to decide what to do. It was the earliest appointment Hillary could wangle.

"*Chee-wah-weetah,*" Mercedes spits out, and picks up her rag. "I never seen such a *aguado*. . . ." She went on muttering to herself about what a wishy-washy I was and lashing the image of a frowning woman wearing a jacket with muttonchop sleeves with a lorgnette pinned to her puffy bosom. "*I* wasn't the one started talking about *pan dulce. I* didn't bring up the subject. Who's gonna know. You think these *muertos* give a shit they shiny or not? You think—"

"Let's go."

Mercedes is at the door, clutching her black vinyl handbag, before I can stand up.

El Mercado, the new version, always jars me. Clean, prosperous, safe for the whole family, it is the exact opposite of the flea-bitten market of my youth. I miss the flat-bed trucks with homemade wooden side railings piled with onions and cucumbers, peaches and grapefruit. The market now resembles a very festive strip mall with roofs of red clay and floors of Saltillo tile. El Mercado has been transformed into a migrant's nostalgic dream of what the old country was like. This revisionism reaches its height in Mi Tierra.

Like the nostalgic builders of the new market, I, too, look for ghosts here, the ghosts of the three most important people in my life—my old roommate, Aurelia; my art teacher, Sister Theonella; and Sinclair. Aurelia and I used to come here when she was homesick and wanted to buy a piece of fruit from the hand of the person who grew it. Sister Theonella let me come along with her several times when she tired of painting bluebonnets and decided to switch to produce. And Sinclair.

Sinclair and I used to be frequent visitors. We would stay up all night roaming around in his International Harvester, drinking, smoking dope, laughing like fiends, then swoop into Mi Tierra, ravenous and oblivious. At the bakery case we stood paralyzed by the infinity of choices: Chulas 30¢, pan fino 20¢, empanadas de polvo 35¢, magdalenas 15¢, nuecito 20¢, semita de anise 15¢, ricardo, always the most expensive at 40¢.

The prices have tripled since then, but one thing that hasn't changed about the new modern Mi Tierra is the noise. Dishes clatter as bus boys sling the dirty ones into a metal cart, perpetually annoyed waitresses slam down plates of *huevos rancheros,* a mariachi singer belts out a full-throated, throbbing rendition of "Malaguena" to a group of embarrassed tourists.

"Mexico with air conditioning" was how Sinclair always described San Antonio. I know that there is too much air-conditioning in Mi Tierra now and not enough Mexico for his taste. Still, as we walk in, I feel his eyes on me and glance around. Of course he is not there.

Mercedes is already at the bakery case talking to the

counter girl. The girl reminds me of Aurelia. She has the same high-born Castillian face as Aurelia, the same thick black hair and eyebrows as a Frida Kahlo self-portrait. Of course, Aurelia never wore ultraviolet eyeshadow striped with lime green. The clerk holds a pair of tongs poised over a silver metal tray, waiting for Mercedes's selection. Together we study the rows of yeast buns, plain or chocolate topped, the slices of jelly roll soaked in red syrup and rolled in coconut, the stout brown gingerbread pigs, the orange halves marinated in sugar syrup, the gooey squares of pumpkin candy, the cookies knobby with nuts and raisins.

I am as paralyzed with indecision as I used to be with Sinclair in front of this same selection. Suddenly, however, the indecision becomes much more than that. My hands and feet begin to tingle. My vision is splotched with patches of bright light. A zone of numbness spreads out from my crotch. A feeling of true paralysis creeps up through me. I wonder if I am having a stroke.

"What you want, Truthee?" Mercedes's voice sounds very far away. It is the first time she has used my name. *Truthee.* That is exactly how Aurelia and the other girls from Mexico used to pronounce it.

"Truthee, you don look so good, girl. You better lie down. Truthee, you passing out? Truthee!"

Truthee. I hang on to that pronunciation even as the bakery case, and the counter girl's lime and violet striped eyes and Mercedes's round face are all consumed by the patches of brightness until they become as shimmeringly radiant as a white beach at noon.

"Oh, chit, she's passing out!" are the last words I hear.

The blinding white clears and I can see that I'm back in my dorm room at Our Lady of Sorrows. I am the only

boarder whose parents live in town. By age fourteen my
academic and attendance record is already too spotty to get
me into anything other than a special education class in
public school with all the "hoods," so my bewildered Lutheran parents find me a place at Our Lady of Sorrows.
Sister Tabernacula, the principal, a formidable woman rendered positively terrifying by acres of black shrouding and
lips permanently pursed over ill-fitting dentures, matches me
up with another new girl, Aurelia Gojon, from Morelia, Mexico, and assigns me the job of teaching her English. Most of
the other boarders from rich Mexican families know a little
English. All Aurelia knows when I first meet her are "jes"
and "no." By the time of her abrupt departure three years
later she knows "rat fink," "twink," "dip," and "yucky."

We are both redheads, *pellirojas,* Aurelia tells me when
we meet, touching my caramel tufts. I am honored to be
included in the same category with her vibrant titian tones.
She thinks our hair makes us sisters. When we get to the
point that we can discuss more than hair color, I find out just
how sheltered Aurelia is. She doesn't even know what a
queer is and when I tell her about homosexuality, she
doesn't believe me. She isn't much better informed about
regular sex, and I am the one who has to tell her where
babies come from.

In our room, we each have a narrow single bed made up
with sheets and a blanket worn thin from years of launder-
ing. We each have a small, rickety desk and a child's dresser
drawer. The dorm, built in the 1870s, has no closets so we
share an armoire. We have five hangers apiece. Our navy-
blue nylon cardigans with the blue and white Lady of Sorrows patch goes on one. Two of our three white blouses take
up two more hangers. One is for our Marymount plaid,

knife-pleated skirt. We keep one hanger for a civilian dress. Our polished black and white saddle oxfords are lined up on the floor of the armoire. Underwear, socks, hankies, scapulars, mantillas, extra rosaries, holy cards, and other personal articles go in the drawers.

On Aurelia's side of the room are a large picture of Our Lady of Guadalupe, roses spilling from her blue mantle onto a kneeling peasant; a cross of palms blessed on Palm Sunday by her parish priest back in Morelia; a brightly colored picture of her and her eight brothers and sisters, parents, both sets of grandparents, and various aunts and uncles, all formally posed around a wedding couple in front of an archway of yellow and red roses. But the place of honor on Aurelia's wall is occupied by a picture of the boy Aurelia loved above all others, Tony Perkins.

Her narrow bed is covered with dolls with poufy knitted skirts of yellow and pink; a stuffed dog with a slit in its stomach for hiding her pajamas during the day; small, hard pillows covered with scratchy aqua lace. On her dresser top is a fantasy world of filigreed glass creatures: a family of raccoons washing their dinner; a herd of wild horses, manes flying in the wind; a four-masted schooner, sails puffed and billowing; a baby fawn capering after mama doe while daddy buck scents the air for danger.

My side of the room is as spartan and bare as it was the day I moved in. I had to leave all my projects stored back in my parents' garage. That was part of the deal when Sister Tabernacula agreed to take me. My parents feel that my projects have taken over my life and that I must give them up.

Suddenly our tiny room fills with chattering and Aurelia's family floods in from Morelia. Her mother carries six dresses puffy as clouds made of baby blue, mint green, lozenge pink, lemon yellow. They are for Aurelia's *quinceañera*, for her and her attendants to wear the Mass and party celebrating her fifteenth birthday. I am the head attendant.

The talk is all about basque waists, bouffant skirts with lace tiers, lace capelets, simulated pearl crowns, white fingerless gloves. The soft, female purr is even puffier, even airier and dreamier in Spanish. *Cinturas estilo princesas, faldas abullonadas cubiertas con tiras de encaje, capas de encaje, tiara con perlas de fantasia, guantes blancos, dedos descubiertos.*

Shy, gentle Aurelia becomes a different person in the bosom of her boisterous family. I am surprised to learn that in Morelia, she is considered to be quite a puckish lass with the hot temper *pellirojas* are noted for. When Aurelia introduces me, her relatives roll their eyes and shake their heads, speculating on the havoc and high jinks we two *pellirojas* must have been getting up to together. Aurelia laughs, apparently believing that we two church mice have truly been leading the poor nuns a merry round. Then only the women are left.

"Make your mouth *como* me," Aurelia tells me, bringing her face close to mine and stretching her lips tight over her teeth.

"Sister's going to know," I warn her.

"This?" She holds up the tube of lipstick in her hand. "This little pink for babies? *Es casi nada.* Make your mouth this way."

I imitate Aurelia, and she drags the lipstick across my mouth, holding her own tight the whole time. Her hands are warm and soft. Her breath puffing against my face smells like bread out of the oven. Without asking, she smooths on eyeshadow no bluer than an old workshirt and daubs rouge pale as seashells on my cheeks. She stands back and inspects me. She is very pleased with her handiwork, very pleased with me.

"*Qué preciosa!*"

The other attendants cluster around to view me and whisper about how beautiful I am. I am happier than I have ever been. As long as Aurelia never really learns English, she'll never find out that in America I'm a dip and we'll go on being friends and *pelliroja* sisters. But the girls chatter louder and louder and I pick the word *embarazada*, pregnant, out of the din. I know that if Sister finds out, I will have to leave.

"Shut up," I order the girls.

"Don she got a funny voice?" a familiar voice asks.

"It's cute. All high and squeaky. Kinda like Minnie the Mouse, you know."

"When I was pregnant with Alejandro I was passing out everywhere. I passed out in the H.E.B. I passed out in the Solo Serve. I passed out in the McDonald's."

"Now you just pass out when Alex Junior brings home his report card."

"Hey, he didn't do so bad this last time. Got him a B in spelling. I never could spell to save my life. . . . Hey, look, you guys, her eyes is open."

"You ever see a person white as she is that wasn't in a coffin?" Mercedes asks. I wonder what she is doing in my dorm room. "Look at them eyes. Like a big, old Siamese cat." Six pairs of brown eyes stare down at me.

"Why am I on the floor?" I ask.

"You passed out," Mercedes tells me.

The counter girl with the striped eyeshadow hands me a

Coke. "Sip it slow. It's what I always drank when I was expecting and didn't feel too good. It'll get your blood moving to your head again, then you'll be okay."

Mercedes helps me sit up on the floor. I haven't been allowed near a sugared drink for the past few weeks that I've been at Hillary's, and the Coke tastes wonderful.

"Hey, look, the color's coming back into her cheeks already," Mercedes tells the women hovering above me. "Okay, upsy-doozy." She struggles to her feet and extends a hand down to me.

Other hands reach down to me, and I ascend as effortlessly as the Virgin Mary rising up to heaven at the end of her immaculate life. They take me to a table, sit me down, and cluster around again. A skinny woman in her seventies opens her purse, pulls out a small plastic travel bottle and squirts the clear liquid on a hankie. She hands the hankie to Mercedes, waves the back of her hand in the direction of my face, then, wordlessly, pats her own.

Mercedes wipes the cool hankie across my forehead and temples. It smells of lavender.

"Agua colonia," the women murmur in unison as the fragrance reaches them.

"I coon go out of the house without my *botellicita,"* a busty woman wearing a waitress's fiesta dress uniform says. "Everything I smelt made me sick. I was dropping like flies."

"How you doing, hoe-ney?" the hostess asks me. I'd noticed her when we came in, standing behind a podium, studying a seating chart, then gathering up menus and beckoning diners to follow her. She has thin lips over which she has drawn in fuller versions in watermelon-red lipstick.

By this time I'm feeling fairly substantial, but I shrug in

a whey-faced way. I don't want the women to leave or for Mercedes to stop patting my face with *agua colonia*. I'm living a continuation of my passed-out dream with Aurelia smoothing pastel baby powders on my face. I want more than anything to remain in this booth with soft, friendly bodies pillowing mine.

Mercedes stops sponging my face and confides to the others, "You know why she fainted?"

"Her blood's thin," the double-lipped hostess answers. "The baby takes out all the minerals. I lost a tooth for every one my babies. They just take 'em. Lucky I stopped at five, I'd be living on oatmeal."

Mercedes nods. "It's these people she's staying with. They got her eating all this health food. Tofu, bean curds. Things like that."

"Can't build up the blood on that." The hostess shakes her head at the Goettlers' ignorance.

"No way," the counter girl agrees. "You know what got my blood built up? *Menudo.*"

A couple of the women groan and flap their hands, dismissing the tripe stew solution. "The smell. *Qué olor.* And the way it looks. Looks like—"

"Don say it," the hostess warns. She turns to me. "Red wine. That's what you need. Plenty of good red wine."

"Yeah, just what she needs for a little *borracho* baby," the waitress hoots. "No, eat whatever you want, just cook it in a cast iron pan."

"But don't cook nothing before the sun goes down," the hostess adds. "Sunlight's what kills your iron."

"Sunlight?" the waitress mocks. "Where'd you hear that? Back in Michoacan? You're so *ranchera.*"

Before the hostess can defend herself against the country-bumpkin charge, an insistent *ding-ding-ding* intrudes. A crowd of tourists is clumped in front of the bakery case. A skinny man with liver spots wearing a light blue golf jacket glares at us and pointedly continues to throttle the bell on top of the case.

"*Cretino,*" the counter girl snaps. "Them Winnebago people. No *tienen corazón.*"

The others agree that tourists have no heart and reluctantly hoist themselves up off the vinyl. They all speak sweetly to me before they leave.

"Take care yourself."

"Come back, see us again, Truthee."

"Do like I say, make you up some *menudo.*"

"You want a boy, don't eat no more tomatoes."

The women shuffle back to their duty stations throughout the restaurant.

Mercedes remains next to me, pressed close. She honks off a snorting laugh. "*Ay-chee madre,* what kinda cow would she have if she found out you been passed out on a dirty restaurant floor and now you drinking Coke?"

Mercedes never says Hillary's name. Thinking of her, Hillary suddenly seems like someone I knew a long time ago. My life at the Goettlers', the Bonus Meals, the exercise bike, my Laura Ashley room, even being pregnant, they all seem distant and hard to recall. I am overwhelmed by the feeling that my real life, that the only people who care about me, are here, in this booth at Mi Tierra. I never want to leave.

"We better shuffle off the buffalo." Mercedes heaves herself out of the booth.

Tears jump into my eyes. I don't have the strength to slide across the vinyl, to stand up, to climb the stairs to the second floor of the Goettlers' house, to live up to my part of the deal with Sweet Pea.

Mercedes plops back down. She pulls a wad of napkins out of the silver dispenser on the table and blots up the tears leaking down my cheeks. *"Eee, Truthee, ojos vemos, corazón no sabemos."*

I translate through hiccuppy sniffles. "Eyes we see, hearts we don't know?"

"I didn't know you was so sad. But I gotta tell you, this is a weird deal you got going. I don't think it can end good. We ain't factories. Put in your calcium and tofu at one end, plop, out comes a baby at the other end. Lot more to it than that. Lot more. Too much. Ask me, I know. What is it? You don't want to give your baby to them?"

That, I assume, would be the normal reaction. Luckily, most people take it for granted that you are basically like them. If money is what makes their world go round, they'll figure you're into amassing too. If it's sex, they'll smirk at everything you say knowing what you *really* mean. Mercedes, obviously, thinks I'm like her and could never give up my child. What would she think if she knew that the concept of a baby was as remote to me as Pluto. I put on a suitably mournful expression.

Mercedes, of course, has a saying for the occasion. *"Ay, dios, no más el que carga el saco sabe lo que lleva dentro."*

Only he who is carrying the bag knows what it contains. I nod as if my sack contained a hundred pounds of rusty nails.

Mercedes slides out again. "We gotta roll, Truthee. They can't fire their own baby. But me . . . pffft. Going in the wind."

As I start to leave, the waitress rushes up to me. "Don't

ever kiss the baby upside. He'll go crazy or the devil will get him."

Outside, the world seems to have expanded and lightened. A corona of light shimmers around everything: around the fat pigeons pecking at popcorn spilled on the concrete, around a couple of maintenance men resting on a planter drinking Dr Peppers, around the broad bottom of a tourist woman fingering the hem of an embroidered dress hanging in the doorway of a shop.

Mercedes stops and looks back at me. "Hey, *guera*, the sun getting to you? Last person I seen grinning like you was my aunt San Juan, and she dresses her cat up like the Infant of Prague."

I look around, blinking. "It's just such a pretty day."

"You *gringos, loco* about weather. Prolly cause you never had to get out in it and pick bush beans. You do that a few seasons, you're never so cheerful about weather again, I'll tell you that much for sure. Come on, you get me fired."

I dawdle after her, noticing for the first time in months the glittering flurry of discarded objects on the pavement shed as carelessly as butterflies dropping jeweled wings. I'm prying a beautiful St. Christopher's medal out of a crack in the concrete when Mercedes trudges back to ask why I'm digging trash out of the street.

"But it's a perfectly good medal." I hold up the silver disc showing the baby Jesus riding on St. Christopher's back.

Mercedes clucks. *"Unos nacen con estrella y otros nacen estrellados."*

Some are born under a lucky star, others are just born with stars in their eyes. Something like that. I don't have to ask which category she thinks I fall into. I don't happen to agree with her, but I don't say anything. I pocket the St. Christopher's. He was always my lucky saint. Even after the pope demoted him.

9. My breasts have taken on a life of their own. They tingle and itch and want to be touched. But lightly. Ever so lightly. I scream if the Laura Ashley sheet settles too heavily upon them. I scratch them with a feathery touch and the feeling is bliss. But they want more. During the day they push out of even my largest bra, squeezing over the sides, plopping out of the top like muffins overrunning the tin. At night they take over my dreams.

My breasts have zero imagination; the dream is a straight memory with no embroidery of imagination stitched through to decorate it. I am back in my apartment, where Sinclair and I sleep on a mattress and box spring on the floor and never make the bed. I am bathed in medieval cathedral light from the window over the bed which I have painted with glass stain. Instead of St. George and the dragon or Joseph with his carpenter's tool, though, I have chosen the Silver Surfer as my motif and rendered him hanging ten across the cosmic void of the love nest I share with Sinclair. Because my breasts are dictating this dream, we are in bed and Sinclair is doing what my breasts want done most: stroking them softly.

The bed takes up nearly the entire room, with only the narrowest moat of floor encircling it and that covered by dirty jeans, T-shirts, a half empty box of animal crackers. Curtains made of strings of apple seeds hang at the door. Sinclair stands on a chair painting constellations on our ceiling with phosphorescent paint. Those stars are still on my ceiling, but they have bleached out so much that they no longer glow in the dark. They shimmer like cat's eyes in my dream. I marvel at the magic in Sinclair's fingers.

That part was true too. Sinclair could certainly paint. I don't know exactly how old he was when we met. Early thirties I'd guess, though he could have passed for twenty-five. He had a reputation; he was on his way to being a famous artist. Maybe he is one now and I just never heard. But there was all kinds of magic in Sinclair's fingers. My breasts want him to channel some their way, but Sinclair keeps painting stars. That wasn't like him. In real life any excuse could get him off the track. That was because painting was labeled work. If drinking and making love had been labeled work, Sinclair would have been sneaking off to paint.

I wake up with the familiar lump of missing him, missing his hands on me, clumped in my chest. The pale light of a February morning turns the windows periwinkle. The melancholy color makes me wonder what has become of Sinclair. Once he got back together with his old girlfriend, I completely stopped going anywhere that I might have seen him. This cut me off pretty completely from the few art connections I'd managed to make as well as from some of my favorite old haunts, like Schilo's deli.

I think about Schilo's German beer cake and an astonishing realization comes to me: I am not nauseated. For the first time since October, I don't feel as if I'm on a ship rolling through high seas. I listen to the sounds of a house where I am not quite a guest, not quite a servant. Where I am not part of the family but carrying its newest member. Downstairs the dishwasher is humming. The pipes in the wall behind my bed gurgle. The heater clicks on and a burst of hot air from the ceiling vent ruffles the canopy on the four-poster. The temperature has dropped into the sixties, but it is not really cold enough for the heater. I have started to think of Hillary as wasteful and a bit spoiled.

My breasts don't want to think about Hillary, they want to continue thinking about Sinclair. Sinclair loved my body when I was pregnant that first time. He loved how spindly my arms looked next to my hydroponic breasts. Suddenly all the craving for sweet, soft touches flowing through my body goes to my teeth. A ferocious desire for a candy bar from the

Segovia Candy Company made of coconut and from several forms of sugar molded into a bar of green and white and violent pink stripes comes over me.

Sister Immaculata, the biology teacher whose dream was to serve in the Congo, used to sell these candy bars at lunch along with other homemade-looking candies like clear mercury-red cinnamon suckers formed into a deadly dagger point and soggy peanut patties dusty with chalky sugar residue. But it was the coconut bars Aurelia and I splurged on, sending our nickels and dimes to support the work of the missionary arm of Sister's order.

I'll bet that wherever Aurelia is now, she's craving a coconut bar too. We always had the same cravings. After a few weeks of living together, we started getting everything together: cravings, periods, dreams. I suppose it was the nonverbal factor. We couldn't communicate in words, so our pheromones or neurotransmitters or something reached out to each other. Anyway, we synched up in amazing ways. I'd have a dream about buying gardenias in the plaza from a man with no legs and wake up and Aurelia would have tears in her eyes from homesickness. Or she'd be studying and out of nowhere I'd say, "It's 'notebook.' The word for *cuaderno* is 'notebook.' " And she'd say *"Gracías"* and finish her lesson.

I didn't know that Aurelia was receiving as well as transmitting until the third week we lived together. I was sitting on my bed, trying to read *Gulliver's Travels,* but all I could think about was a coconut bar. It was evening, though, and Sister wasn't selling, so I kept trying to read. Without a word Aurelia left. Half an hour later she came back chomping down a coconut bar and handed me one. Neither one of us had the right words so that she could explain where the candy had come from or how she'd known that that was what I was craving. Of course, if we had had words, we never would have needed to link up the way we did. Or else we would have said "Weird" and gone back to more normal communication.

The memory sharpens my need for that taste of concentrated sweetness mixed in with a slurry of ground coconut and undercut by the chemical tang of red dye. I must have a coconut candy bar from the Segovia Candy Company. There can be no negotiation. Hormones do not compromise.

I look out the window. Arnufio hasn't allowed Mercedes to take the LeMans today. The disappointment nearly fells me. I have no other choice. I must walk or take the bus to my apartment, get my bike, and cycle over to the ice house where I *must* purchase as many coconut bars as I can carry. I jump out of bed, surprised by my new energy. None of the clothes I brought fit me anymore. They're all too tight around the waist. Naked, I look like a fifth-a-day alcoholic, my arms and legs and butt are as skinny as ever, but my tummy pooches out like a wormy pup's.

Until now I have resisted the new prego clothes Hillary has hung in my closet, half a dozen sweat suits. They arrived by express mail a week ago after the elastic in my black stretch pants gave out and I appeared at breakfast with my pants and blouse pinned together. Hillary ordered the suits out of a catalog. They're not actual sweat suits, they're all-cotton Go-Togs! made in California in luscious colors: grape, jade, teal, cobalt blue, emerald, and deep rose. Like a bear hunter wearing a bear claw necklace, I put on the rose one in honor of my search for the red-striped coconut bar. The thick cotton feels expensive.

Downstairs in the kitchen, Mercedes is leaning over the

counter, the *San Antonio Express* spread out before her, a mug of coffee in her hand. She tips her head back to read the front page headline, "3 Skinned Dogs Discovered amid Satanic Designs." Then she flips back through the paper to check and see if her Wingo number has won.

"Chinga!" she exclaims when her number doesn't match. "Ain't going to retire today." She looks up at me. "You better put on something warm, *flaca,* norther's supposed to come through today. Go through them skinny legs like a duck through butter. You get a chill it go right to the baby."

"It will?" I ask. Before Mercedes can elaborate, Hillary calls my name. I wince. What is she doing home?

She pushes the swinging door open and bounces into the kitchen. "You haven't forgotten our appointment?"

"What appointment is that, Hillary?" I struggle to be polite. The last two weeks, ever since she found out how old I am, have been a struggle to be polite.

"The genetic counseling."

I had forgotten.

"We'll be waiting out in the car for you." Hillary breezes out of the kitchen.

Every molecule in my body is poised, screaming to be bathed in sweet coconut syrup. I look out the back windows and consider hopping onto the first tourist boat that passes by. I'd like to simply float away. Float south all the way down to Mexico and live on coconut bars. I feel heavy and discouraged and out-of-place. I miss what there used to be of my friendship with Hillary. I miss admiring her. I move toward the back door.

"Oh, Trudy." Hillary pops her head of sleek black hair back in. "Don't worry about your breakfast; we're picking it up on the way over. Wholewheat blueberry pancakes," she chirps, as if I'm supposed to get excited about Eat for Your Life's purplish green urp mat–looking concoctions. "You ready?"

I follow her out.

"Remarkably good health on the mother's side," the counselor says with undisguised skepticism as she taps her pencil point along all the "nones" I'd filled in for history of heart disease, diabetes, arthritis, cancer, and a couple dozen other infirmities. Unlike everyone else I have met in the baby business, she is not cheery or comforting. She has thick black bangs that hang down over her eyebrows. Her lips are flaky with bits of chapped skin stained orange from rubbed-off lipstick. Her nose is raw from what appears to be either chronic allergies or a bad head cold.

"Really *quite* an incredibly good family history," the counselor repeats suspiciously, grabbing for a tissue. With Hillary so upset about my age, I thought it more important than ever to boost her morale with a spotless family health history. Without taking her eyes off the form I'd filled out, the counselor dabs at her nose, pulling her upper lip down over her front teeth to allow greater access to the stretched nostrils, wads up the damp tissue, and tosses it into the wastebasket on the far side of the room. The basket is filled with balled-up tissues and there is not one on the rug. Whatever her social deficiencies, and there appear to be plenty, the counselor is a great shot.

"Just lots of fresh air, fresh food, and farm living," I say cheerfully. The counselor looks up, startled, then glances at Victor and Hillary to make sure that my voice is not some kind of put-on, some joke on her. Reassured that it is not, she snuffles liquidly and moves on to the form Victor has filled out. Apparently Hillary and Victor don't care if the counselor knows about our arrangement, since we're obviously not pretending that I'm a single mother. The counselor doesn't seem to care.

I try to read Victor's form upside down, to learn what frailties he harbors beneath his handsome suits, his British suspenders, his tight and toned shoulders. He sits between Hillary and me, long legs jammed against the side of the desk, shifting in his chair. He is clearly used to being on the comfortable side of the desk. I decipher that he has a cousin with lupus.

"History of early heart attacks on Dad's side," the counselor says, peering up at Victor as if he should apologize. "Father, uncle, two first cousins," she adds like a prosecutor making her point when Victor doesn't answer. She looks back down at my form. "Nothing on Mom's side cardiacwise. Thank goodness."

"Well, there would have been," I blurt out, not wanting Victor to feel his contribution was flawed. "If my father hadn't retired." The truth of the matter is that, after my father retired—more from his morning treasure hunts through doughnut shops and convenience stores than from work, which was always a secondary diversion at best—my mother with her skimmed milk and Special K gained control of his diet and he shrank over the years from 380 to 250 pounds. With losses continuing to this day. Of course, I don't mention any of this.

"Anyway, no heart attack," I say, dismissing the subject.

"Moving right along," the counselor says. "You're not at any higher risk for birth defects other than those related to advanced maternal age. Okay." She snorkels in a mucoid breath, slides several charts across the desk, and goes into a canned spiel. "Both the mother's egg and the father's sperm contain twenty-three chromosomes, each carrying many genes. What we check is to make sure each pair of chromosomes is complete." She taps one of the charts. It shows pictures of chromosome pairs, lines of fuzzy gray dots twisting off in odd directions like caterpillars going after dewberry leaves. She calls our attention to the X pair.

"Now, here's where Down syndrome shows up. As an extra X. Okay, the mother." She ignores the tissue and drags the back of her hand across her nose. "That's you, right?" She is having trouble grasping the irregularities of our arrangement. Victor shifts in his seat, bristling at the counselor's question, her abrasive manner.

"Yes," I answer.

"And you're going to be, what?" She glances at my record. "Thirty-nine? At delivery?" I nod yes. I have a birthday coming up in April. Well, actually, that's not my real birthday. My real birthday is the day after Christmas. But when I started at the museum, I told everyone that it was April first, April Fool's Day. The reason was group office presents. Every job I'd ever had I was always getting hit up for five, ten dollars to contribute to a present and party for someone in the office. Sometimes I barely knew the person, but I'd always chip in because of the lunchroom dissections of anyone who didn't. "Cheap" was the nicest thing noncontributors got called. Being blackmailed into contributing was bad enough, but what really annoyed me was that since my birthday was almost always a holiday, my turn to collect the group present never came around. So, I moved my birthday back a few months.

The counselor pulls out a graph and twirls it around to

face me. Her pencil point stabs the square where Maternal Age at Delivery, 39, and Incidence of Down syndrome meet: one in 130.

"One in one thirty?" Hillary gasps and leans forward for a closer look. I feel like a brass ring that Hillary bought believing it was gold, turning green on her finger.

"Yep," the counselor chirps. "Odds really start jumping when you go into the kiddo biz after about thirty-six, thirty-seven. I'm surprised you didn't know that."

"Nevertheless," Victor says in his lawyer voice, the calm, unflappable one he uses on the phone. "That's still less than a one percent chance of encountering a problem in this area."

"Oh, yeah," the counselor agrees. "Chances are this kid'll be healthy and driving you up a wall. I'm just here handing out worst-case scenarios." She smiles for the first time, showing an inappropriate glee.

"Okay," she continues. "The procedure is basically pretty painless. The area is numbed first, then a needle is inserted somewhere between the navel and pubic hair line depending on where the doctor sees the baby is on the ultrasound. Don't want to spear the little guy. There will be some cramping as the needle passes through the uterine wall. It's muscle down there, and you stick any muscle and you'll get cramping."

The counselor bobs her head from one side to the other as she ticks off the steps. "Okay, twenty ccs of amniotic fluid are withdrawn. It gets shipped to the lab. The cells sloughed off by the fetus are cultured. In ten to fourteen days, bingo, we ought to have some news for you. Any questions?"

I suddenly have many questions, but she doesn't look up and plows on ahead.

"If you do get the black bean, you have, basically, three options. One, go right on ahead with the pregnancy and use the time to educate yourself about Down syndrome. The second, put the baby up for adoption. And, third, terminate the pregnancy. That can be done legally up to twenty-four weeks. . . ."

"Terminate?" I ask. "You mean have an abortion."

The counselor bobs her bangs at me. "Well, a D and E. Dilation and evacuation." She claps her hands on the desk. "Well, if there aren't any other questions, and if the mom has a full bladder, and if we still all want to go ahead, we can do the procedure whenever Dr. Patterson's ready."

Hillary jumps up. "We're ready." She glances down at me. "I mean, the odds are what? Four times what we'd anticipated. Trudy? This is okay with you, isn't it?"

"They stick a needle in me and take out some fluid?" I ask, still not entirely clear.

"That's all." Hillary heads for the door, as if everything were decided.

Victor sees the perplexed look on my face. "You okay with this? If you want to take some time. Think it over." He speaks softly. His voice is very calming. I can see why he has so many clients who trust him so much. I don't like keeping everyone waiting, but I really can't figure out how I feel. Ever since I fainted in Mi Tierra, I haven't felt quite the same about anything. I know, however, that nothing is going to come clear in the next few minutes, so I nod yes, and follow Hillary into yet another examining room.

Shortly after I am settled on the table, a doctor in a white lab coat sweeps into the room. Victor and Hillary stand. The doctor is a slender East Indian man with black hair, beautiful brown cow eyes, long dark lashes, and skin a beautiful bluish-toned brown.

"Good afternoon, all," he greets us bouncily, a hint of a British accent on the chirpy syllables. "I am Vijay Poonwalla." Starting with me, he shakes everyone's hand.

Victor and Hillary glance at each other but don't say anything until he turns on the monitor beside my head.

"We were expecting a Dr. Patterson," Victor finally says.

"Yes, and Dr. Patterson was indeed looking forward to attending. However, the discourteously ill-timed labor of another patient has unfortunately called him away. I shall tell him of your disappointment." Humming a tune that sounds like a hive of bees swarming, Dr. Poonwalla bustles about, preparing the ultrasound equipment.

Hillary bugs her eyes at Victor until he holds up his finger. It wobbles uncertainly in the air for a good while before Victor speaks. "Uh, Doctor. Uh, pardon me, Doctor, but where did you train?"

Dr. Poonwalla stops his preparations and cocks his head brightly. "I have completed my residency at Duke University. I believe you will find it to be an institution held in the highest esteem. In addition to a most rigorous training program, I bring excellent hand/eye coordination to my work. And what of yourself, Mr—" Dr. Poonwalla quickly checks the chart. "Mr. Goettler? I see you are an attorney. Where did you receive your training?" Dr. Poonwalla asks the question as if good manners demanded no less.

"Where did I . . . ?" Victor is caught momentarily off balance. "Uh, here. At UT."

"Oh, a fine institution, indeed. Not one of the top ten, of course, but certainly a most creditable institution. Are you comfortably situated?" he asks me. The whites of his eyes are blue and his breath smells like clover. I nod.

"Good, then if you have no objection, we may begin." He holds an instrument that looks like a giant burnisher with a rolling ball on one end. It takes me a second to realize that he is waiting for my permission.

"Sure. I guess so."

He blinks twice, surprised, I'm sure by my voice. "Excellent. Then if you will be so good as to raise your upper garment . . ." He pauses as I hike up the rose cotton until he says, "Fine, fine. And now the lower . . ." I push down the elastic waist until my stomach pokes out, pale as dough and only the tiniest bit raised.

Victor starts for the door.

"Victor." Hillary stops him. "We're going to get to see our baby." Victor opens his hand and points it, palm up at me. He widens his eyes at Hillary and leaves. I appreciate his consideration. Dr. Poonwalla's expression doesn't change, so I can't tell if he knew already about our arrangement or if he's trying to piece it together even as he picks up a tube and prepares to squirt a plop of goo on me. I brace for the icy squiggle. It is warm as a cat on my stomach.

Dr. Poonwalla smiles at my surprise. "So much more agreeable when warmed a bit, don't you find?" He reaches over and dims the lights to cocktail lounge level, flips on a screen next to the table, and begins to run a monitor over the lower part of my belly. What looks like a weather map appears on the screen. Patterns of black, gray, and white swirl around like cold fronts meeting areas of low-lying precipitation.

"Oh, we're in luck today," the doctor grins at the screen. "We've caught the little nipper in full profile. Can you see?"

I attempt to make out a face in the swirling gray blotches. But it is like trying to see the Virgin Mary in the scorch marks on the tortilla that turned up as an object of reverence in South Texas. She's much clearer in my Tortilla Goddesses.

Then, as suddenly as when you finally see the wineglass in the famous optical illusion, I see the unmistakable profile of a tiny human being. My breathing stops dead. I trace the big forehead, the curve of an ear. Nothing else on earth exists for me at that stunning moment.

It startles me when Hillary crowds in to get closer to the screen. She stretches forward even farther and bumps the doctor's hand. Suddenly he's monitoring my bladder and the little face is gone.

"Hillary," I say sharply, much more sharply than I have ever spoken to her before. She moves away and the doctor finds the tiny skull again.

I am spellbound. I would not have been any more surprised if the outline of a Galápagos tortoise had appeared on the screen. Least surprising of all would have been if the doctor had rolled his instrument over every inch of my stomach and finally said, "I'm sorry. There's nothing in there. You're not really pregnant." But there is a baby. Sweet Pea is there.

"Oh, look," Dr. Poonwalla says, delighted. "The little cricket is sucking."

The tiny mouth opens and closes.

"What is the baby drinking?" I ask, surprised that I've spoken my question out loud.

"It's own urine," Hillary answers. "They all do that. It's all sterile."

For a second I am embarrassed that my child has been

caught gulping its pee. But Hillary says all babies do this. I did it. Dr. Poonwalla in his mother's womb did it. Yes, I make the final leap, even Hillary was a pee gulper at one time. That thought and the vision of the guppy within me slurping away at its watery world make me immensely jolly.

"What's the sex? What's the sex?" Hillary crowds in again.

The doctor rubs the instrument around, trying to zero in on the pertinent area. "Oh, the little cricket has turned away from us. The sexual parts are hidden. It is impossible to discern."

Hillary's shoulders slump. "I wish we could have found out."

"Why?" the doctor asks. "Do you have a preference."

"Not really. Well, probably we'd prefer a boy if this is going to be the only one. But it really doesn't matter. It would just be nice to know. For decorating. Presents."

"Don't fret. The sex is revealed in amniocentesis. Shall we proceed?"

The doctor wipes the goo from my stomach and paints it with an oversize Q-Tip saturated in orangy-brown Betadine solution. Then, holding up a syringe of novocaine like a dueling pistol, he tells me I'll feel only a little stick.

The prick of the needle breaks me out of the trance I had fallen into. With the syringe still in my stomach, I sit up. The doctor, startled, pulls out the needle.

"Trudy?!" Hillary says, trying to push me back down. But I've already pulled my pants back up, permanently staining the front of them with an orangy-brown square of Betadine.

"Uh, okay. I'm not going to have this test. Okay?" I start backing away toward the door. "If there's anything wrong with the baby, you don't have to keep it. And, uh, of course, you don't have to pay me anything."

"You are changing your mind about the procedure?" Dr. Poonwalla asks. "If there is some doubt about my professional qualifications. My hand-eye coordination . . ."

"No, no, nothing like that," I assure him. "If I was going to ever have it done at all, you'd be the one I'd have do it. It's just that—"

"Trudy, let's talk about this." Like Victor, Hillary uses her professionally calm voice. "All we want to do here is prepare ourselves for any problem."

"Uh, there's really no point. I have to have the baby." That was the deal with Sweet Pea. There weren't any riders on the contract that said, okay, if I turn out to be defective, you can send me back again. No, that is out of the question now, now that he is here, gulping his pee.

"Yes, Trudy, of course. Nothing's cast in bronze here. Everything's open to negotiation, no matter what we find out."

"Uh. No negotiation." I leave the room. Victor is sitting in the hall on a chrome-legged chair.

"Trudy?" he asks.

"Uh, I changed my mind."

"Trudy." Hillary comes out of the examining room. "Trudy, don't you feel you owe it to me to at least discuss this?" There is an edge on her words that I feared when I was her assistant. It no longer matters, though, what my feelings in the matter are. I speak for Sweet Pea. The case is closed.

"No," I answer. "No, I don't."

"Discuss what?" Victor asks.

She turns a look of bewildered betrayal on Victor. "She

refuses to have the test. We thought we were getting a twenty-eight- maybe twenty-nine-year-old mother. Trudy's almost thirty-nine and she won't even test for the greatest age-related risk."

Hillary thinks that I am a devious, selfish shit and it suddenly makes not the tiniest bit of difference to me. Victor turns to me and I prepare for the sound of his lawyer voice, the deeply sensible one he uses to soothe distraught clients. "Trudy, what is your objection to having the test?"

"There is no point in further discussion," I answer, and shrug. I say what I must and the words ring with the finality of a judge's gavel. "I'm not having the test."

Victor and Hillary stare at me. I pivot and walk down the hall, aware of every inch of slate blue industrial carpet that passes beneath my feet. Aware of the Dahlhart Windberg prints of broken wagon wheels and weathered windmills hanging on the walls. Aware of the music, a heavily Muzaked version of "Under the Boardwalk." But aware, more than anything, of the guppy fluttering within me.

Sweet Pea can't wait for that red-striped coconut bar.

10.

Net Monthly Income After Deductions:	$1,000

EXPENSES:

Rent	$375.00
Utilities and Phone	100.00
Food	160.00
Subtotal	$635.00

ADDITIONAL EXPENSES:

Child Care	$240.00
Diaper Service	50.00
Formula	65.00
Subtotal	$355.00
Grand Total	$990.00
Art Supplies	35.00

GRAND GRAND TOTAL = $1025.00   —$25.00 per month

(medical and clothes not included)
(or movies)
(or Laundromat)

When I was young, and even fairly recently, I used to dream about having the ability to get inside another person's mind and see the world as they saw it, as a normal person saw it. I thought it would be like wearing glasses. That I would find out what normal people focused on, then I could make compensatory adjustments in my own vision that would bring it more in line with everyone else's. Later on I realized that for the most part, everyone else is just as fuzzy as I am. Still, I thought it would be interesting to travel into someone else's mind.

Pregnancy has given me that ability. I become aware of this gift as I look up from my figuring to stare out of the window of the bus whisking me away from Dr. Poonwalla's office. Away from Hillary and Victor. In the past I would have been one big frayed nerve ending worrying about what I'd said to Hillary, about what she must think of me, about what I was going to do now to make amends. But even with intense concentration, I can't make myself worry. I think, "So this is what it feels like to be a calm person." Because I am. Calm as a cow in a meadow. Lulled by the rocking of the bus, I just sit and watch the stops go by. It's not often I get this far out into northwest S.A.

At one stop there's a message on the bench: "Pregnant? Need to Talk? Call Vicky. Texas Cradle Society." I am glad I am taking this vacation in the mind of a calm person or that message might upset me. Before I can write down Vicky's number, I let the bus rock me back into a snoozy daze. There is so much I don't want to think about, starting with that long needle. It is wonderful to be on public transportation again. I'll figure something out.

At North Star Mall we pass the giant brown and white cowboy-boot sculpture. Each boot weighs five tons. The bus stops and a gaggle of preteen Chicanas boards. At first I take them for scouts of some sort in their Bermuda shorts and jaunty caps. Then I notice the grieving insignia of Our Lady of Sorrows on their cardigans. They're Catholic-school girls, but they all wear neon rainbows of makeup, stripes of lapis lazuli and violet eyeshadow, puffs of fuchsia blusher, streaks of raspberry lipstick. The chemical floral scent of hair conditioner hangs over them. They chatter and giggle and make me miss Aurelia.

I used to get occasional glimpses of her life. They came to me like movies projected in my mind and I knew they were from her life, though I could never figure much out from them. Once I got a plate of breaded fish on a cafeteria tray. Another time a rack of Easter dresses in a department store. The only thing I could figure out was that this was what Aurelia was looking at when she thought about me. I tried for years to find out from her family where she was, but all my letters came back unopened. I, along with everything else *norteamericano,* was considered a bad influence and purged from the Gojon's universe.

It happened our junior year. Frank was Aurelia's first boyfriend. I personally never saw the appeal. He wore his hair in a crew cut like all the other boys from the Catholic military school across the street from Our Lady of Sorrows and kept his pants tucked into black, lace-up combat boots. His ears stuck out and he had a long upper lip like a chimpanzee. But Aurelia took down all her pictures of Anthony Perkins and replaced them with Frank's chimp face.

At first she frisked around, high-strung as a colt, giddy about Frank, covering her notebooks with his name and boring me to death with tedious details about his every tiny like and dislike. Frank was the first enthusiasm Aurelia and I didn't share. I think I was jealous. Anyway, we weren't as close once they really started going together. I suppose that's why I didn't notice when Aurelia became quiet. I assumed she was just hugging some new and wonderful information about the luminous Frank to herself. It didn't even register with me when she started throwing up in the mornings. I mean, Aurelia was a girl who, only last semester had writhed with disgust when I told her that there might come a time when a boy would try to put his tongue in her mouth.

I don't know what I would have been able to do if I'd figured this out in time. I don't know if I even would have stopped her from going to see the school nurse, Sister Immaculata, who really wasn't even a nurse, but the biology teacher whose entire medical training consisted of a first aid course in tropical medicine back when she was briefly a candidate for a spot in the order's Congo mission. Sister diagnosed *Entamoeba histolytica*. At least I could have told Aurelia what her problem was. It was Sister Theonella, my favorite teacher, who discovered what the problem was just by asking Aurelia a few obvious questions. Once the discovery was made, things happened fast.

In her last few hours at Our Lady of Sorrows, Aurelia and I became friends again. She came back from the doctor's, pale and trembling, too stunned to cry, and told me that she was *embarazada.* It took me a while to make out that she was considerably worse off than embarrassed. Her parents had already been called and were driving up for her. Her last act was to write Frank a letter. She wrote his full name on the envelope and entrusted it to me to deliver. As soon as she handed it over, Aurelia was whisked away by a father trembling with rage. Her mother, who had patted my face with powder the last time we met, wouldn't even look at me.

I delivered Aurelia's letter to her jug-eared Frank. He read it and looked up at me as if I could tell him what to do. He was so young and Aurelia was even younger.

I moped around for the rest of the year. Sister Theonella was the only one who acknowledged Aurelia's absence. My teacher let me hang out with her in the art room even more than usual and went out of her way to say nice things about Aurelia even after we were forbidden to mention Aurelia's name. When all my grades dropped, Sister Theonella took up for me with Sister Tabernacula, the principal, and kept me from getting kicked out.

I go to sleep remembering Aurelia. The bus jerks and I wake up. A large medallion of drool spots the front of my sweatsuit. A woman in her fifties with the thin lips and offended nostrils of the severely religious sits next to me. She sniffs disapprovingly as I cast a bleary glance in her direction. I know she thinks I must be either on drugs or drunk to be sleeping on public conveyance.

"Boy, being pregnant sure does make a person sleepy," I mumble.

The hard line of her mouth goes from disapproval to a kind of know-it-all satisfaction. "You think you're sleepy now, just wait till after it's here. At least you get a chance to sleep now. You can forget that after it's here." She tucks her chin into her neck in a signal to me to mark her words.

"How many do you have?" I ask, because I know she wants me to.

"Four, and I'll tell you what, take your rest now while you can."

"They keep you pretty busy, huh?"

"Busy isn't the half of it. But I wouldn't take for them. Not even Ronnie Junior, and he's the real wild one. Born that way. Even the judge said he was provided with a good home life. Even with all of that, all of the heartache and disappointment and them stealing money right out your pocketbook, they're still a blessing. This your first one?"

"Yes. My husband and I tried for years, but the Lord waited a long time to bless us."

She shifts around to face me. "He moves in mysterious ways. You have much of the morning sickness?"

"Oh, a little."

"Eat you a cracker before you get out of the bed, that'll help settle your stomach, let you put some real food on it."

"You don't say. I hadn't heard that."

"You try it. Just get you a pack of plain crackers and keep them right there by the bed. See if that doesn't do the trick. It didn't work for me. Nothing worked for me. I threw up from day one right through to the end. I actually lost thirteen pounds the first three months. They had to put me on an IV to get my electrolytes back up where they were supposed to be. I was that dehydrated."

She glances out the window. We are downtown again. The woman swears an approved Christian curse, "Oh, Jiminy Cricket!" then lunges to pull the bell cord. "I missed my stop. Serves me right for running my mouth. You shoulda just told me to shut up."

"Oh, no. I appreciate the advice. This is all new to me."

The woman hefts herself out of the seat and sways in the aisle as the bus hisses to a stop at St. Mary's and Travis and warns me sternly, "Get that husband of yours to pamper you. It'll be the last chance you get, believe you me."

I laugh and the woman moves to the door, then stops and looks back. "Flat 7-Up is good too. Just shake up a bottle till the fizz's gone. That's a good clear liquid. Help with the electrolytes." Then she's gone.

A lot of people, probably most, wouldn't think it very cozy to make friends with a sour-faced religious zealot spouting unsolicited advice, but most people haven't had the problems making friends that I have. There are a lot of drawbacks to pregnancy, but I'm starting to see that being instant friends with any woman who ever was or wanted to be a mother may nearly cancel them all out.

Being pregnant is like knowing the secret handshake to the biggest sorority in the world. It astonishes me how easy it has been to walk into this mammoth network that I never realized existed even though it's been right in front of my eyes. I imagine it's similar to being gay.

I want to stay on the bus forever, passing from one sister to another and never going back to King William. There is so much I am not up to dealing with. The sisters would adopt me and bring me plain crackers and clear liquids. They would take me home to my apartment on Laurel but would never leave me alone. They would put me to bed on sheets that they'd just pulled piping hot from the laundromat dryer.

When they were sure I was resting comfortably, they would organize into squads and defrost my refrigerator, chipping out packages of frozen peas embedded in frost and wiping away black pools of liquified vegetables. They would throw away all the plates dotted with dried daubs of cat food I had scattered around for the cat that left. They would vacuum and scrub. They would cook meals and pack them into freezer containers, each one a nutritionally complete individual serving neatly labeled. They would put soaps made from avocado and almond oil by my sink and bathtub. They would do for me all the things no one did for them when they were pregnant, and it would be as if they were reaching back in time and pampering their own nauseated, tired, discouraged selves.

At the next stop I haul myself off. We're heading south, and I don't want to get any closer to King William. The norther Mercedes warned me about has blown in. The thick cotton of the rose-colored sweat suit now feels as thin as a pair of panty hose, and a shiver goes through me. I start walking just to warm up. In a few blocks I am at the Main Plaza. Fat pigeons waddle about the limestone plaza. Across the street is San Fernando Cathedral. The blue-gray clouds bullying their way in from the north stream past the cathedral's twin spires. I feel more at home in the shadow of the cathedral than I have in weeks. Going to Our Lady of Sorrows made me an honorary Catholic, which, in immensely Catholic San Antonio, made a person practically an honorary Latino.

San Fernando was a favorite destination for processions. I liked marching through the city streets behind a statue of whatever saint we were celebrating, part of a plaid-skirted army of Catholic-school girls. Aurelia always marched next to me and we compared notes about which of the Central Catholic School boys in their paramilitary khaki uniforms was the cutest. That was before Frank. Jug-eared Frank Whatsisname.

A car alarm warbles in the distance. Sheets of the *San Antonio Express* whip past my legs. I catch a brief glimpse of bodies being removed with welder's torches from a tangle of snarled auto parts and remember what Sinclair always used to say about San Antonio journalism: If it bleeds, it leads.

I grab the paper, Sunday's, and chase after the other sections blowing in the chilly wind. Once I've collected an armful, I sit down on the edge of a low limestone wall encircling a garden area, where the bare branches of tall pecans are being whipped by the wind. I fight the wind trying to rip the papers out of my arms as I paw through them, looking for that week's Wingo numbers. I have to force myself to be practical, to consider my finances. If I'm going to raise a child, I'll need much more than I currently have in the way of capital assets. Winning Wingo would be a good start. Unfortunately, the numbers are already torn out.

It's true, though, that what God takes away with one hand, he gives back with the other, and I spot a vendor on the far side of the plaza. His cart is loaded with Bart Simpson balloons on sticks, bumper stickers that advise the reader, "If You Don't Like My Driving, Call 1-800-EAT-SHIT," and, hallelujah, the red, white, and green striped coconut candy bars that I crave.

I sprint across the plaza. It is getting late and I am hungry, having missed lunch. I buy five candy bars from the vendor. He is missing the top part of his thumb, but handles the quarters I give him with more grace than most fully-fingered people. Because of the missing digit, I watch him return my change and so I notice that he gives me one more quarter than I am due. I offer it back, but he waves the coin away.

"Keep it," he says jauntily. "A valentine."

It *is* Valentine's Day.

I settle back on the nearest bench and peel off the clear cellophane wrapping on the first bar. As I do, a chant sung in high, girlish voices comes back to me:

> *Trudy, Trudy Red Mouth*
> *She just ate a dead mouse.*

Patti Macafee and her crowd of young Catholic harpies used to like to crowd around me and sing that little ditty after the red dye from the candy bar had stained my mouth.

"*Qué están diciendo?*" Aurelia would ask me.

"It's kind of hard to translate," I would tell her, pushing past the cat-calling girls. That little chant was my reminder of what my whole life would have been like without Aurelia and the rest of the Mexican girls. It kept me from forgetting that my own kind still knew who I was.

The first bite of the candy bar is better than anything I have ever eaten. My teeth hurt from the sweetness. Whatever oil they use to keep the bar from getting brittle coats my mouth and throat. I stuff as much of the candy as I can into one bite, so that every taste bud is bathed in the sugary coconut taste. My face heats from the rush of sugar up my neck into my cheeks, my forehead. One more crammed bite and it is gone. I chew like a dog, barely noticing the little girl who comes up to stare at my feral eating.

"*Ven, ven aquí!*" her mother calls her back.

A police car, frosted blue and white with a big yellow star on the door, cruises past the plaza. The mother stops yelling and watches until it passes. Her little girl hurries back to her.

As soon as I swallow the pulped wad, I am crushed by disappointment. Candy was not what I wanted. Just as all the sweet touches I craved in my dream went into my mouth, the flow of desire filters back to its source, and I ache for Sinclair. It is Sinclair I want. I toss the remaining four bars into the trash can next to the bench. Desolation comes upon me so swiftly that I weep. Mood swings. I read about them in Hillary's library of prenatal-care books. To stop crying, I get up and begin walking east on Commerce. Behind me the cathedral bells toll out four o'clock, tea time, an affectation that Sinclair used to be fond of. The German beer cake at Schilo's was a particular favorite.

Sinclair liked Schilo's for a number of reasons. He liked the Texadeutsch menu with the jalapeño cheese sandwich right there next to the knockwurst and Reuben sandwiches. He liked the deli's watery way with a cup of coffee. He liked the fact that every Sunday evening a duet of middle-aged men in lederhosen with hairless legs would entertain on tuba and accordion, playing "Doe a Deer" and "La Vie en Bleu," "Wooden Heart," and "The Ant Song." They would always end the evening when the tuba player said, "We gotta go now, otherwise my wife will think I'm out with a blonde!" What Sinclair liked most about Schilo's, though, was their prices.

Schilo's met Sinclair's fifty-cent criterion. You could buy a dessert such as homemade apple strudel or German beer cake or a side dish like spiced beans or homemade potato salad or a deviled egg for under half a dollar. Sinclair frequented establishments that met this criterion as they came as close as possible to supporting his firm belief that for a man of his beauty and charm the essentials of life should be free.

Not that Sinclair was cheap. If a man who never, ever, had any money can be said to be extravagant, Sinclair was extravagant. But only with items in the luxury and enchantment department. The mundane essentials of life—food, utilities, shelter, in short, all the things which women, starting with his divorced mother, usually supplied—those things merely annoyed him. The kinds of things Sinclair preferred to supply were, for example, a pair of white kid gloves, opera length, with pearl buttons that cost more than his half of the rent. Which was one reason why he never had his half of the rent when it came due. Not that I seriously cared. Anyway, the German beer cake was a particular tea time favorite.

The memory of the taste of the cake mixes with the taste of Sinclair's skin, and I know clearly what I must have. What the baby in my stomach is demanding. Schilo's is only a few blocks away. It is a relief to move toward something, to finally have a destination of my own. I feel that if I don't keep moving and moving quickly toward my destination, Hillary's will might overtake me again. That I will understand why it is so important that I have the long needle put in my stomach. I hurry on to Schilo's.

The Solo-Serve on Soledad has a display of red and pink construction-paper hearts in the window. Just beyond, the river pops out like a varicose vein. The walls of the buildings on both sides of the river are covered with gang graffiti. Overhead, grackles, black and nearly as big as ravens, circle back to their home in the trees in the plaza. The temperature drops by the minute. The chilly winds blow customers into the Esquire Bar at the corner of South St. Mary's and Commerce. Sinclair used to love going to the Esquire to drink a draft at the wooden bar, long as a bowling alley. It was authentic enough for him, which meant that outsiders could get authentically knifed. Sinclair believed, however, that he should be welcome anywhere and as with so much in life, this belief overpowered reality. I peek in the window. Perhaps Sinclair now spends tea time at a bar.

He's not there.

Two blowsy white women, one of them pushing a flimsy stroller holding a towheaded baby boy, all three of them underdressed, hurry down the street ahead of me.

At the corner of Navarro and Commerce, the taste of

fresh-baked white bread fills my mouth, my nostrils. A cluster of businesspeople, men in suits, women in suits with skirts, rushing toward the river, toward an early happy hour, bumps past me. I barely notice as I remember the Saturday mornings Aurelia and I used to ride the bus downtown and get off on this very corner, across the street from Woolworth's. For some reason, it was our idea of a great treat to share one of the loaves of bread that Woolworth's, for reasons nearly as inexplicable, used to bake and sell. We would walk up and down the wooden aisles, our mouths wadded with bread, fingering the Tangee lipsticks and cut-glass pendants.

It has been a long time since Aurelia communicated with me, but, standing next to the old Woolworth's, my mind fills with an image. Like watching a movie, I see what Aurelia is seeing. Unlike most movies, however, the vision is less than thrilling: linoleum. Instead of the crowds jostling past or the grackles winging through the gray sky overhead, I see the ugliest kitchen linoleum I've ever encountered. A starburst pattern of gold and blue, it has a bumpy, waffled texture. Aurelia is waxing it and thinking of me. I am seized by the certain knowledge that she is near.

Then the ugly linoleum flickers away and I am left staring at La Cocinita de Pik Nik Foods. A convenience store occupies the building where Woolworth's once was. TACOS 2 FOR 99¢. 1/4 LB HAMBURGER $1.19.

Of course, neither Aurelia nor Sinclair are inside, but I check anyway.

The window of the Alamo Area Tours and Gift Shop is crammed with edible mementoes of the Lone Star State: Texas Beer Jelly. Indian Paintbrush Jelly. Tyler Red Rose Jelly. A trio of young men, boys, really, borrowing men's muscles pass me. Their short haircuts and arm-punching attempts to hide their awkward nervousness mark them as servicemen. It touches me to finally realize what brawny, confused children they are, these defilers of young Catholic womanhood the nuns had warned us were the most dangerous of all the corrupters we could "go to the river" with. I want to speak to them in a friendly, motherly way as an apology to all the lonely boys I shunned out of scared chastity.

The river is only a block away. Everything and everyone in San Antonio eventually comes down to the river. I glance behind me at the First Interstate clock suspended over the sidewalk at Presa and Commerce, 4:10.

Half a block from Schilo's, I stop and duck out of the way, almost expecting to see Sinclair open the front door. There is a sign outside advertising the special of the day: TURKEY AND DRESSING, TWO VEGS. $3.75.

The first time we came here together, I had the special of the day, which also happened to be turkey and dressing. When I observed that the gelatinous slice of pressed turkey parts, olive-green canned peas, and greasy, oversalted dressing tasted like the most indifferent of school cafeteria fare, Sinclair laughed.

"Taste? Taste!" he hooted that first time. "You don't come to Schilo's for *cordon bleu*, Trude, my girl. You come for gemutlichkeit. You come for the Heidelberg meets Luckenbach ambience. No, no, Trudenda." He exalted in my delicate parts. It was an affection that any woman would have found winning.

"One does not expect taste from Germans. Germans are root diggers. Eaters of pig fat slathered on black bread. They're a square-jawed, massive-boned people lacking the *buoyancy* to ever *ascend* to haute cuisine. Expect no lighter-than-air vol-au-vent from the Germans. No, one comes to the Germans for substance." He held aloft a soup spoon mounded with Schilo's Famous Split Pea Soup. "Substance, my girl, aye, that's what you'll be looking to the Krauts for. Substance." I loved Sinclair's little filibusters.

Schilo's was one of the major places I avoided after Sinclair left. I haven't been here in almost ten years. For several minutes I lurk about the parking garage next door, then, heart pounding, I step forward and peer in the window. He's not there. My body sags with disappointment and I feel again how heavy it is. I go inside.

Nothing has changed. It is warm and smells of stale beer and sauerkraut. The ceilings are high, fifteen feet maybe. The walls are painted dark green and white above the dark woodwork and booths. I slide into a tall-backed booth by the front window. On top of the red Formica table are the same bottles of Cajun Chef Sport Peppers, Louisiana Hot Sauce, and one squeeze bottle of mustard with a collar of crust that have always been there. It is a great relief that Schilo's is still the same, that it hasn't become a lawyer's office or a convenience store.

It was stupid of me to even dream that Sinclair might be here. I pick up one of the menus that are always left on the table and try to concentrate, but the space I open up for sandwich selection is seized by this question: What am I going to do with a baby? The question alone is so scary that I almost jump up and run back out, back to Hillary. I almost decide to risk drawing the black ball. To go back and have the test. To let Hillary and Victor make all the decisions, take care of everything. But a leaden weariness keeps my butt nailed to the booth. I see the words "Schilo's Famous Split Pea Soup" and my mind wanders.

In spite of all the substance-rich pea soup Sinclair ate, "substance" was the one thing he always lacked. He had a Celtic sort of twinkle about him even though most of his ancestors were German "root diggers." Root diggers and Czechoslovakian farmers. Somehow, out of that stolid genetic heritage he had pulled the coal-black hair, rose and white complexion, and leprechaun airiness of the Black Irish. He also had the weakness around the mouth and chin that so many Irish men do. Few women—myself not among them—got far enough past his lashes and mossy green eyes to notice such minor imperfections.

Sinclair did nothing to counter the impression that he was Irish. When in his cups, or bowl, depending upon the substance being abused, or when he just generally felt expansive, an Emerald Isle lilt would ruffle his speech and he would call me "my girl." It never seemed phony or affected to me because by all rights Sinclair Coker *should* have been born Irish.

And, if there was one thing that held us together, it was our shared belief in lending full support to what *should* be in this world and in ignoring what was not as it should be. At the moment we met and fell in love we were both struggling artists. What we *should* have been were struggling artists at the foot of a path that would climb straight to glory. Consequently, we each spent a lot of time making the other promise that he or she would still speak to the other when he or she was fabulously famous. Our other hobby was composing the artist's biography which we would have to supply the *New York Times* when our work was selected for the Whitney biennial. This belief that the world should pay more attention to you than it pays to a "normal" person is, I've found, the major quality needed to be an artist. A deep desire to be famous will fill lots of holes where talent should be.

Now, sitting in Schilo's Delicatessen almost ten years later, trying to figure out what on the menu I can afford, with a baster baby inside of me gulping his own pee, I can see that neither Sinclair nor I were ever on any path to glory. At best I could say that my path was a cross-country meander with a few shallow dips and some barely perceptible rises. And what of Sinclair? Unless I've missed more than I thought I had, he never made it to the Whitney biennial either.

"We ready to order here?"

I jump, startled out of my strange mix of lethargy and panic. The candy has left me light-headed and hollow. I imagine Sweet Pea down there slurping away at a sugar solution and feeling dazed and unable to cope. "I'll have . . ." I scan the menu, wishing I'd paid more attention to Hillary's nutrition bulletins. I'm going to need them now that I'm on my own. "A deviled egg and"—I look for something in a green and leafy vein—"an order of cole slaw and . . . a glass of milk and . . . an order of beans." I shut the menu and the waitress starts walking away, still scribbling. Then I see again the little mouth that had formed like a face in the clouds from the blotches of the sonogram. It is like a newborn puppy's rooting for its mother's teat as it gulps again in my memory.

"Uh, miss. Uh . . ." I lean back to read her name tag. "Connie." She stops.

"Something else?"

"Yeah, I don't know, I've just been extra hungry since I've been pregnant."

"You're expecting? I never would have guessed." She ducks her head around to peek under the Formica. "You sure aren't showing much. How far along are you?"

"Four months."

"So you're finished with the throwing up part and are ready to get down to some serious eating."

"I guess so. I've never been so hungry in my life. If it slows down long enough, I'll eat it."

Connie laughs. I have never made a waitress laugh before. Sinclair did it at least once before every meal I ever saw him consume. It was a ritual with him, like saying grace. But, until that moment, I've never even tried.

"I remember that phase." Connie pats her hips which jut out heroically from her waist. "I still have these to remind me."

It's my turn to laugh.

"I was as skinny as you are before I got pregnant. Not that you're skinny," she adds quickly, thinking she might have hurt my feelings. "It's better to start out a little under. Just don't end up like me. I put on fifty-three pounds with my first and sixty-five with the second. The doctor had me on diuretics, diet pills, the whole nine yards. Nothing helped. I retained water better than Hoover Dam. You getting much swelling?"

I look at my hands. Front and back. "Not really."

"I was working Denny's back then, and they keep you moving. Not like in here." She points the pencil in her hand behind her. The only thing moving is an ancient ceiling fan trailing cobwebs. "No, at Denny's I was on my feet every second of my shift. It got to where you couldn't tell my ankles from my thighs. My legs were just these columns went straight into my shoes, no time out for bones. You working?"

"Yeah."

"Where?"

"At Sears. I sell candy, nuts, and popcorn."

"So, you know what I mean about being on your feet."

I roll my eyes to indicate painful familiarity.

"It's the back that'll get you. Just wait'll you put on the pounds out front, you won't believe the backaches. You'll need good, solid arch support. Get a pair of lace-ups from the SAS outlet."

"Oh, that's all I wear when I work," I assure Connie.

She nods approval. "Every little bit helps." She turns back to her order pad. "What else can I bring you?"

"Uh, I think I'll have the special."

"And cancel the other stuff?"

"No. With the other stuff?" My tone is apologetic.

"You go on and eat. I just stopped listening to those doctors and threw the pills away. I say nature is telling you to eat. Eat. I had two healthy babies, and if I had to get these battleship hips to do it, well, that's just the way it has to be. So, you order anything your heart desires."

"Well, all right, then." We are united against doctors. "Bring me another glass of milk with that."

I have polished off most of the special—turkey still a queasy union of parts, dressing still oversalted, peas still olive green and tasting of the can—and am starting on my side dishes by the time I think to check my wallet. I haven't had to worry about money for the past few weeks living with the Goettlers. It has been a surprisingly easy habit to lose. I dig through my purse, chasing crumpled ones and the rattle of loose change.

My head is buried in my purse when I first notice the change in the atmosphere. Suddenly the air has the pressed-down feeling to it that comes before weather of tragic proportions. It's the sort of heaviness that makes rabbits dig into their burrows and long-reformed alcoholics go on mean drunks. A chill pierces me, and I am almost scared to look up and find out what it means.

When I do look up, my heart lurches and I stare directly into the ersatz Black Irish face of Sinclair Coker. Sinclair seems so close that I can smell his breath. It always smelled like a combination of roast beef and marijuana, even when he went lactovegetarian. The first thought that comes into my stunned mind is "I wish I'd worn mascara." But it's a movie closeness, and like the familiar idols who press you deep into your seat, Sinclair is actually on the other side of the large room with no more awareness of my existence than, say, Tom Cruise.

Once my pulse stops spiking, I realize how unsurprising his appearance really is. It is tea time and Sinclair has come to Schilo's. For all his bohemian ways and dedication to life on the edge, Sinclair always was a man devoted to his cozy comforts and little rituals.

I scoot into the far corner of my booth, where I can peek out at him but where there is no chance of him seeing me, and this calms me. His profile is to me. I am pleased to note some puffiness around the jowls, a delivery on the promise of a weak jaw. He is still lean, but in the unmuscled way of a man who never exercises and indulges more in sweet treats than protein. He has the aging cherub look of Paul McCartney, of a man who has put on years but refuses to take aboard any ballast to give them some heft. He is the same old Sinclair trying to skate through life on charm and good looks except that both have become shopworn.

Connie comes by to take his order. I pull my menu out from behind the napkin dispenser and guess that he will order either the hot apple pie or the German beer cake since they are the only selections under a dollar. I imagine that ten years has at least doubled his fifty-cent criterion.

Connie doesn't even take her order pad out. Sinclair tips his chair back and looks up at her like the dissolute young viscount flirting with a serving wench. I wait for it to happen. In less than a minute Connie, Connie of the swollen ankles and battleship hips, mother of two, is giggling as delicately as a geisha. I wonder if Sinclair is still a lousy tipper. It wouldn't matter. He could come back to a restaurant week after week and always get a smile from the waitress even though he stiffed her on the tip every time. So I expect Connie to laugh.

What I don't expect is to feel my heart lift out of my chest and go to Sinclair Coker like a homing pigeon finding its true nest. I'd expected heat, lust, physical attraction, wild infatuation for all the wrong reasons. But not this bedrock emotion, this geologic certainty that Sinclair and I were meant to be together. That it is destiny.

He is still handsome. He'd established a style decades ago that suited him and has stuck to it yet. Just as it was when I first met him, his hair is in a ponytail. Unlike most men who were around for the first wave of ponytails, however, Sinclair does not come across like a grizzled throwback with some Willie Nelson braid that looks as if its main function is to keep the hair out of the way while the person stamps out license plates. No, Sinclair's hair is slicked back into the perfect samurai warrior squirt arcing above his neck.

Like the ponytail, his clothes have a timeless quality: a white linen shirt of a vaguely buccaneer cut, a black vest, jeans, also black. In this unplaceable outfit, Sinclair would look equally at home at a TriBeCa art opening or singing "Sole Mio" from the back of a Gypsy caravan.

Clear as the bottle of Cajun Chef Sport Peppers on the table in front of me, I see the meandering path of my life split in two before me. I can go back to the Goettlers and keep on carrying this baby for them. Or I can get back together with Sinclair and we can raise the child that I now clearly see we were meant to have. I can't decide. My life has been one wrong choice after another. This decision is too important for me to make. I decide to let fate choose: If Connie brings Sinclair the apple pie, my baby will be Sweet Pea Goettler. I'll give him up and disappear forever. If, on the other hand, Sinclair has ordered the German beer cake, then we are meant to get back together and raise the child we postponed ten years ago.

I wait for Connie's return, aware of every second. I try to distract myself by reading the label on the Sport Peppers bottle: Hot peppers, vinegar, salt, alum, 1/10% sodium benzoate (as a preservative), yellow no. 5 food color.

Connie comes back. She slides a plate in front of Sinclair. My view is blocked by a barricade of napkin dispenser, coffee cup, and salt shaker. I must wait until Sinclair lifts the first bite up to see what he has on his fork. He raises his hand. Stops. Studies the forkful. Plucks a hair from the morsel. The fork rises again. Sinclair parts his lovely lips and slides in a bite of . . . German beer cake.

I am rejoicing, the name Sweet Pea Coker is cannonading through my mind before I admit what a nitwit I am. There is no decision to be made here. The decision was made when I put Victor's wigglies into my body. There is no choice. As for destiny. Destiny, shit. It was a fluke that Sinclair and I were ever together in the first place. He wouldn't give me the time of day now.

I wait, hidden in the far corner of the booth, for over an hour until Sinclair finishes and leaves, throwing a kiss to Connie from the cash register. More than anything, I want to go back to my apartment. However, as it takes every cent I can track down in the bottom of my purse just to pay my bill, I return to the only place I have left to go: King William.

APRIL 15

11. "You can't hurt the baby, but that baby can hurt you."

Our childbirth instructor, Rachel, is telling us how to sleep. Her eyes, popped as an amphetamine addict's, bore into the class. Hillary is the first to scribble her words down on the back of the Birth Right! Way of Birth class syllabus. Some of the fathers scramble around for writing materials. Me and the other big ones lying on the floor, our mounds shimmed up with pillows, are exempt from scrambling. Our job is to lounge around and incubate.

Rachel has already imparted a number of compelling insights: her labor pains felt like nothing more than especially bad menstrual cramps, my uterus will expand to five hundred times its normal size before this is over, she prefers the birth partners be called "sherpas" rather than "coaches."

"Birth," Rachel told us in the first class, "is not an athletic event. We in Birth Right! don't care much for a competitive, sports-oriented model. We view birth as an exploration with the mother scaling new inner heights and the 'sherpas' driving in those pitons, snapping in those carabiners."

Hillary came across Birth Right! after, naturally, much research. She studied statistics from all the different childbirth education classes and found that Birth Right! had the most drug-free deliveries. Hillary does not want her baby contaminated in any way. Birth Right! also teaches you how to keep your doctor in line with episiotomies and epidurals. Hillary decided that we should keep on seeing Dr. Worley, since his healthy baby stats are the best in the city, but she makes him toe a strict line.

Hillary and her birth plans are irrelevant to me. I don't plan to scale any inner heights while another human being emerges from my body. No, I'll be yelling for drugs like Elvis when my time comes. I've heard all my life from Randi that childbirth is something best experienced in a vegetative state, and I believe her. I went back in body to King William after seeing Sinclair at Schilo's two months ago, but my spirit has never returned.

Birth Right! I don't like classes that turn into imperatives. I'm not much for orders these days.

"On your sides, please!" Rachel, the frog-eyed teacher, instructs. We big ones heave over. "There's a major artery running underneath your tummies. Right here." She holds up a pelvis bone and pokes her finger up through it. "It's called the vena cava."

Hillary writes down the Latin words as if she's going to be doing bypass surgery later that day. My irritation with Hillary has reached such a peak that I can barely speak to her anymore. I know that it's myself that I'm really irritated with. That I'm mad enough to chew nails for letting myself get in this situation. Even knowing all that doesn't stop me from throwing the irritation back on Hillary. Pregnancy has impaired my lifelong ability to take the other person's side. I care now only about me and how I feel and how I mostly feel is pissed off.

"Lie down on your back and you put that baby's weight plus the weight of his little aquarium right smack-dab on top of that vein. Know what happens next?"

I look around at the five other couples in the class. They're all so young. This could be an SAT study group. Except for me. One girl at the start of the class asked if she could arrange for makeup sessions since she'd be having finals in May in a few weeks. I try to believe that she means college, but I'm not certain.

Hillary and I aren't the only female couple. The other maleless pair is composed of a sherpa with a black panther tattooed around her left ankle and a big one dressed in a leopard print maternity top. They both have the stringy, used-up look of topless dancers who were once pretty. Before I have time to speculate on what their situation might be, an even more curious crew walks in—one pregnant woman, one unpregnant woman, one man. All three are in their early twenties and look like Bedouin tribespeople in their flowing tie-dyed regalia. The women carry many pillows.

We all gape at them, even Rachel, who started off the class by sharing her personal belief that there is "no right or wrong way of doing things, just ones that seem more or less comfortable." From the way Rachel is gawking, I'd have to guess that a trio of Bedouins falls in the "less comfortable" category for her.

Rachel catches herself and jokes, "Just pull up a floor."

The other two help the pregnant woman settle on pillows. Lank red hair hangs like faded drapes on each side of her doughy face. Only the ring through her nose makes her face memorable. The nonpregnant woman is strikingly beautiful. Her dark hair is wound with brilliant bits of fabric and piled onto her head. She moves like a ballerina, plumping the man on his pillows, then she sits on the floor beside his feet.

All I can think of the curious arrangement is that I'm certain Sinclair would love it. In the two months since seeing him in Schilo's, Sinclair has become a prism that I refract all my thoughts through. The young man reminds me of Sinclair at that age: petulant, self-absorbed, expecting the adoration the two women heap upon him. Of course, what saved Sinclair was a sense of humor, which the pouty young man doesn't seem to have.

"We were just getting into why all you mothers need to be sleeping and resting on your side," Rachel says to the redhead, who is lying back on the pillows. "Stay the way you are for very long and you know what'll happen?"

The three look at each other. None of them has an answer. Rachel does.

"First there'll be the pins and needles. Then your legs'll go completely numb. You'll depress your return flow and you know what that'll do to oxygen levels in the blood going to your baby who's in there trying to develop a brain."

The redhead rearranges herself, shifting over to her side before she turns her child into a retard.

"That's it," Rachel congratulates her.

"You don't sleep on your back, do you?" Hillary whispers to me, alarmed.

"Never," I assure her, even though I've fallen asleep every night that I've been at her house staring at the canopy wafting above the four-poster. For the past two months I've gone to sleep dreaming about winning Sinclair back in spectacular ways. I dream that I hit big in Wingo and Sinclair, dazzled by my photo in the paper, is compelled to seek me out. I imagine myself warbling enchanted songs of my own composition to him over the beige plastic radio he used to keep by the bed we once shared and my angelic voice draws him to me. I pretend that I can soar into the clouds and sail above Sinclair, who beholds me and instantly recognizes the inevitability of our love.

I am having a delayed adolescence. I loaf around all day, sulky and lost in a dream world, suffering from rampaging hormones and a delirious crush. I don't recognize my body. I think about sex all the time and I eat like a lumberjack. My skin is broken out and I have hydroponic breasts where once there was dryland farming. I try to think and plan and usually end up taking a nap or having a snack.

I see the looks that Hillary gives Victor when she asks me a question and I just shrug my shoulders. We never discussed the day I walked out of the amniocentesis. We never discuss my new distracted personality. They believe I am holding their baby hostage. That there is nothing they can do. I don't do anything to alter that belief.

The experience of having power is new to me. In the moments when I am lucid or energetic enough to think about it, I am fairly disappointed in how poorly I am handling it. I struggle to get ahold of myself, but my mind is in brownout mode, flickering faintly as all my energy is drained away to swell my breasts and belly. I can't put my hands on my waist anymore because it has filled in solid from armpits to hips. I no longer resemble a spindly alcoholic, I now have the look of a gout-ridden eighteenth-century lord in dancing hose with my great pot of a belly mushrooming over the frail stalk of my pale legs.

"Trudy?"

I look over at Hillary, who is kneeling beside me. All the other big ones are down on all fours with their sherpas kneeling beside them like patient cowherds.

"Come on, everyone. Let's practice those pelvic rocks." Rachel directs her comment to me, and I obey.

"Okay, sherpas, put your hand on her back and make sure she's doing it right. We want to feel those backs round, then sag. Round, then sag."

All the other coaches put a hand on the mother's back. The man and nonpregnant woman in the Bedouin trio each put a hand on the mother's back. The nonpregnant woman softly sweeps a lank strand of red hair out of the mother's face and hooks it behind her ear. The skinny woman with the black panther around her ankle puts both her hands on the mother's back and gently helps her tip her pelvis back and forth. All the other sherpas are happy for a chance to put their hands on the mother. I can feel Hillary's reluctance to touch me. It is more than equaled by my reluctance to have her touch me.

"How we doing here?" Rachel leans down to check on us and Hillary finally puts her hand on my back. After a moment's hesitation I pivot my pelvis up and down. Sinclair was always impressed by my flexibility. I wonder how much limberness I've lost and experiment with a few deep rocks.

"Your arch is a bit too extreme," Rachel warns.

"It's more of a sag," Hillary coaches.

I nod and go to a less-fevered tempo.

"That's it. That's it," Rachel congratulates.

All around me the other big ones down on their hands and knees tip their bottoms up into the air and down.

"Come on," Rachel tells the group. "Let the moms know what a good job they're doing."

A couple of husbands give their wives a good Bossy pat on the flanks. Most murmur words of praise. The two non-pregnant members of the Bedouin trio both kiss the redhaired mother. "*Ex*cellent pelvic rocks, Patrice," the young man says in a too loud voice. Patrice tilts her head around to look up at him and becomes beautiful at that moment. The other woman watches the exchange and reaches out to stroke the hand the young man has on Patrice. The complexities of their arrangement dazzle me. I feel I could tell them everything about my situation. If Sinclair and I were together, we could all rent a large house together in my old neighborhood and raise our babies to accept casually the intricacies of life. Except that I know Sinclair and the beautiful one would sleep together and break my heart.

Suddenly I sit straight up on my knees.

"Trudy, what is it?" The look on Hillary's face alarms me and I check to make sure there's nothing terribly wrong with me.

"Something's pulsing in me," I tell her.

"Pulsing? Like, like blood?" The word alarms her and she really touches me. For a second I break out of my adolescent sulk and see her clearly. There are more tiny lines around her eyes than I remember there being. The fluorescent lights buzzing overhead wash her skin out to an ashy green.

"What is it? What's wrong?" Rachel intervenes.

"Something's pulsing in her," Hillary explains for me.

"Pulsing? Where?" Rachel puts her hands where mine are over my rib cage.

"There," I answer.

"What's it feel like?" Hillary crowds in next to me.

"It's just this deep, rhythmical pulsing." I mark the beat throbbing inside of me with my hand. "Dum-dum-dum-dum. Can't you feel it?"

Rachel pulls away smiling. For a second I think it must be my voice. "You know what that is?" She is much too pleased with herself. "That's the baby. Hiccuping."

Everyone in the class crowds around me, wanting to feel the baby hiccup, but I'm the only one who can. I am almost as surprised by this latest proof of Sweet Pea's existence as I was watching him in the sonogram. The shock makes me realize how much in limbo I've been for the past two months.

"That is awesome," the young man says with such a look of wonder on his face that I change my mind about him. Maybe he isn't the spoiled narcissist I'd taken him for.

Maybe he doesn't want to have a baby just to increase the population of his adoring mass by one.

"Haven't you been feeling the baby move?" Rachel asks, clearly surprised that I should be caught so off guard by the hiccups.

"Well, yeah, I guess." My voice is extra high-pitched. The trio of Bedouins now look at me the way everyone looked at them at first.

"You have?" Hillary asks, sounding betrayed.

"I think. I mean, yeah. I guess." In fact, I've not only felt Sweet Pea move, I've watched him swimming around under my skin. I just haven't been in the mood to hike up my blouse and show Hillary. If I had, she would have wanted Victor to see, of course, and, although it is their baby, it is still my stomach surrounding him.

"What does it feel like?" Hillary wants to know.

I've read articles in the baby magazines Hillary has scattered all over the house by pregnant women who are mightily annoyed at being asked how they're feeling by strangers in polite conversation. I like strangers asking me how I feel. It is Hillary I can't stand to report to. Strangers have no interest in taking over my feelings. Hillary wants to make every twinge her own. The more I shut her out, the fewer communiqués from the front she receives, the more frantic she is for information. With the entire class clustered around me, waiting for my answer, I have no choice but to let Hillary in too.

"It feels like . . ." I think back to another baby magazine article. "It feels like bubbles. Little bubbles rising up inside of you."

Rachel smiles. She's read the same article or maybe even had the bubble feeling herself.

"Bubbles," Hillary mutters, obviously trying to work herself into a sympathetic carbonated moment.

I get a tiny pang at how easy it is for me to lie to her now. Sweet Pea moving doesn't feel anything like bubbles. He feels like an otter slithering about inside of me. He feels happy inside me. I want now to keep him in there forever. I am no longer able to think about the time when he won't be inside me.

"Can you see anything yet?" Rachel asks. "Any movement on the outside."

"No. None." I answer curtly, cutting off Hillary's eager expression.

"Oh, just wait until you see the baby move," Rachel coos. "It's just, just . . . I can't describe it. The wonder of it."

"I can't wait." Hillary gives me a moony look.

I can't bear to even consider the cozy little tableau that I know she has in mind: she and Victor, hands clasped, staring fondly at my stomach, waiting for a precious little hand or foot to goiter out. Various protrusions have, in fact, been lumping up for the past week or so. When mothers talk about these protrusions, the movie *Alien* always seems to come up.

I wonder if Sinclair would be entranced by the spectacle of a tiny human burrowing beneath my skin, humping it up like a cartoon mole digging through the earth? Would he want to spend hours gazing at my belly, waiting for Sweet Pea to do a bit of spelunking? Would he be amused if I told him these sudden bunchings of my flesh remind me of a Popeye cartoon where the sailor man gulps his can of spinach then the atomic vegetable travels to his bicep, transforming it into an anvil? I dream that he would be. I want Sinclair to see this baby moving around inside me.

"My first one kicked so hard he knocked my ex-husband out of bed." The woman in the leopard print top speaks to me.

"Had better taste than you did," her partner with the black panther tattoo says. Her laugh sounds like coffee and cigarettes for breakfast.

"He'd rear up in the middle of the night all mad and go, 'Quit kicking me, Renee.' I'd go, 'I'm *not* kicking you. *He* is, and if you think he's kicking *you,* you should feel it from this side.'"

"Okay, everyone," Rachel calls out. "For next week I want you all to fill in your diet sheets. Especially, *especially,* count your grams of protein. Okay? And listen everyone, do those pelvic rocks and squats. Forty minimum. Every day. Remember, we're all climbing this mountain together and we'll do it without drugs!" Rachel calls after us as we file out into the night.

A breeze ruffles the spring air carrying the scent of pink blossoms, mimosas, and Indian hawthorne. There is a mimosa outside the bedroom window of my apartment. Every year when it blossoms, the scent takes me back to the spring Sinclair and I spent mostly in bed together beneath that window. I believe I might have shaken loose of Sinclair sometime during the past ten years if the mimosas didn't bloom every spring.

"Well, what did you think?" Hillary asks once we're in the car.

"About what?"

"The class."

"Seems okay."

"What about the little menage à trois that came in late? Looked like they'd all just escaped from a Grateful Dead concert."

"I didn't notice." All my hormones jump for glee at my purposeful grumpiness. Hillary doesn't try to make any more conversation and I glaze over, pretending I'm driving through the night with Sinclair at the wheel and that there is no baby making everything so impossible.

I wake up the next morning hung over with remorse for my snittish behavior of the past two months. I leave my bedroom determined to make amends. From the stairs I see Victor and Hillary are in the living room. Hillary is holding up a swatch of bunny print material against a swatch of bunny print wallpaper. Victor is pulling a knot into his tie and trying to see around Hillary to his reflection in the mirror behind her.

"Do you think it would be too coordinated to have the bumper pads match the wallpaper?"

"Bumper pads?" Victor asks.

For the past month Hillary has been obsessed with decorating the room she is turning into a nursery. She already has it outfitted with a white wicker crib and matching changing table that look as if they came out of the czar's summer palace. She just can't decide now on a "motif" and makes occasional references to how much easier the whole process would be if they knew the sex. If I'd had amniocentesis. That makes me really snarly.

"Bumper pads," Hillary repeats. "You know, bumper pads!"

"Oh, right, bumper pads."

The pattern we've developed seems to be that Hillary absorbs my sullenness and Victor takes hers. Probably Victor's secretary goes home at night and berates her potted plants.

"So, do you like the circus motif or the ballooning motif better? Or what about this one? Peter Rabbit."

"Hillary, I don't care," Victor finally snaps. "Circus motif, yeah, fine. I mean, what does it matter whether the kid upchucks on sheets printed with clowns or Squirrel Nutkin?"

Hillary's response is muffled.

Victor's is swift. "Don't cry. I'm sorry. Hillary, please. The bunnies. Definitely." Another muffled comment. "Well, if the research shows that infants respond more to black and white than pastels, go with black and white."

"You don't think that's too stark for a baby's room?" Hillary sniffles.

"Stark?" Victor pauses, trapped. Should he support black and white or pastels? He looks up and spots me on the stairway. "Trudy," he booms out. "What do you think? Black and white too stark for the nursery?"

I don't know what to say either. I've always decorated by accretion. Objects I like just seem to wash ashore in my apartment. The concept of going out with a scheme in mind and purchasing component parts is utterly foreign to me. But as my act of penance, I force myself to talk about the nursery with Hillary.

"Well, it would be different," I answer. Hillary's face falls. "But not in a bad way."

Hillary turns to me. There is something undeniably poignant about a woman who can mount major museum exhibitions being undone by bumper pads.

"All the research shows that black and white is actually the most visually stimulating environment for an infant," she tells me. "I mean, I'm not into any super baby thing here or anything. It's just that these first few months are the peak time for brain development and why not make the most of them?"

"Why not?" I answer gamely.

My effort pleases Hillary.

The phone rings and Victor grabs it.

"Darrell, hey, I'm on my way right now. . . . Darrell, now is not the time to waffle, hombre. . . . Typical IRS intimidation tactics. So some weasel told them about the Lamborghini? That's a legitimate tool of your business. We can justify that. What? You're supposed to meet prospective investors in a Hyundai? . . . No, Darrell, no. Steady on. One does not 'work with' the IRS. One works 'with' the Mafia. One works *around* the IRS. Darrell, call me back on the cellular, I got to bolt."

As soon as Victor hangs up the phone and grabs his gym bag and briefcase, the cellular phone in its leather pack rings. He picks it up and starts talking to Darrell again. Pecking Hillary on the way, he leaves.

Hillary and I go out into the kitchen together. Mercedes jumps up and whisks the pink and orange Dunkin' Donuts box she had been picking through away under the counter. For the past two months she's been bootlegging me doughnuts in the morning. The headline on the *San Antonio Express* spread out on the counter reads "9-year-old Gives Birth on Playground."

"Qué pasa, calabaza," Mercedes greets me.

Our deep-fried delights do not escape Hillary's notice. Without a word she reaches under the counter, pulls out the

Dunkins, and dips in. Watching her befoul her fine-tuned system with a chocolate doughnut, I realize just how badly she wants in the club, and I renew my pledge to make up for my sulkiness.

"So you think black and white?" she asks, a daub of cheap powdered sugar icing jumping up and down on her lip as she speaks.

"Well, yes, if that's supposed to be the most stimulating."

Mercedes, well-versed in the endless nursery motif discussions, starts rattling dishes around in the sink, pretending she's not listening.

"I want your involvement. Your input," Hillary says.

"Well, the brain development and all. That's important."

"Key."

"Yes, brains are a major thing." As I stumble on, fishing for "input," I have a vague recollection of Hillary pleading with her volunteer docents from Alamo Heights for the same thing, for "input." In that case it meant she was launching another fund drive.

"Black and white can be very interesting. Like in that diorama you had constructed for the carved gourds from Nigeria." The memory of that exhibit reminds me of the first Hillary I knew, the one who was so good at her job. The one who made my job fun. It seems a long time ago.

"Did you like that?"

"Some of your best work," I say heartily. Perhaps too heartily for, practically before I've finished nodding approbation, Hillary is on the phone with the museum designers getting names of painters, stencilers, seamstresses.

She pays them extra and has all the work finished over the weekend. By Monday we are standing in a nursery that smells of fresh paint and of the fabric sizing stiffening the new curtains flounced along their rods. The walls are painted in a black and white zebra pattern. The sheets on the white wicker crib are a black and white jungle print. The bumper pads and curtains match. A mobile of black and white animals pirouettes over his crib. Penguins and zebras and black whales with white stomachs stalk one another across the border stenciled around the top of the walls. It reminds me of a cocktail lounge in Matamoros Sinclair used to be fond of. Club Safari it was called. Supposedly, if you stayed around long enough, women got chummy with burros and the like, but we never caught the late show.

"It's great," I say.

Hillary puts her arm around me. "I've loved working with you again. I've missed that."

I smile at her, pretending that me standing around all weekend telling her all her ideas were great is working together. My sulky silence was much more honest. Hillary gazes fondly at the mound. I have on a big T-shirt and elastic-waist shorts and could be just an ordinary person with a barrel-trunked build. Hillary, however, knows that not to be the case.

The fond gazes make me squirm, make me want to run away. I wish I had somewhere to run. I wish I had Sinclair. He is the only constant in the ever-shifting constellation of possibilities I study endlessly. With her arm around me, I almost tell Hillary that we have to call this whole thing off. That I cannot endure another minute of it.

When we really were working together, Hillary was always good at organizing me. She was like a prosthetic sense of direction getting my enthusiasm and energy all headed down the same trail. Without her I am a shambling mess of indecision, my ideas sprinting off into the thicket. I wish I could plug back into her focus again. Get her opinion on a number of vital issues.

Mostly I want to ask her if she thinks I am equipped to be a mother. The question beats through me, but even I know that Hillary is the last person I can ask it of.

"Trudy, you don't look too well. Oh, my God!" Hillary shrieks, pushing me out of the nursery. "You were breathing paint fumes!" She steers me to the window above the second-story landing, guiding me toward an untainted breeze. It is so dense with the smell of mimosa blossoms that the breath clots in my chest. I have to do something. But what? I need guidance.

"I think I'd better go lie down," I say woozily.

As Hillary helps me into my room, I ask her for the cordless phone and she delivers it to me in bed along with a tall glass of milk.

"Thanks," I whisper wanly, dialing before the door closes behind Hillary. The phone answers on the second ring. In the background I hear the theme music from *The Price Is Right.*

"Hi, it's me," I say, nervous, hoping my familiarity is not misplaced.

"Oh. Hi," Randi answers. "Are you calling from work? They check the bills, you know."

"No, I got the day off. Heroes of the Republic Day."

"You Texans get more state holidays. I wish we had half the holidays in Indiana you Texans have."

This talk of state holidays almost makes me hang up, but I don't really have anyone else to talk to, anyone else to help me figure out what to do.

"Hey, Randi," I say, trying to sound as if the question

had just that second popped into my head and, more important, as if it were a casual, totally abstract question. "Do you
want grandchildren?"

"Grandchildren?" She repeats the word as if I'd asked if
she wanted diverticulitis. "Shouldn't we be married before
we start thinking about all that?"

"I wasn't 'thinking' about anything. I just wanted to
know if you ever think about having grandchildren. If you
care one way or the other. Besides, not everyone is married
these days."

"Well, I hope to smash that 'everyone' who isn't has
established some security before they start thinking along
those lines. I hope they know their employer's policies and
aren't thinking their parents have anything put aside in a
case like that."

"Sometimes things can't be planned out that neatly," I
say.

"Nowadays they can. Nowadays it's the person's own
decision. It's not like the way it used to be when a person
had no choice in the matter. Not like the way it was for me.
A person has choices now."

I don't have to worry about fooling Randi into believing
that this was a discussion in the abstract. None of our conversations ever got exactly personal. Still, I risk a question,
"Did you like it?"

"It?" my mother stalls.

"Being a mother?"

"Oh? What about being a mother? There's a lot goes
into being a mother. You can't just say 'it.' Did you like 'it.'
You have to be more specific."

"Anything. Did you like anything about motherhood.
Having a baby? Raising it? Being pregnant?"

"Being pregnant? Did I like throwing up for eight months straight?" I was premature, so she got that ninth month off. "Did I like getting grapefruit-size piles? Hard to find much good to say about being pregnant. Well, no, I take that back. There were a couple of good things."

"What? What were they?" I can't keep the eagerness out of my voice. I want to know about the joy I might have brought my mother and where to look for some for myself.

"Well," Randi continues. "No periods for one thing and, for another, I got to clean the lint out of my belly button."

I am so deflated by her answer that I can barely rouse the energy to tap on the phone to simulate the click of call waiting. "Oh, sorry, Randi, I've got another call coming in."

"You have that call waiting? That's a good feature. I've thought about getting that. How much's it run you a month?"

I throttle the receiver. "Uh, I got to go."

I hang up and sag into bed. No periods and getting to clean the lint out of your belly button. That is not much of a mothering legacy for me to build on.

I sit up until I can stare out of the back window at the river toiling along its concrete banks. On the other side of the electric fence a couple of men lounge among the Indian hawthorne and pass a tallboy of malt liquor in a paper sack back and forth. In the next clump of bushes over, a couple grapples. His straight black hair is held in place with a net. Hers tumbles over the grass. His hand slides up between her legs. They are "going to the river" in a big way. A bargeload of tourists pass by. A woman tourist wearing an umbrella on a hat crown snaps off a couple of pictures. The river is a magic passage that allows winos, horny Chicano teenagers, and flotillas of tourists access to the back side of the ritziest neighborhood in the city.

I stare out the window, motionless, until three boats pass by and think about Sister Theonella. About how nice she was when Aurelia had to leave. How nice she always was to me. How she guided me, encouraged my projects. How she stood up for me when my grades slipped. Downstairs, the door opens and closes. Hillary leaving for work. I need guidance. I need a mother. I must find the one woman who ever truly was that to me. I push the covers aside and stand up.

12. From the moment I set foot on the campus back when I was twelve years old, I loved Our Lady of Sorrows. My memory of it is one of cool serenity. Even though none of the buildings were air-conditioned, they all sat in the shade of pecan trees grown to an enormous size off the water they slurped from the river. The limestone walls always felt cool to the touch, even in August. Inside, the floors were dark and shiny and smelled of wax buffed to a high gloss, and ceiling fans turned lazily just beneath the high ceilings.

The school now smells of stale beer, which makes sense since it has been turned into a brewery. I jump out of the way of a beer truck with a spurting bottle and the name Alamo Beer painted on the side. Mine was the last class to graduate from Our Lady of Sorrows. The diocese decided that the hundred-year-old boarding school was too expensive to maintain and put it on the market, keeping only the convent. Our Lady went through a succession of owners until it was purchased by the heir to a local brewing fortune who publicly proclaimed his intention of showing his father that beer shouldn't taste like cat piss. He turned the old classrooms and dormitories into the state's first microbrewery and started making his Alamo beer.

Everything else is the same. More the same, in fact, than it was when I went to school here, since the heir spent a good chunk of his fortune-to-be restoring the place in a historically accurate way. It now looks pretty much the way it did in the middle of the eighteenth century when the first group of nuns arrived from New Orleans to teach the daughters of San Antonio's finest families. The original architect had given the place a French Quarter look so that the Sisters wouldn't be too homesick, clustering the two stories of classrooms and dormitories for 160 girls around an airy courtyard.

"Help you, ma'am?" A security guard approaches me as I wander up to the main building.

I tell him I used to go to school here and have come back to visit.

"You're welcome to tour the grounds. But all buildings are restricted." He checks to make sure I've understood. "You can't go inside."

I tell him I hadn't planned to, and he leaves me alone.

I look up to the bell tower on the chapel and remember the day I first met Sister Theonella, the art teacher. Because the principal, Sister Tabernacula, was sick, she had been given the job of showing us new girls around the campus. The first landmark she pointed out was the convent tower. There was a clock on three sides of the tower, but there wasn't one on the north side.

"Do any of you girls know why they would not have put a clock on the north side of the tower?" she asked us.

I looked around at the thirty other new girls. They were divided into two groups, Anglo and Mexican. I stood in a thin isthmus between them, terrified of what was going to happen when they found out I was a spy. I didn't know anything about Catholics, not even why my mother called them "mackerel snappers." I wished I could have gone to reform school, which Randi had said was my only other option. I barely breathed fearing that at any moment they would find me out. That something about the way I wore my knee socks or the way my patch was sewn onto my beanie would give me away as a Protestant. I pondered that term "mackerel snapper." It grew sinister in my imagination.

"Well?"

Sister Theonella was the first nun I'd ever seen in person. I couldn't get over her clothes, her "habit," the sheer quantity of that much yardage up and ambulating. The laundry and personal hygiene complications held me spellbound.

The only parts of her that were visible were her face and her hands. They were small hands and a small face enlivened with quick eyes. I assumed that beneath the billowing black and white she must be a small person, but I couldn't prove it. Sister had dark brows and eyelashes, perfect, smooth skin, and a nose like a newt with tiny uptilted nostrils. Her shoes scared me. They looked like crippled children's shoes.

"No one can guess why there's not a clock on the north side?" She looked at us, then squeezed the back of her thumb against her pursed lips and stifled a giggle. I was mesmerized by her witch's cackle. Would there be torture if no one came up with the right answer? Would panties be yanked down? Would a cat-o'-nine-tails sing through the air?

"Give up?" Sister asked with a glee that raised the hackles on the back of my neck.

"Because they didn't want to give the time of day to the damn Yankees!" Sister held her face straight for a moment or two, then turned away. Her snuffling chortles soon turned to great honks of mirth. Now the other girls became alarmed. They glanced at one another and made faces that asked what was going on. The Mexican girls buzzed attempts at translation that all ended with big eyes and little shrugs. They moved closer together. Aurelia was among them. We'd spent only one night together and hadn't become best friends yet.

Sister turned back around and faced the general consternation she'd caused. "Don't you get it? The Sisters were Rebs. From New Orleans."

Nobody said anything. The mirth drained from Sister's face and she flipped her hand through the air. "Oh, well, it doesn't matter. They moved the mother house to St. Louis years ago anyway."

Then I got it. Of course. Time of day. Damn Yankees. I laughed. Even for me it was a screechingly memorable laugh. All the girls turned and gaped at me. Aurelia twitched an alarmed glint of rabbity tooth. Sister blinked twice and cleared her throat starchily.

The chapel still has the three-faced bell tower I laughed at that first day, but now a plaque screwed onto the outside wall identifies it as "main warehouse." The door opens and a man in a khaki work suit emerges backfirst. I hold the door for him and he pushes out a dolly loaded with cases of Alamo beer. I slip inside.

For a second my memories of the endless daily Masses I endured in the chapel collide with the sight of its present incarnation, jamming in my mind like slides caught in a projector. I remember rows of wooden pews facing an altar laid with golden vessels and vases of gladiolas, clouds of incense rising over it like ghosts too bored to move in the still air. The pews have all been removed and rows of stainless steel beer barrels now gleam in the soft light dancing from the high clerestory windows. The main altar has been replaced with a wire mesh cage, where a shipping clerk sits absorbed in filling out forms. But the stained glass window is still there, the one Sister Theonella pointed out to us that first day.

High above the western nave the window gleams. It depicts a beautiful young woman clutching a baby lamb and drenching the beast with bloody tears. The first time I saw it I found it riveting as only a twelve-year-old whose sexual stirrings are tinged with a distinct sadomasochism can. I was particularly drawn at that age to accounts of the Holocaust and had read *The Diary of Anne Frank* several times.

"This window was sent over from the mother house in

Arles, France, in 1894," Sister Theonella had started off. "It illustrates the sorrow of St. Agnes. The lamb is a traditional symbol of purity often used to represent—"

Sister stopped dead and stared at the window as if seeing it for the first time. As she cocked her head to the side, a look of distress came over her face, and she shooed us along. "I don't think we really need to spend any more time on this. Okay!" She clapped her hands and turned away from the window to face the chapel where I was to spend untold hours on my knees in daily Mass.

"Girls! Tell me! What would you do if a hostile party of renegade Indians were outside that door?" Sister pointed to the thick plank doors and grinned eagerly.

All the well-behaved little Catholic girls stared silently at the door. None of them spoke until a tall girl with silky white-blond hair curling into a pageboy on her shoulders raised her hand. I would learn that her name was Annette and that she was the ultimate realization of a peculiarly Catholic sort of overachiever girl. The sort who would ask after reading *Lives of the Saints* where one might purchase a hair shirt.

Sister pointed at her. "Yes, yes! The savage redskins are out there cutting the night with bloodcurdling cries and sharpening their tomahawks for some lovely blond scalps. Tell us, what do we do?"

Annette stuck her pointy chin in the air and answered with the confidence of a strict party-liner: "Offer a novena to the Blessed Virgin Mary."

"Offer a novena? Do you know what it sounds like to get scalped? First the Indian cuts around the section to be taken. A section just about the size of the one covered by your beanies." Several girls touched their heads. "Then, when the brave yanks the section free, there's a distinct *pop.*" Sister recreated the sound with a tongue clucked loudly against the roof of her mouth at the same time that she pulled an imaginary scalp off her head.

"Ew-yuck," Annette said quietly.

"Yuck, indeed. What do we do?" Sister asked urgently.

Having been powerfully seized by the image of a mohawked brave in bear grease *popping!* off a rondelle of my hair, I began to babble, waving my arms about to indicate directions. "We should push all the pews up here against the door. Then stack some other ones so that we can climb up to those windows and throw stuff down. Then we ought to, we ought to . . ." I looked around the chapel for weapons. I couldn't believe the stupid Catholics would be out here in Indian country without weapons. "We ought to"—I pointed to the altar, gleaming with candlesticks and crucifixes—"melt those down and pour the molten lead on the Indians. Then we tear off all our petticoats and rip them into long strips and wind them up real tight and melt wax on them, then light them on fire and hurl them out . . ."

I noticed that everyone was staring at me, transfixed. I heard someone behind me mutter, "Weird." The Mexican girls were trying to piece together a translation.

"Great defense," Sister finally said.

"Is there something I can do for you? Ma'am? Ma'am. Ma'am!" It takes the shipping clerk three attempts before he can capture my attention. When he finally gets it, I wave distractedly and wander out of the chapel.

I can almost feel Sister Theonella's hand on my back as I leave. I'd been the last girl out of the chapel that first day and Sister had stopped me as I passed her. "You're the girl who likes art, aren't you?" she asked.

My curbside finds had been discussed at length during negotiations to have me admitted to Our Lady of Sorrows. Randi maintained that they were the reason I "lived in a dream world." The principal, Sister Tabernacula, took her suggestion that my treasures be banned altogether from the campus. Randi seized upon the opportunity to purge my room and stow everything in the garage. At least she didn't throw my things away.

I missed them terribly. The night before, Aurelia, who had yet to say one word to me, had cried herself to sleep. The only possession she'd unpacked had been a picture of her teeming family, so I knew she missed them. I'm glad she cried first, because then, when I thought about Lizzie, my blue-tailed lizard, making scritching sounds in her coffee can in my room at night, and my map of the Lower Antilles I'd found in the Dumpster behind the high school and pinned next to my bed, and my mosaic of a butterfly on a lantana flower that I'd made out of crumbled eggshells dyed with food coloring and old coffee, then I could cry too.

"The principal mentioned your love of found objects to me. I teach art. From four until five every afternoon I paint. Please feel free to join me anytime if you'd care to pursue your own projects." She patted my shoulder and moved to the front of the group.

The heat that fall broke records that had stood for a hundred years. Sister Paul, a bowling ball of a woman who taught us civics, passed out in class the first week. I was used to air-conditioning, as Randi had declared that if she had to live in the state of Texas, she wasn't going to stew in her own juices while she was doing it and had ordered two window units, one for each of the bedrooms. I couldn't sleep in the stifling heat of our dorm room. I stayed awake long after Aurelia cried herself to sleep, waiting for the temperature to drop enough that a breeze could struggle in over the windowsill.

I trudged through that first week in a haze of exhaustion and near heat stroke, terrified of being found out for the Protestant I was. Though traps lay everywhere, daily Mass at six in the morning was most dangerous of all. Too sleepy to be alert, I either forgot to genuflect before filing into the pew or stumbled through an awkward, obviously antipapist curtsy. Sharp fingers poked me in the back if my weary butt sagged onto the pew during the interminable kneeling. My hands couldn't pick up the rhythm of the Sign of the Cross that the other girls waved over themselves so fluidly.

Even Catholic food was strange. Lima beans with ham hocks. Fried okra. French toast. Creamed spinach. Chicken-fried steak. And fish. A piece of fish had never appeared on Randi's table in the entire span of my life. Nor had my calorie-obsessed mother ever served anything fried, creamed, gravied, or battered. That first week I missed my watery bowls of Special K every morning, the dry, unadorned cuts of lean meat and steamed vegetables in the evening. But mostly I missed coolness and the anchor of my stuff.

The beer smell swamping the brewery brings me back to the present, and I find the tall windows that mark what once was Sister Theonella's art studio. There are four high arched windows bowing up toward the twelve-foot ceiling, one on the west side, one on the east, and two on the south. Both south windows face onto the river, each one catching a different bend in what was back then more a canal. Through the east window could be seen the grape arbor the wine-loving French Sisters had planted a hundred years ago. The west window looks onto the courtyard. I stand on tiptoe in the Burford holly and peek in.

A gleaming stainless-steel vat studded with gauges and tubes stares back at me. The clutter of the old art room I'd loved is gone: The lumps of clay drying whitish on the potter's wheel. The bisected blocks of ceramics molds streaked with grayish slip. The little platoons of vases and ashtrays and poodle figurines drying on racks. The easels layered with decades of paint. The watercolors curling up at the edges tacked over every wall. After a week in my barren cell with my mute roommate, it was the clutter of Sister Theonella's studio that drew me like a rat to her fuzzy nest.

I remember the first time I went to the art room. I sat quietly in the back and watched as Sister, sleeves rolled up workmanlike to display a shocking amount of naked arm, swayed in front of the easel, turning caterpillars of green paint into the lacy foliage of a pecan, a spiky mat of grass. Sister's master plan, I was to learn, was to move her easel to a different window each time the season changed. To capture the view from each window in each of the four seasons. Then to begin again. The year I came, she set up for fall in front of the southeast window, looking down onto a grove of crepe myrtles along the river, their hot pink blossoms lacy and cool in the heat.

I waited eagerly for those vibrant blossoms to appear on her canvas, but, once Sister roughed in the background of pecans and river, she brought out a tube of blue and spotted the foreground with a field of bluebonnets, stippling their centers with garish yellow pistils. I had to speak.

"Uh, where are the, uh . . ."

She didn't turn in my direction. She didn't even stop

dotting her lovely canvas with the horrid flecks of yellow where the lovely pink should have been.

I cleared my throat. Still no response. "Uh." I tried out the word that seemed so foreign and false. "Uh, Sister." She didn't turn. I walked over to her and spoke up boldly. "Sister." She looked my way.

"So that really is your voice," she said. "I thought you might have been making fun of me." She stared, waiting for me to continue.

"Sister, where are the pink blossoms? The——" I pointed out the window. "There aren't any bluebonnets."

"Bluebonnets sell better. At the mother house in St. Louis. That's where all my paintings go. Do pretty well too. Especially if they have bluebonnets in them."

With that, she turned back to her canvas and continued meticulously adding a field of bluebonnets to the scene, petal by perfect blue petal.

When fall arrived shortly before Christmas and Sister moved to the southwest window, I waited eagerly to see the silver dollar leaves of a giant cottonwood appear on the canvas. But Sister made the cottonwood a spring green shading a field of bluebonnets.

We rarely ever spoke. I already knew about the narcotic joy of creating another universe and escaping into it whether that universe is the ceiling of the Sistine Chapel or a tin tray tole painted with a bowl of fruit. Or a field of bluebonnets. I didn't ask permission to start collecting again. One day I simply appeared with a handful of pecans and asked if I could use some paint and a brush to turn them into a family of tanned sharecroppers with little overalls I made from a pair of jeans I found on the riverbank. Those were the days when the river was still a muck of carnal delights getting especially heavy use from servicemen who needed a place to neck with local girls who didn't have the Sisters of Our Lady of Sorrows to protect them from the young soldier's fast and easy ways. The bank was always littered with titillating bits of stray clothing.

"We could sell those at the mother house for Christmas decorations," Sister Theonella said about my first batch of pecan-faced sharecroppers. "Probably do better, though, if you made them angels. Nice pink satin gowns. Pipe-cleaner halos. Angel hair, fluffy white angel hair, of course. Maybe a minuscule harp with fishing-line strings."

It was a compelling vision. I just never ran across any pipe cleaners, angel hair, fishing line, or pink satin lying on the bank of the river or off in the construction site. So I stuck with the sharecroppers until I had a sprawling clan of hillbillies. When a few cool breezes started to ruffle the torpid air, I moved on to leaf collages, using golden cottonwoods and scarlet Chinese tallow leaves pressed between layers of waxed paper and tissue sealed with diluted Elmer's Glue. Then there were rock people decorated with Sister's leftover oil paints. At Christmas I made tree ornaments out of blown-out eggshells with intricate patterns of corn kernels, rice, poppy seeds, sesame seeds, and peppercorns glued onto them. I made bamboo wind wands for Aurelia, for all my teachers, for the bus driver who took us on special excursions like the one to the Buckhorn Hall of Horns at the Lone Star Brewery. I was particularly impressed by the collection of deformed horns. Disease had warped them so that the antlers looked like twisty stalagmites. Anyway, the driver was the most appreciative of any of my wind wand recipients. The element of surprise, no doubt, played a big part in his gratitude.

The first piece I did that I could say really had my stamp on it was when Sister Immaculata went to St. Louis for her tropical medicine course, hoping to be placed on the Dark Continent. I got a soup bone from the cafeteria and set it out so that the ants would clean it. Then, after soaking in a bleach solution, I painted ships, planes, and trains and the words "Bone Voyage" on it. Everyone thought it quite clever.

The two longest periods of happiness in my life occurred in these places, in my apartment on Laurel Street when Sinclair lived with me and in the art room when I worked on projects with Sister Theonella.

13. "Call me Cece," Sister Theonella requests. "No one's used my nun name for years."

Sister Theonella, without the tarping, *is*, it turns out, a tiny person. A tiny, *brisk* person.

Walking up the steps to the convent, I had prepared myself for a shriveled senior citizen. I'd made some calculations and estimated that Sister would be anywhere from sixty to eighty years old. I factored in the possibilities of physical infirmities, mental instabilities. I was ready for most anything except this hummingbird of a person who darted out to meet me. Freed of a bolt or two of black cotton, I could see how minute Sister truly was in her modern habit of knee-length skirt, white blouse with the sleeves pushed up to the elbows, and black scarf covering her ears and the back of her hair. A pompadour of black hair threaded with silver puffed up over her unlined forehead. Except for a pair of glasses, Sister Theonella looked twenty years *younger* than she had last time I'd seen her. Mostly it is the nimbus of energy oscillating around her that makes her seem so youthful.

"Sister Theonella?" I ask, and she chirps right up and tells me to call her Cece. In the next instant she recognizes me and buries her face in my breasts.

"Trudy Herring! Come back to the old alma mater." She grips my arms and pushes me back for a look. "Did you get tall or did I shrink?" I'm wondering the same thing. I'm certain I reached my full height before I left Our Lady, but I don't recall Sister being so diminutive.

"I'm probably shriveling up," she says, amused. "Probably end up a dust bunny. They'd like *that* at the mother house. Save them the price of a coffin. They'd like it if we *all* just shriveled up and blew away, all us senior Sisters. How is a person supposed to live on ninety dollars a month?" she asks me.

As I look into her eyes, magnified and swimming behind her new glasses like fish in an aquarium, I see an otherworldly misfit. How could I have not noticed her daffy distractedness when I was a child? Probably because it is so much like my own. I have made a mistake in coming.

"It can't be done," Sister answers her own question. "Not in this capitalist society. Where's our retirement plan? What did we get for all the sweat equity we poured into that school? A brewery, Trudy. The diocese sold us out for a few six-packs. We live on Top Ramen noodles here and the bishop is swimming in beer. Where's the justice in that? Come in, come in." She pulls me inside the convent.

In the four years I attended Our Lady of Sorrows, I set foot in the convent only once. Back then the Sisters' personal residence was like a museum filled with lovely Chinese vases, Oriental rugs, sumptuous wall hangings, velvet drapes, settees, and devotional paintings in rococo, gilded frames. More than any other place in the school, the convent gleamed, smelling of floor wax, furniture polish, and Windex. I tried to imagine the lives of the thirteen women who lived there, what they did in the evenings after school. Did they watch television, educational programs like Mutual of Omaha's *Wild Kingdom?* Play board games like Yahtzee? Or did they just kneel and flagellate themselves in their little rooms, preferring to do their time in this world rather than the next? Aurelia and I and a couple of the other Mexican girls spent hours devising plans to sneak into the convent. We were dying to see a nun naked.

The convent, however, is as changed as Sister. A large poster of an upraised fist bursting through chains dominates the foyer. The wooden floors that gleamed and smelled of wax in my memory are dusty and scuffed. I follow Sister in. She pushes aside a Guatemalan tapestry and we enter what was once the living room. The sedate arrangement of antique furniture I had seen on my one prior visit to the convent shimmers in my memory like an oasis on the desert before being replaced by the current reality. Six folding tables are set up around the room with three metal folding chairs behind each one. Across the tables are strewn stacks of flyers, pages of pamphlets, a metering machine, staplers, envelopes, accordion-folded strips of computer-printed mailing labels.

"This is the dissemination center," Sister—Cece, says. With every word out of her mouth, Sister Theonella is crowded farther and farther out of my memory by this "Cece" individual. "We coordinate all our educational efforts here. We're in the middle of a big mailing to Congress right now." She hands me a pamphlet entitled "Legislative Update."

"The Mideast has pushed Central America out of everyone's mind. Everyone except the people down there getting killed. So, tell me, what has the best art student I ever taught made of herself?"

Still flipping through the pamphlet, her comment takes me by surprise. Best art student she ever had?

"Obviously," she continues, "you left San Antonio, or I would have read about you. An opening. A grant. At least you would have come by to visit. I'd hoped for something a bit sooner than this, but better late than the memorial service, right? When was the last time? You were close to finishing your degree at SAC."

"I did. I left. Shortly after graduation as a matter of fact. Things got a bit rushed what with moving and all." That part was true, except it wasn't me who moved. It was Sinclair.

"So you left right after you graduated. A job?" she asks.

"Postgraduate work, actually. The Chicago Art Institute."

She beams, her cheeks pushing her glasses up. "Wonderful! Wonderful! The best art student I ever had went on to a career in the field."

"Well, yes, I did. Sort of. I mean, I met Derek in school. No one thought in a million years that it would work. The artist and the engineer."

Cece chortles merrily at the delicious incongruity of it.

"But, well, you know, the stability, I needed that, I always needed that and, boy, is Derek ever stable."

"Just who we want building our bridges and such, eh?"

"Actually Derek's in EE, electrical engineering. Bridges are in civil engineering." It always astonishes me how good my memory becomes when I lie. When inventing, I can pull up conversations I'd had with strangers ten years ago. "Anyway, after graduation, he got a job in Minneapolis with a big farm-equipment manufacturer. About that time I started doing miniatures, just as a hobby. But they caught on. I mean, I haven't achieved any measure of true fame. No retrospectives at the Whitney or anything." We both laugh at my charming self-deprecation. "But I am known regionally. By collectors. A couple of galleries in the twin cities area represent me and I have one in Chicago and"—I allow a note of enthusiasm to creep into my voice—"and a gallery in New York wants to handle my work."

"Ah, Trudy." Cece beams at me. "I knew that if any of my girls would ever carry on and pursue a career in the field, you would be the one to do it. So what's brought you back to San Antonio?"

"We moved back. Did I mention that Derek comes from San Antonio? That's how we met actually. At a Lone Star Students get-together in Chicago. Anyway, Derek has this huge family. Most of us all live within blocks of each other over in the King William District. Derek's Catholic. And we just wanted to be closer to them now with the"—I gesture vaguely toward my stomach, swaying my back at the same time—"the baby."

"A baby?" Cece stares quizzically at my stomach as if unacquainted with the particulars of human reproduction. Hers is the most subdued response I've gotten. In my disappointment, I realize how much I'd been looking forward to Sister's approval.

"Don't you think that's a good idea?"

"Good. Bad. How should I know? I guess I'm just surprised."

"Surprised? Why?" I snatch at these crumbs of information about myself, my state, as if they might be a trail leading out of the dark forest I am lost in.

"I would have expected you to pursue your art to the exclusion of all else. We used to have that in common, didn't we? That ability to let our art hurl us onto another plane."

Hurl us onto another plane? Jesus, she's talking about paintings of bluebonnets and pecan face sharecroppers. I see how futile and stupid it was of me to imagine I could learn anything from this crackpot spinster. I notice that there is white, gluey stuff at the corners of her eyes and mouth, the kind that only old people produce.

"Gosh, I'd love to stay longer—" I start, but Cece cuts me off as if I hadn't been speaking.

"Talent is almost immaterial alongside that ability, isn't it? Or is it more a compulsion than an ability? A need for escape? Isn't that what we both used our art for? To escape?"

Her goggling eyes search my face for answers. I can't believe she doesn't see that all I have are questions.

"Trudy, I wish I'd known how to encourage you back then. Hah! I wish I'd known how to encourage *myself* back then. You were unique, Trudy. You had something special."

"I did?" Why had no one ever told me that before?

"Oh, yes. I never had another one like you."

"You didn't?"

"Oh, yes. You had it. What you could have been in different circumstances. Different parents. Ah, well, if we all had the power to rewrite our bios, eh? Still, things turned out well for you. House in King William. Engineer husband. A little one on the way. Well, what do you—"

Cece stops suddenly and jerks her head as if she'd heard a voice. I don't want her to stop. I now want her to go on. To tell me what I need to know about myself. I had something special? What? What?

"What?"

Just as I speak, Cece pivots smartly on her heel and rushes out, leaving me alone in the big room amid the tracts. I remember that Cece, back in her wimpled days, was devoted to Joan of Arc. I wonder if she, too, hears voices, for not a sound has reached my ears that would explain her sudden evacuation. I pick up one of the tracts covering the folding tables and read about the death-squad activities our tax dollars are supporting.

"Who are you?" The question is sharp as a jab into a sagging twelve-year-old backside from the cane of Sister Tabernacula.

Reflexively I straighten my spine and turn to meet the glowering gaze of my former principal. The once-fearsome dictator of my youth, a canopied black circus tent of a woman, has shrunk even more than Cece. Instead of the draped dirigible who cast an ominous shadow over the entire campus, there is in front of me a querulous pudgeball in a black pinafore. Sister Tabernacula's shoulders and neck have disappeared, and her big, jowly head is planted now square on her chest.

"Trudy Herring, Sister." I supply the full identification we were always required to give. "Eighth grade. Sister Mary John's homeroom" nearly pops out of my mouth.

Another black-pinafored figure crouches behind Sister Tabernacula and yells in the overly-loud voice of the hard of hearing, "Is she one of Sister Theonella's people? Is she with them? She doesn't look Spanish." It is Sister Immaculata, the biology teacher/school nurse/tropical-medicine specialist manqué. Sister Immaculata had started off sharp-shinned and beaky-nosed and had gotten down now to the size where her large finger and wrist joints are the only rounded shapes on her bony body.

Sister Tabernacula yells back at her, "No, it's Trudy Herring. Remember? Sister Mary John's homeroom. The strange one with that unearthly voice."

"Oh. Her. The Protestant." Sister Immaculata tilts her head back and from side to side, drawing a bead on me. "Is she expecting or just fat?"

"I wouldn't know," Sister Tabernacula yells back.

"I'm pregnant!"

The two nuns stop dead and stare at me, then at each other. Sister Tabernacula regains the use of speech first. "I remember that voice. Have you seen anyone about that voice?" the old principal asks me.

Before I can answer, she grabs my arm. "Hear that?" She puts a finger up and cocks her head. I listen.

"You mean that mewing sound?" I ask.

"She hears it!" Sister Tabernacula informs Sister Immaculata.

"She hears it!" Sister Immaculata repeats, her bony face lighting with excitement. "Does she say what it sounds like?"

"Mewing! She says she hears mewing!"

"She can't tell us we're hearing things now!" Sister Immaculata yells triumphantly, then clutches at me with her bony claw of a hand. "She tells us we're hearing things! Did you ever see the movie *Gaslight?* The one where the husband tries to make his wife think she's gone round the bend? That's her, that's Sister Theonella! Tells us we're imagining things! Cats yowling, keeping us up all hours of the night and day, and she tells us *we're* imagining things! That *we* need therapy! She's the one! She needs more than therapy! She needs to be reconciled with the church! Guitar masses! I knew it would come to no good."

Sister Tabernacula clutches at my other arm and hisses in my ear. "We never had pets before. Mother Superior would never allow it. Thin edge of the wedge. Anarchy. Would never allow it. Now she keeps packs of them. Packs. Uses all our food allowance for milk. Special powdered milk. Smell that?" Sister wrinkles her beaky, heresy-sniffing nose and nods for me to do the same.

I oblige her with a sniff.

"Cats, huh?" Sister Tabernacula nudges me. "She can't tell us we're imagining that, can she? Can she?"

I shrug. The source of the odor I detect might indeed be cats and spoiled milk. With the Sisters crowding in on me from either side, however, it's hard to tell. It might just as well be two old people who aren't as fond of the feel of water and porcelain as they once were.

"Catching up on old times?" Cece bursts back into the room, yelling her question. The two old Sisters jerk away from me as if I'd become electrified. "Did you all get reacquainted? Did Trudy remind you that she was Aurelia Gojon's roommate? Remember Aurelia, Sister Immaculata? The one you diagnosed with *Entamoeba histolytica.*" Cece zings in a jab almost a quarter of a century old.

Sister Immaculata starts to open her mouth to defend her diagnosis of tropical parasites, but Sister Tabernacula shoots her a sharp glance and she seals her lips into a tight line and turns away from Cece.

"Should we invite Trudy to stay for dinner, Sisters? Huh? Huh?" Cece badgers. "Should we? Should we have our old student stay for dinner?"

The two Sisters stare in stony silence at each other, pointedly avoiding even glancing toward Cece, who continues to dance around them like an impatient third-grader asking, "Huh? Huh? Should we? Should we?"

Cece zips about, taunting the two nuns like an overwrought terrier herding big black and white cows. Then, like cows caught between annoyance and terror, the two Sisters look at Cece, roll their eyes, shift their weight, and, noses pointed sharply into the air, make a slow exit that they would like to be dramatic.

Cece dogs their heavy footsteps all the way out into the hall. "Sister, what do you say? Dinner with an old girl? Just like when you'd return to the mother house back in St. Louis?" The old nuns pick up their pace and hurry away. Cece continues to yell after them. "Pot au feu with Mother Superior, wasn't it? And always a cake from scratch! Never any of this store-bought package stuff!"

Cece comes back in. "They think they're punishing me."

She practically shivers with glee. "Punishing me by denying me their company. They haven't spoken to me in five years." She hugs herself and grins. "Solitude. Just being left alone. It's what I prayed for for thirty years. They disapprove of my Central American work. They think that their disapproval has weight. Why did it take me so long to realize that the specific gravity of disapproval is zero? But you always knew about that, didn't you?"

"About what?"

"About not being who the world wanted you to be."

"I did?" This is what I've come to find out. I tense, waiting for Cece's answer. I know it will guide me. The honk of a car horn startles me. Cece darts to a window and waves to a van that has pulled up in the parking lot.

"Heriberto! Javier! Mateo! Jorge! Justicio! Manuel!" she yells down. *"Un momento."* The driver switches off the engine. The side door slides open and five slightly built men whom I assume are Central Americans get out and stretch.

"Can you come with us?" Cece asks.

"Where?"

"To the archdiocese chancery. To protest the bishop's chicken-shit stand on El Salvador. The more Anglo faces we can get on camera, the more seriously viewers will take us."

Not only do I want to go with Cece, I suddenly want to move back into my old school. To stay here until I can win back Sinclair. Then, maybe, he could move in too. He could be the groundskeeper and I could do some light housekeeping. I'm pretty good at germ and dust control; it's simple clutter that defeats me. It's the perfect solution. I don't want to go back to King William. I want to stay here and figure everything out. "Come with you?" I ask, wanting her to repeat the invitation and to extend it in perpetuity. "Right now?"

"No, of course it's impossible."

"Why?" I wonder.

"Well, your husband."

"Oh. Right. Derek." The lie traps me. "He likes me to be there when he gets home. He likes to talk over the day. He calls it 'debriefing.' Of course, now, with the baby . . ." The lie takes on a momentum of its own, and I roll my eyes with loving exasperation at the thought of doting Derek. "He practically bursts through the door, runs in, and talks to my stomach. Pretty silly, huh?"

Cece gathers up the placards leaning against the wall without so much as a comment on my fuzzy fantasy. "Well, take care of yourself, Trudy. You have always been very special." It takes me a second to realize that Cece is leaving, just like that. I run after her.

"I have?" I ask.

"Have what?" She glances over at me, surprised that I am still there.

"Been special. Always been special." Because I need to know so much, I can't stop myself, can't think of a subtle way to ask. "How? How am I special?"

"How? Your art. Your . . ." Just before she reaches the door, Cece finally stops and faces me. "Just everything. The way you are. You are blessed with a child's heart. The Lord grants no greater gift."

"Should someone like that . . . Should someone like me . . . Should I be having a child?"

"Something of a fait accompli at this point, isn't it?"

"Oh, yeah. Sure. Just wanted, you know, to get your opinion. Should I be a mother? Would I be a good mother?"

"Would you be a good mother? I suppose that depends on who's doing the grading."

She reaches out to open the front door, and I put my hand on hers to stop her from turning the knob. "No, Sister. I need a real answer."

Cece lets the bundle of placards slide down to rest on the floor. "Trudy, that's like asking me if you would be a good lover. I imagine that given the proper motivation and hormones, a person could be either one."

She picks up her placards again and bounds out the door. I run after her, remembering my other important question. Cece, however, moves much more quickly than I can in my condition. Before I get down the front steps, the side door of the van slides open and a couple of the slight men in slinky polyester shirts that flap about their whipcord arms, and pants that ride low on their skinny hips jump out and help Cece in.

"Sister," I yell after her. "Whatever happened to Aurelia?"

She turns and gives me a startled look.

"Did she keep her baby? What happened to her?"

One of the men slides the door shut with a bang.

"I feel like she's nearby. Sister, do you know? Is she in San Antonio?"

The van starts up and Sister holds her palms up to me, helpless. They roar off and I am left standing in the doorway of the convent that once bustled with the orderly lives of thirteen women of God. All I can hear now is the far-off sound of cats yowling from a distant floor.

14. I live now in a body bloated up like a dead steer's left in the hot sun. In the seventh month, growth became exponential. I used to think that pregnant women played it up with that duck-footed waddle. Now, in my eighth month, even when I try very hard, I can no longer walk any other way. From my position inside a pregnant person's body, I observe all sorts of things. I've observed, for instance, that what appears to others to be serenity is, in fact, a lethargy known only to Galápagos tortoises and gestating women.

It is May. The mistakes in my life have become clear to me: Rubbing, not patting, my face dry. Not reading the Greeks. Not keeping a journal. Becoming a person unfit to be a mother. Letting my butt muscles turn into pudding. Making that bargain with Sweet Pea. And most especially, being pregnant in San Antonio, Texas, in hot weather. I can't believe I have two more months left. I already feel as if every ounce of the added twenty-five pounds I'm carrying is all in bituminous coal. Blistering, blazing coal. Enough coal to heat Dublin for a winter.

"How about a smoothie?" Mercedes offers Hillary's approved drink. I stab halfheartedly at the Greek salad in front of me. Or what is supposed to be a Greek salad. Though, if you substitute garbanzo beans for the calamatta olives and chunks of tofu for the feta cheese, I don't see what's so Greek about it anymore.

"Thanks. I'm not real hungry."

"It's the heat. Can you believe it's in the nineties already? The heat's tough on you *pellirojas*. Never bothered me a bit. And, I tell you, Truthee, you think it's hot here. You ain't seen nothin' till it's middle of August in Los Indios. No running water. Of course, no air-conditioning, and you're nine months pregnant. Now, *that, cuate*, is hot. Boy, we was eating chile peppers to cool down, it was that hot. You wanna listen?" She nods up at the ventilator grill.

"Sure." Mercedes and I generally tune in every night while I pick through my dinner.

She pops the grill open. Victor is speaking.

"Geoffrey Prescott? Hillary, tell me you're kidding." They've been arguing about names for the past few weeks. "Why don't we just call him Tweed Jacket? Or High Tea? Why mess around? Go full out Anglophile."

"And Theodore is so much better?"

"Theodore was my grandfather's name. He was a great guy. Possibly the only great guy ever produced in my family. I'd like to remember him."

"Wonderful. I applaud the sentiment. I want our child to have a rich sense of his family mythology. But, really, Victor, he's going to end up being called Ted."

"So?"

"So, think of the connotations. Ted Bundy. Ted Kennedy. Teddy bear."

Connotations. I read recently that children with certifiably goofy names, Virgil, Bertha—Trudy, Gertrude, wasn't on the list, but I'm certain it qualifies—these children don't do as well in life as the Jasons and Jennifers. It's not the names, it's having parents who think about connotations. I know it would have been hard to work with Herring, but adding Gertrude to the front of it didn't help matters. Oh, well, a couple of movie stars not too long ago named their daughter Dakota Mayi. At least I don't have the same name as a cigarette marketed for young women who wear vests. I try not to let myself think of names. Not until I've made my plans. All I know is that I hate Theodore only slightly less than Geoffrey Prescott.

"Okay," Hillary says. "Let's put the first-name discussion on hold. What about the last? Is it going to be Goettler-Murkoff or Murkoff-Goettler?"

"Do we really want to do that to a child?" Victor asks.

"What are you saying? That we drop my name? Why does it have to be my name? Why does it always have to be the woman's name?"

"I didn't say that it did."

"Victor, if you start using that tone with me, I am going to scream. I hate that tone. That calm, reasonable, we-are-dealing-with-a-lunatic we-must-not-disturb-her tone. I've been under a lot of stress. You leave everything unpleasant for me to deal with. I'm caught in the middle. You've got the luxury of being remote. I'm the one, I'm always the one who has to deal with, with . . ."

Me. It's gotten to the point where neither one of them ever says my name. Connotations.

Hillary starts sobbing. The last few months have been rough on her. She's gained weight. A lot of weight. Instead of Norma Kamali knits, she wears caftans from Pier One. I hear her at night going to the bathroom three, four, always one more time than I have to go, as if we're competing for the smallest-bladder prize. Lately she's also been throwing up. She comes home in the afternoons and takes long naps. Her ankles are swollen into thick baguettes at the ends of her legs.

I was certain Hillary was pregnant until I saw the used home pregnancy kit in bathroom trash. Same brand as I used. The little dipstick was white. Blue means bingo. That word the doctor used, *couvade*, sympathetic pregnancy, comes back to me.

"There, now, there." Victor's soothing voice filters into the kitchen. My head sags onto my hand and I pretend that the voice and the soothing are for me. "I'm sorry, boobah. Come on, now, let's see some teefies. Come on. That's better. We'll call the squirt anything you want. Chadsworth Twittingham, huh? You like that? Little Chad? No, really, you pick. I don't care. Grandfather Theodore, rest his soul, obviously doesn't care. Your choice, lamb chop."

Victor is being a good father. Everyone needs a good father when they are pregnant.

"I guess I'm a little on edge," Hillary says, her voice thick. "The shower tomorrow and all."

"I thought you said it isn't a shower."

"It's not. It's just a simple, casual affair to welcome our child into our community of friends and colleagues. Why didn't I specify no presents on the invitations?"

"Because you didn't want to make the presumption that there would be presents. You were going to mention it casually."

"But I never got around to it. There will be masses of presents. Baby presents. It will *be* a baby shower."

"Come on. It's coed, you're having margaritas and what, those crab taco things. That doesn't sound like a baby shower to me."

"Okay. You're right. Just help me out a little bit more with . . ." Again the silence where my name should go. "You know, introductions and things. This is hardly covered in Emily Post. Oh, Jesus!" Hillary's voice, suddenly loud, startles me. "I almost forgot, Rachel moved the birth class to tonight. Shit! It starts in ten minutes and we're doing episiotomies. A birth class on Friday night. Isn't that the most ridiculous thing you've ever heard? Why should all of us have to accommodate Rachel's schedule? Trudy! Trudy!"

"Show me how you blow your nose." We are all nestled on our pillows for class discussion. Rachel hands Renee, the mommy with the black panther tattooed around her ankle, a handful of tissues. Renee is having a problem with nose-bleeds. Not uncommon at all, Rachel has assured her.

"No, no." Rachel stops Renee after a bit of energetic honking. "First, gently close one nostril with the thumb. The thumb," Rachel corrects when Renee presses an index finger against the side of her chip of a nose. "Then carefully blow out the opposite side. Carefully, now." Renee puffs lightly into the tissue and Rachel congratulates her. "Perfect." She turns to us. "You've all got to take extra care. You've got incredibly high levels of estrogen surging around in your body, getting everything softened up and ready for delivery. That increases blood flow to the mucous membranes. So take care. You can also expect some stuffiness. Perhaps a postnasal drip you never had before."

Beside me, Hillary coughs gently and dabs at her nose with a Kleenex.

"Any other questions?" Rachel asks, looking around the group. The beautiful, nonpregnant woman in the tribal trio glances at the doughy, redheaded mother and hides a smile. Then, with a foot bare except for several rings around the middle three toes, she kicks the father.

"Timothy?" Rachel, noticing the prodding, asks the father. "Did you have a question? A concern?"

"Uh. Sort of. We've noticed this pattern that's probably real normal and fine and everything. But for about an hour." He turns to the two women for verification. "An hour, right?"

Patrice inclines her head questioningly toward Yvonne, the beautiful one, who stares up into space, calculating. "Yeah. About," she answers.

Timothy continues. "Well, for about an hour after Pa-

trice experiences orgasm, the baby stops moving. That probably doesn't mean anything, does it?"

Rachel doesn't miss a beat. "Just that the baby likes to
be rocked. No, really, rhythmic motion tends to soothe the
baby. She probably just went to sleep."

I love coming to classes and staring at Timothy and Patrice and Yvonne, the beautiful one, and imagining their life
together. Timothy's question adds a whole new dimension to
my speculations. Who would have thought that Yvonne
would be the one good at numbers?

"Now that you bring it up," Rachel goes on. We are all
sitting on the floor around her like kindergarteners at story
time. She tucks her feet under her, getting settled for a
particularly good yarn. "Childbirth is a lot like making
love."

Patrice, Timothy, and Yvonne huddle together and lean
forward as a unit. Hillary and I both stiffen and tilt ever so
slightly away from each other.

"In both, the key to a pleasurable experience is learning
to give yourself over to the physical. To surrender the cere-
bral to the corporal."

"Really," Timothy affirms in the enthusiastic manner of
someone listening to someone else express his very own
views. "We think birth is going to be the ultimate orgasm."

In the silence that follows, Patrice puts one hand on her
mound and the other on Timothy's shoulder. Yvonne
stretches her neck and gazes about like a gander warding off
intruders. I recall this activity. Long ago it was called freak-
ing the straights. I have a sudden desire to share the exten-
sive irregularities of my own life with Patrice, Yvonne, and
Timothy, to prove to them how freakproof I am.

"Well," Rachel says. "It's all about unfolding, isn't it?

Relaxing. That's why the flower imagery I've talked about is so important. Why it's so helpful to visualize your cervix at delivery as a rose, gently unfolding its soft pink petals as new life surges through it."

I pray that Rachel won't start with the Birth Affirmations in which we have to say things like "Birth is a wave I will ride to shore" and "My body is my friend." I've tuned out all of Rachel's affirmations and flower lectures, all of her creative visualization exercises in which we lie on the floor and imagine we're floating on some aquamarine tropical sea. It annoys Hillary when I start snoring, but since the point is relaxation, I don't see the difference. Besides, I've got my money on major pharmaceuticals anyway. Absentmindedly, I scratch my stomach. Rachel, searching for questions to fill out the class, notices.

"Itchy tummy?" she asks.

I look down at my hand as if it had been acting on its own. "Sort of," I admit.

"That's the skin stretching. Makes it dry," Rachel explains. "It only gets worse."

Out of the corner of my eye I see Hillary sneak a hand down to her own gut and rake gently. For some reason her sniffling and coughing and scratching make me so mad that I want to bite her hand.

"What about headaches?" Hillary asks, fondling the spot between her eyes.

"Very common," Rachel answers. "Another side effect of all those hormones bopping around."

"And insomnia?"

Rachel looks at me sympathetically, as if Hillary were asking all these questions on my behalf. "The expectant mother's curse. Try eating a complete protein before you go to bed."

"What should we do about heartburn?" Hillary asks.

"Headaches *and* heartburn," Rachel says to me. "I sure hope you don't get the mother's other H too."

"What's that?" Hillary asks eagerly.

"Hemorrhoids," Rachel answers authoritatively.

Hillary shifts on her pillows and I struggle to my feet as quickly as I can.

"Bathroom," I explain over my shoulder as I rush from the room.

The class is held in an elementary school. The hall walls are covered with crayon drawings on large pieces of newsprint. Wire mesh covers the windows. Vandalism. The sweaty smell of school cafeteria enchiladas and spaghetti lingers. The green and black speckled linoleum wavers beneath my feet as my eyes fill with tears. I push myself to move faster.

The kid-size sinks in the bathroom hit me just above my knees. The mirror is a piece of polished sheet metal screwed into the wall. The kind they use at highway rest stops. It makes me sad that schoolchildren can't even have a real piece of glass to comb their hair.

I hike up my extra-large aqua T-shirt, pull down the stretchy waistband of my white shorts, and unsnap my bra in front. My image in the wobbly metal is something out of a fun house. My arms are sticks next to the kettledrum of my mound, and the pendulous hammocks of my breasts with their eggplant nipples. My stomach is a mountain of lasagna with tomato red stretch marks bursting through my mozzarella white flesh.

I am pregnant. Not Hillary. Me. I am the one having a baby. Not Hillary. Me.

It is obvious I am upset on the drive home and Hillary doesn't make her usual strained attempt at conversation. Back at the house, I hurry upstairs, turn off the lights, strip off my clothes, and get into bed. Though I try to block out the sound with pillows over my head, I can hear Hillary crying downstairs. I know that Victor is holding her. I don't have to see his hands, the hands I put far too much stock in, to know that they are roaming around on Hillary's flesh, puffy from her imaginary pregnancy. I don't have to hear his voice, lawyerly yet loving, to know that he is cooing words of comfort.

I touch my breasts and pretend that my hands belong to someone who dreams of me at night and thinks of our baby during the day while he works making a living for the three of us. I put my hands on my stomach. My belly button is popping out. I hadn't noticed. I unearth a nugget of lint packed hard with thirty-nine years of cheesy bodily oddments. So this was the highpoint for Randi. I try but can't imagine her whippet body puffed out like mine, her belly button turned inside out.

I rub my palms along my hips, where the ligaments are stretching and the joints ache. I stretch my leg out on the clean sheet that Mercedes changed that day and gasp when a stitch of pain catches my breath as the muscle cramps up. I hop up to stand and straighten the kink out. As I bounce on the fisted muscle, it occurs to me that Victor would be massaging Hillary's leg right now if this happened to her. Rachel has told the class that these muscle seizures are a symptom of calcium shortage. That they will go away if we up our intake of milk, yogurt, and cheese. They don't feel like a mineral deficiency to me. They feel like a touch deficiency. Like they would go away if I upped my intake of hugs, caresses, and kisses.

The cramp subsides and I stand in front of the mirror on the back of the door and study my body. My body *is* my friend; Rachel got that much right. And my body is a friend who is seriously down in the dumps. She's someone I have just run into again after a long separation. Someone who has been ignored and rejected. The tender touches and fond embraces my friend needs are being siphoned off by a pretender. I look at my body and try to think how I can possibly get for my friend what she needs. She has been neglected too long. I can't let this unkindness continue.

Hillary's crying has stopped. I hear the click of the lock being turned on their bedroom door that means they are going to make love. That click is an alarm going off in my fogged mind. I wake up knowing what I must have. What my baby must have. We must have tender touches. There is, of course, only one person I care to get them from. Sinclair. Whether or not he will be interested in providing them becomes almost inconsequential beside my crushing need to have them.

I go to the closet. Hillary puts clothes in it that she would want to wear if she were pregnant. I flip past all of them. I am tired of wearing tasteful, well-made clothes of thick cotton. I find the pair of jeans I wore the last time I walked out of my apartment. Of course, they don't come anywhere close to buttoning. I leave them open and my extra large T-shirt hides the gap in front. I dress quickly, methodically, like a woman going out to buy milk or get some other necessity.

Downstairs, I don't bother to be quiet. I flip on the

lights. Hillary and Victor keep their car keys out, hanging on a wooden cutout of an adobe house that they got on their last trip to Santa Fe. I decide: Victor's keys, and pluck them off the rack.

Outside, the moon is nearly full and fills the earth like a shallow bowl with luminous, milky light. It tangles around my feet as I walk across the spongy grass. I smile. My heart hums. Sweet Pea tickles me from inside with a foot in my ribs. The moon tugs on the lagoon inside of me, pulling it up, taking the weight from me. My walk goes from a waddle to a march to a spring. I bound forward, my tummy in high tide, my step light as a ballerina *en pointe*. Pink clouds of mimosa hang over my head, sweet-smelling halos sanctifying my every move. I am doing what I have to do. It's bad for the baby to deny yourself what you must have. Everything will be all right.

I jump into Victor's pewter gray BMW and immediately roll down the windows to air out the smell of Spanish leather, German engineering, and American yearning. I want to smell the moon and the mimosas. I am going to Sinclair. I am less nervous than I would be once I realize that I have been holding an ace in the hole all this time. I mean, how can Sinclair resist me now that I am so obviously that which he finds most irresistible: another man's woman.

15. "Oh, hon, Sinclair hasn't been by in, I don't know . . ." Connie, the waitress, blinks as she computes. "A month? Month and a half? Something like that." My heart sinks. "You're definitely pregnant now, aren't you?" She steps back to look me over.

"You remember me? Just from that one other time?" This surprises me.

"I've got a memory for faces. And voices. You ordered what? The turkey special. Bunch of sides. Two milks. No, you were memorable. Most women come in, order a dinner salad and leave me a quarter tip. You left a good tip too. Sinclair involved in this . . ." She waves in the general vicinity of my stomach.

"No. No."

"Well, you know Sinclair.".

I would have had to do an awful lot of detective work to get all the information Connie just packed into those three words: "You know Sinclair." I now know that coupled or not, he is still a runaround. Well, that's good, because if he is married, I would never have a chance if he'd turned faithful.

"He hasn't moved, has he?" Panic grips me.

"Sinclair? I wouldn't think so. He's just out doing the circuit again. It's that time of year."

Circuit? Is Sinclair with the rodeo? Surely, he hasn't turned to preaching. Connie and I are standing in the back of the restaurant. It was locked up when I got there. The manager, a Middle-Eastern man with dark shadows under his eyes and a twitchy manner, was closing out the register when I knocked at the glass door. He yelled that they were closed and I told him I needed to talk to Connie. Luckily, she was still in back, doing her set-ups for breakfast the next day.

The manager switches the lights off and on.

"We're going, Habib!" Connie yells to him. "Keep your fez on," she mutters under her breath, grabbing her purse and moving toward the door.

"Circuit?" I ask, hurrying after her. "What kind of circuit?"

Connie turns around to look at me just as Habib switches off the light, shoos us outside, and locks the door behind us. "How good did you say you knew Sinclair?"

Even in the dim glow from a light down the street I can read the suspicion in Connie's face. My automatic impulse is to lie, but I don't have time for that anymore. Besides, if Connie doesn't know the precise lyrics to my song already, I'm sure she could hum the tune. "We used to live together. We lost touch and I just wanted to, you know . . ."

"See if the flame still flickers? Before you have that baby and the gate swings shut forever? Same impulse overtook me with my first one. There was this boy. God, how long ago. Twenty? Twenty-five years? Davey Lanier. Good, *good*-looking boy. My first love. The one that got away, you know. From the minute I got pregnant with little Carl, all I did was think about Davey Lanier. *Dreamed* about him. Can't say why. I guess he seemed like a way out."

One of the rules of the mommy club is that you can say anything to another member.

Connie heaves a sigh for good-looking Davey Lanier and says, "Renaissance fair."

"Renaissance fair?"

"That's the circuit Sinclair does. The Renaissance fairs. I've only ever been to that one they have outside Houston in Magnolia. Loved it. You feel like you've gone back in time with the jugglers and minstrels walking around plunking away on their little mandolins and lutes and everyone in costume. Ladies in pointed hats, men in tights. It's all very authentic. Historically accurate."

"And Sinclair just goes around to these fairs?"

"He works them. Does the face-painting concession."

Face painting? In a way it makes sense. Sinclair always was a good painter. And he liked traveling. And brief, inconsequential encounters. In another way, though, it's sadder and worse than me ending up a temporary office worker and surrogate mother.

"Makes good money at it too," Connie assures me. "You'd be amazed. Averages fifteen, twenty faces an hour at five bucks a pop. Virtually no overhead other than the paints. Wish I made anywhere close to that."

"Is he going to be home anytime soon?"

"Who knows with Sinclair. He pops in and out all summer. Check the La Fonda."

"La Fonda Agua Caliente?"

"Yeah, *agua* something or other. Look, I gotta run." Connie hikes her bag onto her shoulder and starts to back away, heading toward the parking garage next to Schilo's. She takes a couple of backward steps, looking at me as if she wants to say something else but can't think of what it might be. Finally, she flags me a wave. "Good luck." She turns and, hanging on to the strap of her purse with both hands, walks away.

La Fonda Agua Caliente. Hot Springs Inn. Just hearing that name is like sitting down in the hot, sulfurous spring the old resort was once famous for. I feel weak from the memories washing over me. The night we discovered La Fonda Agua Caliente was like one of the beautiful, diseased horns at the Buckhorn Hall of Horns, strange and unforgettable.

A night unlike any other in my life, it was also a night radiant with moonlight. Sinclair and I had been bumping around the back roads behind the state hospital in the old

International Harvester. It was a perfect November evening, one of the first genuinely cold days after a long siege of summer. We'd gone to a couple of our favorite spots. The Shrine of the Black Madonna, where the Sister told us about all the famous Polish Catholics in America like Bobby Vinton, the Polish Prince. The twenty-foot tall concrete pig across from Mission San José for dinner, where Martin Flores sold *barbacoa de cabeza.* Sinclair and I visited Martin and the concrete pig whenever we lapsed from the vegetarianism we were trying to practice in those days. He was licking salsa off his fingers when an attack of the Warren Beattys hit.

"Let's find a spot."

We were right across the street from a drive-in movie, but that was too obvious.

"Mission Espada?" he asked. "Have we ever done it there?"

I suppose I should have been offended that locations and participants rested so lightly on Sinclair's memory, but it's hard getting huffy with a twenty-foot pig looking over your shoulder. Besides, I loved Mission Espada. It's the southernmost of the four missions the Spaniards built two and a half centuries ago along the San Antonio River and the one least likely to have a Gray Line tour bus parked outside.

As Victor's BMW purrs through the night, I make a parallel journey in my memory, joggling over back roads in the big truck, Sinclair spinning the driver's wheel as if he were captaining a steamboat, open bottle of Gallo Rosé between his legs. We passed the bottle back and forth. I sloshed the pink wine all down the mint-condition Fair Isle sweater I'd found at the Disabled Veterans Thrift Shop and almost chipped a tooth when the rim of the bottle hit me in the mouth as Sinclair rocketed over Old Espada Dam. Usually thrashing with brown-skinned men and women, girls and boys swimming in cutoff jeans, the ponded water shone flat and silver as a mirror beneath the full moon.

"Hmmm," Sinclair said, studying our destination, the low-slung adobe buildings of the Mission Espada. "What do you think, Trude? Not much here to set the blood boiling, is there? No, tonight's not the night for wattle and daub. Tonight a more *inventive* setting is called for, don't you feel it, Trude? Can't we do better than this slave camp for Indians?"

"Here's to inventiveness." I toasted Sinclair with the bottle of pink wine, although the mission seemed amply inspirational to me. Perhaps that was part of the problem, I wasn't elusive enough. Where Sinclair was concerned, setting was immaterial. Where Sinclair was concerned, I could have made Warren Beatty seem like a man with a war wound. But Sinclair had more in common with those bird watchers who keep life lists of where they spotted what bird. I think he just needed new locations to keep his list spiced up, so he ground a few gears and we rumbled off into the night.

Every time the road branched into an even more overgrown, twisty, path of a byway, Sinclair would yell, "The road not taken!" and turn off. The old truck groaned and leaves whipped the windshield as we bounced over these donkey trails until we found ourselves in front of a locked gate with the name La Fonda Agua Caliente twisting over it in rusting wrought iron.

"Hot Water Inn?" Sinclair translated the name illuminated in the cockeyed glare of his unbalanced headlights. Sinclair sniffed. "Smell that?" I sniffed. All I smelled was the green fungal dampness of river-watered vegetation. "Sulfur. There's a hot spring in there."

"Sinclair, I don't think you ought to—"

Before I could finish, Sinclair nudged the truck forward enough to pop the cheap padlock off the chain wrapped around the gate. We pulled off the packed dirt trail onto a road that had once been paved but was now deeply fissured. Weeds, yellow asters on tall stalks, grew up through the black cracks. The road curved and the headlights splashed across an overgrown garden that seemed to have been transplanted from Mars. I told Sinclair to stop. Plants, especially rare, exotic ones, are a great source of material, and these were the rarest, most exotic plants I had ever seen.

"That is a most curious plot of vegetation," Sinclair said as the cones of light steadied on plants that bore thin-armed white stars for flowers, and miniature rams heads for thorns, then filled in all the spaces in between with ferns that brontasauri surely nibbled. They were all illustrations out of the botany books I sometimes turned to for design inspiration. Even the names were magical: Peruvian ice lilies, Arizona devil's claw, Borneo fern.

Sinclair drove on, and a couple hundred yards farther on we were pulling into the circular drive that looped in front of a crumbling three-story hotel.

"What do you make of this, Trudaloo?" Sinclair asked, spellbound by the crumbling edifice. He saw past the CONDEMNED sign and the sagging front porch hanging off the hotel like a bit of torn lace. "Can you imagine how grand she was in her day? Probably peaked in the thirties, wouldn't you say? God, look at those bay windows. Those sloping dormers. Isn't it great? That decayed elegance? That sinister grandeur?"

"Yeah." I took another tug of wine and leaned over and kissed Sinclair on the neck. His smell made me feel weak as a month of malaria. I slipped into the cozy coma that getting next to him put me in and chewed on the big tendon behind his carotid artery. It was tough and resilient between my teeth. I unpopped the top snaps of his faded denim cowboy shirt so that I could touch the fine bow of his clavicle. Sinclair had skin like a Southern belle. Soft and white as a magnolia, it felt like sin with small pores beneath my fingertips.

Still studying the old hotel, Sinclair gave my breast a perfunctory squeeze. His lack of interest had a strongly aphrodisiacal effect upon me. My underwear was sopping and I was dying for Sinclair to put his tongue in my mouth. I craved the flavor of his mouth. Especially when he'd been drinking or smoking marijuana. But Sinclair's thoughts were several decades away, back in the glory days of the moldering pile of lumber we were parked in front of. He switched off the headlights and the old place fell into dark shadow. Sinclair's "sinister elegance" started to look flat-out creepy. Sinclair opened the door. The creak sounded abnormally loud.

"Let's find the hot springs." He jumped out, tugging on my hand.

"Sinclair, I—" He pulled me out of the truck. The place had a different feel to it than the rest of San Antonio. As cold as it was that night, the air was still dense with a tropical heaviness. It was hard to breathe, as if too many plants were using up too much oxygen. I inhaled. It felt as if I were sucking the depleted air through a wet blanket. My heart tripped at the prospect of suffocating to death in this miasma. Jerking my hand out of Sinclair's, I raised my arms so

that I could take in a really good lungful. After several panicked breaths I calmed down, then turned to discover that
Sinclair was not beside me in the circle of moonlight.

"Sinclair," I called into the shadows blackening the hotel.

Though not the slightest breeze stirred, a shutter dangling from a second-story window creaked on its rusty hinge.

"Sinclair, this is—" I was going to tell Sinclair that I
didn't think that creeping around a condemned hotel was
such a great idea, when I jumped at the sound of a loud click
beside me. My pulse hammered in my neck. It was just the
truck engine cooling.

"Sinclair. Okay, Sinclair, this really isn't funny. Sinclair? Sinclair!" There was no answer. I listened until I
heard footsteps rustling through dried leaves and followed
them. The Agua Caliente, built around the circular drive,
seemed to embrace me as I moved toward the front porch.

"Sinclair?" A floorboard squeaked loudly from inside
the hotel.

"Sinclair. Come on. This isn't safe. It's condemned. Sinclair? Sinclair!" Something with many legs scurried across
my sandaled foot. The word "scorpion" flashed in my mind.
I shrieked. That was it. I'd put up with a lot in the way of
indignities and cavalier treatment to have Sinclair's tongue
come visit mine, but this was too much. I was stomping back
to the truck when I heard the first splash, then a booming
"Ah, bliss!" and stopped cold. He'd found the hot springs.
Snakes are attracted to warmth. I calculated how long Sinclair would be gone. Without alcohol, half an hour tops.
Drinking, however, always amplified Sinclair's love of the
grand gesture. Given the bottle of pink wine we'd consumed,
I had to figure he'd be gone an hour, at least.

The prudent course would have been to wait in the truck. And I would have if Sinclair and I had been equals. But we weren't. I knew that. Sinclair was the god who came down from Mount Olympus to sleep with the shepherd girl. I knew that I was a novelty item for him. That he'd ascend again soon. Or that there would be other shepherd girls. That he'd bring the whole flock to cavort at the springs he'd discovered. The springs, no question about it, were going to figure heavily in the Sinclair Coker mythology. This was my one chance to enter the annals. I stepped forward onto the sagging porch, as prepared as St. Agnes had been to give her all for the one she adored.

Picking my way across the rotted-out floorboards, I discovered that a dark pit loomed beneath the few strips of rickety board. The hotel smelled like a chicken coop. A ghostly presence fluttered past my head, and I screamed, almost falling off the board. A perturbed cooing answered my scream. Mourning doves. I inched forward.

A sign hung upside down by a single nail behind what must have once been the reception desk. BATHS it read with an arrow pointing straight down. While I was figuring out which way the arrow had originally pointed, a loud splash clued me in and I headed to the right down a long hall. Most of the doors to the rooms had been removed and squares of moonlight fell across the floor, giving me islands of safety to help the crossing. The end of the hall, however, was dark as a tomb.

"Sinclair?"

A cloud scudded across the moon and, as if a switch had been thrown, all the islands of light behind me snapped off and I was surrounded by darkness.

"Sinclair. Sinclair! Get your butt out here! Right now!"

No, the shepherd girl wasn't ready for the ultimate sacrifice after all. But there wasn't a sound. I knew I was close. The air was damp and sulfurous. "Sinclair!" My voice sounded high even to me. High and scared. In the total darkness I saw a sliver of light and crept toward it.

It was a door, large and heavy. I had to press my full weight against it before it creaked open, and then I was standing within an orb of radiant light. The springs were enclosed in a room of glass with all the panes miraculously intact. The moon had cleared and shone through the steamy glass, making the room glow like something nuclear. The springs bubbled up into a swimming pool that must have been alive with some sort of phosphorescent plant because even the water gave off a serenely eerie aqua-green glow. It was so beautiful, I forgot to be scared. I listened to the deep, comforting burble of the steaming water flowing from where the earth was still warm and young. It took me a minute to realize that Sinclair was nowhere to be seen. I called out his name and got nothing but the giant aquarium sounds of the hot springs in response.

"Sinclair?" I didn't like the way my voice echoed off the sweating glass. "Sinclair." His name was dribbling off into a teary choke when Sinclair stepped out of the shadows into the light, naked as a newt, pale as a turnip, and hard as a rock. He looked like an astral projection shimmering in the moonlight, his shadow-ravined face an icon. Only the water puddling at his feet seemed real. That and the erection straining toward his navel.

"Sinclair. God. How did you find this place? It's incredible. Jeez, those are actual lights in the pool. I thought it was some kind of plant, like that phosphorescent plankton that makes waves light up. How come the lights are on? And, look, not one pane of glass is knocked out. Don't you think that's kind of strange? Sinclair, say something."

But Sinclair didn't say anything. Without a word he stepped forward, his body following the erection leading him on. He opened his arms to me.

"Sinclair, come on. This isn't funny anymore. Say something."

He reached me and silently unbuttoned my jacket, letting it slip to the floor. Then he tugged off my sweater. As he was slipping the bra strap off my shoulder, I pivoted away.

"Sinclair, say something. This is a little creepy. Sinclair?" He didn't speak, only continued stripping away my clothes.

I covered my breasts. Maybe the water *was* radiated. Maybe he'd mutated into some sort of soul-sucking incubus. The spell of half a bottle of Passion Pink combined with a genuinely strange setting was strong enough to make me believe that Sinclair had been possessed by an evil spirit. The spell of my love for Sinclair combined with nothing else to make me not care. If he wanted my soul, he could have it.

I opened my arms to him and Sinclair stepped into them, his body cool and wet. He unhooked the metal buttons on my jeans with a practiced hand. I was not the first shepherd girl. I would not be the last. I had to make the most of my moment in the phosphorescence. Sinclair bowed his back to lean down to nuzzle my neck and fine tune my breasts.

I hopped awkwardly out of the hobble of jeans and underwear around my ankles and Sinclair scooped me up to straddle his waist. He loved to strut about the apartment with me appended to him like a toy monkey bobbing up and down on a stick.

The feel of Sinclair inside me jammed my switchboard. I

couldn't feel, hear, see, or think about another thing. All I was aware of was that the world had turned aqua green and that when I died, heaven would be this color. Then I was floating in a bubbling warmth that expanded the boundaries of my body and the sheer volume of pleasure that rippled through me at climax.

"Woooo!" I first had to identify the source of the siren's wail that pierced my aqua green oblivion. When I realized that the unholy howl was issuing from my own throat, the next step was to figure out how to stop it.

"Will you shut your goldarned yap? Sound like a g.d. she-wolf got her tit caught in a wringer. Gone and ruint everything now."

I shut up instantly, shocked at Sinclair's crudeness. But it wasn't Sinclair. His mouth was crimped shut and his eyes sprung wide open in surprise.

"Who's there?" he demanded. His tone meaner and gruffer than I had ever heard it before.

"I just might ask the same question of you all."

I did not like the hillbilly bravado that spiked the words. The banjo music from *Deliverance* plunked menacingly in my mind. The man who stepped into the light might have been a backwoods extra on that very movie. He looked like he trapped badgers for a living. The deep furrows plowing through his face were black with dirt and spiked with an inch of dark stubble. His bushy eyebrows could almost have been combed straight back to blend into his hairline. But the most riveting thing about him was the double-barreled shotgun he cradled in his arms.

"Best I ever saw was when Errol Flynn and his bunch came out. 'Course them people liked to involve a dog or two. Hard to compete with a dog act. But you two weren't bad.

For hippies. Splashing in at the climactic moment at the end like that was good."

The nails on the hand that held the gun were curved and black as a bear's claws.

"What do you want?" Sinclair asked in a gruff, bad-ass voice.

The man cackled. "I already got what I want. Wanted to watch. Already got that, unless you're planning to screw again. You going to?"

"No." Sinclair answered. "Hand us our clothes." I was terrified that the man would shoot us for Sinclair's bossiness, but it didn't have that effect at all.

When he spoke again, a simpering quality cut the danger. "Can I watch?" he pleaded.

"No," Sinclair barked. "You've seen enough for one night. Hand us our clothes and turn around."

The man did as he was ordered and we dressed quickly.

"Who are you?" Sinclair asked, still bluffing in his deep, mean voice.

"The caretaker and you're trespassing. You want to cornhole me?" He bent forward slightly and offered Sinclair the saggy seat of his grease-spotted jeans. Sinclair didn't answer. He finished dressing, then helped me. "You think you're better than Errol Flynn. Errol Flynn wasn't too good to rip hisself off a chunk." He turned around. "You both's a little too bony for my taste. Like 'em with some meat on 'em. Had a linebacker from the Brackenridge High School varsity, the *A*-team, out here last summer. Watched him put it to this big-assed cheerleader. I like a big ass. Man or woman. You'd a been surprised at the ass on Errol Flynn."

"Put that gun down," Sinclair said, "and I'll tell you

about a truck-stop waitress with an ass like a hippopotamus."

The caretaker put the gun aside and opened his mouth expectantly. His front right tooth was missing. "Big puffy pink ass? The kind you can grab big ol' handfuls of?" He made his hands into twitching mitts.

Sinclair's voice twanged with a hookworm accent I'd never heard before. "You could have *wallered* in that ol' gal's backside." The caretaker's tongue flicked greedily around his lips. "Big German gal with enough strudel in the ass to feed the kaiser's army. And bazooms—"

"Naw, naw." He shook his head impatiently. "Just the butt. Just the butt."

"Big, pillowy. The kind a man could . . ." Sinclair cupped his hands out in front of him and nudged me to start edging toward the door.

"You don't need to sneak off," the man said. "I ain't gonna keep you against your will or nothing. You're free to go. I never hold anyone against their will. Specially if the show was half decent."

"So this happens pretty regular?" Sinclair still sounded frighteningly folksy.

"Pretty much a sure thing when the moon's full. I just leave the lights on in here and you moths kind of find your own way to the flame. Them Hollywood people ruint me. Got me to where I like watching best. That is, provided the flesh's still good. I get to see plenty old broke-down stuff with them blue knots of varrycose veins popping out and the turkey wattles aflapping under the chin." He shivered. "See too much of that. 'Course, *she* thinks she's still prime." He prodded a horny thumbnail into the air behind him, gesturing at something off in the darkness. "Thinks she still

ought to have a dozen heinie boys prissing around her, dancing and powdering her nose and zooming in for a close-up."

"Your wife is an actress?" Sinclair asked in his normal
voice. He'd stopped edging toward the door.

"Wife? Wife?!" The man hooted. "Naw. She'll let me
get my plumbing snaked every month or so, but that's as
close as we come to being married. My em-*ploy*-er," he said
with prissy disgust. "The owner of this piss-dripping
shithole. You heard of Larue Reyna?"

"*Damsels in Distress? Ladies' Man? Something Borrowed
Something Blue?*" Sinclair rattled off the names of old black
and white movies we'd stayed up late watching on cable.
Sinclair had recited most of the snappy dialogue along with
Larue Reyna, a fiery actress whose Latin heritage doomed
her to hoop earrings and flared nostrils. Sinclair's mother
had cultivated in her son a worshipful awe of the screen
goddesses of yesteryear. "That Larue Reyna? She owns this
place?"

"She's Mex, you know. Them studio dicklickers put it
out that she was from Spain. Not a word of it. Tee-wanna.
Mother was a whore far as I can make out. She sure acted
like she was the daughter of a whore. She done it with Errol
Flynn. Wouldn't have no part of the dogs though. Whore's
honor. You gonna come back? That linebacker and the big-
butt cheerleader came regular all fall until she got to likin'
being watched a bit too much for Mr. Jockstrap. Know what
I mean?"

"I think I do, Mr.—"

"Call me Pettigrew. Ain't my name, but it'll do."

"You must have seen it all, Pettigrew," Sinclair said in a
way that invited elaboration. This was getting much too cozy
for me. Sinclair liked to cultivate "characters" as if his life

were a movie that needed the texture of oddballs. I'd heard him say, "You must have seen it all," to bums in Brackenridge Park, winos on the stool next to him at the Esquire Bar, long-haul truckers who picked us up hitchhiking. It was the net Sinclair used to collect weirdos and their stories. Afterward he'd always ask "Wasn't he great?" I suppose that collecting weirdos is fun for someone who's always been securely on the right side of normal all their lives.

"Sinclair, let's go."

"Huh? Oh, yeah." To his credit, Sinclair put his arm around me and we headed immediately for the door.

"Hey, come back during the day. Larue'll give you her autograph. Take her about five hours to slop on enough makeup to come outside, but she'll do it. Make her happy."

"Yeah, okay," Sinclair said.

"Here, take this." Pettigrew handed Sinclair a flashlight nearly as long as a baseball bat. "Leave it on the porch. Think I'll wait a while longer. May catch me a double feature." Pettigrew hacked a phlegmy laugh that followed us out into the long hall. "Come again," he called to Sinclair. "Find you a piece with a big butt and come again when the moon's full. I'll be waiting."

For the first time since I'd known him, Sinclair locked the door of the truck. As we turned around the circular drive, I saw a light on in the wooded area beside the rotting hulk of the hotel. It was coming from a trailer. A woman stood at the open door and watched us leave. We heard traffic noise and followed it. It turned out that we had come in the back way and that the front entrance, though completely hidden, was almost directly across South Presa from the San Antonio State Hospital at 5050 South Presa.

Sinclair snorted when he saw the sign and shook his

head as if trying to clear his vision. "That was real fucking weird," he said.

I never had a place to put the memory of that aqua-green night. I suppose the normal reaction would have been to feel violated. But I never did. Once I found out that Pettigrew wasn't going to hurt us, I bore him no grudge. After Sinclair left me for his old girlfriend, I dated a man who wore a V-neck T-shirt under his clothes and never took it off, even in bed. We slept together even though I wasn't attracted to him. When we went to bed I sometimes imagined Pettigrew lurking in a dark corner watching us, and that helped excite me. Mostly, though, with the V-neck T-shirt and with all the others, I thought about Sinclair.

He's all I think about now as I drive down South Presa. The state hospital is still there at 5050 South Presa. I tap on Victor's high-performance brakes and the car jerks to a neck-snapping halt. I feather a toe over the accelerator and it rips forward. The BMW's skittishness compounds my nervousness. After I pass the hospital, I strain to find the road Sinclair and I drove out on in the International Harvester truck ten years ago. I pass it two times before I spot the overgrown path and swerve Victor's car off South Presa, jackhammering the precision suspension as I bounce onto the potholed trail.

I make two turns, brush scraping the windows and sides of the car, and there it is, La Fonda Agua Caliente. The gate is locked. A light shines in the darkness behind the overgrowth. For the first time since Connie told me that this is where Sinclair is living, I stop. I know why I am going down this dark path. I could even write off the forces driving me toward Sinclair as mere hormones, bald lust. But Sinclair? What has brought Sinclair back to this peculiar place?

16. I park the car outside the locked gate and squeeze through the metal slats. The instant my toe hits Agua Caliente property a pack of snarling dogs descends upon me. They all appear to be pit bull/Doberman/rottweiler crosses with some poodle thrown in for extra hyperactivity. I put my arms around my stomach and freeze. The dogs halt their advance, too, and hang back, barking as if they are being tortured.

A door creaks open in the dark. A switch is flipped. A floodlight above my head bursts on, wiping out the moonlight with the purplish glare of a crime light. The faces of the dogs look like sea creatures, sharks with flat eyes. A sharp whistle causes them all to abruptly pivot their heads. On the second whistle they turn and lope away, slack as factory workers at quitting time. The door clangs shut in the darkness.

"Hello!" I call into the darkness. There is no answer. I feel eyes on me. But they're not Sinclair's eyes, they're Pettigrew's. A branch snaps in the silence. I begin to back away. "I'm leaving," I tell the depraved hillbilly. I turn around and make myself walk slowly to the gate. My back prickles with the feel of someone's eyes on me. I keep my arms wrapped around my stomach. "I'm going now."

"Well, shit me out and call me a brownie. Trudy Herring, is that really you?"

It's not Pettigrew. It's Sinclair. I stop and turn. Sinclair steps into the light. Dust particles dance in the violet illumination between us. I pull my arms more tightly around my other body.

"Little Red Herring. Jesus, woman, the years have gone light on you. You haven't changed a bit."

I'm a deer frozen in the beam of a headlight. I can't make anything work. Not my legs, my eyes, my voice or my mind. "Me?" I finally squeak out.

"The voice certainly hasn't changed. Tinkerbell on steroids. Look at you." He steps closer. "Haven't changed a bit."

"Well, there is this." I unwrap my arms, exposing the swell of my belly.

"Oh, well, plumped up a bit in the midsection. You always did have a fondness for sweets."

"Sinclair, I'm not chubby. I'm pregnant. And it was you, you were the one with the sweet tooth."

"You? A baby?"

"Yes, me. A baby." It comes back now, the way Sinclair had of making every conversation, every conversation with a woman, into a game, teasing, pretending to misunderstand, drawing you into playing with him.

He comes forward. Of course, he's not wearing a shirt. As long as icicles weren't forming, Sinclair had his shirt off, displaying his exquisite shoulders. They are as I remember them, broader than the rest of his almost delicate frame with a perfect upholstering of muscle. Not that he ever did anything to deserve them, there was no weightlifting, no sweating. God simply hung a perfect pair of shoulders on him like antlers on a buck.

His face does not fare as well in the purple glare of the crime light. The ultraviolet calls forth blue vessels and pouches beneath his eyes. Shadows channel the lines beside his mouth and nose into ravines. I am deeply grateful for these signs of decay, as they bring him closer to my league and make him less a god, more a shepherd. My only concern is how ravaged I appear to him.

Without asking my permission, he puts both his hands on my belly like a fortune teller holding a crystal ball. "You *are* pregnant." He looks up at me, bemused. "Thought for sure you'd turned into a boozer. You always did have a weakness for the wee drop. Lots of boozers'll go that way. Belly like the Happy Buddha, the rest of them you couldn't use for kindling."

"Sinclair, I was never a boozer. I never drank. You were the one who drank."

"Of course, you always were on the wispy side." He takes my wrist in his hand and circles his thumb and forefinger around it. A perfect manacle. It doesn't seem odd at all that he should touch me this way. "Would there be a father in the picture?"

"Yes. Yes, there is. Of course. Derek. My husband." At the same instant, we both glance down at the hand he's trapped. The left hand. The hand typically adorned with a wedding ring if the owner of said hand is married. I take my naked hand back. "Gosh, they're so swollen. Can't even wear my ring anymore. My wedding ring."

"So, just paying me a social call after all these years?"

The crime light illuminates the crime in Sinclair's eyes. He is much too casual. I haven't used the element of surprise well. I feel the ground slipping out from under me already.

"I was just out. Took Derek's Beaver for a spin." From the way Sinclair glances away from me to check the car parked on the other side of the gate, I know that I've gotten the nickname wrong. "Anyway, just happened to be cruising down South Presa and sort of wondered if this old place was still here." I look about me with perky interest. "And it is. And you are. What are *you* doing here?" I seize the offensive.

"Now, *that* is one long story, little darling. You want a drink?" He points to the trailer. "We'll hit the high points."

"Oh, well. One. Then I've got to . . ." He is already walking away.

The trailer sways as we step in. It is tidy as a showroom model with a tiny chrome sink gleaming in the kitchen nook and tiny crisp curtains over the tiny windows. We sit at a built-in table with a fake wood-grain Formica top. Sinclair assures me that this is not the trailer the movie queen lived in. She died over five years ago and left Agua Caliente to slimy little Pettigrew, who, apparently, didn't care to inherit the tax bill that came with it and slithered away. The resort has been tied up in litigation ever since.

Sinclair discovered that the place was abandoned—I try to imagine that voyage of discovery, the crew members—and moved a trailer out here. The prospective heirs attempted to evict him, but Sinclair talked them into letting him stay in exchange for chasing off interlopers when he was in town.

Sinclair in a trailer with pouches under his eyes. I wait for these deficits to fill me with a sense of superiority, but they don't.

Without asking, Sinclair makes the mixture of Buckhorn beer and Plaza lemonade that we existed on the summer we were together. He puts a foaming glass in front of me.

"Hope you still have a taste for shandies."

"I'm not really supposed to drink alcohol. Derek is pretty strict about that." Sinclair replaces my glass with plain lemonade. It tastes salty and fake.

Sinclair sits down and edges his chair around so that we face each other across the very corner of the built-in table. "So what month would you be in? I'd put you in the eighth."

"Seventh," I lie just so that he won't be right. Sinclair always knew too much about women's bodies. I loved him and hated him for it.

"Derek, is it?" He speaks to the foam at the top of his

glass. "Sounds like an upright fellow. Erect, one might even say. Agush with virility. Derek. A veritable geyser of spurting manhood. Quite the man to be a father. What does this Derek do? Stevedore? Pipefitter? Astronaut? How does one harness such an excess of testosterone?"

Sinclair always had a gift for the flighty filibuster. He could tee off on just someone's name and create an entire identity. "Derek is in real estate law."

"Handles a lot of bankruptcies, does he? Talk about a bottom feeder. Whoa! Bankruptcy law. What would that be? Capitalism's ultimate expression or its dying gasp?"

"Sinclair, I can't sit here and let you speak about my husband that way."

He puts a palm up. "Sorry. I'm sure he's a wonderful guy. Applied himself in school. Did extra-credit projects. Polished the old apple. Smooched the right butts. Moot court. *Law Review.* Beautiful wife. Fine German automobile. Though, if I had the money to be tossing away on a premium vehicle, it wouldn't be a Krautmobile. I'd show a bit more imagination than that. Real estate lawyer. Never would have thought you'd have ended up with a real estate lawyer, Trudy. Where are you living these days? Alamo Heights."

"King William."

"King William. Well, now. Historical restoration, all that? You get one of the famous ones. Doubt Derek would have gone after any but a famous one."

"We're living in the old Schier place."

"Well, well. The Schier mansion. So tell me, Trudy, what happened? Did the river get to be too much? Is that why you climbed out onto the bank? Bit drifty on the river?"

All this river talk came from Sinclair's view of the world which he had formulated in the sixth grade after reading *The*

Adventures of Huckleberry Finn. It was his metaphor for life. He and a few other charmed ones, he'd decided, were "river people" floating down an endless highway of adventure, unanchored by space or time. "Bank people," on the other hand, were those stolid folks who lived, rooted and unmoving, at the edge of his wondrous life. Bank folk might occasionally have a walk-on role in one of the adventures, a bit part to add some local color, a sense of the place being passed through, but mostly they were the audience that we river folk played out our bolder drama in front of. Now, I'd gone and married a bank person. Or so Sinclair thought.

"How did it happen, Trude? How did you end up in the Schier mansion with a real estate lawyer?" Sinclair leans forward, his face empty of expression, waiting to be filled up with a story, my story. And I want to tell it. Desperately. I want to present the past ten years to Sinclair as a gift. I want him to take them, be amused by them. I want him to cancel them out. Such is the quicksand inevitability of Sinclair's charm. He always had the ability to draw a person out, then into his universe. Within minutes of meeting someone he could have them confessing secrets they wouldn't tell their therapists. If that someone was a woman, they'd generally do the confessing without clothes getting in the way.

But I can't tell him anything about my real life. Not yet. "Well, had you heard that I went to the Chicago Art Institute for postgraduate work?" I act as if there was never any chance that our "circles" might have overlapped. As if my "circle" had ever been anything more than a pinprick.

"Chicago Art Institute? Very impressive. But you were talented, Trudy. You were always bouncing signals in from other planets. Can't say I stuck with the art for long after we parted. No." He thumbs away a bead of water trickling down the side of his glass. "No, lots of complications on the art front, lots of tangents."

"What is your current tangent?"

"Actually, I am painting again."

"Oh, really?" I wonder how Sinclair will embellish face painting to make it sound grand and impressive.

"Yes. Small canvases. Small pieces. Very portable." He looks up at me, deciding. "Faces. I paint faces now in Renaissance fairs."

It takes my breath away that he chooses to tell me the truth. For the first time real hope flares up. "I'll bet you're good at it."

"I am, actually. I am. It's all just temporary. I've got some other opportunities cooking. But for now it's quite enjoyable."

"How did you get started?"

"Ah. Fell into it, really. I had a friend. Es-mer-*al*-da." Sinclair trills the syllables, mocking their plummy exoticism. "Old Esmie was a belly dancer going thick in the middle. Not quite in top form. Not up to club engagements and bachelor parties, but still adequate for the semi-pro standards of the Renaissance fair circuit, if you catch my drift. Her pièce de résistance was this technically adept move where she'd flutter her solar plexus like a butterfly's wing. Riveting."

I wonder how many women over the years he's enchanted with my story, my quirks, my physical oddities. "So you traveled with her?"

"Esmie had this Gypsy wagon, and we ambled about the country going from fair to fair. Have you ever been to one? A Renaissance fair."

"No."

"They're actually pretty Middle Agey. Drinking corn

syrup "meade" and eating turkey leg "haunches of deere." Most of the regulars who traveled the circuit with us, the glassblower, the jester, tarot card reader, most of them were just misfits looking for an excuse not to take a bath from one month to the other."

"And you became the official face painter."

"Not right off the bat. But Esmie just kept getting thicker and thicker around the middle until her butterfly-wing flutter looked like a bad case of the dry heaves and she finally called it quits. She told me she'd be out of commission for three more months until the baby came. Baby! That was the first I'd heard about any baby. She told me not to worry. It wasn't mine and she didn't want anything out of me except that if I was going to stick around, I'd better figure out how to pay for some groceries.

I take a sip of lemonade. Sinclair continues.

"That all happened in Magnolia, just outside of Houston. Only one of the biggest dates of the year. Anyway, I gathered up every tube of lipstick, every stick of eyeshadow, every pot of eyeliner Esmie owned, made a sign, and I was in the face-painting business. One of my more inspired moments, if I do say so myself."

Sinclair pours my rejected shandy into his glass.

"Amazing how good I turned out to be at it. My specialty was young mommies with pretty little girls. I'd seduce them with visions of kitty faces. An asteroid belt across the cheeks. A unicorn horn on the forehead. In quick order I equipped myself with a palette of official, nontoxic face paints. Loved those jewel colors. They reminded me of the glass stains you used when you painted. . . . What was that you painted on the window?"

"The Silver Surfer."

"The Silver Surfer. Of course! God, that was great. I loved that. The Silver Surfer. Classic Trudy. Anyway, believe it or not, Trude, I do some good pieces. Some good faces. I'm proud to have them walking around on this earth for a day or so. I've had customers tape Saran Wrap over their paintings to try and save them."

"Really?"

"Really. Of course, that only creates a little sauna bath that steams them away even faster. They never last. They can't. I don't care. I much prefer being the best face painter ever to an anonymous mediocrity working with more permanent media. I've a genius for the temporary. But you know that. For the first ten minutes I meet anyone, I'm golden. After that my staying power becomes taxed."

Sinclair stares into his murky brew for a moment that extends by a fraction of a second into the theatrical. "Staying power, Trude, that's the name of the game now, isn't it?"

"What happened to the baby? The belly dancer's baby?"

"Charlie? Charlie was what we called him. She named him Charlemagne. Uh, they're in Tulsa now. Esmie left the circuit. Left me. For a woman. Jody. I guess after all those years as a semi-pro, lesbianism was a nice kind of retirement for her."

There is no theatricality in the distracted stare Sinclair gives his glass this time. I wonder who it is for, Charlie, Esmie, or Jody? He holds up his mug and speaks heartily.

"By all rights, this should be Dom Pérignon. Trudy, I'm telling you, I was set up, ready to show the U.S. Mint how to make money. There would have been a *fleet* of BMWs in my driveway if I'd have wanted to waste my money that way.

But that pack of thieves at the concessionaire's union blind-sided me. And only a week before Riverfest."

Sinclair knocks back his shandy and tells me the sad tale of how his Mad Max Margarita franchise would have put him on easy street if the villainous union had not stepped in and yanked his permit. The tragedy of the Mad Max Margarita is followed by a litany of other near misses. His "Yucatogs" importing venture, bringing in fabulous woven garments from the Yucatan Peninsula of Mexico, would have bought him "more Krautmobiles than your Derek could have washed in a day" had a crew of larcenous customs agents not impounded his entire fall line at the border. Then there was the time-share deal in Cozumél that the attorney general went after because of a personal grudge against one of the holding partners.

Sinclair is describing how he came up with the idea for accordion-folded, cardboard car window shades long before anyone else when I see, clear as a movie, the life I would have had with him. There would have been a succession of garage apartments, all jumping-off places for the glamorous new life that he would have made me believe was just about to start. I would have worked at temporary clerical jobs to finance Sinclair's enterprises. I would have provided the "seed money," "the grubstake." In essence, my life would have been exactly the same, except that I would have sup-ported Sinclair's dreams instead of my own.

I also see the string of women I would have been jealous of, would have grown dowdy in front of. Sinclair would have told me that it was always them who started it. That would have been the point of honor that kept me staked to a man neither one of us believed I deserved: He never made the first move. But, of course, he would. The joke with the waitress who brought him his German beer cake. The personal instruction for the female bartender in how to create the perfect shandy. The smile, the twinkle that told any woman in range, "I'm available. I'm going after Beatty's record."

It should be a great relief to see what might have been and to know that you took the right path after all. But still I would have eaten hot rocks for the opportunity to take the wrong one.

"I just couldn't find an investor with enough vision." Sinclair concludes the tale of his near brush with window shade fortune. "Trudy, you know what the greatest burden in the world is?"

I take a tight-lipped sip of my salty lemonade and shake no.

"Great potential." He stares into the empty mug with a melancholy look of hopeless yearning. One of the many reasons I adored Sinclair was for this deep streak of melancholy that I thought was terrifically romantic and Byronesque. "The burden of a great potential, Trude, it's crushed better men than me. Too many doors were open to me. I tried walking through all of them and didn't stay long enough in any room to really get settled. So, tell me, how's it feel to have done all the right things and come out with a good, solid American life."

Listening to him, I have a minor revelation. "Gosh, Sinclair, I never realized what a whiner you were." The words simply slip out when I see that what I took to be an exquisitely spiritual yearning is nothing but a highly evolved brand of self-pity.

Sinclair widens his eyes in mock amazement, then huffs out a weak chuckle. "No, please, Trudy, don't hold back. Tell me what you *really* think."

I laugh. Sinclair could always make me laugh even after I heard him tell a truck driver we hitched a ride to Austin with, "Make a woman laugh and you're home. Make a *married* woman laugh and you'd better be sure her *husband's* not home."

"A whiner, eh? Has marriage to this paragon, this *derrick of rectitude* made you so harsh in your judgments? I don't remember that in you, Little Red, this harshness, this love of the stoic."

"Ten years change a lot of things."

"Don't they just. May I touch the baby?"

I shrug, not agreeing, not protesting. My body hasn't belonged to me since I put Victor's sperm into it. Then, since it became apparent that I was carrying an extra occupant, my belly has been public property. People seem to want to tousle a child's hair even before he's born.

With Sinclair, though, it is what I want. It is convenient for both of us to pretend that my flesh will not be intervening. So, when he leans forward and places his hand lightly atop the aqua T-shirt bunched in my lap and says he can't feel anything, I tell him to go ahead and feel underneath my clothes. Sinclair kneels in front of me and slides his hands underneath the T-shirt. Like a basketball player taking a free shot, he puts his thumbs on my navel and splays his hands around my big stomach.

"It always surprises me, how hard it is." Sinclair speaks simply, something he doesn't do very often and almost never when he's been drinking. His voice is softer than the beer would have made it. He rubs, trying to feel the contours of a minute body. The feel of Sinclair's hands, cool from the shandies he's been holding and rough from working, is just right against my hot, itchy belly. When Sinclair touches me,

I know how lonely we've been, me and Sweet Pea. How loneliness has been so constant and so enduring that I've stopped noticing it like a faucet dripping in the night. Sweet Pea's need to be held is in my bloodstream amplifying my own. I list toward Sinclair's hand.

I know what a dog Sinclair is when he presses this advantage and his hand covers my breast. I'd assumed passion had withered like an unused muscle within me during the years of celibacy and am stunned to feel its swooning heat. I force myself to remember that I am supposed to be the adored wife of a King William lawyer. "Sinclair. Stop." My protest is weakened by Sinclair's knowledge that only full-out arousal can bring my voice to the nearly normal register it is in now.

Sinclair kneels sacramentally beside me. My belly sits next to him like a friend who doesn't know when to leave. He maneuvers around it and unsnaps the front fastener on my brassiere. My breasts loll out. He thumbs a nipple and currents frozen for years within me run warm and sweet. I am drunk on the smell of sweat and bravado that pours from him. The light from the cheap fluorescent fixture above the sink brings out the squiggles of broken capillaries on his cheeks, the red, wounded look in his eyes. The muscles of his shoulders bounce beneath his pale, freckled skin as his hands work at my breasts. He dares me with his eyes to make him stop.

"I . . . Derek will . . ." I mutter, goading him to go on by invoking the name of his rival, the successful man he can beat, if only in bed. The dogs bark beneath the crime light in the yard. A June bug buzzes against the screen. The smell of the river, like mushrooms, like semen, seeps in the window. Sinclair pushes my aqua T-shirt up underneath my armpits and brings both of my purple nipples to his mouth. My heart pumps violently.

I bury my face in Sinclair's hair and ten years slam shut like a boring book I'd been reading to fill up the decade. My life, my real life, the one that was put on hold when he walked out on me and Sweet Pea, begins again. The three of us are back together. I fill myself with his smell. Sinclair always smelled liked the two sides of yeast: fresh-baked bread and sour beer. The memory of his hair is in my palms. Soft and flossy, Sinclair has the hair of a choirboy, so fine that it fizzes into dark, damp curls at his neck when he sweats.

He looks up at me, dazed, questioning. This is new. Sinclair never asked before, he always proceeded with the assurance of a professor giving an anatomy lesson. The unfocused, smudged look on his face stabs me with desire. He puts his hands in front of my breasts as if shielding them from sight, then leans forward, swaying around the mound between us, and kisses that part of my body he claimed to love most: the scoop between the clavicles. There was a night when he trickled Drambuie into that hollow, then licked it away.

He is licking now, continuing up to my lips. All my life before Sinclair I'd been told I had no bottom lip. I do, the lower one is just indented in a mirror image of the top. Sinclair was the first person to tell me I had a double cupid's bow. That two cupid's bows meant I had a very sensuous nature. And with Sinclair I did. His approval sanctified my body and I offered it to him to use any way he chose.

His tongue flicks across the bottom bow of my lip, then plunges into my mouth. It's as if I have had nothing in my mouth for all these years, that I should have perished of starvation without a taste of him. He presses both his palms against my cheeks, making me give him more of my mouth.

I have been short of breath for the last three months, but now I am close to passing out. I hiccup shuddery gasps when he moves his mouth away. He stands and draws me to him. Or tries to. The mound prevents us from getting any closer than Catholic teenagers at a parish dance. I cling to his shoulders. I pull him tighter. I want him wrapped about me closer than my own skin, but we remain separated by the aquarium of flesh between us. He cranes down and around and finds my mouth. With our tongues wrestling, Sinclair twines a hand down to the zipper of my jeans and finds that it is already open. He holds his hand motionless over my pubic thatch for a second like a stranger approaching a dog until he feels the slippery wetness, then he begins a patient massage.

Because I will die if he stops, I whisper, "Sinclair, no . . . I . . . Derek . . . he . . ." At the mention of the man whose woman he believes he is possessing, Sinclair slides three fingers inside of me. They fill me like nothing since Sinclair has, and I surge onto them, pressing myself against Sinclair's palm. Then my hands are at the waistband of his jeans: I want to feel him. Times on the Renaissance fair circuit must have been tough, for the jeans hang slackly across the bumps of his pelvis bone. I stretch around my stomach to inch my hand farther into his pants. Apparently worried about squishing the baby, Sinclair pivots away, arching back from both my stomach and my hand while simultaneously slithering his own deeper into me. Thought is blotted from me and my hand loiters, paralyzed by plea-sure. I reach farther into Sinclair's jeans, searching for him.

We are both bent over now like kids playing a party

game, passing a beach ball between us without using our hands as we stretch around my stomach, hands out and groping. I keep reaching. His zipper rasps against the back of my hand. I inch through a mat of crisp pubic hair and find . . . nothing, only a limp testament to a one-sided passion. My hand rests against Sinclair's soft penis. I'm too embarrassed to go on or to withdraw. Sinclair solves the dilemma by backing away from me until my hand is excised from his jeans. It drops at my side. I feel like a cow. A huge, ridiculous, panting, dripping cow.

As if enthusiasm could erase the evidence of his lack of desire, Sinclair quickens his pace, dipping in and out of me with a manic fury. I back away from him, but he follows, his hands still firmly lodged within me. I push him away at the shoulders. He stands, stooped, in front of me.

"I've got to . . . I'd better go."

"Trudy." His face droops. I fasten my bra. The squalid disaster that is my life appalls me. I have come to this trailer with its crummy wood-grain Formica table for this? To have the hand of a pouchy-eyed Peter Pan inside of me waving to the baby he once cast aside. Sinclair removes his hand. I am mortified by its dampness, by its smell. I turn my back to him and open the door only a foot or two from where I stand. Sinclair stops me with that moist hand.

"Trudy. Don't." He pulls at me and the trailer sways beneath us as the great load of my middle is pitched off balance and I stumble into his arms. He clasps me to him from behind and begins shuffling us both toward the bedroom.

"Sinclair, no. I want to leave." Desperate with humiliation, I hold my arms out toward the door, but he keeps shuffling me away from it.

"Uh-uh," he mutters into my hair.

"No, really, Sinclair, let me go. I want to go."

"Uh-uh, uh-uh, uh-uh." This time it's a croon. He crosses his arms in front of me and snags a breast in each hand. He fondles, shuffles, and nuzzles my neck all at once. It is an attention-getting performance.

Most of the space in the bedroom is taken up by a bed covered with a tangle of peanut butter tan sheets and a butterfly quilt that I know some woman made for him. He turns me to face him, then, using a surprising knowledge of the principles of leverage, lowers my amplitude onto the bed. On the nightstand are toenail clippers, some balled-up Kleenex, a brochure advertising a bicycling tour of the pubs of Ireland, and a motel glass with a red crust of dried wine on the bottom. Old issues of *Omni, American Film,* pamphlets about network marketing, and clumps of dirty jeans and dingy boxer shorts litter the floor.

"Quit taking inventory," he tells me, reaching over and switching off the lamp. The small room fills with silver moonlight. I sit up.

"Sinclair, I'm leaving."

He clutches at me as I stand and topples me back into bed. The whole trailer creaks when my bulk hits the mattress, a wobbly cheap affair like the one I have back in my apartment. My four-poster in King William is as solid as a banker's desk. Sinclair's cheesy bed depresses me. The fact that I've come to it seeking asylum depresses me much more. Tears are pooling in my ears before I realize I'm crying. How could I have wasted my life collecting other people's trash?

"Aw, Trude." Sinclair snuggles up to me. He knows

about crying women. I am in the hands of an expert. "Is our Derek a wee bit freaked out about the addition?"

It's a reasonable theory. I honk wetly.

Sinclair kisses my cheek in a sweet, brotherly way and pats my damp cheek. "He's trying, Trudy. He sounds like a do-right guy. He's just not getting marinated in the same hormones you are." Sinclair strokes my flanks like a jockey calming a skittish horse. "See, you've got all these wonderful juices swirling about, dissolving you from within, turning you all rubbery. Does it ache here?" He rubs my hip. I nod yes. "Ligaments. They're getting stretched out. Everything's getting stretched out, opening up to accept this new life that's being wedged into you. Derek doesn't have that chemical advantage. His trip is all mental. He's stretching dry, do you know what I mean?"

I nod and sigh, a look of wifely forebearance on my face. Sinclair is good at cheering women up. The best. He always was. When he got back with his old girlfriend, he worked hard to convince me that it wasn't my fault and that I was a wondrous human with a fabulous future ahead of her. I knew I could depend on Sinclair for some bolstering. If I actually had a negligent husband, I'm sure I would be much comforted.

"Hey, you hear the one about coyote love?"

I give my head a tiny shake to indicate that I haven't.

"First trimester this couple does it the regular way. Missionary. However. Second trimester, they're doing it doggie style. Third trimester, the husband just lays by the hole and howls."

"Sinclair, that's—"

"Gross and awful and stupid, but at least you're talking to me again. Okay, so Derek's not even into coyote love.

Maybe he's been making you feel about as desirable as Ma
Kettle these days."

Sinclair stops for confirmation, but all I offer him is a
loyal silence that proves his hypothesis.

"He's wrong, Trudy." In the moonlight I can see an
authentic gleam in his eye. "You are a marvel. A wonder!
They talk about a glow, but you, Trudy, you are luminous. A
pregnant woman is cooking, all the rest of us are raw, pallid
slugs. Look at you!" He circles his hand around my stomach
like a fortune-teller tuning in a crystal ball. "Look at this
gargantuan mountain of life you're hauling around. You are
thrumming and throbbing with life! You are the last fire in
the last hearth on a cold and lonely planet, and every freez-
ing man with enough wit to recognize that he's a walking log
wants to warm his hands at the heat of your ripening."

Sinclair's hands undulate over my gargantuan mountain
of life, producing a very warming effect. "You are a goddess,
a wellspring. You are a veritable 220 line into the cosmos
and the only way we pathetic males have of plugging into
infinity. Derek is an idiot!" he pronounces fiercely, and
pushes back my shirt to kiss the nub of my popped-out belly
button. The tip of his tongue slides down a stretch mark that
slithers like lava flowing from the erupted summit of my
stomach. He continues on, deftly pushing aside intervening
garments until he is lying sideways beside me, his knees
next to my ears, his face buried between my legs, where he
commences slurping with the undisguised enthusiasm I
loved so well and never found again.

Pinned beneath the weight of Sweet Pea's sauna, I can
only manage to prop myself up on one elbow and clutch at
Sinclair's arm. I try to push him away. "Don't do anything
out of charity. You know, just to cheer me up."

Sinclair peeks at me from around the hillock, grabs my hand and puts it on what feels like an Idaho potato. "In my own bed, I do only what pleases me. Now, lie back."

I sink into the too-springy bed, wondering what Sinclair means. That in other beds he does what pleases the owners of those beds? Will I be expected to pay at some point? Has he turned that corner? What *is* Sinclair's pleasure here? Taking another man's woman? The surrender of an old girl-friend? Proof that the Coker magic holds its potency for two decades? Then Sinclair puts a hand on my bottom and tilts me toward himself even more. His head parts my legs, his nose pokes into the slippery wetness, and what little resistance I'd mustered dissolves along with conscious thoughts.

As his tongue works at me, my mind fills with lipstick colors: fire and ice, meltingly melon, partyline pink, planetary plum, mocha berry, coral frost. They swirl together the way they used to when I'd melt down all the last, leftover chunks of old lipsticks then pour the glistening liquid into a foil form I'd made myself, where it would harden into a new tube. The molten ruby of a deep red is just beginning to stain the shimmering pastel of a frosted pink.

Sinclair stops and looks at me. In the moonlight we are both barely twenty again. There are no pouches under his eyes, and my stomach is flat as a gymnast's.

"We'd have had a beautiful child, Trudy, you and I." He continues to stare while I peruse the lost worlds contained in that sentence. "Your eyes. My hair. Your nose for a girl." He touches my nose. "Mine for a boy."

"Your eyes," I say, as if we might actually be ordering.

"Mine? They're pissholes in the snow up against your peepers."

"Sinclair, I've missed you." It's more than I'd intended

to say. He wriggles up to me and rests his head on my shoulder, a couple of weary campaigners, the only two from the platoon to make it out alive.

"I've missed you, Trudy. More than I can say. Your Derek is a lucky man. Had I but applied myself, perhaps, I'd be a lucky man today awaiting the birth of my child."

I catch his eyes. The truth of my situation, not the particulars, but the essential truth that he could have his wish is so apparent in my face that Sinclair divines it. I know he does, because I feel his body twitch beside mine.

"But it's babes, not babies, I want." He chuckles the nervous laugh of a man who never wants to be taken seriously. Not *that* seriously.

I notice that I have gone numb. My feet and legs are effervescing with a pins-and-needles dullness. As Rachel predicted, if I lay on my back, the baby would hurt me.

17. I feel like a thief walking into my apartment on Laurel in the middle of the night. It has the still quietness of a place that no one has been in for months. The smell of gas lingers in the airless rooms. I wonder what a person with gas space heaters on the floor billowing out blue flames in the winter does if that person has a crawling baby.

The panes in the door rattle when I shut it behind me. All that is left of the Silver Surfer I painted on that glass when Sinclair lived here are a few tracings, ghostly in the moonlight. I switch on the light. The apartment seems like a cave after so many months in Hillary's airy, high-ceilinged rooms. My garage sale and Salvation Army finds—a yellow sofa with the dirt spots hidden by pillows and arm covers I made from a dashing floral-printed fabric, a forties armchair and hassock covered in the original scratchy rose-colored upholstery, the little red wagon I use for a coffee table, the chip-can end tables holding the Day of the Dead skeleton puppets that I wired and made into lamps—all look tacky and unsanitary. Even worse are the towers of project materials stacked everywhere. I notice a few of the more recent additions, the old sample books cadged from a carpet store, some silver film cans and black-lined printing paper boxes found in back of a photo studio, a pile of Formica sink cutouts the lumberyard was tossing out, a few decapitated bowling pins from Holiday Bowlarama.

I slump into the armchair. My giant hand costume holds up a welcoming palm from the corner. I can no longer remember the person who constructed all the curiosities that surround me—the Varmints-à-Go-Go, the Missile Toads, the Dino-Sardines—or why she felt compelled to waste her life on them. Sweet Pea karates me one to the right ribs. He doesn't need to point out how unsuitable this place is. I stayed too long in my own childhood to prepare one for anyone else. Why wasn't I getting useful training? Hanging out with prosperous men? Contributing to an IRA? How could I have squandered my life on giant hands and dreams of a man even more stunted than I am?

"Babes, not babies."

I did not know I had been dreaming until those words woke me up. Without ever admitting it, I had been hoping that Sinclair would somehow save me. That he would know what to do and want to do it. How could I have expected Sinclair to be different, better, than me?

I sit for a long time and watch my stomach writhe. I am surprised to discover a small mole that must have been hidden all my life inside my navel has now been forced into view. I turn out the light and sit back down with both my hands on my stomach. I don't allow myself to do this very often, to really be with Sweet Pea. In my circumstances this is dangerous; it can lead to attachment. My little otter is playing, tumbling around in his tiny water park. His head feels like a croquet ball caroming from one wicket to another. It pokes out on one side until my stomach squares off.

I catch myself cradling his head and heave to my feet. Once again, I have no choice. I drive back to King William.

From my window I watch as the caterer's van arrives at first light and pulls around to the back of the house to begin setting up tables for Hillary's not-a-shower baby shower. A middle-aged woman with a long braid down her back bursts from the van and directs her helpers, three college boys in fluorescent surfer shorts and high-tops, to begin setting up tables in the backyard.

A moment later Victor hurtles out the front door, rushes to his car, yanks the door open, and plunges inside. He sits down in the front seat and punches in a number. As the conversation gets under way, his right hand automatically lifts to the steering wheel.

I should go down and apologize, make up an explanation for why I took the car in the middle of the night. But we've reached the point of such strained politeness that I know neither Victor nor Hillary will say anything to me about it. I put my hand on the knob of flesh Sweet Pea extrudes and try to make out if it is a little hand or a foot. I realize what I am doing and stop myself.

Though I chase them away, visions of Sinclair's trailer keep popping into my mind. Something is not right with them. Something is missing. I search through my memories until it hits me: Sinclair's trailer was totally devoid of any female touches. Subconsciously I had expected the smell of perfume, frilly underthings tucked at the foot of the bed, lipstick stains on half empty glasses. But no. There wasn't so much as a bobby pin in evidence. More than the lack of physical clues, though, was the dispirited aura of sexlessness a place gets after a protracted period without a visit from someone of the opposite sex. I know that aura; my place is drenched in it. So there *are* no babes. Sinclair lied to me. Not that it matters. The will, the desire, that's what matters.

"Trudy?" Daffodil yellow sunlight is filling my room by the time Hillary knocks on my door several hours later. "People are going to start showing up in about half an hour. What are you wearing?" She makes her voice sound chummy, as if she's not checking to find out when I'm bringing the mound down. I know Hillary doesn't want me at her party. But she does want the baby to come. I've turned into the thorny cactus surrounding her sweet red prickly-pear fruit.

"Haven't decided," I call out. The effort of matching her

tone exhausts me. It would take more energy to resist than I can muster, so I get up and waddle into the bathroom, where I pour half a bottle of Hillary's Bain Moussante into the tub. I slip simultaneously into the bubbly water and a deep reverie that is broken only by the sound, both lugubrious and heavenly, of a chamber music group playing in the backyard. I towel off to the clink of champagne bottles against fine crystal and slip on an airy summer sundress printed with sprigs of lilac that Hillary has put in the closet for me, then stand at the window and watch the party for a while. The backyard has filled with couples made up of women with imaginative haircuts who look artistic and men in expensive cotton who look wealthy. Though she resists, Hillary is pushed to the front of the group and squeezed out onto the riser where the chamber group is seated. Presents have already been heaped there. When she is well into the unwrapping, I finally walk downstairs feeling shattered and ethereal.

"Oh, how precious!" Hillary is gushing as I slip into the last row of partygoers clustered around the low wooden riser. In front of her are a high chair, a baby swing, a car seat, and several large pieces of molded plastic whose functions I can't identify. A miniature pair of red hightop Reeboks dangles from Hillary's index finger. Violin bows and stringed instruments sag in the laps of the musicians seated behind Hillary.

I step onto the pad of St. Augustine grass that carpets the backyard and stand behind a woman with hair that plumes out like a secretary bird's. She is wearing what appears to be an intricately batiked pair of pajamas with a horse's show halter around her neck. A dashboard statuette of Our Lady of Guadalupe dangles from her right earlobe. As Hillary puts the baby hightops back into their box, the woman leans in to whisper to a man wearing a black polo shirt, khaki pants, and polished loafers.

"Strange, isn't it? Watching someone with less of a tummy than your average triathlete opening booties. Did I tell you Joanne and Carla and I tried to get a shower together, but no one could figure out how to handle it. You know. The other mother. All that stuff."

Eyes forward, hand covering his mouth, the man beside her nods knowingly, then leans down to ask, "Where is she anyway? The real breeder?"

I try to step away but am boxed in by a group behind me.

"Cuteness! Cuteness! Cuteness!" Hillary announces, pulling a doll-size sweater knit with a pattern of tumbling bears from a froth of tissue paper.

"You can bet no third world hands touched *that* little creation," the polo-shirted man says behind his hand to the plumage-headed woman.

"The ultimate power-shower gift," the woman whispers back. "Something hand knit by a white person. They're going to hate our present. We should have gone in with Phillipa and Arnold on the stroller. But, Christ, a hundred beans apiece!"

"I don't know, Steffie, could have been worth it if Hillary sponsors your grant."

"She's going to hate our present."

"I love it!" Hillary unwraps what appears to be a large orange gourd giving birth to a small orange gourd. "Steffie, it's wonderful! This is going to the hospital with us!" She clasps the gourd assemblage to her chest. "It will be our talisman."

The plumage-headed woman and Hillary grin meaningfully at each other, then Hillary tenderly repacks the gourd creation.

"Wow, she liked it." The woman is thrilled. Her partner puts an arm around her and squeezes.

"Champagne?" One of the college boy helpers, now wearing a pressed white shirt and black pants, holds a tray in front of me. I shake my head no, pointing to my stomach, then change my mind and grab one as he walks away. I press it to my lips so that I can feel the bubbles and smell the wine.

"This is adorable!" Hillary holds up a mobile with a porpoise, a golden-cheeked warbler, and several other endangered species dancing from it. "This defines adorableness!"

"Not to mention environmental awareness!" a man in a madras plaid shirt and the kind of wire-rim glasses that John Lennon used to wear and have been taken up now by stockbrokers calls out. Everyone laughs more than is warranted.

Hillary waves the mobile around. "Todd, Melissa, thanks, you guys. This is great!"

"And all proceeds go to the Sierra Club!" The man crosses his arms in front of his chest, and again everyone laughs as if he'd made a joke.

The next four gifts are all things called Stim-Mobiles. They look like black and white No-Pest Strips but are actually infant stimulation mobiles. For the first three Hillary gushes convincingly, saying, "This is perfect!" and suggesting places where they will hang, the crib, the changing table, and the stroller. By the fourth one she's run out of places, and Victor steps up and says, "Hey, this kid is going to be more stimulated than Redi-Kilowatt."

"I am overwhelmed!" Hillary beams to the crowd at

large, the gifts all opened. *"Mil gracias, mil gracias, mil gracias, mis estimados amigos y amigas."*

I look around. The only brown face in the crowd belongs to Mercedes, who has slipped onto the riser and is bundling up the presents. Hillary nods to the chamber group, the music starts again, and the cluster breaks up. Most everyone heads for the buffet tables, where chefs wait to serve tacos from your choice of smoked duck or crab in ancho pepper sauce on blue corn tortillas. Above the guests' heads flutter a menagerie of piñatas all commissioned by Hillary: baby pandas, baby penguins, baby calves, most of the young members of the stimulating black and white animal families.

It was me, I was the one who originally found this piñata maker and arranged to have his work shipped up here from his tiny village in Chihuahua when we did the exhibition, "The Art of the Temporary: A Celebration of Moments." I am wishing that I could be back in *that* moment, on the phone with the shipping company in Tres Piedras, my life simple and pain free, when Hillary, flanked by several friends, appears before me.

"The guest of honor!"

A strain that goes beyond the strain of having to pretend to be excited about four identical black and white mobiles stiffens the smile she turns on me. I suddenly feel just as sorry for Hillary as I feel for myself and want to hold her hand and transport us both back to a time when I could have actually helped her. I am powerless now before what we have done, and so is she. All either one of us can do is march forward according to the plan we tricked ourselves into.

"Trudy." She puts her hand on my shoulder. "I'd like you to meet some friends."

I put my hand out to people who suddenly have no faces. They murmur, I nod. There is no place in any of our experiences to fit this introduction. My child will know these people, they will be part of his world. They are not of mine. When the introductions are finished, no one speaks. These are people who are graceful with the help, but I am help of a sort they cannot categorize.

"Uh." My voice is high and strained. "I'm not feeling just real great."

"You do look a bit pale." Hillary speaks in her real voice instead of the keyed-up, peppy one she'd been using to express gratitude. "What can I get you? Something to drink? A big fruit juice sparkler?" She glances at the glass of warm champagne still in my hand and I put it down.

"No, I think I'll just, you know . . ." I point to the house behind me. "Go in and lay down."

"Hydrate, hydrate," Hillary calls out to me as I leave.

Not even caring if Hillary sees, I tack off away from the back door and head out for the side of the house. I have to get away. I don't care where, just so long as it's not back upstairs to the canopied bed. I march down the sidewalk, humped up by the roots of centuries-old trees. The street, King William, the kaiser's street, is lined with spears. The barbed wrought-iron pickets of the fences are spears. The weather vanes spike the sky with their twirling spears. The burglar bars crossing over windows are spears. The canna lilies are flaming spears of orange and red. I don't belong here. The entire neighborhood is prodding me out. Even the silver painted fire hydrants could be bullets aimed at me. I quicken my pace and don't slow down until the fencing changes to chain-link at the end of King William Street.

I look back. No one follows. I stop to catch my breath in

the shade of an old magnolia. There is no shade cooler than that cast by an old magnolia tree. Sweat dribbles down between my breasts. The purple blossoms of a mountain laurel perfume the air I pant with a smell like grape Kool-Aid. Some of the blossoms are already turning into scrotal-looking seed pods. I struggle onto the next oasis of shade, a small park wedged into a fork in the road. A woman in a khaki skirt pushes a stroller up to the gazebo at the center of the park. Her baby is pink and chubby and wears a sunbonnet. Sweet Pea will play in this park. Perhaps with this baby. I walk faster.

When I reach St. Mary's Street, I breathe easy again and catch the first bus headed north. I slump into the first empty seat and scoot over next to the window. The mound magnetizes a woman in back of me, who leans forward and asks when I'm due.

"Middle of the summer," I tell her. "End of June, actually. But I start counting summer in April."

"It's hot enough, isn't it?" She sighs gustily. She's in her mid-sixties and wears glasses that magnify her eyes to the size of poached eggs. "I hope you don't go the way my sister did. She delivered in August. Up north in Waxahachie. And that was before air conditioning. Hottest summer in fifty years. When that baby came, no one could believe it. The heat had dried up every bit of her waters, and that baby was just the leatheriest little old thing. Skin like a handbag. And a full set of teeth to boot. What do you make of that?"

I can't speak. In my mind I see the shriveled walnut face of Tutankhamen, the boy pharaoh of Egypt, grinning his death's-head grin into the face of eternity.

"Little boy grew up to be a sailor. A sailor from Waxahachie, Texas! What do you make of that? Just couldn't get enough of the water. Had to be near as much of it as he could. Shipped out. Forged his papers to join the merchant marines. Trying to make up for the dry time. Never been another sailor before or since in the family. Died in a big storm off the coast of Greenland. She was constipated, too, my sister. The whole nine months. Never had a movement. You have a name picked out?"

"Andrew." As awful as it is, the woman's conversation is better than being left alone with my thoughts.

"Andrew, that's very pretty. You know they'll call him Andy. They always do that. Shorten a name. Michael, Mike. Daniel, Dan, Danny. Edward, Ed, Eddie. Wilford, Will, Willie. Harold, Harry . . ."

When I wake up, the woman is gone. I am ferociously thirsty, there's a crick in my neck, and I have to pee. I stagger off, heading north up St. Mary's. I duck into the first open restaurant I come to and rush back to their bathroom, figuring that I might just be able to make it. When I open the door and see two women in their late thirties waiting in front of the one stall, I groan. I can already feel my bladder giving way.

One of the women, a tall bleached-blonde with tobacco-stained teeth, takes one look at me and pounds on the locked door. "Chug, come on out! *Stat!* We got a gravida needs to void." The door pops open and a third woman steps out, still pulling her shorts up over tanned legs.

"Go on, go on." The blonde shoos me in and closes the door. I sit down and a few teaspoonsful dribble out, plinking into the bowl.

The women all turn out to be labor and delivery nurses having a late lunch before starting the evening shift. They ask me who my doctor is. When I tell them Antoine Worley, Chug with the tanned legs asks if I live in Alamo Heights.

I tell them I live in an efficiency on Laurel Avenue.

"Didn't think Old Squirrely took anyone outside the zero nine zip code," Chug says. The other two laugh.

"At least it's not Teeter," the tall blonde answers.

"Good Old Tee-Time Teeter," the third nurse says. When she speaks, you can see more gum than tooth. "Did I tell you about his latest? Induced after three hours at five centimeters so he could make an eight o'clock tee time. Overdid the pitocin. Uterus set up like concrete and he ended up having to do a section."

The words "set up like concrete" echo in my mind.

The tall blonde turns to me. "Don't worry, Worley's got his peculiarities, but he's not knife happy. You'll be fine."

I think of the pink rabbity face outlined with its black stippling of hair transplant scabs that peers at me from between my legs every week now. I never speak. Dr. Worley has accepted Hillary as my vocal cords. I barely listen anymore while she asks all the consumer advocate questions that Rachel has brought up. The questions don't have to do with me. They are for the baby. For a healthy baby. That is the way it should be.

"What hospital are you using?" Chug asks.

"Uh, you know . . ." I snap my fingers. The hospital is another detail I've let Hillary handle.

"Baptist Memorial?" the tall blonde suggests. "Worley is practically on staff there."

"Yeah, Baptist Memorial," I repeat. "That's it."

"Hey, great," the one with big gums says. "That's where we work. Come in on our shift and we'll treat you right. Extra samples of Tucks pads and everything."

I laugh along with the three, pretending that I get their nurse joke.

The tall blonde comes out, washes her hands, and the three nurses head for the door. I want to go with them. Chug pauses and turns to put a hand on mine. "You're going to do just great." She squeezes my hand.

"I am?"

"Oh, yeah. I can always tell." She is the last out the door.

Outside on the sidewalk, the heat makes me gasp. Asphalt dust and exhaust fill my mouth. I can't decide which way to go. I'm so tired I want to stretch out on the bus stop bench, but I trudge up St. Mary's until I reach the limestone wall enclosing the grounds of what used to be my alma mater. A beer truck nearly squashes me as I totter in the entrance. As soon as I am inside the wall, I can smell the river. The same damp, green smell as the breeze blowing in Sinclair's trailer.

"Are you from Wildlife Rescue?" Sister Tabernacula asks when she opens the door. "About the cats," she explains to my blank look. "Though it may be raccoons, we shouldn't rule out raccoons. Or possums. Badgers, for that matter. They're wild, though, I can guarantee that. You're needed here." She crowds in on me and takes my hand. "We can't handle them. Neither Sister Immaculata nor myself are up to it. I broke my hip this previous autumn and am not constitutionally equipped to deal with trapping wild animals." She leans in close to me. "She feeds them. Stinks of sour milk up there. They yowl all night long. SPCA wouldn't come out. You have to do something. It may not be cats. They sound wild. Where's your equipment? Shouldn't you have stout boots? A falconer's gauntlet? What's that about your middle? Protective padding?"

"She's pregnant, Sister." Cece appears behind her. "That's Trudy, don't you remember? Little Gertrude Herring?"

"Ah. The Protestant." She leans toward me. "You don't do animal removal, do you?"

"No, Sister." I answer. "I don't. I'm sorry."

Sister Tabernacula shoots Cece a curdled look over her shoulder, sticks her nose into the air, and trundles off.

Cece pulls me into the convent. "Trudy, I was just thinking about you. Do you believe that every particle of matter in the universe emits a vibration? That if we could just decode those vibrations we could communicate with . . ." She glances around her. "This door?" She knocks on it. "I think we already do it with each other, you and I. I think about you and you appear on my doorstep. The person we want to see least in all the world, the person we think the deepest, darkest thoughts about, pops up every time we go to the grocery store. Do you believe that? That we are all sending out messages all the time?"

"I believe that." My answer seems to close the discussion and Cece turns and walks away. She is halfway down the hall before she looks back and beckons for me to follow.

The big sitting room that Cece has transformed into her political action center smells like mud. It is the smell of many pots of gritty poster paint sitting open.

"You're just in time to help me finish up," she says. Propped up along most of the available wall space are placards with various denunciations drying on them. Cece hands me a brush and I begin coloring in the penciled outlines of "No More Unjust Wars!!"

Cece is immediately absorbed in her sign: CESA LA REPRE-SIÓN! and seems to forget again that I am here. For a few minutes I paint in silence, almost able to surrender to the discipline of filling strict borders with color. But the placard painting reminds me too much of the hours, the days, the years of my life I threw away on my meaningless projects. I am so lost, I can't keep myself from scratching for a clue, for any scrap of wisdom.

"Sis—Cece. Cece." It takes two tries before she lifts her gaze from her painting. "Whatever happened to all the blue-bonnets?"

"Season's over." She returns immediately to her work.

"No, I mean the ones you painted. Your paintings."

"Mother house, every one of them."

"Every one? You didn't keep even one?"

"Property. We weren't allowed to own anything other than a comb, a toothbrush, and a rosary back in those days."

"Do you regret it? The time you spent painting them and now they're gone and you. You've got—"

"Nothing to show for it? Not even regional fame as a miniaturist?"

For a second I wonder what she's talking about. Then I remember my lie.

"I'm like Edith Piaf, *je ne regrette rien,*" Cece answers. "And that's the truth. There was a reason I had to do all those bluebonnets. I'm not sure exactly what it was. But they were my meditation, my joy. They kindled me and kept the chill out. Should I have been studying for a law degree? Should I have"—she studies me—"been having children? Would those things have validated my existence? I don't know."

She sags and the nimbus of energy that whirs around her

like electrons around the nucleus of an atomic particle slows for a moment. "You want my story, I'll tell you my story. I wanted to be an artist. Then I thought I wanted to have been married. To have had children. To cook breakfast every day of my life for a man. I filled up then with irises and orchids and all manner of labial flowers, and that's when I stopped doing the bluebonnets. I also stopped being Sister Nicey Pie. Stopped saying my devotions. Stopped eating. If I could have found the switch, I would have stopped breathing.

"They sent me away to a special place for broken nuns up in the Jemez Mountains of New Mexico. I liked it there. Most everyone drank. I took that up for a while. We were just up the hill from an ashram. I liked going down to eat brown rice and half-cooked vegetables with the rich kids living poor. They told me I was a bodhi, a sage. I wasn't, I was a depressed old woman who thought I'd thrown my life away. That everyone had gotten more than I had. I was ready to cash in my rosary beads and take my chances as a bodhi, when I realized the kind of job security I'd be giving up. So, I accepted what Paul VI told us: 'If you want peace, work for justice.' World peace, that seemed to beat bluebonnets as a reason for existing."

"So, you've never regretted not having children."

"Never," Cece snaps, the atomic particles starting to whir again. "You think painting bluebonnets is tedious. Every little pistil and stamen. Every yellow grain of pollen. Try changing six thousand diapers. That's how many a baby goes through." She gives me a sharp look. "I hope you're planning to use cloth. Get this Derek to spring for a diaper service."

She paints the R on *Represión* a bright royal blue. "The strange thing is almost no one believes a woman if she says

she doesn't want children. They think it's your secret tragedy and anything, *anything* you do with your life is just to
salve your aching heart. You know what children are for? To
teach us how to die. And isn't that the best way to learn how
to live? That's why women die with so much more grace
than men. You've already done it once giving birth. But I've
gotten in all the transformation-of-self experience one person
needs in a lifetime. No, it isn't children I regret not having,
it's sex. I was a virgin when Father Van Overbeek and I
came together as one."

" 'Together as one?' With Father Van?" I am incredu-
lous, thinking of the bald-headed priest, dandruff and chalk
dust powdering his black cassock, who came in once a week
from Central Catholic Boys School to teach us theology.

"Ah, yes," Cece answers, rapturous in her memory. "Father Van." She sighs. "All those years we wasted. I was fifty-
three and he was what? Mid? Late seventies? Such a short
bit of time we had before his juices dried up. He said it was
the blood pressure medicine. Still, he was an exorbitantly
sensual man."

I remember now the enthusiasm Father Van had shown
when recounting the fate of Sodom and Gomorrah. And Sister Theonella became this man's love slave? I see how ridiculous it is to pretend I am living a perfect life with a perfect
adoring husband eagerly awaiting the birth of our perfect
child.

"I don't have a husband," I tell her.

"No husband," she repeats. "Generally for the best,
wouldn't you agree?"

"The father is married."

"Um. I wouldn't encourage divorce if I were you."

"No, he and his wife are planning on keeping the child."

"Make sure the wife's heart is genuinely open to this."

"But maybe I should keep the child. Except that I'm not married."

"Many a fine child has been raised without his or her real father. Consider Jesus."

"I had an abortion ten years ago and never came to see you again because I could not have stood your condemnation."

"You did the right thing. Ten years ago I might have condemned you. Not now. I've seen too much of the world. I wouldn't condemn any woman for not bringing a child into it."

"How can you say that? Don't you believe that all life is sacred?"

"Life *is* sacred. Too sacred to be distributed so arbitrarily. I've seen too much, Trudy. I've seen babies born without enough wit to suck a tit because their mothers had nothing to eat except *tortillas de pobres,* poor people's tortillas. You know what the second ingredient is after corn? Sand. You don't have to go that far south of the border to see women, their teeth ground down to nubs from eating tortillas stretched with sand. What chance does a child have? You can't grow a brain in sand. No, the greater crime is imprisoning a spirit in a broken body. A broken life."

Breath that has been trapped in me for ten years puffs out, and a locked, stale place deep inside fills with clean air.

"Cece, my life is such a mess. I don't know—"

She stops me with a finger jabbed into the air and listens again with that Joan-of-Arc-hearing-voices look on her face. By the time that I, too, hear the distant yowling of cats, Cece is hurtling out of the room. I follow her into the hall. The smell of floor polish still lingers on the scuffed wood. She disappears around a corner. Her heels clack as she goes up the stairs. I remember going up those stairs for my one dinner with the Sisters. All the girls were invited. Sister Tabernacula's favorites were invited back. Aurelia was asked regularly. Annette, the school suck-up, was invited every week. I never had a return engagement. The refectory was on the second floor. The vats of stew and apple brown Betty they ate were hauled up via a dumbwaiter that creaked and groaned in its shaft.

I sat beside Sister Theonella, my hostess that night. She sat at the end of a long table with half a dozen women on either side all shrouded in their habits. I knew enough by then to be quiet during grace, but Sister Immaculata, sitting beside me at the head of the table, rapped my knuckles with a spoon when I piped up with what I considered to be an engaging remark after grace was said. The food was served in silence and eaten in silence broken only by the precisely enunciated words that Sister Immaculata read from *The Story of the Scapular.*

I follow Cece through the refectory door, expecting to see that long table that was the site of so many silent meals eaten while worthy tomes were read aloud, but it is gone. Instead, there are four spindly-legged bassinets, three rocking chairs, two changing tables, and a pyramid of Huggies disposable diapers.

Cece turns to me. "It's impossible to use cloth under these circumstances."

I am too stunned by the discovery that the refectory turned nursery is occupied by three spiky-haired infants to say anything. One black-haired baby is being rocked and given a bottle by a Hispanic woman with a gentle manner. One is sleeping, his face screwed tight in concentration, a balled fist next to his mouth. The third baby is wailing, his hands twitching spastically in the air.

Cece speaks to the woman minding the infants, addressing her as Nasaria. Nasaria answers and Cece scoops the unhappy baby out of his bassinet, taking him to the changing table. His diaper is filled with a surprising substance that looks like a mixture of mustard and cottage cheese and smells like Swiss cheese.

"Their little poo-poos don't really start stinking for a few months," Cece says, as if that question were uppermost in my mind. "Has something to do with the enzymes. There you go, you little poo-pot. All dry now. All dry, *mijito.*" She puts her face down right in front of the baby's, and he goggles a froggy stare at her and grabs onto her thumb with fingers tiny and curled as popcorn shrimp. Cece looks at the little hand, then touches a faint red row of scratches beside the baby's puffy eyes.

"Whose babies are these?" I ask, wondering if Cece is running some sort of clandestine day care center.

Instead of answering, she coos to the baby whose hand she is holding, "Oo, who is doing your nails these days, *mijito?*" She presses a little finger into her mouth and nibbles off a parchment scrap of nail. Using her front teeth, she nips off the other nine nails. "There now. Don't let your manicurist get so lax again." She cradles the infant to her chest and strokes his bare back.

"Your mamma is coming for you, Rubén," Cece whispers to the squalling baby. *"Tu mamá viene. No te preocupas."* She looks up at me. "The other two aren't so lucky." She holds Rubén out to me. "Do you mind? This little buckaroo needs some num-nums."

He is so light, lighter than I could imagine even the

tiniest human ever being. He seems to weigh only what the idea of a human body should weigh. The blueprints. My hand covers his entire back. Cece snaps a plastic bottle liner off a roll, tucks it into a holder, adds a couple scoops of formula powder and some distilled water from a plastic jug. She screws on the nipple, shakes, hands me the bottle, and points me to a rocking chair.

"But I've never—" I start to protest.

"Just like in the movies. Plug him in. Nothing to it."

I settle the baby on the pillows Cece piles onto my lap and push the nipple into his mouth. Rubén knows his job and tugs away like a baby billy goat at the petting zoo.

"I wish my little babies could be on breast milk." Cece sighs, watching Rubén suck at the bottle of formula. "So much better for them. Of course, it would be so much better for them to be with their mothers."

"Why aren't they?" I ask. My curiosity about this astonishing setup is diluted by the necessity of making sure that Rubén doesn't choke or drown.

"Oh, death squads, empty stomachs. Measles, mumps, chicken pox, silly diseases here that kill children down there. A future. That's the big reason they aren't with their moms. Their mothers send them north for a future. Can you imagine how much those women must love their babies? Oops, time for a bubble."

The bottle is empty. Cece gestures for me to put Rubén on my shoulder and pat his back. Before I have the warm lump settled, he unlooses a blaster belch next to my ear that leaves my shoulder sopped with curdled milk. Cece takes him.

"We feel much better now, don't we? Our tummy is full and the bubble is all gone." The baby curls into a ball against her chest and is fast asleep when she slips him back into his bassinet. At that moment the third baby, a scrawny scrap of a creature, wakes, screaming.

"Poor little Rudolfo has colic," Cece says, rushing to pick him up. He arches his back and writhes in Cece's arms. She drapes the baby over her forearm, his head in the crook of her arm, his skinny arms and legs dangling, his diapered rump in her palm, then she bounces. "Panther in a tree," she tells me, raising her voice to be heard over the wails. "Works every time."

Rudolfo's screams pick up to air-raid-siren level. "Except this time," Cece says, shifting him onto her chest. She begins a jerky jig, Rudolfo's head bumping her collarbone with every springy step. A strange accompaniment seems to come out of nowhere and fill the room with a deep, rumbling bass that drowns out even Rudolfo's shrieks. Only when his cries stop do I realize that the rich, guttural sound is coming from Cece as she jigs forward five steps, hops, jigs back five steps, hops, and comes forward again.

"Shoo, shoo, shoo la roo. Shoo la back shack, shoo la baba coo." Her lullaby is more chant than song. "When I see my Sally babby bee come bibbling along shy loreen." Five more verses and Rudolfo is fast asleep. Cece puts him down.

"Twelve children and six of us had colic," she whispers to me. "My mother sang and danced like that until she literally dropped from exhaustion. Was her mother taught her the words she'd learned from her mother and so on right back to Eve, I suspect."

"What?" I gesture at the stack of diapers and sputter out my questions. "Where? Who? There are others? What happens to these babies? How did you get them? Cece, what is going on here?"

Cece looks around. Nasaria is putting down the sleeping baby. All is quiet. She shoos me out and locks the door behind us.

"We keep it locked. There's not much danger of the Sisters getting up to this floor, but we can't take any chances of them finding out. I don't think they'd understand."

"Cece, *I* don't understand."

"I suppose it's a blessing the Sisters can't climb stairs anymore," Cece says as we go downstairs, paying no attention to my question. "They think I keep cats. Since Rudolfo arrived, they suspect larger game. Would you have ever imagined how close your old teacher was, Trudy, to your very own situation? Proves my theory, doesn't it? About vibrations. We all put them out. We all pick up on them. You knew I'd understand. And I know you'll understand."

Back in the main room on the first floor, Cece goes to a locked filing cabinet, pulls a key from her pocket, unlocks a drawer, and opens it. From the drawer she pulls out a photo album, sits on the floor, and beckons for me to join her. Awkwardly, I squat down.

"This will help explain." She hands me the album and I flip through page after page of smiling couples holding babies. Nearly all of the couples are mixed, Anglo and Chicano. All the babies are brown.

"The families I've created," Cece says.

The light dawns on me. "You're running an adoption agency."

"Unofficially. *Very* unofficially. Though, I must say, that since nearly all the adoptive mothers are either old students or their sisters or best friends, no agency could ever know their candidates as well as I do these girls. I never set out to do this. It was thrust upon me. Nasaria, the woman upstairs running the nursery, started it all. She came to us through my Central America work."

"And she had a baby," I guess.

"No. Nasaria's aunt was pregnant when Nasaria fled the country. Shortly after the baby was born, the aunt learned that she and her husband were on a death squad list. We helped them smuggle the baby, Josefina, out to Nasaria. Both parents were murdered. Nasaria is raising the child. Josefina is seven now. She was the first. Word spread. We helped whenever we could. How could we not? For a while we got quite a few Salvadoran babies. Lately, most of our babies have been coming from Guatemala. Every country down there seems to have its season of desperation. Some last for decades. Though there have been months when all the bassinets have stood empty."

"Cece, this is amazing." I look up from the album. There are dozens of family portraits. Questions buzz through my mind. I snatch at the first one that hums past. "How do you pay for it all? Diapers? Formula?"

"Diapers and formula are nothing. It's the fake papers and bribes that really mount up. Oh, bribes, *las mordidas*, are our major operating expense. The new parents help us out. The refugee community does what it can."

"How do people, parents, how do they—"

"Find out about us? Women wanting babies can smell a child who needs a mother. At first we were just a refuge for babies who had relatives who'd escaped and come north. An address. A safe place on the other side of the river. Then we got Hector. He was our first who arrived with no one to go to. Ostensibly. I knew before I ever saw the little mite, though, who he was intended for. Only a week before, a student I hadn't seen in years appeared at my door. A student you knew."

"Aurelia. You saw Aurelia."

"Of course I can't reveal anyone's name. Far too much is at stake for that."

But I know. I know.

"Oh, we chitchatted back and forth, my old student and I. Wonderful husband. Regional manager for a credit bureau, as I recall. Lovely house. Three bedrooms. Then I asked if there were any children, and she burst into sobs. Mixed race marriage. The agency she was working with wasn't optimistic. The agencies were much more rigid back then, you understand. A week later Hector arrived, and my first family was born. Desperate parents talk to other desperate parents. Secrets come out. My old students are drawn back. They don't know why. I do. Look, the image of his father."

Cece points to a baby grinning a toothless smile into the camera. The man holding him grins the same grin with teeth. I flip through the album, starting at the back with the most recent photo. As I go back six years in time, I watch the mothers' hairstyles change from mostly short and curly with Olive Oyl poufs of bangs at the front to mostly long and straight with earmuffs of hair sweeping back at the temples. The dozens of photos begin to look like the same three-person family photographed against a variety of backgrounds.

I flip faster and faster until a photo of a jug-eared Anglo father and a sweet-faced mother with a mono-brow like Frida Kahlo stops me dead. Aurelia is staring down at what appears to be a sack of potatoes in a tiny sailor suit.

"I can't believe this. Aurelia ended up with Frank. Is she in town? Does Aurelia live here? How can I get in touch with her?"

Sister takes the book back and leans over to return it to its hiding place. "I cannot reveal names. That would threaten my families. You understand. We've had inquiries about your whereabouts, Trudy, over the years. But we had no way of knowing where you were. If there are inquiries in the future, we will know."

"But, Sis—Cece. That's Aurelia. We were best friends. She was my roommate. Remember? She had to leave. Her family sent my letters back to me. We lost touch. She would have no way of contacting me. My phone number's not listed. I don't even have a driver's license. How could she find me? That is her, isn't it? I mean, it has to be her. Cece, I dreamed that she had a little boy. I know what that little boy looks like now. Seven years later. He's chunky, isn't he? Chunky with shiny black hair and his front right tooth is out."

The look on Cece's face tells me that I'm right.

"And, and, they live in a house with . . ." I claw through my memory for some detail from the hazy dream. "With this really ugly linoleum in the kitchen. It has some kind of starburst pattern on it. Blue and gold. This awful waffly texture. But the kitchen is big and the little boy likes to ride his trike there."

"How did you know that?" Cece asks quietly.

"Aurelia showed me. In a dream. It was important for me to know that she had a happy house. They're here, aren't they? They're back in San Antonio. Cece, I really need to talk to her."

"Trudy, I can't tell you where she lives. I'm sworn to

confidentiality. All I can do is tell you a story about an old student of mine, the gentlest, softest soul ever placed in my care. The girl really wasn't of this world. Which is why we were so slow to realize that a baby was growing in this angel's body. That was long ago, and we did all the wrong things. Her family came for her and we didn't hear another word for a year. Then I learned through a cousin of this girl's that the baby had grown in the wrong place. Ectopic pregnancy, it's called. The girl thought it was part of the punishment she deserved and didn't say anything to anyone until the tube burst. The girl lived, though she didn't want to."

"Oh, shit, Aurelia." I think about how fluorescent green my old roommate used to turn each month just from cramps and want to weep for all that innocence and pain.

"The girl didn't do well after that. Everyone in her village said the half-Anglo baby she'd been making had taken too much of her blood. That she couldn't make new blood because her crying had dried out her body. After a year, the girl stopped crying. She was too tired for tears. Then she was too tired to eat. Then too tired to sleep. Finally, when she became too tired to live, her mother gave the girl a stack of letters from Norteamérica.

"The lovers had parted as children. When they met again, they were both older in ways than their own grandparents. They told the girl's parents that they would marry. That they would both die before they would be separated again.

"They wed and moved to the boy's country. He found a fine job and bought them a fine house, where they waited for their children to arrive. But no other baby would grow in the girl's damaged body after the first. Years went by and the girl came to see me. Though I told her the crying from upstairs was cats, she smelled the babies and could not sit still. She paced and stared at the ceiling. She cried when she told me she had no children. A week later Hector came to us."

"Aurelia was your first family. Aurelia and Frank. God. Those ears."

"Oh, well. Love doesn't always look like Gregory Peck."

Why hadn't I fallen for a jug-eared guy who would chase me to the ends of the earth? Who would have died to be the father of our child? I am happy that Frank turned out to be that guy for Aurelia. My desire to see Aurelia wanes. Too many years have passed. Too much has happened to me that she would never understand.

"Here." Cece hops to her feet and holds out a hand to help haul me to mine. I breathe heavily when I am upright, exhausted by Aurelia's past and my future.

I hang on to Cece's hand. She clearly wants to be off, though, painting placards, checking on her babies, demonstrating in front of the chancery, working for peace through justice. But I won't let her go. "Why did I do this?"

"Trudy, don't worry. All pregnant women experience some degree of ambivalence."

"No, this goes way beyond ambivalence. I know I made the wrong choice."

"I'd better tell you the secret, then."

"What? There's a secret?"

"It wasn't your choice. It's not you that brings them. It's life. When these little souls are ready to come, they come."

"But is he coming to me or to Hillary?"

"How should I know?" Cece frees her hand from my damp grasp. "No one's filing any travel itineraries with me. I have no listing of the ports of call. I'm just a deck steward, Trudy. I'm not the captain." She gathers up her placards. The paint is not dry and some of the words smudge. She doesn't stop to fix them. She bustles out the door, all her particles whirring.

I think of myself as a conduit, a vessel for passing along life. The thought does not cheer me up. I slump onto the floor and listen for a while to the babies on the second floor who have wakened and are crying. Even knowing that they're human babies, they still sound like far-off cats yowling.

18. All the shower guests' cars are gone and Hillary is sitting on a bentwood rocker on the front porch, waiting, when I walk back down King William Street. As I come closer, I see that the porch is crammed with what I take to be the caterer's plants. Hillary jumps up when she spots me and runs to the gate. Everything she's been holding back for all these months starts pouring from her in a rush.

"Trudy! Where have you been? I thought you went upstairs to lie down. Then you never came back down. I see now that the shower was a mistake. I wanted to be open. I should have considered your feelings more. This must have been difficult. I just wanted everything out in the open. I thought the support of a loving, caring community . . . . Oh, I don't know what I thought."

"You wanted a baby shower."

The tense energy drains out of Hillary. "I wish you would have told me you were leaving. Trudy, we can't continue like this. Tell me what I'm doing wrong. I know you're not happy. *I'm* not happy. I know that the hormones change everything. I've read about the mood swings, the irritability. I've tried to make allowances. But this is more than that." She touches my forearm. "Trudy, tell me about it. Come on. We fixed a lot of things in the past. You and I. Working together. Where there's a problem, there's always a solution."

Involuntarily, my eyes squeeze shut. "No. No, Hillary. Not always. Sometimes there's just living with it." I open the gate. As I approach the porch I see that what I took to be the caterer's plants are really a small forest of the strangest plants imaginable growing in rusting coffee cans: starry-flowered ice lilies from Peru, horned devil's claws from Arizona, lacy fairy fern from Borneo.

"Do you know anything about this?" Hillary asks, studying my face.

I have no breath to answer. Remembering the night Sinclair and I stumbled upon Agua Caliente, my mind freezes in the beam of his truck's headlight falling on these unearthly plants. My nose fills with the rich fungal smell of the river far to the south, far past the concrete banks.

"No," I finally answer. "Where did they come from?" I ask as if I'm not one of the two people in the world who knows the answer to that question.

"That's what we're trying to figure out. They just appeared while we were all in the back. Probably from one of the artists. Maybe something to do with the gourds in labor."

"There wasn't, you know, a note or something?" My voice is high and tight.

"No, there wasn't anything. Just this." She holds up a tape cassette. "For the Mother-to-Be" is written on it in black marker. The sight of Sinclair's handwriting causes my heart to jig.

"Probably Nahuatl birth chants or something equally earthy," Hillary says. She slides the tape into her pocket and starts into the house. "I guess I'd better have Mercedes clear these off. Trudy, are you all right?" She catches me leaning forward, my hand reaching involuntarily toward the pocket where Sinclair's tape rests. "I have to tell the caterer where to put everything right now, but can we set aside a time to really sit down and talk this through?"

"Sure."

"Mercedes!" Hillary turns and shouts into the house. I know we will never really sit down and talk anything through. "Mercedes, can you come and clear all this foliage off the front porch?"

There is a mumbled question from deep inside the house.

"I don't care where you put them. Just get them off the

front porch. Have the caterer's boys clear them away. No!" Hillary yells to someone inside the house. "That's Grand-mother Goettler's punch bowl. It doesn't go there." She rushes in. A moment later one of the college boys appears with a roll of brown plastic garbage bags. He cracks one open and unceremoniously tosses in an ice lily. The star-shaped white flower quivers when the rusty can it is planted in hits the bottom of the bag.

I think of Sinclair making coffee from that rusty can. I think of him uprooting the rhizomes clumped beneath the earth, then gently breaking apart the bulby mass. I think of him digging rich earth by the river, mixing it with peat moss and vermiculite, filling the can with the mixture and setting the rhizome in it. I think of him caring for new life.

"Stop."

The college boy doesn't hear me and reaches for a fern. The plant's delicate tendrils tremble in his hand. I try again.

"Uh. Didn't anyone tell you? Mrs. Goettler wants those moved to the . . ." I glance around. "To the carriage shed."

He stands up, annoyed. "What's a carriage shed?"

"That." I point to the shed in the side yard. "That over there. That's where they're supposed to go. Just bag them up carefully and lay them out on the floor."

"You know, we didn't bring these. We're not supposed to be moving around stuff we didn't bring."

His hightops are monstrously large, laces undone, swol-len tongue hanging out. The big shoes make his long, nearly hairless legs seem almost delicate.

"Oh, you're right. It is unforgivable to ask you. Here, I'll just gather them up and . . ." I throw my legs wide apart and roll from one to the other like a drunk sailor making the aquarium slosh wildly from side to side. I put my hand on my back and lean forward, grunting as I reach for the first can.

"Never mind." He takes the plant from my hand. "I'll do it." When he's bagged a dozen or so, he totes them to the shed. I follow.

In the backyard Hillary is occupied pointing out to Mercedes which presents stay and which go to Goodwill. I wonder what the handicapped workers will make of the gourds. In the confusion of cleaning up, no one notices one more college boy carrying one more garbage bag. In four trips the porch is clean.

Once all the plants are safe, I return my attention to the tape. The tape for the mother-to-be. The tape for me.

Hillary is in the backyard, on the riser, pointing to presents and pronouncing their destinations to Mercedes: "Goodwill. Goodwill. Keep. Goodwill." She dispatches a poly-blend creeper suit, a stuffed bear in a football jersey, and a vinyl diaper bag to charity. Mercedes gathers up the indicated items and tosses them into a bag that will go directly to Letitia, her pregnant daughter.

"Goodwill." Hillary points to a picture of a toddler kneeling beside his bed, his hands folded in prayer, the seat of his Dr. Denton's down, revealing a cherubic, pink bottom.

Mercedes stops and glares at Hillary until Hillary remembers that Mercedes gave her this picture.

"Good! We'll keep this is what I meant," Hillary hurriedly corrects herself. "Good, we'll keep it! And put it in the nursery," Hillary adds brightly, picking up the picture framed in wood-grained plastic. "Right over the crib."

The clear plastic edge of the tape case pokes out of Hillary's pocket. What is on that tape? What does Sinclair want me to hear? Whatever it is, I don't want Hillary, I don't want anyone, to hear it. Once, without my knowledge, Sinclair taped us making love. He called me at the Department of Motor Vehicles, where I was working as a clerk-typist, and played it back for me. The sounds I made surprised me, like a Berber widow keening with wild, desert grief.

I sidle up next to Hillary. While she's deep in thought, contemplating the disposition of the four black and white mobiles, I slither a hand out and touch the edge of the cassette. She jerks away as if stung and looks sharply my way.

"Oh, Trudy, I didn't notice you there. How many mobiles do you think the baby will need?"

"Two? Three?"

"Hills!" Victor appears at the back door, holding up the cordless phone. "It's for you." He covers the receiver. "Janine."

"Janine," Hillary whispers. "Oh, God, not now." She trots off to the house. I pick up a big plastic container with a puck of deodorizer in the lid for the cloth diapers Hillary plans to use and follow her into the house. I time it perfectly so that Victor is just handing Hillary the phone when I squeeze past her. In the crush I attempt to slide the tape out of her pocket and into my hand, but the diaper pail gets in the way and the tape clatters onto the Saltillo tile floor, landing at Hillary's feet.

The cordless phone at her ear makes her look like an insect missing one antenna. She glances from the cassette bumping against her big toe, to me, and bends down to pick it up. Catching the edge of panic in my expression, she says to the caller, "Janine, I'm going to have to call you back," and crunches the antenna back into the phone.

Still staring at me, she hands the tape to Victor. "This was with all those bizarre plants. Let's find out who they were from. Trudy, you want to listen?"

The living room is stacked with the gifts Hillary is keeping. A green Babar the Elephant stuffed toy with music box pokes his head with a yellow crown out of a box lined with tissue paper. A navy blue Victorian-looking baby carriage with chrome trim and bouncy wheels festooned with streamers and bows is parked beside the turquoise coffee table. A wooden high chair with a black and white cowhide backrest stands next to the leather couch.

Victor pops the cassette into the tape player. Sweat that has nothing to do with the heat drips off my elbows. I try to make my face a blank as Victor punches the play button and leader tape hisses through the machine. Hillary continues to watch me. In spite of myself, in spite of having given up on him forever, my breathing turns shallow as I tense, waiting to hear Sinclair's voice again. One last time. At that moment, if I had ten thousand dollars, I would give it to be alone listening to this tape.

The hiss stops and the room fills with music so lush that it turns the very air around me to velvet and transforms me into a concubine, a prisoner of pleasure in a potentate's harem. I listen to "our" song, "A Whiter Shade of Pale." Even ten years ago, when Sinclair and I were together, it was an old song. I see every image painted in the song. Sixteen vestal virgins leaving for the coast. A miller telling his tale of a face at first just ghostly turning a whiter shade of pale. I never knew what any of it meant, just that it was voluptuous.

Hillary and Victor exchange puzzled looks. "Fast-forward it," Hillary says. "Let's get to the message."

A high-pitched squeal stops the music, then it starts

again. Victor speeds through a couple more sections. Finally, he just lets it play.

Sinclair and I were listening to this song the first time we crowded together in the tiny shower in my tiny apartment. We had to stand because there was no bathtub, just the shower. Still, being naked *and* wet next to his body was almost more than I could endure. There should have been more. Like Cece, I regret the lack of more. There should have been years and years of more. There should have been a bathtub.

"That's it?" Hillary asks Victor. "What's it supposed to mean?"

"I'm sure Gourd Lady could tell you. The significance escapes me."

I know exactly what the significance is; it is a song from a trailer park potentate whose harem has abandoned him. It is Sinclair's call to me.

"Trudy? Are you okay?" Victor's softly spoken question startles me.

"Um-um." I nod, wiping away the tears streaming down my face.

Hillary, too, speaks softly. "Have you eaten today? There's all kinds of leftovers from the shower. Maybe a piece of cake."

Hillary's offer touches me. Only if she were genuinely concerned would she allow a sugared substance.

"Uh, thanks. I think I'll just go up and rest for a while. Didn't sleep too well last night. Uh, I'll . . ." I point up the stairs even as I mount them. I have less and less idea what to say to either of them. I glance back from the top of the stairs. Victor is staring at Hillary, asking for an explanation. Hillary hikes her shoulders up almost to her ears to signal her continuing bewilderment and exasperation. Victor holds out his arms and Hillary sags into them.

Later Mercedes brings me a tray piled with leftovers from the shower, bits of smoked duck and sun-dried tomatoes filled with pesto cream cheese. She sits down on the bed while I nibble and fidgets until she can no longer hold in what she has to say.

"Truthee, you wish you never started this deal?"

I give Mercedes a tight nod that could mean anything.

"Ay, Truthee, *'Yo no le suelto la cola aurque me cague la mano.'* 'You can't let go the tail even if your hand's getting shit on.' " She shakes her head and clucks several times. "This what happens with too much money. Arnufio don't believe me, but it's true. *'Ningún jorobado se ve la joroba.'* 'The hunchback don't see his hump.' "

Hunchbacks and shitty hands? It is obvious to me now that all my life I have had bad advice. I don't think I can be blamed for failing to develop good judgment in such a climate.

"Truthee, what's wrong?"

"I'm in love with a man who never grew up. Who wouldn't be a good father. Who wasn't even a good boyfriend. But if he were standing outside in the middle of a ring of boa constrictors and scorpions and he opened his arms to me, I'd jump out of the window to get to him." I don't see any reason to short-change Mercedes on the truth.

"Is that who sent them weird plants with all them spiky deals?"

"He wants me back. What should I do?"

"Truthee, this is not a simple situation. You got the baby to think about now."

"What if it were Arnufio? What if you and Arnufio had been apart for ten years and he finally came for you?"

"And I was pregnant? Depend if he wants just me. Or he want the baby too. Depend if he got a job. A house. 'Course, none of that matters if I was going to jump through a window for him. Then you just gotta do what you gotta do."

"Could you give me a ride somewhere?"

Mercedes shakes her head. "This is not going to end good."

Hillary and Victor are gone when Arnufio comes to pick up Mercedes that evening. But even if they had been home, I wouldn't have cared if they'd seen me loading the exotic plants into the trunk and backseat of Arnufio's LeMans. I leave a note for Hillary that says my mother is in town and that I might not be back that night. I know I'm going to the wrong place for answers, but I'm doing what I have to do.

It is dusk by the time we reach South Presa. If we go over thirty, Arnufio's raked and chopped Pontiac scrapes on every bump in the road and sends up a rooster tail of sparks. He rests an arm tattooed with "Mercedes" on the open window. The seats are sunk down so low that his eyes are almost level with the bottom of the window. The steering wheel is a shiny length of chain welded into a saucer-size loop. His three granddaughters sit beside me.

The girls are playing a game, slapping palms, then turning their hands over for a slap on the top side, all the while chanting, "Give me five. On the backside. In the hole. You got the soul. Give me five. On the backside. Cut the cheese. You're Chinese. Give me five. On the backside. Break the pickle. You get a tickle."

When the game degenerates into serious slapping, with serious screaming, Arnufio, without turning around, fans his hand around the backseat, swatting ineffectually at his giggling granddaughters.

"Indios!" he yells at them. Being called Indians makes the girls giggle even more.

Arnufio gives up his efforts at discipline and asks me, "You got a boyfriend at the state hospital?"

"What'd she tell you?" Mercedes snaps. "He lives *across* from the state hospital. Maybe you the one should check in."

"Who's the one got an aunt dresses her little yappy poodle dog up like *El Infante?* No one in *my* family's got dogs wearing little red velvet capes. Little blue satin gowns. Little black shoes with gold buckles."

Arnufio turns all the way around to look at me in the backseat holding on to the plants that wouldn't fit into the trunk. His granddaughters peer at me, their eyes sparkling. The wind from the open windows blows their Indian-straight black hair around their faces, where it catches in their mouths. "Who do you think ought to check in, huh? Who's the crazy one in this family?" he asks.

The three little girls laugh. The youngest, Nikta, covers her mouth, hiding the empty space where her front teeth have fallen out.

"Ay qué madre!" Mercedes screams, grabbing the shrunken steering wheel and jerking the Pontiac and swerving back into the right lane just in time to avoid an oncoming Honda. The small car's horn shrieks into the window as it passes. "You the crazy one! *Cabrón,* you gonna get us all killed!" Mercedes continues in Spanish to the delight of the three girls, who keenly appreciate the flamboyant manner in which their grandmother details all the ways in which their grandfather is an idiot and a crazy man.

"That little pimple of a car? The Japs don't make a car can even put a *dent* in this machine."

"That's it!" I point to a gate across a dirt road almost hidden in the dense undergrowth.

"Hang on! I'm a whip a Louie!" Arnufio yells. Though he swings his arms wildly in theatrical imitation of a man maneuvering a shrieking curve, he actually turns slowly, wallowing the boat around and backtracking to the dirt road.

The gate is open. Sinclair's truck is gone. As we pull up, the pack of devil dogs swarms around the car. Arnufio gets out and starts kicking at the pack. They scatter immediately, quick to recognize a dog-kicking hobbyist.

Mercedes studies the trailer. A broken screen is hanging from one of the windows. The siding is buckled and warped. Streaks of rust dribble down from the roof. "Don't count on any them black and white baby mobiles here."

I nod and get out, hauling several plants with me. The little girls insist on helping unload the rest. As we finish, Nikta shyly puts her brown hand on my pale forearm and pats it lightly.

Mercedes laughs. "Nikta, you trying to rub off Truthee's freckles? What do you think those little spots are? Dirty water? Huh?" Nikta gives a gap-toothed smile and pats my hair with a gentle, dazzled touch.

"Don't go messing up the lady's hair," Mercedes scolds.

"Ith thoft," Nikta says, her voice barely audible.

I pull a windblown strand of the little girl's black hair out of her mouth and brush it back behind her ear. "I wish I had nice, strong hair like yours," I whisper to her.

"Hey, you gonna be okay out here?" Arnufio asks. Dusk is already beginning to weld the trees into a solid, dark canopy.

"Sure. I'll be fine."

He points to the trailer. "You wanna wait inside till this guy shows up?"

I try the door. "It's locked. That's okay, I'll be fine."

"Nothing to it." He reaches the door, makes a fist, and, "Just . . ." bangs once above the handle. The door pops open ". . . knock once."

"Oh, well. Thanks."

He helps me up the steps, then grandparents and grandchildren pile back into the Pontiac. A spray of golden sparks showers out behind them as they drive into the night.

I go inside to wait. Sometime after two, I hear Sinclair's truck pull up. The dogs yap in an excited frenzy. What I hear next surprises me. I expect the sound of Sinclair's voice, drunken and gruff, yelling at the dogs to shut up. Instead, I hear a tender "How's my boyos? Huh? How's my big boyos? Treats! Treats all around!"

I peek out and see Sinclair kneeling in the purplish glow from the crime light surrounded by the devil dogs, pressing scraps into their mouths. They crowd to get in close to him, to lick his face. Some even ignore the scraps he pulls from a take-out sack in their delight at his presence. He pats every member of his flock, scratches ears, makes sure the timid ones get a nibble and stops only when he notices the rows of plants lined up in the shadows. He stands slowly and looks around, dogs bouncing up to lick his hand. I drop the curtain and move away from the window.

A second later Sinclair comes in, a plant in each hand. His face, knotted and dark, lightens when he sees me. "Trudy."

He is so surprised that he doesn't use a funny version of my name. He doesn't hide his pleasure. I am very happy I came. He holds up a plant and speaks in the highblown way he does when he's drunk.

"So, you came all the way out here to reject my sodden roots. Was Derek the Upright offended by the thought of any other living organism assuming an erect position on his premises? Eh? Was that it? Did Derek the Tire Tool order the turgid shafts out of his sight?" He is in good form.

"No, it had nothing to do with Derek."

Sinclair puts the plants down, staggers over to me with open arms, catches me in his grasp, and keeps on going until he lands us both in his bed. He stretches out in back of himself to push the button on a tape player and the tuna can of a trailer fills with a purple ocean of sound.

"Trudy, I'm glad you came back. I've missed you. For all these years I've missed you and didn't even know how much until the other day. You bring something with you, girl. You make me feel like a sophomore." He laughs and shows his teeth, dulled a bit by sluicing decades of Schilo's coffee over them but bright enough still on a dusky evening in a dim trailer. He puts out a comradely arm and pulls me to him so that I nestle in his armpit. He punches a button on the tape player beside his bed. A part of me that has been stretched for ten years relaxes and goes slack as I lay in Sinclair's arms and listen to "A Whiter Shade of Pale."

The song immediately traps me in a fantasy that lasts only a fraction of a second. A fantasy of being in a potentate's harem. Of the hundred women in captivity, I am the favorite. The potentate ignores the other ninety-nine and comes to me twice, three times a day. Servants live to do nothing but anoint me. Every breath of harem air I take is perfumed with an aphrodisiacal incense much like patchouli oil. I have a maid whose only job is to rub my skin with sweet almond oil. She takes particular care with the pinkish welts left by the potentate's love bites. When she is finished, another servant dresses me in silk so light that when the potentate removes it, it takes a full minute to float through the air and land on the floor beside my feet. My undergarments have been taken from me.

Soon the potentate is coming to me four times a day. His hands never leave my body. He feeds me dates while he is inside of me. We bathe together in water warm as blood and scented with rose petals.

Then the potentate comes to me five times a day. When flesh can no longer express the enormity of his longing for me, he sings, ". . . the truth is plain to see."

The song ends and Sinclair speaks. "I knew the song would bring you. Even Derek the Colossal couldn't keep you from me once you heard that."

"It brought back memories," I admit.

"Memories. Memories? Trudy, 'A Whiter Shade of Pale' brings back an entire kingdom, the kingdom of the senses where we once reigned supreme and unchallenged." He stares up at the ceiling and rubs my stomach with a fond familiarity I wouldn't have expected.

"We had some . . . some good times."

"Trudy. Trudaloo. Trudenda, my little red herring, what Dionysus and the nymphs and satyrs had was a 'good time'; what *we* had was epochal. It was the apex of a moment unlike any the world will ever see again." He rolls over and grabs me with both arms, burying his face in my neck. "It was fucking phenomenal. 'Good time.' Is that what you and Derek have? A good time? He slips on the old bologna bayonet for a quick round and thinks he's done his part, eh? That it? Derek a bit lacking in imagination? Generosity? A touch of the dreaded Madonna complex creeping in? Do these belong to baby already?" He covers my breast with his hand as he asks the question.

"Trudy, they're so big. So immensely"—he pulls open my blouse and laps at the stretched-out nipples—"nourishing." His hands move up the back of my thighs, clamping onto my bottom. He tries to haul my pertinent parts in next to his, but manages only to bounce my beach ball of a stomach against his.

"All right," he says, pushing himself up on all fours. "I admit it, Derek The Maypole may, indeed, be working with a slight handicap. Still . . ." Huffing, he maneuvers over me and drops in a heap at my back, where he molds himself to me, leaving no doubt about his state of readiness. The breath he exhales over my neck, in my ear, is hot and beery. Zippers and waistbands are fumbled with. He tips my pelvis backward to meet him and, moaning, slides in.

For a few seconds I hear nothing, see nothing, and feel only Sinclair inside me. As he begins to move, I realize that this is the destination I have been marching toward for all this time. Pleasure ripples through me as I press back against him. Bliss oozes through me until it reaches a toe-curling height. At the exact moment the toes do curl, a bolt of pain shoots up my leg.

"Ee-yah!" I scream, jacknifing over to grab my foot which has cramped into a rigid spearpoint of agony.

"Jesus Christ, Trudy!" Sinclair yells, scrambling to move with me. "You're going to fucking snap it off!"

"Ah! Ah! Ah!! Ah!!!" My staccato cries pick up in volume and stridency when I can't reach my seized-up foot. Sinclair disengages with an audible pop and jumps around to the afflicted area.

"Christ, Trudy, what is it?" He hovers above me, searching. "Scorpion? Fire ant?"

"My foot's cramped up!"

Sinclair springs off the bed, kneels beside it, and grabs the flexed appendage. He presses it back up and tells me, "Push against my hand."

I can't stop yelling, "Ah! Ah! Ah!"

"Come on, push!" Sinclair orders.

I do and the spasm begins to subside. Sinclair digs his thumbs into the ball of my foot, releasing the knotted muscle. He massages my foot and calf, then switches to the other one. The feeling of a well-executed foot rub compares very favorably with actual penetration. I sink deeper and deeper into the bed. Sinclair is doing sublime things to my calf muscle when he asks in a studiedly casual tone, "What are you going to name the little polliwog? Sinclair?" he teases. "Sinclair if it's a boy and Derek if it's a girl?"

I pull my leg out of his hand and scold lightly, "Sinclair."

"Let me guess. You want something along the lines of Guinevere and Lancelot, Tristan and Isolde. Those would be your sorts of names. Fantastical, enchanted names. But what of Derek? He's probably in favor of Jason and Heather or whatever the latest version of good, solid American names are. There are conflicts, Trude, aren't there?"

"What marriage doesn't have conflicts?" It is a wise and true question, as it should be, given all I've read on the subject in *Woman's Day* and *Family Circle* magazines.

Sinclair snakes back up onto the bed and nuzzles his head against my stomach. "Hello in there, Baby Heather. Watch out, your paragon of a dad will have you barbecuing before you can tie your shoes."

He kisses my stomach, my breasts, then sits, cross-legged, and tries to lift me up to him. "You're so substantial, Trude. You could keep this can I'm living in anchored in a hurricane, couldn't you?" He squeezes me. "I can't believe it. You have a home. A family. This is what it takes. This." He spreads his fingers across my belly. "This weight. Without this weight, this ballast, a man is lost at sea. Most men anyway. I'm sure Derek, that model of rectitude, would have found his way regardless."

He leans over me and kisses my neck, my cheeks. "Did you see that PBS program about termites? There's this immense, luminously pale, dough wad of a queen, tucked away in the heart of the colony, doing nothing but squirting out eggs. Then there're all these tiny crumbs of workers scurrying about, servicing her majesty."

"Whatever could have brought that to your mind?" I ask as we both stare at my immense, luminously pale, dough wad of a stomach. "The termite queen," I say, running my hands over the egg-production center. It makes me laugh. Laughing feels as good as the foot massage, as good as Sinclair inside me. I try to remember the last time I laughed.

"There's helium in your laugh, Trudy. A man could inflate many a dream on that sound. Does Derek know how lucky he is?"

"I . . . we shouldn't talk about that."

"No, of course not. I had my chance. Like every other treasure the gods handed me, I tossed it aside." Sinclair enjoys a moment of melancholic self-pity. "Does Derek know a treasure? Should I write him a note?"

"I'd better get home."

"And just where does Derek think you are? La Leche

League meeting? Little get-together to meet the other obs in your doctor's group practice?"

"Membership committee meeting of the Argyle Club." I drag out the name of the Alamo City's toniest social club.

"No! You married a man who'd belong to the Argyle Club?" Sinclair hoots in derision, then shakes his head sadly. "Trudy, Trudy, Trudy, the passage of a little time couldn't have changed you *that* much. Tell me it isn't so. Tell me you're not *really* a clubwoman."

I grace him with a small smile that makes us conspirators against the Argyle Club, a group that Sinclair would secretly give his life to be asked to join but would give his immortal soul to turn down and sneer at. I've just presented him with that gift.

"Leave it all, Trude," he whispers in my ear. "Leave it all and come to the forest to be my Gypsy bride."

I turn to look at him and he closes his eyes, grins, and rolls onto his back, letting me know that he is drunk and can't be held accountable for anything he says. His breathing slows and gets heavier. I think he has fallen asleep until he asks: "Remember the way you used to wrap your legs around my waist and we'd go jigging about the apartment? Where was that apartment?"

"Laurel. West Laurel. The Maryland Apartments. Number Nine."

"The Maryland on Laurel. That was it. The Laurel Theater next door. Remember how we'd sneak in? Spend the entire day there sucking up the air conditioning?" He bounces up to a sitting position. "Hey, let's go sneak in right now! Come on!"

"They tore the Laurel down over five years ago."

"Tore the Laurel down? I didn't know that. Of course, I

don't go that far north in the city very much. Surprised you'd have kept up with the old neighborhood like that. A few trips down memory lane, eh? That it? You cruising memory lane in Derek's Beaver?"

I have started to hate this Derek person.

"What am I to you, Mrs. Derek?" Sinclair whispers in my ear. "A momentary diversion? A thrill from the wrong side of the river?"

"Sinclair, we both live on the same side of the river."

"Allegorically, Trude. Allegorically. You went ashore. I never thought you'd go ashore. We are river people, Trudy, you and I." Mixed in with the drunken self-pity is a genuine note of betrayal. "River people never go ashore and mix with the bank people. Not permanently. Not genetically. You're going to end up having a little amphibian."

Having a baby is the biggest betrayal a river person could commit.

"I'd better go, Sinclair. Thanks for the plants. Sorry I can't keep them." I start to stand and Sinclair grabs me.

"Don't go," he pleads, and I know he means it. With sudden clarity it hits me: he is lonely. "What is Derek going to say? Really. You can't tell him you and the La Leche ladies were up until four in the morning expressing milk."

"You know an awful lot about having babies."

"Ah, well, you know, lactation, that was one part of motherhood Esmie could handle. Didn't care for much else about it. Raised little Charlie like a spider monkey. Didn't believe in shackling his individuality with niceties like school or toothbrushes. He was as close to a savage as it is possible to raise on this county's interstate highway system."

Sinclair smiles at the memory. "He was a bright little boy though. First word out of the kid's mouth was 'dah!'

Took him almost another year to get around to 'ma-ma.' Drove Esmie bats since she was going off men in general and me in particular around this time. Charlie. Be six years old in August." He swats away the thought and turns to me. "Trudy, what are we doing here?"

An even bigger violation of the river-person credo than having a baby is defining the exact nature of a relationship. I am stunned to hear Sinclair attempt to do exactly that. Stunned and exulted.

"You'll have to tell *me*, Sinclair," I answer, realizing at that moment how true that is. There is nothing more I can do. If anything is going to happen, Sinclair must be the one to make it happen. I stand. "I'd better go home." The cheap aluminum front doorknob is turning in my hand before I remember that I have no means of transport. I turn around. Sinclair is behind me.

"Can you give me a ride home?"

"How did you get out here?"

"I got a ride with the maid." I hate it when the truth is so vastly more dishonest than any lie.

"That sounds a bit dangerous," Sinclair teases. "Dicing with discovery. Maybe you want Derek to find out."

"Maybe I do," I answer wearily. I am sick of "Derek." "Will you give me a ride home?"

Outside, the land is quiet and as cool as it will get, waiting for the sun to come up. The dogs start to bark.

"Put a lid on it!" Sinclair yells in the voice I'd expected to hear earlier. He helps me into the truck. *"Wátchale, mamacita."*

We are silent on the long ride back to King William, each of us lost in thoughts we can't put into words. Sweet Pea swims within me, more agitated than he has ever been before. I am sorry for whatever stress chemicals I have stirred into his liquid world.

When we reach the Schier mansion, Sinclair drives on past it, down to the end of the street, where it dead-ends in front of Ernst Altgelt's flour mill. The mill with its tower on top looks like a fairy castle in the bluish light before dawn. Sinclair pulls the truck onto the bridge crossing the river and switches off the ignition. The water glints below us. The jaunty, fake Irish look is gone from his expression when he faces me.

I can't say anything. All the words now must be Sinclair's. But there are no more. In his confusion he grabs me for a sloppy kiss that makes me think of how the males in an elephant herd will try to mate with a sick female. To cheer her up. To keep her with the herd. A person does not do only what he has to do, but what he knows to do.

Then I stop thinking of sick elephants or anything else and Sinclair's kiss is the kiss I wanted to get all those years ago outside of Agua Caliente.

Once his mind is made up, my enormous stomach is no longer an obstacle to Sinclair. With one hand he feels between my legs, with the other he rips open the fly of his jeans and pulls himself out. We are both ready. On the seat of his old truck we fit together smoothly. When he is inside me, he asks, "We should be together, shouldn't we, Trudy? Don't we belong together?"

I can't answer. I have said and done all that I can. All the words from now on must be Sinclair's. We make love like teenagers, though, joining together as effortlessly as two people can.

The sun is starting to come up when I open the truck door and slide down onto the bridge.

"Trudy," he calls to me before I can close the door. "Will we be together again?"

I close the door and walk back to the house. Sinclair will have to answer that question. He is still parked on the bridge when I turn at the door before going in.

Upstairs, I lay beneath the canopy and listen for the sound of Sinclair's truck starting in the distance. For all the months since the sonogram, I've forced myself to stop thinking about Sweet Pea, to make a blank in my mind where his future is. But, without my permission, the empty space fills in. I see a little guy in diapers playing in an enchanted forest of lacy plants. I see myself sewing a tiny Harlequin costume with bells stitched onto the turned-up toes for Sweet Pea to wear as he goes about drumming up face-painting business for his father at a Renaissance fair.

I allow myself to hope. I know Sinclair. I know that he covets me, that right now I am a prize to be taken from another, a better man. But I also know that he loved me. He loved me then and he is starting to love me now. At the right time he will claim me even if there isn't a line in front of my booth. Me and the baby we were meant to have ten years ago. I can feel it. But he must come to me, he must claim me. He has to do at least that much. I know he will. I know it because Riverfest is coming.

The only person I've ever known who loved Riverfest as much as me is Sinclair. The year we went together, he wanted to stay out even later than me, his feet never hurt, and he could always find a Portosan.

New Orleans has Mardi Gras. San Antonio has Riverfest. The only difference is that San Antonio doesn't have to share her party with the world. But I'm biased. I love Riverfest. If I had my way, Riverfest would be the normal way of life and once a year there would be a break for a week or so when people *didn't* wear costumes, eat corn on the cob in the street, drink Big Gulps spiked with rum, and wander the plaza cracking eggshells filled with confetti, *cascarónes,* over strangers' heads.

Riverfest implies amnesty, a time for cleaning the coins out of the fountain and granting a few wishes. It tends to be the focus of my life. Under normal circumstances I would have spent the past eight and a half months getting a costume ready for the Rey Antonio Costume Contest. I'm sorry I don't have anything to wear this year. This year is special. Not only is it the one hundredth celebration of Riverfest, it is the three hundredth birthday of San Antonio. Surely on the one hundredth Riverfest of all time, I'll get just one wish granted.

I am falling asleep by the time I hear Sinclair start up his truck and drive away.

19. Long before dawn on the first day of June, with less than a week to go before San Antonio's three hundredth birthday, I awake to find that the sledgehammer of an Alamo City summer has landed, and even though I have lived for twenty years without air-conditioning, and even though Hillary keeps her thermostat set at sixty-five, I swelter. The Laura Ashley sheets are limp rags beneath my steaming body. It has been three days since Sinclair dropped me off. A hormonal heaviness presses down on me with a weight that settles around my eyes and temples and pushes me into a dangerous state of glower. And, of course, I have to pee.

I accomplish this, then watch at the window until the sun is fully up. Exhausted, I go back to bed and sleep on sheets that now feel cool and crisp. I wake twelve hours later, unable to figure out why there is a ruffly cloud of material floating over my head. Gradually I remember that I am in my ninth month of pregnancy and the hormonal glower returns.

The glower is made worse by the hum of activity outside. King William has its own miniature Riverfest every year, the King William Fair. This year it is scheduled for the second day of the real Riverfest, eight days away. The street is already lined with half-constructed booths. Orange extension cords snake everywhere and the sound of power saws rips the air. Committeewomen with lists on clipboards march about, directing men wearing tool belts.

Then, over the hammering and sawing, I hear the unmistakable belch of an old International Harvester truck backfiring and I bounce out of bed, my heart cartwheeling with joy. I run to the streetside window and there is Sinclair cruising past. On the side of the truck he has painted, "River Tours. Call the River Man." He circles for an hour, passing in front of the house twenty-nine times.

"The mystery man?" Mercedes asks, coming up behind me with a stack of clean sheets in her hand.

I nod and keep staring out the window.

An hour later Mercedes comes back and I am still standing in front of the window. Though there is no one else in the house, she slides up next to me and says under her breath, "Be ready at five. We'll take you out, if you wanna go."

I crave Sinclair and am ready to hop into the LeMans, but I can't. He has to come for me. For *us* or nothing will work. "I can't."

"Playing hard to get, huh?" Mercedes nudges me knowingly with the sheets. "That's the way I did with Arnufio. Drove him crazy with love. He was begging me for it. It was pitiful. But I just done like this." She holds out her hand and extends a chubby brown ring finger. "I told him I had to see some gold there before he was getting *any*thing off me." She nods and heads off, tossing back over her shoulder. "You're smart, *gabacha.*"

Smart. Sweet Pea karates a swift kick to my lower left rib to let me know how "smart" he thinks I am. I have to agree. Almost forty years of age, nine months pregnant, mooning over a man living in a trailer. Very cagey indeed. I put my hands on my stomach. It is squirming around like a sackful of cats. I have been still too long. Sweet Pea likes motion. I tread heavily up and down the hall, my bare feet rubbed by the rough weave of the antique Moroccan rug. But my belly keeps oscillating. I know that Sweet Pea is telling me that he doesn't believe Sinclair will come for us.

But Sinclair does come. For the next three days he circles the block more often than the weekend tour buses. He announces his presence with a loud backfire. On the fourth day he parks in front of the flour mill and gets out. He is wearing khaki shorts and a Hawaiian shirt, a floppy tennis hat, tube socks with a stripe around the top, and gray running shoes. A tripod is tucked under his arm. He marches up to the Goettlers' house and pantomimes a seizure of artistic inspiration. Hurrying as if to capture that inspiration, he screws the camera onto the tripod and sets up the whole assemblage on the sidewalk across the street. For the next hour he studies every window of the house through the camera's telephoto lens.

I feel his eyes on me and ache to feel his hands. I flush a sweaty red from the heat, from the extra blood circulating in my body, from thinking of Sinclair. Mercedes comes up behind me and clucks loudly. "This ain't going to end good. I can feel it."

Her words are a curse, but they don't stop the heat or the hope.

The next day Sinclair comes again, riding a ten-speed bike, wearing a long-sleeved white shirt with dark suit pants, and carrying a Bible. I ache to go to him, my Mormon missionary lover. Each succeeding day he appears in a different guise. He is my itinerant gardener lover pushing a lawn mower down the street. Then my insurance claims man lover taking pictures of hail damage on a roof with a Polaroid camera. In between times he circles the block in his truck. I think he goes unnoticed in the general clamor, but that evening Hillary proves me wrong.

"We've got to do something about that maniac in the derelict truck" is how she greets Victor when he gets home from work Friday evening.

"TGIF to you too." Victor throws down his briefcase.

"I mean," Hillary goes on, "I have enough to contend with just getting everything organized for the party. God, Riverfest *starts* tomorrow. Then there's the fair Sunday. And one week, *one week* from that is the party. One week, Victor. It's impossible."

Apparently it's a big Goettler family tradition to have a giant party at the end of Riverfest. Hillary has been in a state of near hysterics about it for weeks.

"You've seen him," Hillary says. "He's out there at all hours of the day and night. Wearing disguises. Disguising that truck. I mean, this is not normal. He cruised by the other day with a cardboard pizza delivery sign taped, *taped* to the door. Yes, I'm sure Domino's is using old, broken-down *trucks* to deliver pizza. Victor, I've got enough to worry about. I think the band is trying to back out. The chef wants first class tickets from New Orleans. They don't even *have* first class on Southwest."

I can't hear Victor's answer.

"I just don't know how many more Riverfests I can endure."

Hillary's hatred of Riverfest, a hatred shared by most well-off people I've ever heard discuss the subject, bewilders me. I can't understand turning a party into an ordeal. From the looks of the preparations her neighbors are making, however, it doesn't appear that everyone in her circle shares her opinion. All through the evening and into the night Friday, the neighborhood bustles preparing for the King William Fair Sunday.

I am too keyed up to sleep that night. Then, as excited as I am, the prego hormones sneak up and knock me flat into a tarry pit of slumber that holds me fast until the sounds of Victor and Hillary leaving for their usual Saturday morning brunch at El Mirador wakes me up. Once I'm sure they've left, I get up. All three of us try to avoid one another as much as possible.

Downstairs, Mercedes is already hunkered down in front of the small television clamped onto the bottom of a cabinet, watching the official kick-off event of Riverfest, the Fountain of Flowers parade.

"Oh, God, has it started?" I rush to the set.

"Not the parade, all the other stuff."

I pull up a stool next to her in time to witness the fabulous centennial excesses. Thirty-two thousand marchers, says the announcer, most of them sweating in high-collared band uniforms, have assembled. A skywriting group has spelled out "Riverfest 100" in the sky over the parade route. At the moment the parade starts, ten *cascarón*-shaped balloons, each one thirty-five feet high, release thousands of smaller balloons into a cloudless sky while a twenty-man skydiving team leaps into the bobbing flock of balloons spelling out "one hundred." All over the city, the announcer assures us, hot-air balloonists are ascending.

"Now, *that* would have been worth sitting in the sun and sweating for," Mercedes says as the sky divers touch down. I have to agree. Mercedes didn't have the choice, though, as Hillary has conscripted her to come in today and work extra on party preparations. There is a lot of Goettler silver to be polished before next Saturday.

A close-up of this year's Rey Antonio, the king of Riverfest who reigns over the ten days of abandon, appears on the small TV screen leading the Fountain of Flowers parade. As always, Rey Antonio looks like a leader of a Third World country in sunglasses and a white uniform jacket adorned with gold braid. Spectators eddy around his convertible limo, diving for the specially minted gold-colored coins he tosses into the air. Right behind him is Brackenridge High School's Mighty Eagle Band pumping out "Land of a Thousand Dances." When the television camera moves in for a close-up of a girl flute player, you can see sweat streaming down her face onto the collar of her heavy white and purple wool uniform.

"Nah, nah, nah, nah," Mercedes sings along, as the rows of sweating teenagers pass by the camera.

A float that is a flatbed-sized wedding cake trimmed with a beautiful Texas blonde in a vaguely sari-like gown burps and heaves into view. The train of her gown is larger than a living room rug and depicts a jewel-green peacock preening itself on a field of yellow flowers. The announcer tells us that the blonde is the Maharini of Consummate Artistry and that she is, "of the house of Bradshaw." Maharini Bradshaw waves her hand in the prescribed window-washing figure eight and smiles as if she actually enjoyed riding on the back of a flatbed truck wearing a couple hundred pounds of yellow rug in ninety-degree weather. It's not my kind of costume, but I have to admire the execution.

"You think she bleaches her hair?" Mercedes asks. We study the screen, but the maharini rumbles out of sight before a definitive call can be made.

"What'd they say she was? Maharini of what'd he call it?"

"Consummate Artistry," I answer.

"What's that supposed to mean?"

I shrug. The names of the themes that the Riverfest princesses design their gowns and floats around are works of art in themselves that I have learned over the years not to question. I recall a Queen Empress of the Court of Eternal India, a Maharini of the Vision of Paradise and Golden Oriole, a Maharini of Persian-Inspired Gardens, a Maharini of Himalayan Wildflowers, a Maharini of Revered Artistry, a

Maharini of the Hymn to the Universe, a Maharini of the Splendor Add to Splendor, and a Maharini of Marbled Filigree. A lot of people think that the themes are stupid. A lot of people think most poetry is stupid unless it is bound in leather and tucked away on some library shelf, and even then they're not too sure.

After the parade I go back upstairs and watch the street below as the finishing touches are applied to booths. Mostly, though, I wait. I wait for the waiting to end. Riverfest has begun.

The next morning, Sunday, Hillary invites me down to join them on the front lawn and watch the neighborhood parade that opens the King William Fair.

"Not too warm?" she asks me as we settle into our lawn chairs atop the viewing platform they'd had constructed so that we could sit and still see over the heads of the crowds on the other side of the fence.

"No, I'm fine."

"Something to drink?"

"Just had something before I came out."

"Great. That sun too much on you?" Hillary jumps up and adjusts the beach umbrella over our heads until most of its shade is cast on me, leaving Victor and their guests baking in the sun. Victor shoots Hillary a look and she sits down. It feels very strange to be on the grassy side of the fence instead of out on the street with the crowd.

It is easy to tell the outsiders from the neighborhood residents in their weekend outfits of khaki and madras, the women highlighting their khaki skirts with brightly colored woven sashes. Simpson T-shirts and neon-colored surf wear are more popular with the former group. Also, the King

Williamites all keep their hands in their pockets more than chronic masturbators.

"Oh, look, here they come," someone shouts out.

A fife and drum corps in Revolutionary red coats marches into view, tootling and tapping out "Yankee Doodle." I lean forward in my seat. An El Camino follows with a banner across the hood announcing "The King of King William Fair." In the back of the truck is a man in khaki pants and madras shirt. He is tossing corn chips instead of coins into the crowd. The next member of the "court" of King William is a young woman standing up in the back of an open Jeep. Her banner reads "Maharini of Unceasing Sanitation, Ethel of the House of Mertz." She is draped in Hefty bags with a train that twines out behind her.

Hillary's guests call out to the woman, who recognizes them and does a simpering imitation of the figure eight wave of the real princesses. Behind her is another "Maharini" draped in wallpaper. I don't care to stay and read her banner.

"I think I'm going to wander," I tell Hillary. I have to use both hands to lever my bulk up out of the lawn chair.

"Are you sure you . . ." Hillary starts, but Victor puts his hand on her forearm and she stops. "Watch the sun," she calls out after me as I make my way over to the booths.

Eating from booths is one of my favorite Riverfest pastimes. I typically drift from gorditas to funnel cake to corn dogs. Suddenly, my taste buds start beating out an all-points bulletin for a corn dog.

The first booth I come to is sponsored by the Lutheran General Hospital and offers a free cholesterol screening. This is not a good sign. All around me are attractive white people enjoying family fun. They carry their small children in backpacks and stop at booths that sell monograms and give away information on recycling.

The food booths all seem to have been stocked by Eat for Your Life. There are booths selling Red Zinger iced tea, gazpacho, fruit kabobs, tabouli, tofu fajitas, sorbet, and potato skins. There is even a booth selling nothing but spritzes of Evian water to the overheated. It is a diabolical plot to thwart my craving for grease and meat by-products. There is not a corn dog to be had. I drag myself back to the Goettlers and slip in the back way. The King William Fair is a big gyp, but there is still a whole week more of real Riverfest. A whole week of the biggest Riverfest ever. I go to my window to watch and wait.

"Did you hear about the . . . those . . . you know, those three people?"

I eavesdrop on a conversation between several of the college children in the Tuesday evening Birth Right! class.

"I have a friend who works over at Presbyterian. They came in night before last."

"I thought they were planning on a home birth."

"Well, they were, but the mother freaked out. Made them take her to the hospital. She couldn't handle it. My friend says she was screaming for drugs from the moment she came in. The father goes, 'Release your negativity about the birth experience. Imagine that your cervix is a flower blossom gently opening.' Then she bit him."

"She bit him?"

"On the forearm. Exposed the bone. He passed out, the mother's still screaming for drugs. The nurse comes in with the Demerol, sees Dad on the floor, puts the pills down and the other one, the other woman, steals them."

"Weird."

There is much less gloating than you might expect. A part of all of us wanted to believe that birth might, just conceivably might, be the ultimate orgasm.

Around six Wednesday evening Mercedes calls to tell me that my Styrofoam-boxed delight has arrived. I am pleased to discover that it is the best of the lot—low-salt whole wheat "pizza" festooned with eggplant and red peppers. I pull the white box over to my kitchen listening post and monitor that evening's dinnertime conversation between Hillary and Victor as I wolf down the pizza. Cultivating hopes for the future has given me an appetite.

"I'm not the one who insisted on having this party," Victor says.

"The Extravaganza is a Schier mansion tradition dating back to the twenties." Hillary is on edge.

"What do you want me to do? Without going into my many grievous character flaws, just tell me what you want me to do."

"If you'd just talk to the band. Tell them I'm truly sorry about the death of the bass player's father, but that we've planned everything around a Cajun theme. We're doing a whole bayou-swamp motif with the alligators and the moss. We've got the crawfish, the Dixie beer. We have a chef coming in to do his world-famous mudbug étouffé. They can't cancel. Please, there will be a lifetime to grieve after the party."

"Okay, I'll tell them to put the lamentations on hold."

"Victor." Hillary chides him for chiding her.

"No, no, I think your request is legitimate. We have a contract. Have you invited—"

The pause. Their stand-in for my name.

"I don't think it's the sort of thing someone in their ninth month of pregnancy would be interested in, do you?"

"Well, just as long as she's invited," Victor says, closing the discussion. I am pleased by his ultimatum. I want to come to the party, any party.

All that week teams of carpenters work to construct a dance floor and several bayou shanties. Working along with them are designers from the museum and crews of laborers who drape the yard in Spanish moss and arrange stuffed alligators and blue herons in strategic locales. When the carpenters finish with the dance floor, they create a crude "gumbo stand" for the chef to cook in.

And every day Sinclair appears, a tool belt tugging down his jeans as he mingles with the carpenters, a tank top showing off his estimable shoulders as he trails Spanish moss about with the landscapers. Unfortunately, Hillary has taken the week off to supervise, so I can't appear and give Sinclair his opportunity to beg for me. For us. But I don't mind. The finale is coming; Sinclair's sense of drama will demand it.

I love the idea of a party in a swamp. For me, it fits the mood of Riverfest perfectly, dark and funky, sweaty and full of the danger and the magic of the night. By Friday the promise that Riverfest always holds out has captured me. I am so certain that Sinclair is coming that I forget everything and begin to plan an impromptu costume for an evening of swamp party fun. I think about smearing myself with a mixture of cocoa powder and cold cream and going as a fertility symbol. Then I decide on a sort of swamp goddess motif. I go to sleep dreaming about ratting my hair out into a bushy nest and twining flowers into it.

On Saturday morning the chef arrives early from New Orleans with five helpers all carrying enormous cast-iron skillets and kettles. As the day progresses, the backyard fills with long tables covered with pressed and hemmed pieces of burlap and centerpieces made from pussy willows and twisted chunks of mangrove root.

I spend my time experimenting with makeup and wafting fluttery bits of fabric about myself. Once my hair is done, I step back and notice something that had escaped my attention during the long months of funk: I am beautiful. I have a glow on me like a saint on a pillar. My wispy hair has a glossy authority and knows to curl about my flushed face in fetching ways. My face has overflowed its usual bony borders into a smudged and serene fullness. I am ready for Sinclair. I am ready for a party.

But Hillary never gets around to inviting me to her bash. By that evening when Hillary appears, her hair blown into a wind-tossed mane with flowers twisted into it, diaphanous bits of fabric wafting about her in a spectacular swamp goddess costume, it is clear that she has read my mind, stolen my costume idea, just as she has appropriated all the other bits and pieces of my mental state over the past months, and now she is not even going to invite me to her party.

My hormones are stirred into full glower by the exclusion. By the time the guests begin to arrive, my chest sizzles with heartburn and the space behind my eyes throbs with a hormonal headache as I watch men in coonskin caps carrying Kentucky long rifles romp into the yard, where they are met by women dressed as riverboat floozies and men decked out as gamblers. Cardsharps, trappers, strumpets abound. There is even a Huck Finn in a straw hat. For one night the drivers of Volvos, the checkers of collateral, the owners of leather couches, have all transformed themselves into river people, and I am stuck on the bank.

I see then that I have waited too long. Sinclair has not persevered. I will watch forever from a window. Except that I don't have forever. I touch my stomach. I have two more weeks. Probably more. Everyone says first babies are always late.

Smoke curls out of the chef's gumbo shack. The chef, ladling étouffé onto china plates, is a patchwork of blinding whites, starched toque, toothy grin, napkin tied around his thick neck. Piles of red crawfish are heaped on the table next to baskets of crackers and bottles of Tabasco sauce. The band starts to play "Louisiana Man," "Muskrat hides hanging by the dozens . . ." Because this is Riverfest, guests crowd onto the floor from the first notes to hop about with a boisterousness that comes only once a year.

At the center of the rollicking crowd Hillary floats like a bit of cottonwood floss twirling serenely through a high wind. She beams up at Victor, radiantly sure that hers will be proclaimed the best party of Riverfest. She has lived up to, exceeded even, the Schier mansion once again. Victor kisses her cheek. I go to the bathroom and throw up. Supremely irritated, I am starting to wipe away my makeup when the whine of the fiddle calls me back to the window.

The frolicking crowd breaks into pairs that sweep around the floor as the singer begins "The Jolie Blonde Waltz." As the fiddler saws swooping laments from his instrument, I hug Sweet Pea and let the tears leak. Which is why my first glimpse of a certain Mississippi freebooter is somewhat misty. At least, I take him for some sort of seventeenth-century pirate in his white buccaneer shirt and leather jerkin. It is only when I am able to make out the very curious puffy diaper-looking breeches and tights that I place the period more accurately: Renaissance.

"Sinclair," I breathe. I stop myself for one second to weigh the strategic implications of my next move, then hurtle down the stairs. Sinclair has come for me. I knew he would.

The night is dark and muggy with a viscous pheromonal funk hanging in the air that makes everyone eighteen again. Eighteen and ready for life to start.

I sneak up behind him and bump him with my stomach. "Buy me a corn dog."

Sinclair turns, and a slow smile spreads across his face. "Trudy. You've come. Great party. Trudy." He looks around, for "Derek," I suppose, then puts his hands on my shoulders. He slides them to my face. I know that feeling of wanting to suck a person in through the palms of your hands, wanting to touch them until you fuse together. I am overjoyed that Sinclair has that feeling in his palms.

"Buy me a corn dog," I repeat.

Sinclair swashes all his buckles. " 'Twould be my distinct and immense pleasure."

"Come on, let's get out of here."

"Derek?" Sinclair asks, his dark eyebrows twitching the question as he searches the coonskinned crowd for the man he has bested.

"Derek be hanged." I give the verdict the saucy fillip of a wife throwing it all away.

"Trudy."

I knew that Sinclair wanted me back, and the proof is there in the way he says my name. He takes my hand and we move out of the party lights into the darkness beyond.

20. Fajitas, candy apples, agua frescas, caramel apples, nutty buddies, raspas, fudge, picadillo tacos, guacamole tacos, tripe tacos, beer, gorditas, cotton candy, popcorn, corn on the cob the Mexican way with sour cream and chili powder, exquisitos "Hot Dogs" calientitos, but not a corn dog to be had on San Fernando Plaza.

"I don't like this," Sinclair intones ominously, gazing through the smoke from the fajita vendor's fire at the rows of booths clumped about the plaza. "My darling wants a corn dog, my darling *gets* a corn dog."

I am dazed by the heat, the crowd. By being with Sinclair. He turns and kisses me.

"We're back on the river again, you and I. The way it was meant to be."

He puts his finger under my chin and I nod up at him. Yes, we are on a river. Standing there on solid pavement, I rock and sway to currents that are running now out of my control. Nothing will ever be the same. I am terrified and exhilarated. I wish I'd at least taken a change of underwear with me. My toothbrush.

The Oasis Band, five guys in white pants, royal blue shirts, and white ties, starts playing "Never Gonna Give You Up" on the stage set up at the far end of the plaza, the end where Luby's used to be.

"Come on now," the lead singer exhorts the crowd gathering in front of the stage. "Put your hands together now." He beats and spins a tambourine. No one in the crowd claps along with him. "That's the way!" He sings about never giving this person up and finishes, "No, no, no! No, no, no! Yeah!"

Sinclair claps wildly and alone.

"All right! Thank you! Thank you very much!"

The next song is "Tell It to My Heart." Three little girls in fluffy white Communion dresses join hands and bob to the music. A beer-gutted street whack, bare-chested under a heavy overcoat, joins them, throwing his arms over his head like a fisherman casting a big net. The girls stop bobbing, mesmerized by the man's exotic motions, look at one another, and bend over to hide their grins in their poufy skirts.

A polka with more *conjunto* than Krakow in it brings the couples swarming onto the floor.

"May I have the honor?" Sinclair extends the crook of his elbow to me.

"Sinclair, it's just barely possible for a woman in my condition to lumber. Forget polkaing."

"Roll out the barrel," Sinclair sings. He grabs me around what was once my waist, and slowly spins me onto the floor. *"We'll have a barrel of fun."*

"Sinclair, no, I *am* a barrel."

"Boom tah ter rah rah." His song is low and insistent next to my ear. *"We've got the blues on the run."* The slow spin graduates to a gentle twirl that I actually have to hop to keep pace with and, though, I'm still fighting it, "The pregnant lady polkas!" Sinclair crows.

The street whack stops, weaving for a few seconds before he catches his balance. He grins a boozy, toothless grin at me, pushes the sleeves of his overcoat up past his wrists, and claps at my clodhopping efforts.

I try a few more tentative hops. One, two, *hop.* One, two, *hop.* Perhaps because Sinclair is holding me so tightly, I feel all of a piece again. The mound doesn't keep undulating as it usually does like a sprung-off diving board long after the initial movement. Together Sinclair and I do make a big, rolling barrel. I put a bit more oompah into the hop. Sinclair holds me tight, riding out the crash of the tidal wave of my body against his. Gravity has lost its hold on me. For the first time in far too long, my heart is not a stone weighing me down. We surge upward. We make a snug, jolly unit, the three of us, dancing together.

The dance area is too small to contain the cavorting excesses of our reunion. Sinclair detours off the crowded floor and onto the plaza. His ponytail lofts and falls as he swings me past a black man in a wig of silver tinsel selling huge inflatable crayons and red and yellow rabbits feet. The Exquisito's Hot Dog Calientitos vendor with his apron proclaiming "The Diet Stops Here" blurs past me. The customers lined up in front of Alejandro's Gorditas clear out of our way as we whirl past.

Little boys set off bottle rockets that screech into the air and explode over our head. A shower of silver sparks rains down on us, and the ruffle-shirted lead singer of the Oasis Band announces that Sinclair and I have won that round of the dance contest and to "stick around" for the finals. There is clapping, but before I can graciously acknowledge the cheers of the crowd, Sinclair twirls me into a patch of darkness at the side of the cathedral, where he collapses, panting, against the 240-year-old limestone wall. He pulls me even closer and buries his face in my neck.

"You smell like Trudy now. I had to get you breathing hard, had to get Derek out of your pores. Now you smell like Trudy."

"What does Trudy smell like?" I ask, my face buried in his neck.

"An earth angel. A twinkling, gossamer sprite who sweats like a washerwoman. You smell like the middle of the enchanted forest where all the pixies and nymphs go to shit. Kiss me full on the lips, Nymph Shit."

I don't have much experience in congratulating myself, so I enjoy the novelty as much as the congratulations.

Though both less than the kiss. Even before our mouths have taken leave of each other, Sinclair is pulling me out of the shadows back to the brightly lit vendor area.

"Stay here," he tells me, turning me around so that I face a limestone wall. "And no peeking."

I am studying the square, lighter than the surrounding stone and set off at its four corners by bolt holes, where the sign for Luby's cafeteria used to be, when a mane of colored ribbons brushes against my neck. Sinclair digs the comb holding the crown of ribbons into my hair.

"There," he says, turning me to look at him. "The Maharini of Nymph Shit." He takes my hand and we drift through the crowds between the plaza and El Mercado. Carnival rides are set up in between: the Kamikaze, Tilt-a-Whirl, Fun Slide, the 4X4. The lights seem to shine more brightly as it gets later.

Ahead of us is a Chicano couple holding hands. He is wearing a black denim jacket with a grinning skull and the name of the heavy metal band, Anthrax, written below it. His girlfriend's long hair, bleached orange, brushes her thighs. Gang boys in bandannas throw balls at weighted bowling pins trying to win giant stuffed teddy bears and gorillas. A jowly man with a gut that almost hides his tin belt buckle passes by wearing a T-shirt that promises "Instant Sex: Just Add Alcohol." His wife follows in plastic thongs and a pink maternity dress with a little girl bow tied in back. A pair of cops lean against the yellow star painted on the side of their blue and white cruiser.

"Top of the evening to you, Officers," Sinclair says as we pass them.

"Hey!" One of the policemen yells after us. I freeze, wondering how much he knows, if he has the power to make me go back to King William. "Your wife is losing her dealy-bopper there."

I touch my head, but Sinclair is already disentangling the ribbon crown from the few strands of hair it was hanging on by. He anchors it again, calls cheery thanks to the cop, and puts his arm around me in a protective, husbandly way. Obviously pregnant and apparently married, I glow within the halo of approval that shines about me.

We slip in with the stream of humanity flowing down Commerce Street, back past the cathedral, past Solo-Serve, past La Cocinita Pik-Nik, down to the river.

As we get closer to Paseo del Rio, more and more costumed revelers join us. In front of me is a tall, thin woman in green tights and leotard. She wears a Medusa headdress with dozens of snakes twining out. Beside her is a Quasimodo, misshapen eye and mouth drooling below the hump rising off his neck. A covey of schoolchildren, all in the same dime-store skeleton costume tied at the back of the neck, runs past. La Llorona, the weeping ghost mother of Mexican legend, also passes us, her face a death mask, a wild white wig flowing out behind her. Dracula, Frankenstein, a giant cockroach, all pass us by. In fact, everyone is passing us. Sinclair, trying to walk as slowly as he can, looks back. We have almost reached Schilo's.

"Is this too much for you? You'll have to tell me. I need reminding. Maybe you've had enough for one night."

"No!" I can never have enough of this night. I try to hurry, but the message is lost somewhere between my brain and my pelvis. It is impossible to hurry with a bowling ball lodged between your legs. An odd electrical sensation shoots down from my crotch along the inside of my left leg. I duck into the doorway at Schilo's until it passes.

"Trudy?" Sinclair asks, putting the back of his hand to my flushed face.

"No." I push off from the delicatessen door. I have to make it to the river. At the stone stairway leading from the street down to the riverwalk, I cling to the railing and the crowd closes in on me. With no effort on my part, it sweeps me up and delivers me to the water's edge.

Torches planted along the concrete banks burn twice, casting wobbling reflections in the dark water. Fairy lights twinkle from the branches of the tall cypresses. The patios of the restaurants lining the river are wreathed in colored Christmas lights, red, green, blue. I see a short couple dressed as leprechauns. There is a Guinevere in a high, pointed cap trailing chiffon. I am surrounded by wonderful costumes, but I know that if no one remembered it from last year, my hand would win again. No one else is doing body parts and, much as I personally love the fantastical, the gruesome will win every year at the Rey Antonio Costume Contest. The crowd demands it. I don't even consider the Swamp Goddess scraps to be a real effort.

In the tumult, Sinclair passes me. I sneak up behind him and break a *cascarón* over his head. Instead of confetti, however, the eggshell is filled with gold and silver glitter. A wisp of a wind picks the glitter up and whirls it about us for many seconds longer than gravity would seem to dictate. The glitter cloud sparkles like snow sifting down off a limb in the bright sunshine of a morning after a storm. Sinclair turns around.

"How did you get away from me?" He grips me in a bear hug and laps at my neck. "How did you ever, ever get away from me, Trudy Beth Herring?"

"You dumped me."

"Not me, Trudy, that other guy. The stupid, blind one."

"What happened to that guy?"

"Whipped, Tru. Whipped to a bloody, beaten pulp." He presses me back to bring my face into sharper focus and picks specks of gold and silver glitter off my cheeks.

"Have you always been this beautiful?"

"No, I think it's just crept up on me recently. All the extra rest and healthy food. Plus I have fifty percent more blood now."

"Ah, you're juicy as a Stonewall peach." Sinclair bends down to sip at my lips. "You'll never get away from me again."

A few diadems of glitter still float in the air behind his head. Laughing people in costumes jostle past us. We are safe from the real world in this subterranean refuge. Life is finally how I always thought it should be. The moment has come to tell Sinclair.

"We can do it," I say. "We can be together."

"Hah. And just what would our Derek think of that?"

"Sinclair, there is no Derek." I want to start getting the record straight as soon as possible. Sinclair and I don't have any time to waste in attending to the many technicalities that will accompany our new life together. The thought of technicalities and Victor's law degree worries me.

"No Derek?" Sinclair asks.

I believe he is stunned by happiness. I can't hold back another second. "I'm not married. We can be together. You and me and Sweet Pea. By the river. On the Renaissance fair circuit. Painting faces. Grafting exotic plants. There is nothing to stand in our way."

Sinclair blinks and all the noise around me, the gang boys yelling curses, the drunken frat boys yelling back, little girls squealing in mock terror, the muffled bass of the Oasis Band, car horns honking on the street above my head, it all stops. I hear nothing except Sinclair's answer. "The trailer only sleeps two. Actually only one comfortably."

I had expected to see Sinclair's face transformed as if a cloud of glitter were sparkling across it. I hadn't expected to hear niggling details about sleeping arrangements.

"You're not married?" Sinclair asks for confirmation.

There is only one word that can describe his expression, and that word is disappointment. Yes, it was true, Sinclair did want me. But only so long as he was certain he couldn't have me. Or Sweet Pea. I have misplayed my hand. Again.

It is suddenly hot. Far too hot. A drunk stumbles past, bumps into me, and sloshes half a cup of beer down my back. The wafty bits of fabric of my swamp goddess costume are plastered to my body with a sticky film.

"Fuck you, asshole!" I scream at him.

He turns a belligerent, slurred face toward me. I hope he says something, but he sees my mound of maternal holiness and turns sheepishly away. Since he is Chicano, I yell, *"Hijo de la chingada-joto-chingadero-maricón!"* But I can no longer hear my voice. The noise has come back, and it is too loud. The riverbanks fill up with noise that rises around me in a screeching, babbling tide. I see Sinclair's mouth open but can no longer hear the words coming out. It doesn't matter anyway. I saw his handsome face go slack with unhappy shock. Nothing matters after that.

All the benign fantastical creatures are gone. Skeletons and vampires, ghouls and hags, serial killers and Nazis dance around me now. I can't imagine why I ever liked descending every year into this horror show. I have to get out. I have made a terrible, terrible mistake. The worst mistake of the many I have made in my life. I try to leave, but am trapped, wedged in on all sides by the mob. Sinclair reaches out to take my hand, but I can no longer feel his touch.

The tide of noise continues to rise. When it reaches my lips, I know I will die. I am already having trouble breathing. The crowd closes in on me. My mistakes close in on me. The silly illusions that bolstered my life close in on me. They crush and crush against me. The pressure and noise become unendurable. I look up and notice for the first time that the moon is full. Full and pulling the tides to shore. Pulling my child from my body.

"No," I cry, but something pops within me and Sweet Pea's liquid world, warm and tinted pink, flows out onto my thighs.

"No." He can't come out. I have failed to find a good home for him.

I can no longer breathe, nor do I want to. The air is pressed from me and the fairy lights twinkling over my head smear into bright streaks across the dark sky. Just as the smears of light turn to black as well, a door opens up and I fly away through it. Unfortunately, my body must split in two to allow me to escape. It is interesting to discover that the howl filling my ears comes from my lips.

"Why's that lady screaming?"

"Hay-*sus, Madre* Santísima! She's having her baby!"

"*Ay dios, mira!* She's in labor! Somebody call somebody!"

I sink onto a bench. Sinclair sits beside me.

"Trudy, who should I call?" I block out his question. I will never let his voice touch me again. "Who's your doctor?" When I don't answer, he stands. "I'm going to get 911."

I grab his wrist. I will speak to him one last time, then never again. "No. Call the convent of Our Lady of Sorrows. Get Cece. It's only . . ." A contraction forces me to stop talking. "It's only a few blocks away. She'll come for me. Cece will come."

Sinclair leaves me in a place guarded by pain. Nothing else gets through. Not regret. Not humiliation. Not hope. Even time loses its hold on me. There is only pain.

I hear nothing until, "Trudy! Trudy, can you hear me? Trudy, it's Cece. You're not breathing, baby. Breathe! Breathe!" She turns to Sinclair. "Who are you?"

"Sinclair."

"Christ, we've got to get her out of here! How could you have brought a woman in her condition down here? What kind of a dimwit are you? Thank God, you caught me before we left for the demonstration. Jesus, we didn't even have time to get out of our costumes."

Cece is dressed in a child's skeleton costume that ties at the neck. The six Central American men with her wear similar Day of the Dead getups.

She yells at the costumed men. *"Heriberto! Javier! Mateo! Jorge! Justicio! Manuel! Levantase la señora! Ándale! Ándale!"*

The men lift me and I fly up through the air, held aloft by a dozen hands attached to six skeletons. All I see now are the moon and the branches of the tall cypress trees twinkling with fairy lights. Pain turns the lights above my head red, the moon to a blood clot. I writhe and the dozen hands bob to hold me upright and level like the springs on a giant bed. I become a bystander again. Pain horsewhips my body toward a destination that no longer concerns me. There is nothing for me to do except move out of the way.

The noise of the crowd suddenly becomes muted and far away as I burrow deep into the remote corner within myself that is the only space left where I can hide from the pain.

The men beneath me yell out, *"Abranpaso!" Esta señora está dando a luz!"*

The crowd parts. *"Pásale! Pásale!"*

I huddle down in my dark inner closet, barely breathing, not thinking anymore about all the mistakes, but still the pain finds me and drives me from my hiding place. I thought contractions would be like menstrual cramps. Cramps, that was what Rachel had promised. The pain that girdles me is to cramps what a hangnail is to a hanging. It owns me. It colonizes my body and makes me a slave state.

It scares me to see nothing, to see only blackness interrupted with bursts of light. I am slipping away to a place I will never return from. I have no words to call out for help with, to bring someone to my aid so I scream.

Cece yells to the men. *"Apúrense! Apúrense! Ella está dando a luz!"* Hang on, Trudy!" It calms me to hear Cece's voice. She reaches up and takes my hand. I grab it and grip it as tightly as the pain is gripping me. I have to make one other person on earth feel what I am feeling or I will be lost forever. "We're trying to get through, Trudy, but the crowds are blocking us. The costume parade is going over the river now and all the stairs up are clogged with people."

English or Spanish, it makes little difference what language Cece speaks. Pain blocks them all out. She yells, "Concentrate on your breathing!" six times before I obey.

I breathe and am amazed to discover that my lungs have remained free from pain. I rush to the safety of air, hot and humid, moving in and out of my body. A contraction clamps down on me and, though the men beneath cannot move, I rise on a wave of pain that seems as if it will never crest. When it does, I return to the safety of my lungs.

The next wave catches me by surprise, for I have fallen asleep. A bark of surprise and pain grunts from me.

"God, Trudy!" Cece yells up at me. "If that's transition, don't push! Don't push! Pant! Pant!" She yells at the people blocking the stairway. "Can you move! Please! We've got to get this woman to a hospital! You there in the Storm Trooper of Death T-shirt! Out of the way! Move it, sonny! Will you, please. . . . Listen, this is an emergency. For Christ's sake! Move the frap out of the way! Thank you! Twerp."

The street is even more crowded than the Riverwalk. Policeman link arms to push the mob back out of the street. The Rey Antonio Costume Parade is starting.

"Sir! Sir! Mr. Policeman!" Cece must scream as loudly as she can to be heard above the tumult. "This woman is having a baby! Sir, we need help! We need police escort!"

"She's what? She can't! Step back please, ma'am! Ma'am, that's Rey Antonio's limo! You're going to be mowed down! Thank you, ma'am!"

A shower of gold coins tossed by the king of Riverfest patters down on my face. They are light as autumn leaves and stay tangled in my hair.

"Ma'am, there is no possible way to access support services at this time! We've got gridlock from here to the Alamo! Nobody's moving an inch!"

A giant tentacle of pain reaches up from a hundred fathoms deep and wraps around me. My howl makes the siren of the police car clearing the way for Rey Antonio sound like a whimper. When it has stopped reverberating, I hear the scratchy static of a two-way radio.

"Uh, we've got a four nineteen here."

Static.

"I *know* that's a woman giving birth. We need an ambulance. Pronto!"

Static.

"It has *got* to be possible! She's doing it! Now!"

Static.

"No, I am *not* current on emergency childbirth procedure."

"For crying out loud!" Cece's disgust blocks out the staticky conversation. *"Apúrense!"* she yells at the men. *"Vamos al* Baptist Medical Center! *Es bien cerquita! Vamonos! Apúrense! Apúrense!"*

The men in skeleton costumes bearing me like an Egyptian queen on a palaquin follow Cece into the parade. We are behind the float carrying this year's costume contest finalists, a float I have ridden on every year for the past five.

"Wow! Great costume!" Someone in the crowd yells as I pass. "She really looks like she's having a baby."

I close my eyes and grip Cece's hand as the pain changes not in intensity but in timbre, moving from a shrill, piercing pitch to a deeper, more resonant tone that seems to pour out of the earth into me as if I were at the end of a giant root. I grunt a mud-wallowing grunt.

"Jesus, Mary, and Joseph!" Cece yells for the men to turn off the parade route. The bodies, noiseless pistons pumping beneath me, pick up speed, then veer off. The side streets are blocked with cars around which the men in skeleton costumes maneuver. A canyon of buildings hides the sky. At last we break free and I spy a single star shining in the darkness. As we move closer I see that it is, in fact, the five-pointed Lone Star, beacon of bravery gleaming atop the iconic outline of the Alamo. I feel as stalked and desperate as the proto-Texans who died there as the dozen silent feet bearing me along hurry past the hallowed site.

I cannot tell how much time passes. It seems I only close my eyes, then open them and we are loping into the emergency room of the Baptist Medical Center. It is as crowded as a M.A.S.H. unit with the casualties of Riverfest. Pain etches every detail of the chaotic scene into my memory.

A man, stony-faced, holds his right hand in his left. A pool of blood fills the left palm beneath the stump where the top two joints of his right index finger used to be. A skinny teenager lays across four plastic chairs, holding his stomach and rolling over to vomit into a plastic mop bucket. A Chicano family struggles to keep their father, raging, stumbling drunk, his forehead gashed open, from walking out. They cling to him like Lilliputians trying to pin down Gulliver. He shakes off his preteen son and looks up to see me held aloft on the hands of half a dozen bearers like an Aztec virgin being carried to sacrifice. He stands, weaving, and stares long enough for his family to pin him down again. He holds up the one hand they leave free and points it at me as we pass.

A contraction grips me and I am alone again. My cries pass unnoticed in the din.

"Have her waters broken?"

I turn my attention to the clerk standing beside us. When Cece points out the drenched clumps of my costume, the clerk informs us that I have to be on a gurney. Hospital regulations.

The men lower me gently onto the vinyl. Without the

men's warm hands beneath me, the pain grows too strong for me to bear. This is not cramps. This is something that I cannot endure. There is so much I did not agree to. So much I couldn't have known. I was one person when I decided to do this, but I have become another person. A person who was never consulted about what is now happening to her body. I can no longer be held to promises I never knew I was making. I struggle up on one elbow.

"Cece." My voice is calm with the certainty I now feel. "I can't do this. You're going to have to let me out. I'm going home now. To my apartment. It's on Laurel. Right off San Pedro."

"Laurel, right off San Pedro, eh? All right. I'll give the baby your regrets. I'll tell him you would have loved to have been here, but that a prior commitment unavoidably detained you."

I nod. Cece is handling this very well. I try to roll over on my side so that I can heft myself up and return to the life I left behind, but the pain has not listened to me excuse myself. It crushes down, flattening every molecule in my body until I feel like the picture in my eighth-grade science book of the astronaut's face pulled like taffy by G forces beyond my imagination.

When it lifts, a belch rises out of me, then another sow-like grunt.

"Do you feel like pushing yet?" she asks.

"Pushing what?" I ask irritably. It is taking all the restraint I can muster to keep from hitting Cece, she is so annoying.

"You'll know when it starts. But don't push until I tell you to. Pant like a dog if you feel like you can't hold back.

Like this." She puts her face right next to mine and huffs hot exhalations at me.

"Don't breathe on me."

Cece stops panting and takes my hand and pats it.

"If you don't stop—" Before I can order Cece to stop touching me, a monster contraction squeezes the breath from me and the hand that is being patted rises up and slaps Cece's face. She stares at me for one second, then turns to grab the clerk.

"This woman needs a doctor. She's in transition. Do you know what transition is? That's the step before the pushing starts. You get it? She's going to have her baby!"

"Are you a licensed medical professional?" the clerk asks.

"I don't need a license. I've witnessed dozens of births and I recognize the signs of one proceeding with a ferocious velocity."

"Huh?"

"Get us a doctor!"

"All the doctors are busy right now. We got one myocardial infarction. Two stabbings. An anaphylactic shock reaction to a wasp sting. We got delirium tremens and a kid blew his cheek off with a bottle rocket. Which one you want to go ahead of?"

"Put us ahead of the DTs," Cece orders.

"Drugs," I whimper. "Bring me drugs." But the clerk has already left. There is no longer any space between the contractions. The blackness of the pain runs together, completely obliterating the few rays of light shining in on me. I see before me a dark universe of pain with no way out. I will be lost forever. "I need help. Doctor. Drugs." This isn't fair.

I wasn't supposed to do it this way. At last I remember the magic word that will save me. "Epidural," I gasp.

"Someone will be here soon." Cece strokes my hair back away from my sweat-drenched face. "Don't worry. This is the worst. It won't be long now, baby." Her touch feels wonderful now. I want her to stroke my face and call me baby. I grip her hand, my lifeline back and beg her, "Please. Please. Please. Please." But she cannot save me. No one can.

"Thirsty," I whisper to her. She pats me, then rushes to a soft drink machine and quickly returns with a can of Gatorade.

I drink. Nothing has tasted better in my life. Like lightly sweetened sweat. An instant later the pain changes from driver to driven. It becomes something that I can expel from my body and I know exactly what pushing means.

"I have to push," I tell Cece, struggling to sit up.

"Wait! Wait! Pant! Like this." She puts her face next to mine again and makes me imitate her. The quick, shallow breaths make the overpowering pressure recede for a moment. She looks around frantically. Several ambulances have pulled up and even more stretchers are being wheeled in.

"Good God Gertie, a person'd have a better chance of finding a doctor on the streets of Calcutta. This is hopeless." She grabs the gurney and pushes us toward a curtained area. After she closes the curtain around us, Cece tears away the scraps of my costume and my soaking underwear and examines me.

"Christ on a crutch! This baby is ready to be born!" She pokes her head around the curtain and yells into the cacophony of ambulance sirens, screaming drunks, and wailing children, "Someone help us! A baby is being born! Please! Someone! Anyone!"

"I have to push!"

Cece turns back to me and has me pull my knees up as far as they will go and feels inside.

"Oh, my, yes," she says, "you do have to push." She raises the head of the gurney and has me brace myself against it and take a deep breath. Then my body exerts itself. My neck melts away as I strain, my head crunching down against my shoulders. Tears pour from my eyes and sweat from all my pores. From my gut rises a sound that is like a spirit trying to be born through my throat. It forces its way out with a wail that feels as if it will tear my throat apart.

"Look! Look!" Cece yells. "The top of the head! Feel! Feel!" She grabs my hand and puts it between my legs. My fingers touch a tuft of soft wet hair.

Then the pressure stops and the little head slips away. I am left gasping, drained, unable to believe that it did not all end then. But it hasn't. My body gathers itself again and again; the unimaginable pressure bears down on me.

"Push! Push! Push!" Cece yells at me. "Keep up the pressure! Don't stop!"

My face reddens. The veins in my neck stand out. The wail shreds my throat once more. Then it is over and I fall back against the gurney. Each time the urge wrenches my body, then recedes, I am left drained, everything taken from me. Then it starts again. And again. And then I am too exhausted to scream.

"Just one more good push," Cece tells me.

Slowly, I shake my head on the pillow to tell her that there are no more good pushes left in me. She runs her finger around the vaginal opening, massaging and trying to stretch the band of flesh blocking Sweet Pea's entrance into the world. The chains holding up the curtains rattle on their metal track. Without turning around, Cece says, "Doctor, thank God, you're . . . you're not a doctor," she finishes when she turns to find that Sinclair has entered.

"What are you doing here?" Cece asks.

"I followed you."

He comes up to stand by my head. "Trudy, it was so sudden. Springing everything on me like that. I needed a minute. But now, yes, now I'm ready to do this thing."

Sinclair is pale and insubstantial in the fluorescent light, a wraith barely distinguishable from the muslin curtain at his back. He is so irrelevant. So incidental. I close my eyes so that I won't have to see him and I surrender to the force massed within me. This time when the pressure crushes down, I let it pass through.

"Oh Jesus. Oh Jesus. Oh Jesus. A baby. A real baby. Trudy! It's a baby! A baby. Oh, a baby," Sinclair keeps babbling "baby" as the head slides free.

"Pant, Trudy! Pant! Don't push for a second! Let me get this little fellow untangled before—"

But I can no more stop the convulsions than I could have halted an earthquake.

"Sinclair!" Cece, still occupied with the cord, barks at Sinclair. "Stop your gawping and get down here! I can't do everything."

Then, in a gush, the body comes free and slides into Sinclair's trembling hands.

The baby I have tried so hard not to love, not to even think about, is here. The pain leaves the instant its job is done. Already it seems as if I'd pretended, made up the agony. I hold my arms out. Cece looks at me.

"Are you sure, Trudy? Are you sure you want to see her?"

Her? I open my mouth to ask "her"? but the word stays trapped in my throat. Instead, I jiggle my arms frantically and Sinclair tenderly places the tiny creature, still slippery with my watery blood, still attached by a cord to my body, into my arms.

Her. It *is* a girl. I pull away the last shreds of my costume and lay her against my chest so that she can hear my heart and be warmed by my body. She is a tiny little girl, light as a cat in my arms. Lighter. The bumps of her spine beneath my hand feel like a string of toy pop beads. She is not Sweet Pea. And she is not a miniature Victor. She looks exactly like me. I touch her hair to make certain that I haven't imagined it. The little head, the unformed spot on the top bouncing with her life's pulse, it is all covered with wisps of taffy-colored hair.

I tilt the tiny body, drawn up tight as a fist against the noise, the light. I tilt her back to make sure I haven't imagined her eyes, her face. But no, I haven't. She stares up at me with eyes big as a lemur's. This is what I could never have expected. That I would look into the face of my child and find someone I knew. But I do. I see my eyes in her small face and finally know them for what they are: the eyes of a dreamer.

I know this and I know the life she *will* have as clearly as I know the one I *have* had. I don't know dates and names of boyfriends and which bones with be broken. But I know the eyes that will see it all. They are dreamer's eyes. They are my eyes. And behind them is my soul.

I know this child and I know what she needs. I see her future in King William more clearly than I see Sinclair and Cece frozen motionless against the curtain drawn around us. I see that a black and white world, no matter how stimulating, will be a prison to this child. That if she is nourished with crab tacos and all the latest and all the best that her spirit will float right out of the leaded glass windows of the Schier mansion. I see that Hillary and Victor will not know how to protect her dreamer's soul any more than Randi and Gordon did mine.

In that instant of clarity, I see my past as well. I see how the thin gravity of my parents' regimented lives allowed so much of what might have been in my life to simply leak away. That the only way I had of keeping myself anchored in this world was to gather junk. I cannot let this happen to the fragile being curled against my breast. Once I make my decision, Cece and Sinclair unfreeze. Cece leaves to find a doctor. Sinclair leans down to put his face close to mine, to the baby's.

"A baby," he marvels, falling in love. "She looks just like you, Trudy. A clone, a virtual clone." He touches her fist and it closes around his finger. He is euphoric. She turns her otherworldly eyes on him. "Oh, the eyes. Trudy, they're your eyes. She's tiny. She's so tiny. Oh, Trud-a-loo-da-loo, I am ready to do this thing."

Softly, he hugs my shoulders. "Isn't this cozy? I didn't think it would be so cozy. The three of us. An instant family. My family. I never really had a family. Not one I wanted to belong to. Yes, I'm ready to do this." There are tears in his eyes. "We can do like the Indians along the Amazon and rig up a hammock for her to sleep in. Keep the little nipper safe from pythons and such." He laughs, a giddy, tipsy laugh.

"And she'll have the tall pecans for a mobile. None finer in the world. No baby in King William could ever have a better mobile." He hugs me again, more forcefully than he'd intended in his exuberance. "Sorry, sorry." He pats me lightly, apologetically. "Trudy, it's great you're not married. Great that you're free. This will work. I'm ready now. I'm ready. What do you say, Trude? You ready? Come on, you've had ten years to think it over."

I say nothing.

The curtains are slung back and Cece pulls in a doctor, who cuts the cord and clamps off the stump. "I don't suppose you have your own doctor," he says, examining the baby. He assumes that I am one of those women who pretend they're not pregnant for nine months, then give birth in the ladies' room. I want him to assume this and shake my head a shamed no.

"You're lucky. She's healthy." He hands the baby back to me. I try not to notice that her skin is soft as an apricot, her hair as fine as the fluffy down on a baby chick. That her nails are pink and tiny as the smallest shells that wash up on the seashore. I try not to notice that the place I feel the most empty is where my heart once was.

The baby starts to cry and Sinclair cuddles up close and softly sings a song into a pearly ear.

Life could be a dream, sh-boom,
If only all my precious plans
  would come true, sh-boom,
If you would let me spend my whole life loving you,
Life would be a dream, sweetheart.

Ah-ling-ah-ling-ah-ling-ah-ling,

Woo-dip-a-dip-a-dip-a-loo.

Woooo, life could be a dream, sh-boom,
If I could take you up to paradise up
    above, sh-boom,
And tell me, darling, I'm the only one
    that you love,
Life could be a dream, sweetheart.

Sh-boom, ska-diddly-diddly-boom,
Doo-doo-doo-doo-sh-boom!

"The Cords, 1954. 'Sh-Boom.' Life could be a dream," Sinclairs tells the baby. She stops crying and, for a second or two, I believe that life could be a dream. I search Sinclair's face for the minutest scrap of a hope that this man has more than song lyrics to offer. That the empty part of me will not be hollow for as long as I live. I consider Sinclair, a man who paints faces and lives in a trailer. A man of intense but fleeting enthusiasms. A man who would put my child in a hammock and use a tree for a mobile. Then I think of my own ridiculous life. Of the cats I've forgotten to feed who've had to run away to find a real keeper.

The baby's dreamer eyes goggle up at me and I force myself to stop listening to Sinclair's song. I am a mother and I must open my own eyes and see clearly for the first time in my life. Babies need humidifiers and playpens. They need real cribs, not hammocks in the trees. They need their chance to dream.

The admitting clerk is the next to fling back the curtain.

"You should have told me she was so close," she scolds Cece, then hands me a sheet to cover up with. I throw it around myself and tuck it carefully about the baby. "Okay, we got a room. Who's the responsible billing party?"

"Me." Sinclair straightens up and steps forward like a man picking up the tab for a big dinner. "Me. I'll handle everything."

"Okay, come with me." The clerk motions Sinclair to follow her, then she turns to the orderly, a broad-shouldered man wearing a stocking cap and goatee and gives him a room number. He grips the gurney and it glides soundlessly out of the curtained enclosure.

Sinclair leans over as I slide past. "Will you be all right?"

I say nothing.

"Rest your voice, darling. I'll attend to the paperwork, then run out for some things for you. Shampoo, nightgown, tiara. A few wee articles for the babe. Didees, powder, Princess phone." He laughs a giddy laugh. "I don't know what little girls need. I'll have to find out." He kisses my cheek and follows the grumpy clerk.

Cece stands beside my head in the elevator. The orderly turns his back to us, grips one hand in the other in front of his belly, and watches the numbers of the floor ping slowly past. The baby mews and snuffles against my chest. Cece looks at the baby searching for something to suck, then looks at me. I help the tiny mouth fit around my nipple and she applies herself. I want the elevator to go on forever, to never stop. I don't want to have to make the decision I will have to make when the doors open.

But the doors do open and I am pushed into a room barely bigger than a closet. The orderly scoots me onto the bed and leaves. I let the baby nurse and memorize her face, her smell, the way her damp hair curls on her scalp. Then I hold her out to Cece and try to speak, but my vocal cords sag in my throat, unable to bounce words out. I motion to her for paper and pencil and with my free hand write, "Take the baby. You know who to give her to."

Cece reads the note. "Trudy, are you—"

I put my free hand over my ear. It would hurt more than I could stand to hear her ask if I was sure. I hold the baby out again. Cece studies my face a long time. When she has seen what she is looking for, she takes the baby. I can't believe how my arms could ache from holding something so light.

Cece stares at the baby but speaks to me. "Trudy, I've seen more in my life than you will ever guess at. More than I ever wanted to. But of all the misery, none equals that of a mother sending her child to a better life than she can ever hope to give it. I won't argue with you."

It is done too quickly. Cece takes the baby wrapped in a thin white sheet with the words "Baptist Memorial Hospital" printed along the edge and leaves. I have never been taken seriously before. That I am now and for all time stuns me. I start to scream, to stop her, but still my throat doesn't work. I listen to snuffling, mewling baby sounds recede down the hall, then the ping of the elevator, then the doors shutting and my baby is gone forever.

I don't know what time it is when they leave. I don't know how long I stare at the blank screen of the television mounted above my bed, but the sun is coming up when Victor and Hillary enter the room.

"God, you're here," Hillary says. "We've been calling every hospital in the city since midnight. How are you feeling? How far apart are the contractions? Do you want something to drink? Have you called Dr. Worley?"

I say nothing.

"Trudy?" Hillary asks, her tone somewhere between frantic and impatient.

I am glad my voice is not working. I do not want to speak. Not to Hillary. Not now. I want both of them gone.

"Trudy." She strains for evenness. "Could you please tell us what is going on? We'd like to help, but we can't if we don't know what's happening to you. Has your water broken?"

I remember the warm fluid leaking down my leg, the pinkish stain coloring my costume. It seems like a memory from long ago.

"Hillary, she's not pregnant." Victor seems not to believe the words he is speaking. "Look at her. She's had the baby."

Hillary stares at me. "Where's our baby?" She glances around the room. "Where's our baby?"

I say nothing.

"Trudy," she demands. "Trudy, speak to me and speak to me right now!"

"Trudy." Victor's voice is as level as it is when he speaks on the phone to the men who have lost their fortunes, their reasons to live. "Did you have the baby?"

I nod, my mind filling with the images that accompany that answer.

"Okay, okay, Trudy." He holds up his palms to me as if I were pointing a gun at him. "Where. Where is the baby?"

I touch my throat and try to answer. At least to tell them that I won't answer.

"Oh, my God," Hillary moans. "What's happened? Tell us. What happened to the baby? Is he dead? Is there something wrong with him? Victor, get the doctor. Go find some-one. Victor!"

Victor holds his palms up to Hillary. "Just, just one second."

Seeing them both so distraught, I wonder if I was wrong. Perhaps there *would* be enough gravity to hold my baby's spirit in the Schier mansion. Then Hillary begins to cry and I know I have made the wrong decision. I now want to speak. Surely Victor can reverse my decision. Make things come out right. But still no sound passes my lips.

Victor sees that I am trying. "Just nod your head," he tells me. "Is the baby alive?"

I nod yes and the relief that floods their handsome faces makes me believe that they will be good parents after all. I think I can speak. The cords that have strangled me all my life have finally loosened. I will tell them where to go.

But Hillary speaks first. "It's something worse, isn't it? The baby has Down syndrome, doesn't he?"

Worse than death is imperfection.

Hillary sees something in my expression that she takes for confirmation and the blood drains from her face. She turns to Victor, frantic now. "I told you we shouldn't go ahead without the amnio. I told you the risks. The odds. I told you we should have ended it right then. We could have. We should have. She lied to us. She lied from the very beginning. I knew this would happen. I knew it. I knew it. I knew it."

Worse than death is imperfection.

Victor does not speak. He has no reasoned lawyer's words to offer. Finally, reluctantly, he says, "We still have to take the baby. Hillary, we're obligated. We can't just dump it."

"Victor, think of what you're saying. Don't make any commitments."

"There are programs. There are ways to deal with these things."

"Victor, be real. Those people live for ten, twenty years. Victor, we . . . I . . ." Hillary presses a fist to her mouth to stop a sob and turns away.

Victor stares at the fire sprinkler in the ceiling and speaks in a dead voice. "Our commitment stands. We'll still take the child."

Hillary chokes down a sob.

It takes me a minute to find out how to make my voice work. It is deep and scarred. "No. No, you will not take my baby."

"Trudy?" Victor asks. "Was that you?"

"You don't have to take my baby." My voice is dry and raspy, but there are no squeaks, no shrills, no hesitancy.

"She's right," Hillary says. "We don't. We never had a contract. We never signed anything."

"Hillary," Victor says. "Don't be like that. We had an agreement."

I make myself speak. "Yes, but the person you had an agreement with wasn't a mother. Motherhood makes you another person. I know that now. I didn't know it then."

Victor dutifully tries again. "That child is partially ours."

Not half. Partially. A small part that they are allowing to shrink even as we speak. Just as I shrank. I am sorry for what they've been through. I am sorry for being unfair to them. But none of that matters. What they think of me doesn't matter. Only the baby matters.

"She has already gone to a family that is willing to take

a child who's been grown in sand. You want more than a baby should be asked to give."

"The baby is gone?" Hillary asks.

The relief in Hillary's voice reassures me that Hillary and Victor would not be good parents to a dreamer baby, a baby who would disappoint them as much as any genetically flawed child.

"You and Victor will be good parents. Someday. Not now. Not to my baby. She is the wrong baby for you."

"She?" Hillary says. "She's a girl?"

I ignore her. "You and Victor should try some more to have your own baby. Being a lab rat is good preparation for having a baby. You should at least be willing to take your temperature for a few months before you can be a mother. I will pay you back for everything. It will take a while, but I'll do it. I'm sorry."

"Victor." She turns to her husband for wisdom, for a ruling. Victor stares at me. Because of his work, because of spending his life sorting out fact from fiction, he has become a connoisseur of the truth, and what he has heard from me is an especially convincing vintage. He is used to thinking clearly when his guts are churning and his palms sweating and he does so now. I watch his face and see him projecting into the future, imagining an almond-eyed child with a thick tongue poking short fingers at the Ocumicho pottery. Imagining *any* child poking short fingers at Hillary's treasures. I see Victor submit.

"Would you leave now," I ask them. "I'm tired."

"No, we will not 'leave now.'" Hillary is frayed. "We have to get this worked out."

"Let her rest, Hillie." Victor takes his wife's arm. "Come on. We'll come back later." Gently he pulls his wife from the room. As soon as she is away from the bedside, Hillary turns her face from me. Victor pauses at the door, opens his mouth to say something, then closes it. He opens his hand, then lets it drop, and they both leave.

I don't listen to the elevator carrying them away. I touch my stomach. It is still swollen. There could still, almost, be a baby inside. Except that the hum of a second life within my own is gone. I am glad for the incompetence of the hospital, that no one has ever shown up from the nursery. I will be gone before anyone comes. When I stand, watery blood leaks down my leg. There are pads in the bathroom. I am clinging to the bar by the toilet when Sinclair comes in, whistling.

"Are you in there?" he asks, and bubbles on. "Did someone from the nursery come for the baby? When can we go down and see our bonnie lass? I've been about, purchasing a few of the necessaries. Not an easy task, shopping for a newborn at five in the morning. But, the kindness of strangers. It was amazing. The crone at the Quickie-Pickie had her thumb half an inch from the police alarm from the minute I walked in until I invoked the magic word, 'baby.' Then, presto, all manner of impossible goods appeared—formula, bottles, diapers. Am I premature on the Barbie Malibu Condominium set?" Sinclair laughs. "I brought you something to wear. Hope a beach muumuu is all right. The Quickie-Pickie's fashion selection leaves a bit to be desired. Orchids and muscular tropical men bent over their outriggers."

The chatter stops.

"Trudy? Are you all right in there? Trudy?"

He finds me on the toilet. I have no energy left to stand up. Tenderly, he pulls the pad on its elastic strap snugly up between my legs and carries me back to bed. He asks five

times where the baby is. I turn away from him to the wall
when he asks a sixth.

"Those people, the King William people, they took her,
didn't they?"

I let him believe this because it doesn't matter. None of
it matters anymore. There once was an angel spirit in me,
but the baby took it with her. I am glad I had it to give, but
nothing flutters inside of me any longer. Sinclair tries to stop
me when I struggle out of bed and put on the muumuu. He
tries, but his touch is too gentle to have any effect. He
doesn't want to hurt me. I look even paler and more washed-
out against the poisonous green and violet slashed with gold
of the muumuu. My hair snarls about my head. My makeup
was sweated off long ago, leaving only a greasy sheen over
my pallor. I start for the door. It hurts to pick up my feet, so
I shuffle. Sinclair puts his hands lightly on my shoulders.

"Trudy, we'll get her back. Don't worry. You agreed under duress. It will never stand up in court. We'll say I'm the
father. Trudy, I *am* the father. Trudy. Trudy? We'll get her
back. We will."

I hobble into the hall.

Sinclair flaps beside me, crying. "Trudy, talk to me.
Trudy, this is too much punishment for one delayed reaction.
You caught me by surprise. It took a while for happiness to
catch up with me. Trudy, I'm not a decisive person. You
know that. You've always known that. You knew my flaws
when you came back. Trudy, if I'd been a decisive person,
you never would have found me living in a trailer by the
river. Trude, talk to me."

I lean against the elevator button. The doors open and a
nurse pushing a cart with a clear-sided box on top gets out.
The word "Nursery" is printed in green stick-on letters on

one side of the box. She holds the door open for me and we trade places, then she trundles off to my empty room. On the elevator, my legs give way. Sinclair catches me and carries me out to the truck. He props me up against the hump of the door while he rips open the bag of diapers he's bought and spreads several on the seat to make a soft nest for me to sit on.

We drive a slow, twisting route. Sinclair holds out his hand in front of my chest every time we go over a bump. We are passing the Space Needle, heading south before I realize that we are not going to my apartment. It doesn't matter. Destination is of no consequence to me. I stare out into the glare of a day that is too hot before it's even begun. The city is torpid in the heat, exhausted by a hundred Riverfests.

A Chicana mother, dressed up for Mass in a pencil-thin skirt and black patent spike heels pushes a flimsy, cheap stroller with a pink wrapped bundle strapped in it. The woman's mother in a variation of the same outfit, same spike heels, follows. Crews of men wearing orange safety vests and squinting into the glare of the sun sweep up mustard-smeared hot dog buns and bright sprays of confetti crushed into the tarry asphalt. The cathedral bells ring. I lean back and close my eyes against the bright light.

It is shady at La Fonda Agua Caliente. Sinclair carries me into the trailer and arranges me in bed. There is clattering and pounding in the small kitchen, and he brings me a small glass of orange juice he has squeezed himself and poured over a mush of ice.

"I crushed the ice," he says, pointing to the glass in my hand. "Wrapped the cubes in a towel. Clean towel. And beat them with a hammer. It's better that way, don't you think?"

I drink seven glasses before Sinclair runs out of juice

and switches to ginger ale. He brings me magazines and points to a bouquet of pink carnations in a white plastic vase sitting on top of the television set. "Fresh out of long-stemmed roses at the Quickie-Pickie."

It occurs to me that Sinclair is trying to cheer me up. I think of how bright any day in the last ten years of my life would have been if I'd gotten so much as a blade of grass from him. His flowers are lost now in the immensity of the darkness within me, specks of confetti ground into the asphalt.

"Rest now, my little red herring. Then we'll formulate a plan of attack. A family, Trudy, that's what it's all about. It's the only anchor you're allowed when the big one starts to blow."

For the next few hours I notice nothing. Sinclair's ice hammering, the shudder of the air conditioner compressor in the window, the plates of scrambled eggs and toast that sit beside the bed uneaten, the smell of the special coffee imported from Kenya that Sinclair brews for me, they all barely register, like the whispering of someone in the far corner of a darkened theater. The movie that plays again and again in my head is far too compelling for me to care about some distant whispering. Over and over I touch the top of my daughter's head while she is still inside of me. Over and over I feel her slide from my body. Over and over I see the cinnamon tufts of her hair poking out from the hospital sheet as Cece carries her away.

Sometime later I notice that my breasts are swollen and hard as apples. Milk drenches Sinclair's bed and I burn with fever. Sinclair wraps towels tightly around my chest, snugging them in under my armpits to catch the milk. He brings me aspirin to take down the fever, but since I can't even force words past my clenched throat I can't get the pills down. So Sinclair crushes them between two spoons with five drops of water and adds sugar, then holds the spoon out to me.

"Come on, this is the ticket, Little Red. Slurp this down."

The bitter taste of the crushed aspirin slurry mixed with undissolved sugar brings back the smell of Vicks VapoRub steaming in the black plastic cup of the vaporizer Randi had turned on in my room when I had strep throat. For the first time I wish she were here. I can't make myself swallow, and the aspirin mixture dribbles out of my mouth. Sinclair's hand holding the spoon sags onto the bed.

"Trudy, I don't know what to do. You have to get well so we can go claim our daughter. You have got to get well. For me. Trudy, don't leave again. Don't punish me for bad timing. Not this harshly. Trudy, speak to me."

I can't.

"Eat, then. Please." He grabs the most recent meal abandoned on the nightstand and waves a forkful in front of my face. His exuberance repels me. It is unfitting. I turn away from him to face the wall. I have no desire to see anything else of this earth. I want only to watch the movie that plays now continuously in my mind.

Sinclair leaves. Night comes. The trailer is quiet. He is gone a long time. This is good, I don't want to be interrupted. Ever again.

But, too soon, I am. Without speaking, Sinclair comes in and picks me up off the bed. I don't resist, but I don't hang on to him either. I am a lump in his arms as we step out into the dawn. He is sweaty and smells rank. His clothes are dripping wet; there is dirt on his face. He doesn't speak as he carries me out under the canopy of pecan trees and toward the collapsed heap of the old resort. The pile of rotting timber is encircled with an orange plastic ribbon and faded signs reading "CONDEMNED BY ORDER OF THE CITY OF SAN ANTONIO. KEEP OUT. VIOLATORS PROSECUTED."

He ducks under the ribbon and steps onto a makeshift boardwalk stretching across the splintered wreckage of the front porch. Most of the floorboards inside the hotel are rotted away, and Sinclair teeters across the bridge of new boards laid over the holes. Mourning doves coo and flap above our heads, raising clouds of dust that stand and shine in the morning light. We go down the long dark hall. Strips of peeling wallpaper dangle free. At the end of the hallway Sinclair kicks open the door to the pool room and light floods in. About half of the panes in the glass walls have been broken out and those that remain are filmed with dirt, but the aqua-tiled pool is clean and filled with water that sparkles in the radiance.

"You're not going to believe this," Sinclair says. He bounces beneath me with excitement. "I stayed up all night working on it. Cleaning the gunk out of the pool. Wiped it down really well. Had to use muriatic acid to get the really heavy stuff off the pool walls. It hasn't been filled in years. Not since Pettigrew left. The pipes were so clogged, silted in with sediment, I thought they were sealed off forever. But I ran the long snake down them and the spring geysered in like Old Faithful. Then it settled down to a pleasant little burble. But, Trudy, this is the part you are not going to believe. Remember how hot the springs were before? Agua Caliente. Like bathwater. Like soup. Trudy, they're cool now. Chilly as a frosty mug from Schilo's. Trudy, the water's cold."

He waits for the wonder he has laid at my feet to penetrate the gloom. I have no reaction.

"You'll see. When you get in, you'll see." He kicks off his shoes and steps forward. I shake my head. I do not want to go in. He stops.

"Trudy, come on. These are healing waters. The feel of them on your skin is a miracle. Trudy, the gods and goddesses of the silver screen cavorted in these waters. With German shepherds yet. Come on, you'll get your spirit back and we'll figure out what to do. We'll do it, Trudy. We'll make it all come out all right. It's not too late, Trude. Don't make it too late."

But I refuse to go in. When he takes another step forward, I lunge out of his arms onto the rough surface of the concrete surrounding the pool. Sinclair's shoulders sag and he weeps, but his tears do not touch me. Nothing he does or could ever do will touch me again. He is the source of my life's biggest mistakes. I owe him nothing. When I can speak again, the first thing I will say is, "Since you brought me here and since I don't have the strength to go anywhere else, please, just leave me alone." I haven't made the decision to die, but as I don't want to live either, I'm certain natural events will take their course.

Sinclair carries me back into the trailer. He changes the pad between my legs. It is stained an orangish-red. He brings a cookbook with a picture on every page. He points out puffy cheese soufflés and shish kabobs of steak and pineapple chunks strung on skewers and offers to make anything I want.

I turn away from him, back to the wall, back to the images flickering there of my baby's birth. I don't have time anymore for Sinclair's strained joviality. I've missed too much already of the scraps I have of my daughter's life.

"Trudy, Trudy, you caught me off balance. We both wanted to end up the same place. It's just that I was prepared for the trip to take a bit longer. That's all."

It takes no effort to block Sinclair out. He leaves and returns what seems to be only minutes later except that he is carrying a cheese soufflé baked in a battered tin bread pan. He holds his puffy golden creation out to me, and I turn back to the wall.

"Trudy, it's been almost two days now and you haven't eaten a thing. I don't know what to do with you, girl. I know I fucked up. I know my life is a travesty. Punish me any way you have to, but not like this."

It perplexes me for a moment to hear that Sinclair thinks he has so much to do with this. But that wrinkle of bewilderment is smoothed over by the memory of the feel of my daughter's head. Sinclair leaves. I don't know how much later. I am stuck in birth time, where contractions last for hours and hours last for minutes. It is dark when Sinclair comes back in.

"Trudy." He stands behind me at the edge of the bed. "Trudy, they don't have the baby. The King William people. They don't have her. Mercedes told me everything. Where's the baby, Trudy? Trudy? We have to act quickly before attachments can be formed. Before state lines can be crossed. Trudy, look at me."

When I don't turn to face him, he rolls me over. I study his face as I would a mannequin's in a shop window. Definitely not a young face anymore. He has the jittery look of a man whom time has pulled the rug out from under. He sags onto the side of the bed and buries his face in his hands. His misery touches me not at all. He leaves and I turn back to the wall in time to see the doctor snip the cord that had made the baby part of me.

The light of dawn interrupts the movie, and I notice a letter on the bed beside me. Since there is always an intermission at dawn, I open the letter. It is a thick wad of pages, plain white typing paper covered with Sinclair's blocky handwriting done in black felt pen. The sight of his signature used to take my breath away. I would have tossed this fat letter aside without a glance if I hadn't been between shows. But since I am, I read.

My Little Red,

I left you ten years ago to go back to a girl whose father owned a Chrysler dealership. I needed to be taken care of and a rich father seemed the way to go about it. I left her for a girl with an even richer father. This one liked to dress me in shirts with my initials stitched on the cuff and to pat lime-scented aftershave from the West Indies on my cheeks.

Trudy, I never thought twice about you. I never thought about the baby we might have had. I'm ashamed of that now, but I wasn't then. There were too many women and they all had rich fathers. Then there were women rich all on their own. They took me with them to helicopter-ski in Norway and to view the friezes in Florence. I made them laugh. I made them feel sexy. I made them believe I would have paid for it all a thousand times over if the money had been in my pocket.

I gave full measure, I'll say that on my behalf. If there was a breast anywhere on the premises, I fondled it. If the odd bit of thigh poked out from under a slit skirt, I was there to lick it. Sex was always good and guaranteed, but I did the extras too. I cossetted. Once, when a woman was teetering toward a wrist-slitting depression, I brushed her hair, ran the bristles gently over her scalp, for five hours. I sang. Lots of women liked me to croon lullabies to them. The word "gigolo" almost never came up. Because I wasn't. I was simply a performer who played to a very small house. Big house, little house, we all have to make a living.

Of course, the time came when I had to nudge myself toward the fondling, the licking, the cosset-ting, for the breasts were beginning to sag and the thighs, often as not, were stitched with varicose veins, and I was in need of bolstering myself by then.

I'm not like Mick Jagger, Warren Beatty, some of these others who stay too long at the party, who ride too long on tread too thin. I knew when my days as a professional were numbered. I'll always have a way to take a woman's eye, I'll always charm, but I knew when to move into a strictly amateur capacity.

I was casting about for alternate sources of in-come when I hooked up with Esmeralda. Esmie. It wasn't love with us. We'd both had our respective tickets punched a few too many times to go at it as a hobby.

I thought my life was an anthology back then. That all the curious people and strange circum-stances that passed through it were adding up to a collection. That was before I found out that no one was taking notes. I figured back then that a few months on the Renaissance fair circuit would make a zesty addition. Then there was Charlie. I told you about Charlie, Charlemagne. Esmie's little boy. I didn't tell you I broke his heart.

At first I treated Charlie like the leaky sack of tissues he was. Nothing more. Esmie wanted it that way. She didn't want me involved. She knew from the start that I was the sort who wouldn't stick around. She knew it because that was the only sort she ever took up with. So she didn't want anyone getting attached. But someone did. Charlie did.

There was never any chance that he was mine. Not in the technical, biological sense of the word. Which, in those days, I was stupid enough to believe made a shit dab of difference.

Then Esmie took up with Jody. Jody was a big solid woman with a face like an Iowa farm wife, but she rang Esmie's bell in a way no one else ever had. So Esmie moved in with Jody. I wished the couple well and was glad of the extra space.

In exchange for the use of Esmie's trailer, however, I got night duty with Charlie. We thought this was for the best, given that Jody's trailer had only one bedroom, and novelty charged Esmie up like nothing else.

It was a mistake. We were both too stupid to shoot. Kids don't know when you're not in it for real, when you're only tending them for free use of a trailer and lack of anything better to do. All they know is that you're the one who gets them a drink of water in the middle of the night or holds them when they have a bad dream.

You lose track of time. I was still thinking that this arrangement was temporary when Esmie and her girlfriend decided it was time to quit the circuit. That a child needed a more regular life. They left, rented a house, settled down.

I came by a few times and brought toys. Stupid, thoughtless things. A train set you needed a father to put together. Ball and bat. Stupid. The first two times I came, Charlie about jumped out of his pale skin with joy. The third time I came he turned his back on me and crossed his arms in front of his chest like he was protecting his heart.

Charlie loved me as only a little savage can, and I broke his little savage heart. That was three years ago. I don't think about Esmie from year to year, but I think of Charlie every time I wake in the night. These days, there are more nights I wake than I don't. I listen to the river and wonder how I could have tossed away the love of a little savage.

I was stupid, Trudy, I don't have to tell you that. I thought that if I stayed light enough on my feet, I could tiptoe through the mine field. That if I avoided marriage, mortgages, and babies, I could come out clean on the other side. I stayed light, Trudy. I've come through with neither spouse nor spawn, and where has it gotten me? I could spin out of the galaxy tomorrow and there would be only you and Connie at Schilo's to take serious note. The fatal flaw in my frothy life is this: whether I marry or not, whether I have a child or not, I, Sinclair David Coker, am going to get old and die. I don't want to do it alone.

I want a baby because I want to fall in love

*again. I want to hear the squirt crow "Dah!" I want
to wake up eager to get out of bed to see how the
night has changed my new crush. Trudy, it's craven
and it's cut-rate and it's far less than you deserve,
but I want you because I'm lonely down to my toe-
nails. I want to sink into a cozy muck with you and
the baby we were meant to have.*

*I'm through tiptoeing, but there's no reason for
you to believe me, so I'm enclosing the only proof I
have. Find attached the justification for a life lived
on the cheap. It has always been my plan to escape to
Ireland. I thought I'd find the country compatible to
my lightfooted ways. But, say the word, Little Red,
and I'll plant my miserable feet beside yours for
better or for worse. Forever and anon.*

> *Yours if you'll have me,*
> *Sinclair*

Clipped to the letter is a cashier's check with my name
on it for $83,921.23.

My mouth opens and a howl comes all the way up from
my empty belly. I scream for the waste. If Sinclair had given
me enough money to buy a humidifier before, if he'd just
shown he was willing, that he wanted to be a father, everything might have been different. A million dollars wouldn't
make any difference now. A million dollars can't buy back
the moment when I handed my baby to Cece.

The pain is more than I can bear. I turn back to the wall
to lose myself in the vivid movie that never stops playing
there. My cry stops the instant I sink again into the last
night of Riverfest on the Riverwalk. The screen is painted in

tones of black and darker black with slashes of red from brake lights and silver from fairy lights. Constellations wheel overhead. White grins jump out of the black night. The moon pulls the baby out of me. I cannot fight the moon. And then the reel snaps and the screen floods with light. Another movie starts up. I can't stop it. This one is too bright in the way a summer day becomes too bright a few seconds before you pass out. The bleached-out pastels are the same colors as the dresses we attendants wore for Aurelia's quinceañera, powder blue, shell pink, buttermint yellow.

The movie starts in a very ordinary kitchen. I see again that ugly linoleum, the starburst pattern in blue and yellow waffled by a bumpy texture. This time, however, I see more.

Frank, Aurelia's jug-eared Frank, wanders into this kitchen and opens the refrigerator. He has grown into a tall man with a poochy belly and a sagging satchel butt, who combs his thinning hair over his ears in a style that makes him look like a werewolf. In his navy blue Sansabelt pants and white Banlon shirt, he looks like a school principal on his day off. Frank runs his thumbs around the beltless waist of his pants, hitching them up a bit higher on his tummy. They begin to creep back down immediately. He pulls a can of Isomil dairy-free formula from the refrigerator and fills a bottle.

A little boy with tea-colored skin and hair straight and black as a Mayan prince pedals in on a low-slung plastic trike. His mouth is open, singing, but no sound reaches me. Frank says something to the boy, then puts the bottle in a pan of water on the stove to warm.

Aurelia enters and the camera moves in for a close-up. The only thing that has changed in twenty-three years is that my old roommate looks younger now than she did at Our Lady of Sorrows. She smiles at me and I know the way I used to know what word Aurelia was searching for in English that what I am seeing is not a vision. That it is true and happening as I watch.

Aurelia is holding a baby, a flannel-wrapped bundle with tufts of apricot hair sticking out. Aurelia pulls the receiving blanket away from the sleeping face. Aurelia is astonished at how much the baby resembles me. She would have known she was mine even if Cece hadn't told her.

The baby wakes and turns her extraterrestrial eyes to the camera and lets me know that her name is Madalyn and that she is ready to come home. To me. Her mother. Aurelia smiles to let me know that she is waiting as well. All I have to do is come.

My breasts leak milk. My eyes leak tears. I don't know where you are, Madalyn, I tell my daughter. I don't even know Aurelia's last name.

Aurelia smiles and tells me that I do, I do know. I only have to remember. When I remember, then I can come and get my baby. She will keep her for me until then. But hurry, Aurelia warns, hurry. Babies need their mothers.

Madalyn cries in Aurelia's arms and milk runs down over my ribs and pools at the thin dam of my underpants elastic. It spills over, streaming down my thighs and dripping off my knees onto my toes. The smell of caramel fills the trailer and the baby's face disappears in a shimmering whiteness.

"Aurelia, don't go." I am surprised to hear my words. I stand and go to the window.

Outside, Sinclair is sitting in an old green metal lawn chair surrounded by dozens of coffee cans filled with the movie goddess's exotic plants. The long, thin petals of the starry ice lilies bob in the faint breeze. The strong light filtering through the tall pecans splashes shifting doily patterns across Sinclair's face as the breeze catches the branches. He is reading the paper, the classified ads, holding the paper as far away from himself as he can to bring the fine print into focus. I remember when we were buying a used sofa how, crammed into a phone booth, he could read the for sale ad pressed almost against his nose. That was long ago. If it had happened last week, it would have been long ago. Everything that happened before my baby was born is now long ago.

Sinclair stops reading and glances up toward the trailer. The glare off the window screen keeps him from seeing me. He squints into the sun and I know how he will look as an old man, cheeks sunken in, more gum than tooth showing. How odd that I have caught a high-flying kite of a man just as the wind has started to fail him.

Sinclair goes back to reading and a cat, pale as moonlight, creeps up behind him. It is not until the creature is rustling through the foliage of a clump of Peruvian ice lilies that I realize it is not a cat, it is a baby in a long layette gown that trails behind him as he crawls. It is Sweet Pea. He stops and stares up at the whorl of pecan leaves far over his head.

I finally recognize this baby, this little spirit who has visited my dreams for all these years. He crawls toward Sinclair's chair. A tiny hand plops down on Sinclair's foot. Baby knees scuff over them. Sinclair goes on reading.

Sweet Pea dawdles, waiting. Like a porch light left on all night fading at dawn, he grows fainter and everything comes clear. I finally know what he has been waiting for all these years. Sweet Pea was waiting for me to grow up.

My hands itch for two things: the feel of skin soft as apricots and Sculpie clay. Sweet Pea lets me know that all I have to do is ask for them. It is that easy. I see two things: I see my next project, a ceramic bowl filled with ceramic cornflakes and studded with ceramic blueberries: Post's Partum Blues. And I see Aurelia holding out that apricot-tufted flannel bundle.

Sweet Pea looks up at me, waiting, waiting for me to claim my life, and I remember. Hudspeth. Frank Hudspeth was the name Aurelia wrote on the envelope of the letter I delivered to her schoolboy lover. With that memory, all that has gone before ends.

I flip through the phone book and tear out the page that has Frank Hudspeth, 518 Valle Vista Drive, listed on it.

Sweet Pea shimmers. He has accomplished what he came for. He is crawling back toward the ice lilies when he disappears altogether.

I push open the window.

"Sinclair," I call out. The earthy rumble of my new voice no longer surprises me.

Sinclair looks up and sunlight fills in the places on his face that time has eroded.

"Do you know where Valle Vista Drive is?"

Sinclair drops the newspaper, stands, and lopes toward the trailer.

All my regrets vanish. I am here, beside the river. It is where I was meant to be. There are no mistakes, no regrets. Everything that has happened in my life was precisely as it was meant to be.

The milk my baby is waiting for puddles around my feet.

I hear Sinclair before he opens the door. He is singing. His voice is as sweet as a coconut candy bar.

Wooo, life could be a dream, sh-boom,
If only all my precious plans would come true,
If you would let me spend my whole life loving you,
Life would be a dream, sweetheart.

Hello, hello, again, sh-boom,
I hope we meet again, boom-a-boom.

Wooo, life could be a dream, sweetheart!
Sh-boom, ska-diddly-diddly-boom!

ABOUT THE AUTHOR

Sarah Bird is also the author of *Alamo House* and *The Boy-friend School*, which was selected by the New York Public Library as one of its Twenty-Five Books to Remember for 1989. She has written for *Mademoiselle, Savvy,* and *Ms.* She lives in Austin, Texas, with her husband and son.